John
THE BRIDE OF NEWGATE

Carroll & Graf Publishers, Inc.
New York

For Clarice

R.L.S., many years ago, said it best:
    So now, in the end, if this the least be good,
    If any deed be done, if any fire
    Burn in the imperfect page, the praise be thine.

Copyright © 1950 by John Dickson Carr
Copyright renewed 1958 by Clarice M. Carr

Reprinted by arrangement with Clarice M. Carr

First Carroll & Graf edition 1986
Second Carroll & Graf edition 1994

Carroll & Graf Publishers, Inc.
260 Fifth Avenue
New York, NY 10001

ISBN: 0-7867-0102-1

Manufactured in the United States of America

INTRODUCTION

By Bill Pronzini

John Dickson Carr (1906–1977) was a positive genius at the contruction of fair-play detective puzzles, especially those featuring a locked-room "miracle problem" in which a crime—usually a homicide—takes place in circumstances which seem to defy rational explanation. He was also a master of the historical novel, in particular those utilizing his lifelong interest in England's Stuart, Regency, and Victorian periods. He combined his puzzle-making talents and passion for history in more than a dozen historical detective novels—books so good and influential that they firmly established the detective-story-in-a-period-setting as a subgenre. Critic Anthony Boucher said in the 1960's that "the current popularity of this form ... certainly dates back to Carr's *The Bride of Newgate;* and equally certainly no one is consistently so successful [at the form] as Carr." Boucher's assessment is as valid today as it was three decades ago.

Although *The Bridge of Newgate* was billed as Carr's first historical novel when it was published in 1950, it was in fact his third. *Devil Kinsmere,* which appeared under the pseudonym of Roger Fairbairn in 1934, is chiefly an adventure romance with secondary detective-story elements, set in England and France in 1670; *The Murder of Sir Edmund Godfrey* (1936) is a nonfiction study of a famous seventeenth-century British murder case presented as a fair-play detective story, complete with clues and a dramatic unmasking of the guilty party. Actually, *The Bride of Newgate* is Carr's first true mystery-in-historical-costume. It is also the book which marked his transition from a writer of present-day whodunits to one who, over the last twenty years of his writing life, dealt primarily with fictional crimes of the past.

Readers and critics alike hailed *Bride* as one of Carr's most enjoyable tales. *The New York Times* called it "a swashbuckling tour de force"; the Los Angeles *Herald Express* said that it "engrosses, tantalizes and thrills the reader." In a 1990 evaluation of Carr's work, *John Dickson Carr: A Criti-*

i

cal Study, S. T. Joshi opines that "in its vivid characterization, vigorous narration, and real emotional involvement, it may be the best of his historical mysteries."

Carr was a meticulous researcher who prided himself on the exactness of even the smallest detail. Thus his depiction here of London in 1815, just after the fall of Napoleon at Waterloo, is strikingly real: rich in color and fine points, peopled with individuals who speak and act in a fashion absolutely faithful to the era, and sprinkled with a number of actual (if mostly little known) historical figures. Reading Carr's lush descriptive prose, one can virtually smell the dank squalor of Newgate Prison, feel the chill dawn fog as Dick Darwent prepares to fight a pistol duel with one of his adversaries, hear the victims' screams during the riot at the Italian opera and the clung-clunk of sabres in the climactic confrontation inside the house on St. James's Square.

Carr's other strengths as a mystery and historical novelist are sharply evident as well. The plot, which concerns among other wonderful things, a murder by sword thrust in a "disappearing room," is both intricately layered and mystifying. The action is plentiful, at times fast and furious; especially well choreographed is the swordplay, for Carr had an encyclopedic knowledge of swords and fencing techniques. There is an abundance of sly humor, as in the scene in which Darwent breaches his reluctant new wife's bathroom while she is taking a milk bath. There is more than a hint of sex—Carr was one of the few Golden Age writers to inject healthy doses of young passion and old lust into his narratives. There is even a clever sleuth, Mr. Hubert Mulberry, a fat, slovenly, drunken lawyer, who is reminiscent, no doubt deliberately, of another "H. M.": Sir Henry Merrivale, hero of Carr's detective novels as by Carter Dickson (and in this reader's opinion, his most memorable series character).

Above all in these pages there is an aura of mystery, of things dark and dreadful, perhaps even supernatural, lurking just beyond the ken of the characters and manipulating them in devious ways. Mystery was Carr's number one stock-in-trade: no writer past or present could create and then maintain a fever-pitch atmosphere such as that which Webster's defines as "something beyond understanding ... something which baffles and perplexes."

In sum, *The Bride of Newgate* is vintage John Dickson Carr. And that means it is vintage Entertainment, with a capital E.

◇ CHAPTER I ◇

Introduces the Hangman

The hanging of Dick Darwent, outside the debtors' door of Newgate Prison, was to take place on the following morning.

Not until dawn would anybody hear an ominous sound, not even the tolling of the great bell at St. Sepulchre's. At dawn the spectators would hear the dragging clatter of hoofs on cobbles, the bump of wheels as horses drew out the scaffold from the Main Gate. It was a big and heavy scaffold, this one: a dozen feet high, and so broad that ten couples could have danced on its platform.

Its sides, boarded up like a box from platform to jolting wheels, were chastely painted black. Under the direction of John Langley, the hangman, it would be set up outside debtors' door.

At the moment, on that summer night before the hanging of Dick Darwent, it was not much past ten-thirty. But a crowd was already beginning to gather in the narrow street outside.

"Damme," said one hoarse-voiced turnkey, who was on duty in the lodge above the Main Gate, "damme, but this'll be a proper 'un!"

The turnkey was leaning out the window, craning his neck to look left and downward at the gloom of the street called Old Bailey.

A second turnkey, who had held his job for less than a month but whose red longcoat was almost as soiled as his companion's, hurried across to the window. The light of a single candle, burning on a table in the whitewashed room, for a moment showed only the backs of two dirty red long-coats craning outside.

"There won't be no riot!" protested the second turnkey, his voice high as though with defiance.

"W'y not?"

"They likes Dick. They're friendly to Dick."

The first turnkey, called Blazes because of his nose, leaned down and patted the rough-stone front of Old Newgate as

5

though he loved it. His hoarse-voiced chuckle floated from outside.

"And so they was friendly to Holloway and Haggerty," he said, "when Brunskill turned 'em off in '07."

"Ah?"

"Twenty-eight people, as come to see the execution, a-crushed to death in front of the scaffold. Not countin' the ones as wos 'urt, either. And that's not a word of a lie."

The second turnkey, tall and lean Jamy, drew his head back from the window. He knew it was not a lie.

"And 'twasn't a riot," argued Blazes. "Leastways, not wot you'd think of as a riot. Lord, it begins afore the coffin meat comes out of debtors' door, and they all gives the 'Ats Off! shout. It begins afore you knows it."

"But *w'y* does it?" insisted Jamy.

Blazes considered this, still patting the rough-stone front of Newgate.

"They're most of 'em drunk, for one thing." He stated a simple, natural fact. "About daylight they begins a-whoopin' and shoutin' and singing. Maybe a dog nips somebody's ankles. Maybe a 'ooman's stifling to death, or thinks she is. And then—"

Outside the window Blazes' red arms described a whirl. His voice, which had been almost serious, became again a hoarse chuckle.

"But the rarest games, though the crowd don't like it, is when the hangman's drunk too."

"No, and *I* never liked it meself!" Jamy cried suddenly.

Blazes slowly turned round. From the window emerged a large face with little blue veins trailing from the nose.

"W'y, bless your innercence," he began, in a kind of passion, "I've seen old Brunskill—afore Langley come in—so full-up o' brandy-and-water he tried to put the halter round the parson's neck 'stead of the coffin meat's! And that's no word of a lie either."

Abruptly, on the verge of another outburst, Blazes stopped.

Both men were uneasy. Both knew it. But neither would refer to what lay uppermost, like a fear clot, in his mind. And this fear clot had nothing to do with the execution tomorrow morning.

A hanging, to them as to others, was a familiar and almost a friendly spectacle. It was far more edifying than Punch and Judy. Some other disquiet, always there but seldom mentioned except with a jeer, oppressed their hearts as it oppressed all

6

London. It could be felt in the air, and breathed like the smoke from the roofs opposite, on this night of Thursday, June twenty-first, 1815.

A bell on the wall jumped and danced and clattered.

"That's the wicket," growled Blazes. "Inside, too."

"Late visitor a-going out?" asked Jamy, who was hurriedly lighting a lantern at the candle.

"*Werry* late," said Blazes, with a significant look. "If you know what's o'clock, my lad, you'll get somethin' handsome outen him for your trouble."

Jamy, his keys rattling, hastened down the corkscrew stair.

The late visitor, who stood by the wicket gate in the big Main Gate, seemed mostly in shadow even when Jamy held up the oblong lantern with its grimy glass sides.

The visitor's nose twitched, perhaps his stomach twitched as well, at the smell of Newgate. From the Felons' Side you could faintly hear the noise of a carousal; wine or spirits might be obtained at any hour here.

"Late, sir," growled Jamy, in a voice imitating Blazes.

"Precisely a quarter to eleven," replied the visitor, in a dry and even voice.

He was a little, spare, unemotional man, in a coat with several capes; but he wore the black knee breeches and buckles of the last century. An old-fashioned 'un, thought Jamy; a shrewd 'un, as he watched the eyes behind the small gold-rimmed spectacles.

But the gentleman, whose gray hair was clubbed behind the neck, put a shilling into Jamy's hand as the later unlocked the wicket gate.

"Begging your pardon, sir," Jamy blurted out. "Is there any *news*?"

Mr. Elias Crockit, lawyer, of Lincoln's Inn Fields, knew what Jamy meant.

"None, I fear," he replied. "Only rumor."

As the gate closed behind him, Mr. Crockit stood for a moment in the street under a fine if smoke-misted night of stars. He glanced at the house across the way. It was dark. But at dawn the windows would be lighted, and the champagne breakfast set out for that willful beauty, Miss Caroline Ross, and her guests.

It was the fashion of the gentry; no one minded. After breakfast, showing tipsy faces at the windows, they would watch the victim kick his heels on a rope with amusement or tears, according to their mood.

7

And Mr. Crockit must see Miss Caroline Ross now. Most desperately *now*!

A little way down Old Bailey, a hackney coach waited. In a low voice the little lawyer gave the address of Miss Caroline Ross, in St. James's Square.

Inside the gloom of the musty-smelling coach, as it jolted down and turned right into Fleet Street, Mr. Crockit took his hat from under his cloak and placed it on the seat beside him. He leaned back, pushing his spectacles up on his forehead and closing his eyes.

Mr. Elias Crockit was frightened. And he confessed it to himself.

It was not that he cared a groat for Richard Darwent, a condemned murderer. Murderers should be dusted away as snuff is dusted off the fingers. But what Miss Caroline Ross proposed was so shocking, so much a-bristle with possibilities for scandal, that Mr. Crockit feared for his own reputation.

And on his mind, he confessed, rested the oppressiveness which had troubled even that poor brute of a turnkey.

To Mr. Crockit, not as a rule an imaginative man, this oppressiveness seemed like a huge, slow drumbeat: distant, yet approaching until all the drums should strike up.

"News!" he murmured aloud. "News!"

But he did not open his eyes until the cab drew near Pall Mall. With the Strand left behind him, Mr. Crockit felt he could breathe cool bloom and grass again. Much as Mr. Crockit (like others) might feel apprehensive in the presence of the gentry, he was at least permitted to approach.

Pall Mall lay deserted. The feeble street lamps burning coal gas, installed here seven years ago and now common to London, lighted up only dun-colored houses and lines of hitching posts. Mr. Crockit's coach turned into St. James's Square, and stopped before number thirty-eight. Having paid his fare, the elderly lawyer mounted the stone steps to the narrow red-brick house. He had just rapped at the bronze knocker, when . . .

"Come, now!" protested the startled Mr. Crockit, after which he wished he had not spoken.

A covered carriage, with horses nearly spent, smashed at full gallop into St. James's Square, and drew up with a clatter before the door of number eighteen.

Number eighteen was the home of Lord Castlereagh, the War Minister.

Mr. Crockit saw that brief scene at right angles, and some

distance away, by the gleam of a gas lamp. He saw a flash of red coat and two gold epaulettes as a young officer jumped out of the carriage, raced up the steps of number eighteen, and plied the knocker.

Now Mr. Crockit did not know that the young officer was Major the Hon. Henry Percy, aide-de-camp to the Duke of Wellington. But he saw, protruding from a carriage window, what looked like the standards of two captured French eagles. And some emotion squeezed at his withered old heart, such as he had not known for years.

"Yes, sir?" inquired a man's voice, as the door of number thirty-eight opened to Mr. Crockit's knock.

And Mr. Crockit was, first and last, a man of business. Whatever he may have felt was instantly shut up, with a snap, in one of the small innumerable drawers of his mind.

"Miss Caroline Ross?"

He raised his eyebrows superciliously at the tall footman, chosen as usual for wide shoulders and fine calves, who wore Miss Ross's livery and a powdered wig.

"Yes, sir. If you will please follow me?"

The footman led him to the drawing room, up a padded staircase in a foyer softly lighted by candles. Coal gas was too dangerous for domestic lighting; a careless or drunken servant might blow up the house. Mr. Crockit approved such moderation. To him it remained an irritant that young dandies should wear grotesque tall hats, and (to him) the new fashion of trousers.

Clothes. . . .

Another disturbing thought entered Mr. Crockit's mind.

Miss Caroline Ross was determined on a mad, dangerous enterprise. What if bravado prompted her to wear one of the lewd dresses invented by Lady Caroline Lamb?—another Caroline! This dress consisted of nothing whatever except a gown of transparent muslin, dampened with water so that it should adhere to the body.

It was unlikely, of course. Despite her beauty, Miss Ross was widely known for being (plague take these vulgar expressions) as cold as a fish. But she was willful and fiercely stubborn. Mr. Crockit more than suspected she cared not a straw for her reputation.

Nevertheless, after one glance into the drawing room as the footman announced him, he was reassured.

"Good evening, Mr. Crockit," said his hostess's voice.

9

Caroline Ross was a few months short of her twenty-fifth birthday.

"Your most obedient servant, madam," replied Mr. Crockit, bowing low and meaning every word he said.

Both of them waited until the door had closed.

It was a *bijou* room, an intimate one too, decorated in the so-called Roman mode which permitted much green-and-white striping in the upholstery and many austere classical curves in the furniture. Four candles, each one inside a glass container and set in pairs, lighted the room from either side of the white-marble mantelpiece. Two tall windows, facing out over St. James's Square, were closely muffled with heavy dark-green curtains bordered in gold.

"Do you bring me good news, Mr. Crockit?"

"At least, madam, I bring you the news you desire."

The faint flush of triumph sprang into her face as he said that.

"Is there the faintest chance—no, the *tiniest* remote possibility!—that he may not die tomorrow morning?"

"There is none."

"Pray sit down, Mr. Crockit. Do sit down!"

She was being kindly to him now, spreading condescension; and Mr. Crockit, so humble in the presence of the great, keenly appreciated the honor.

Caroline Ross, also after the fashion, wore a white satin gown cut very high at the waist and very low at the corsage; her arms bare, the gown ankle-length. Color touched it only with a scarlet sash, and a single ruby at her breast. Her rich light-brown hair was worn in bands across the forehead, and, at the sides, in short ear-length ringlets. Her eyes were dark blue, with black lashes.

And yet Caroline, so feminine of face and especially of body, seemed to have about her no hint of softness. No animation, no tinge of color except that of the excitement of anger, ever touched her cheeks or her eyes.

And so she sat there, at one end of a low backless sofa, one bare elbow on the curved side of the sofa, her hand supporting her cheek under the ringlets as she inclined her head, with the candlelight falling softly over her.

Her blue eyes watched Mr. Crockit without expression.

"I am told," she said, "that this wretch what's-his-name has *no* tiniest chance of escape. What assurance do you give me?"

The little lawyer looked grim.

"You wished, I believe, that the hanging should be—expedited?"

"Yes, yes, yes!"

"Very well. I therefore made interest with a gentleman whom we shall merely call Sir B."

"Do you mean Sir Benjamin Bloomfield? Prinny's confidential adviser?"

Mr. Crockit was pained to his very eyelids.

"In all else, madam, you may command me. But pray allow me to deal with your affairs in my own way."

"You are rather an amusing old dear," smiled Caroline, still with her elbow resting on the sofa side and her cheek against her hand. "Well! And then?"

"Darwent," said Mr. Crockit, "was condemned to death on the 19th. In these matters it is customary to permit seven days' grace, including one Sunday."

"May I ask why?"

"So that the condemned person may hear the preaching of an edifying sermon, and sit before a coffin as he does so. It is an excellent old custom.

"However!" continued Mr. Crockit, seeming all spectacles and forehead wrinkles as he bent forward. "In this case the death warrant was signed almost at once by the Secretary of State. Whereupon, through the good offices of Sir B., it was shown to . . . to . . ."

"You don't mean to Prinny himself?" cried Caroline.

Again pain twitched at Mr. Crockit's eyelids.

"To His Royal Highness the Prince Regent," assented Mr. Crockit in a low voice.

"And what did Prinny say?"

"His Royal Highness was told the entire story: a fair and accurate account, bear witness! His Royal Highness was filled with indignation; and also, I am told, with iced punch. The murdered man, Lord Francis Orford, was his near friend. Though it would appear . . ."

"That Prinny had forgotten all about him? Yes?"

"In effect, yes. But His Royal Highness was graciously pleased to write across the death warrant, 'This sentence *must* be carried out.' "

"Oh, you are a dear! You are a jewel! You are a treasure!"

"I can but do my best. Madam, God Himself could not save Richard Darwent now."

There was a pause. Caroline sat upright, her hands folded.

11

She seemed about to pour out more congratulations, when annoyance struck into her guarded life.

"Upon my soul," she said pettishly, "I can't have quiet in my own home! What is that insufferable noise down in the street?"

A movement of her eyebrows indicated that Mr. Crockit should ring the bell. Alfred, the first footman, was instructed to inquire about the disturbance. Any urchin in St. James's Square could have told him.

Major Percy, clattering up in his carriage to the door of number eighteen, had found Lord Castlereagh not at home. But the War Minister, they told him, was dining only a few doors away at the home of Mr. Boehm. Abovestairs, still over the wine, he found not only Lord Castlereagh; he found Lord Liverpool, the Prime Minister, and His Royal Highness, the Prince Regent.

But none of the sparks from their talk, now blown and adrift over London, touched the *bijou* drawing room with its dark-green curtains and its white-clad hostess.

"Then I am quite, quite safe!" murmured Caroline.

Whereupon Mr. Crockit lost his head.

"Before you do this," he burst out, "I implore you to stop and consider."

"I have considered, sir."

"Madam, it is a damned outrage!"

Caroline Ross merely looked at him.

"That will suffice, I think." Effortlessly she put him in his place, as though with a candle snuffer. "You yourself," she could not help adding, "told me that my grandfather's despicable and *mean* will could not be contested."

"No man can contest it. It is a good will."

" 'A good will.' " repeated Caroline, and threw back her head. "God save us!"

"Can you bear in mind, madam, that you inherit a very great fortune?"

"As I have always expected to inherit it. Naturally!"

"Well! Under the law, believe me, your grandfather could have imposed conditions much more severe. He might have chosen you a husband. Instead, the only conditions attached to your inheritance is that you are married by your twenty-fifth birthday. Mark that! Married by your twenty-fifth birthday!"

Again there was a pause.

"Do you recall," Caroline said dreamily, "any particular phrase in the writing of that will?"

"I have forgotten it."

"*I* have not. 'She's a stubborn filly, and needs the whip.' — Let us see!"

Mr. Crockit, in quiet despair, made one last plea.

"Come now," he urged persuasively, "there must be a dozen eligible gentlemen, if I may say so, eager to ask for your hand in marriage."

Caroline lifted one shoulder. "I daresay."

"And yet, to avoid the necessity of marrying anybody . . ."

Caroline's soft brown ringlets fell forward as she inclined her head in assent.

"To avoid this," said Crockit, "you would go by stealth to Newgate Prison. You would wed a verminous creature condemned to death. On the morrow, above all, you would watch from a tavern window while he kicks at a rope's end. You would gorge a champagne breakfast, and make sure he is dead. This is not worthy of you."

Caroline regarded him fixedly.

"Worthy or not," she replied, "does it fulfill the conditions of the law?"

"The letter of the law. Yes."

"Will this marriage be legal?"

"This afternoon," returned Mr. Crockit, and tapped the side of his coat, "I procured a license at Doctors' Commons. The Chaplain at Newgate, whom they call the 'Ordinary,' is an ordained clergyman of the Established Church. Yes: it will be legal."

"Can any man *then* contest my right to my inheritance?"

"None in this world."

"Why, then! Let me be married to the convicted felon!"

"As you please, madam. —You do not find it, forgive me, a trifle degrading?"

"Degrading!" exclaimed Caroline, though in fact her cheeks were flushed. She arose from the sofa.

As though to conceal anger by concealing her face, she swept over to examine two framed silhouettes hung on the wall beside the door. After a moment she turned back to the small round table in the center of the room. Standing sideways to her guest, she glanced at him over one bare shoulder, past the ringlets.

"Dear Mr. Crockit," she breathed. "Do let me explain!"

The lawyer merely inclined his head.

Caroline turned round to face him fully. The ruby at her corsage burned with shifting colors by candlelight.

13

"In marriage, it's understood, the husband has a certain 'right.' I will not grant *that* right to any man." She rapped her knuckles on the table, breathing quickly. "Do you understand me, sir?"

"Perfectly."

"That aspect," said Caroline, "I have always considered rather ridiculous and faintly revolting. But, under your precious law, the husband has still another right. Everything I own becomes his property, even to the house we stand in at this moment. And what, pray, do I get in exchange?

"I receive a boorish lout who will stamp home smelling of the stables, rattle out his oaths, and be hopelessly drunk by three o'clock in the afternoon. Or an empty-pated dandy (praise heaven the breed is passing!) who pays fabulous compliments, has a sour temper, and gambles away every farthing at Watier's or White's. If one lives *à la mode*, that's a husband.

"And for *this*," Caroline went on, with bitter disdain, "we're taught to simper, and swoon, and tap coquettishly with a fan, and cry 'Fie!' at some mildly bawdy jest. For wha. purpose? To 'catch,' dear me, a husband who is not worth the trouble to catch!"

Her voice went up.

"It's not fair. It's *odious*," cried Caroline, suddenly becoming human and stamping her foot on the dark-green carpet. "You say, Mr. Crockit, that what I propose is degrading. Very well! Then which is the more degrading: their style of marriage or mine?"

"My dear young lady," protested a much-puzzled Mr. Crockit, "I am not responsible. That's the way of the world."

"Not my world, sir. Not my world!"

The lawyer studied her.

"You have spoken much," he told her dryly, "of feeling and sensibility. Have you thought of your felon-husband's feelings?"

"Pardon me. Of . . . what?"

"We come to him, madam, during the last few hours of his life. We say to him, 'Wed this lady and die as soon as possible, so that she may have fine jewels and painted carriages.' It might well sicken a poor devil on the brink of eternity."

Caroline's whole manner had altered to one of poised coolness.

"This murderer, I imagine, is not *du monde*?" Her sarcasm increased. "He belongs to perhaps a little lower stratum of society than my own?"

"And if he does, madam?"

"Then how does it matter what his feelings are?" Caroline asked simply. "Indeed, he has no feelings."

That was the moment at which, suddenly, they both turned toward the door.

They could not have been more astonished if a tidal wave had swept up over Whitehall. For the door of the drawing room was almost flung open. Alfred, the first footman, stood red-faced and unable to control his voice.

"He's beaten," the footman said. *"Boney's beaten!"*

The words struck across that fastidious room like hammers against glass.

And now they were all aware, as though noises had hovered only at the back of the mind, that a crowd was assembled in the square below. Two-hundred-odd voices were upraised with, "God Save the King."

"You may apologize later," Caroline told the footman. "In the meantime . . . no, no; don't try to speak formally: you'll burst. Simply tell us."

"On Sunday, madam," the footman began formally, and choked. "On Sunday they beat the immortal stuffing out of Boney at some place near Brussels. The Frenchies, they downed arms and ran. Old Boney ran too. We might 'a' had the news Sunday night."

"Sunday night?"

"Yes, madam. Two of our lads, cavalrymen they were, swore they'd ride all night and send the news to Dover by semaphore. They'd got a big semaphore, and a lot of brushwood for a fire to see it by. But in Dover . . ."

"Gently, now. Gently!"

"They couldn't tell, even with the best spyglass, whether the message was, 'Boney beat us,' or, 'Boney beaten.' My brother says an old woman was hurt, and a man dropped dead. But there wasn't anything more until today."

And outside the windows voices rose up:

> *Confound their politics,*
> *Frustrate their knavish tricks,*
> *On Thee our hopes we fix,*
> *God save the king!*

Verse after verse of that anthem, sung in deep fervor, rolled across the square. Mr. Crockit hastened to the nearest window, and threw back the heavy curtains.

Toward his left across the square, over a multitude of up-turned faces, he saw that every window in Mr. Boehm's house was illuminăted. It kindled the trees of the square to spectral green. At the windows they were exhibiting the first trophies, two war eagles and four French battle flags. Out on a balcony moved an indistinct figure, which by its immense fatness could be only that of the Prince Regent. The figure bowed, and bowed again, amid a thunder of huzzas.

Napoleon Bonaparte, so-called Emperor of the French, would trouble this earth no more.

"You may go," Mr. Crockit heard Caroline say to the footman. The lawyer hastened to close the curtains, and compose himself. For here, it is regrettable to state, there were tears in Mr. Crockit's eyes.

"Will you be good enough, Mr. Crockit, to favor me with your attention"

"I deeply apologize," said Mr. Crockit. "I was much preoccupied."

"This victory," said Caroline in a tone of anxiety, "will not disturb *our* plan?"

"No, madam. Why should it?"

"There will not be—oh, what do I want to say!—a rejoicing, a jail delivery for the victory? He cannot escape hanging?"

Caroline's mouth, which was broad and full lipped and should have added to her beauty, had been compressed by sheer will power to a thin line.

"I fear," said Mr. Crockit, "you must take your notions of law from the Minerva romances. No; he can't escape."

"Stay a moment, though! You said, or at least hinted . . . oh, it's absurd! it's incredible! it's impossible! . . . that the man might refuse this offer."

"I had already thought of that, madam. He will not refuse."

"What assurance do you give of this?"

Mr. Crockit made a mouth.

"The last position occupied by the man Darwent," he answered, "was that of fencing master at a *salle d'armes* near Drury Lane Playhouse. He became attracted by a young person . . ."

"Yes, yes, I might have guessed it!"

"This young person is an actress, of sorts. But she is given very small parts, and is near destitution. If it had not been for Darwent—well!"

"Well?"

"He has nothing to leave her. Fifty pounds—an overly generous sum, mark you!—should keep her in comfort for a year. Yes; he will consent.—I have no pity to waste on murderers," Mr. Crockit added curtly. "Yet the man Darwent, one hears, is a good fellow."

"Oh, and indeed? Have you seen him?"

"No. I visited Newgate tonight for that purpose. I also wished to have a word with Darwent's representative, a fat and drunken rascal named Mulberry. But I decided that an approach nearer the last moment would weaken him more."

"Yes! I agree!"

"As for the young person from the playhouse . . ."

Caroline made that sound which is usually described as "faugh!" Mr. Crockit politely ignored it.

"He would die for her, they say," the lawyer mused, and then woke up. "Come!" he added, angry with himself. "I have strange notions in my head tonight. He will die in any case, madam. Have no fear for that!"

◇   C H A P T E R   I I   ◇

Deals with a Blue Coach at Twilight—

The Rev. Horace Salusbury Cotton, Ordinary of Newgate, stumbled once or twice as he hastened over the rough ground of the Press Yard.

A turnkey, carrying a lantern, followed him respectfully. The lantern light shone on the clergyman's black billowing gown, and the neat white bands at his neck.

The Rev. Horace Cotton was a large, rosy, robust man, with two kinds of strength in him. He was a trifle unctuous, they say, and a little inclined to be strong in his hell-fire sermons to the condemned. But this came only from zeal and earnestness; at heart he was a kindly man.

Midway across the yard he stopped, his prayer book in his hand, and looked round him.

The condemned cells were ratholes crowded round three sides of the small yard. "Press Yard" was only a name derived from an older Newgate; no one nowadays was pressed or crushed to death. After dark, as a rule, these cells were light-

17

less. Sometimes as many as fifty persons were pushed, willy-nilly, into the few of them.

But Press Yard was strangely quiet tonight.

"Which cell," asked the Rev. Horace, in his rich voice, "is the prisoner's?"

"W'y sir," answered the turnkey, pointing toward a very faint gleam inside the grill of an arched iron door, "it's that 'un with the light in it. Dick must'a paid something 'andsome for it."

They approached the door. The Rev. Horace cleared his throat, for better richness of exhortation. He could have sworn he heard, inside the cell, the rattle of iron fetters against a wall: as of a man in a convulsion of mortal terror. But this ceased instantly as the jailer's keys rattled.

The Rev. Horace, having forgotten something in his haste, bent close to the turnkey and spoke in a low voice.

"Er—the prisoner's name?" he inquired.

"Darwent, sir. Dick Darwent."

"And his—er—offense?"

"Ain't sure, sir. There's so many of 'em."

Handing the Rev. Horace his lantern, the turnkey unlocked the iron door for the clergyman to enter, locked it behind him, and waited stolidly.

And the Rev. Horace swept in, large and robust and rosy, like a sunrise over a sewer.

"My poor fellow . . . !" he began.

Facing him, sitting back to the wall on the pile of straw which served as a bed, was a figure whose hands were fettered to the wall with long rusty chains attached to iron cuffs. He had one leg fettered as well.

If Darwent had been washed and cleansed of lice, he would have been a middle-sized, lean, very wiry young man in his early thirties. But he had allowed himself to go to seed in detention before his trial. A dark stubble of beard marred his dirty face, and mingled with long greasy hair. His clothes were a scarecrow's amid straw. His eyes—gray eyes, rather bloodshot but steady and compelling—regarded the clergyman with watchful friendliness.

"My poor fellow," continued the Rev. Horace, "I have come to help you during your last hours on earth."

"Good evening, Padre," replied the scarecrow, in a voice of polished courtesy. "It was kind of you to visit me in my somewhat cramped lodgings."

The Rev. Horace took a step backwards, and tightened his

hand on the prayer book. His astonishment held him speechless.

At one side of the cell was a small niche of a seat, reserved for visitors. In this stood another lantern, with a tall candle burning inside. There was no other furniture except a wooden bucket, which the French politely called a *chaise d'aisance,* within reach of the condemned man's chains. In the straw bed stood a bottle of brandy, only an inch or so depleted.

"And before you continue, Padre," Darwent spoke earnestly, "may I venture a small request?"

"Of—of course," said the clergyman.

With some effort Darwent rose to his feet, the chains rattling, and propped his back against the wall.

He was weak, since the condemned were permitted only bread and water after their sentence. He had drunk too much brandy, both before and after trial. The iron cuffs galled his wrists to festering, with ceaseless pain.

"Padre," he said, "I would mock at no man's religion, even the faith of those we are taught to call the heathen. Therefore," —Darwent held up his hand to forestall objection, and pain burned him—"therefore let us discuss all books save only Holy Writ.

"By your look, Padre," he went on, "you are good fellow. By your calling you are a man of education. Let us sit here, like two friends—I am devilish lonely!—and talk together until you're obliged to go. I beg of you to do this!"

Here, thought his visitor, was a very bad case.

The Rev. Horace Cotton had not long occupied his post at Newgate. He had not yet seen, in the condemned cell at least, such a dirt-coated wreck of what was plainly a gentleman. His whole nature and soul became as hard as a rock.

"My poor fellow!" he repeated. Then his voice rolled out. "Do you not credit the reality of the Lord God Almighty?"

Darwent considered this. His gaze moved slowly over the damp stone ceiling.

"I don't know," he replied. "That's the most fair and honest answer I can give. I don't know."

"Tomorrow morning," said the Rev. Horace, "you stand in the awful presence of your Maker, who may condemn you to the torture of fire everlasting and sear you with pain beyond human knowledge. Make your peace with Him!"

The language of the time was not intended to be cruel; it was meant to uplift hearts. The Rev. Horace Cotton thundered at him.

19

"Have you nothing to confess? Nothing to repent of?"

Darwent's gray eyes looked back at him as steadily as his own.

"No, I don't think so."

"Come, then!" the clergyman said persuasively.

Putting down his lantern on the floor, the Rev. Horace took up the other lantern from the seat niche and placed it beside the first. He sat down, his black gown billowing, within three feet of Darwent.

"Come, then!" he urged. "Let me meet you on worldly grounds, if you like. You need not stand in my presence. Sit down."

Darwent slid down the rough-stone wall, amid rusty iron and damp. straw.

"You say there is nothing you repent. Very well! Is there anything you *regret*?"

"Yes."

"Ah! What is it?"

While the clergyman watched him steadily, Darwent reached out for the brandy bottle, took a deep swallow, shuddered, and then held out the bottle in his manacled hand as though thoughtfully considering a toast.

"I regret," he said, "all the books I have not yet read. All the wine I have not yet drunk. All the ladies I have not yet . . ."

"Stop!" roared his companion. "Would you add mockery to your other offenses?"

"Mockery? But I spoke no word of it! You asked me for the truth. Padre. and I told you."

The Rev. Horace, now less rosy-faced, lowered his head. In his heart he was praying.

"And that is all you have to regret?"

"No. Forgive me. I had all but forgotten the most important regret. Little Dolly."

"You—you mentioned a name?"

Darwent put down the brandy bottle amid straw, and corked it.

"I don't know where she is! If she were not ill, or under duress. or God knows what, she would have come to visit me! She is Dorothy Spencer, of the Drury Lane Theatre."

"Your wife?"

"No. I had not the good sense to make her my wife."

This condemned felon, the Ordinary guessed, was holding himself under an almost inhuman self-restraint. Despite his

20

weakness, despite the low tone in which he spoke, his voice had a strength and vibrancy that lingered in the ear.

And then, as Darwent took another swallow of brandy, his mood changed.

"Now the deuce take it, Padre, but we're a pair of solemn owls. Do you know what I've got? Sewn up somewhere in this abominable coat of mine? A bright new half-sovereign that will buy us two more bottles of brandy. Let's make a carouse of it until morning!"

"Would you go to your Maker in *that* state?"

"Quite frankly, yes. I feel the Creator must have enough dignity to make up for lack of mine. —No, stop!" Darwent said suddenly, and deliberately banged his fettered wrist against the wall.

"That was bravado and bad manners," he added quietly. "I should be kicked for saying it. And I ask your pardon."

His gray eyes, growing more bloodshot, looked out across the two lanterns toward the iron door of that little cell. To-morrow he would walk across the Press Yard, and through a door into a room where they would strike off his irons.

"I won't go like a coward," he said, "but I won't go with the strut and bravado which is worse. Let me go quietly, without fuss."

"Now you speak like a man!" exclaimed the Ordinary, and sympathy welled up in his heart. "Let me exhort with you to repent, so that you may perhaps find mercy and salvation. Young man! You lie here condemned of the foulest and most dreadful crime. You lie here condemned of the crime of . . . of . . . I forget precisely what?"

Sardonic eyes regarded him.

"The indictment was for murder. I am supposed to have killed Frank Orford in a duel."

For perhaps ten seconds there was quiet. A rat scuttled in the straw; and Darwent automatically thrashed at it with his ironed leg. The Rev. Horace Cotton sat with his mouth open, his thick knees wide apart, in utter incredulity.

"A duel?" he exclaimed. "And is that all?"

" 'Tis not so deep as a well, nor so wide as a church door,' " quoted his companion. "But 'tis enough. 'Twill serve.' "

Thick veins were swelling in the Rev. Horace Cotton's neck. He surged to his feet in wrath.

"God damme!" said the parson.

The scarecrow was polite enough not to laugh. But a blood-shot eye twinkled.

21

"And now, Padre, *you* speak like a man."

"I am," confessed the Rev. Horace. "May heaven forgive me! I am one of His most undeserving servants, with too many faults. To—to shed blood, I know, is the most grievous . . ." His voice trailed off. "But a duel!"

Here he tugged at the neat white bands at his neck.

"The duel," he went on, "has for centuries been the privilege of a gentleman. That is why the House of Lords fights tooth and nail for it."

Again the Ordinary paused, fingering his prayer book.

"By custom if not law, your crime should have meant a few months in Newgate. Perhaps a year. Even transportation if you had no friends to make interest for you. Had you none?"

"None!"

"But the gallows! I do not understand this! Who was your judge?"

"Mr. Justice Twyford, they tell me." Now Darwent smiled. "This learned judge, in his youth, once engaged another learned gentleman with smallswords. By accident or foul thrust, he was run through . . . well, it is a very necessary part of our anatomy. Don't you find entertainment in this?"

"Bravado," the clergyman said quietly.

"True! Your pardon again." Darwent remained satiric. "Meanwhile, Frank Orford's family . . ."

"You refer, perhaps," interrupted the Ordinary, with an odd glance, "to Lord Francis Orford?"

"That was the man. A lisping dandy who looked so closely at both sides of a penny that he could never endure to spend it. Frank Orford's family, I say, were busy with a tune of clinking guineas for the jury." At last Darwent burst out, with an animal snarl. "Who knows the reason of the verdict? And who cares?"

The Rev. Horace Cotton drew a deep breath.

"A while ago," he said, "you asked that we should sit together and talk like friends. Well! Be not afraid. You have a friend."

For a moment Richard Darwent looked at him, and then closed his eyes.

"I . . . thank you, Padre." He would have said more, but he was incapable of it.

"And now," continued the clergyman, planting himself in the seat niche, "you shall tell me the story."

"Ah, but that's the best part of the jest! And it was never

once mentioned at the sessions house out there. —Padre, there was no duel."

"No duel?"

"On my oath," Darwent spoke with intensity, "I am neither drunk nor mad. Someone murdered Frank Orford, and put the blame on me. I never touched him."

"But, man! Did you not speak—no; you may not speak— well! Did you not write a deposition of this for your trial"

"No. I dared not."

"For what reason?"

"I was advised (and rightly, I think) that what the truth was could not be told in a sessions court. It's a brief tale; but it's too full of goblins and wizardry for anyone to believe in our day. Besides, I—detain you from your duties."

"You are my only duty. Speak!"

Richard Darwent settled back against the wall. Since brandy padded his senses against festering wrists and ankle, it seemed to him that for a little time—in imagination which almost became reality—he could be outside this rathole. The dream of green grass and trees! The dream of Dolly Spencer!

He saw again the rural immensity of Hyde Park, where cows and deer grazed under the trees by day: where there were few paths, yet all the world of fashion came to ride at five o'clock in the afternoon.

"It was nearly eight o'clock in the evening," Darwent said drowsily, "and growing dark. To be exact, it was on the Piccadilly side of Hyde Park, and on the evening of May the fifth.

"I had gone for a long walk as far as open country. I saw nobody. The fashionables of Piccadilly would already have sat down to dinner, and wouldn't stagger up from the table until midnight or one in the morning. On that side of the park, if you recall, there is a white-painted wooden rail like a paddock, with a broad open space so that carriages may pass through.

"Well, I walked perhaps ten yards into the park. And then I saw that damned coach."

Darwent hesitated. The Rev. Horace, who knew that this long-haired patchbeard was half in a dream, forbore to interrupt him.

"It moved towards me along the path, out from the twilight trees in the park, like a coach from ghostland. It was no hackney coach. It was painted a rich dark blue edged in

23

gold, with yellow wheels and, I think, someone's crest on the panels. The horses were two fine bays.

"But the coachman, instead of resembling the wigged archbishop he usually seems, was a thin shabby man in a low-crowned hat, his scarf drawn across his face under the eyes.

"Mark you, now, I had no thought of deathliness or danger. Merely a passing wonder at so odd a driver on the box of so fine an equipage, and why anyone should drive in the park at this hour. I stood aside on the grass to let the coach pass towards Piccadilly, and continued to walk on the grass.

"And I didn't hear the coach stop, except in a preoccupied manner. For there I strode along, whistling, my hat in my hand, under twilight becoming darkness. I was a happy man, you apprehend. A very happy man—until then.

"I did not hear the coachman approach me from behind, until he spoke through folds of the scarf. What he said was: 'Are you ready?'

"We have mad moods in our happiness, Padre. Without thinking I cried:

" 'Ready for anything!'

"And, as I was in the act of turning round, a blow across the back of my head caught me fairly, or unfairly; and knocked me as senseless as ever Tom Cribb felled Molyneux."

Once more Darwent ceased speaking.

"Do you find my tale," he asked, "incredible so far?"

The Rev. Horace Cotton, his pale blue eyes wide open, hesitated, moistened his lips, and looked unhappy.

"I do not doubt you in the least," said the Ordinary. "In fact—"

"Yes, Padre?"

"I live here amid crime and sin, with even the poor debtor rattling his cup against the door for alms." The parson's voice sounded despairing. "My duty? What is my duty? Yet I learn. . ."

"You learn?"

"Other men have seen your ghost coach. Yes; and ridden in it too."

Something which was not quite hope, because no hope existed, struck into Darwent's heart.

But the Ordinary quenched it by waving a big hand in front of his own face.

"Pray don't question me. Continue!"

And Darwent shrugged his shoulders, and again he crouched like an animal above the brandy bottle.

24

"Well!" he said. "When I came to my senses, inside that coach, I was slung there in a seaman's hammock. My legs and wrists were tightly tied; but with soft cords. Gently, do you see? I wasn't gagged, but blindfolded; even my ears stopped. You may well ask how the devil I knew I was in the coach.

"But I knew it, Padre, and more which I could prove. I knew where we went.

"The coach carried me exactly nine miles into the country, to a house near Kinsmere in Bucks. It was Frank Orford's country house; or, more precisely, it belonged to the old Earl, his father. It's the only house of its kind within fifty miles of Kinsmere.

"Let me omit, under favor, the reasons why I knew this. The tale sickens me, I would make it short.

"Two persons, it seemed to me, lifted me out of the coach before the country house. I was carried up the front steps. They put me on my feet well inside an entrance hall, turning me gently sideways towards the right.

"Remember that I was still blindfolded and even my ears stopped up. Imagination (which proved to be correct) conjured up a door in front of me. My leg cords were cut with a knife. I was impelled forward towards an opening door; its panel brushed my right arm as it swung.

"Now how shall I describe a—a mere impression of the senses?

"It seemed that, in an instant, all things stopped as a clock stops. As though the persons with me, if there were more than one, stood paralyzed. The hand on my back, impelling me, rested motionless. I counted a dozen heartbeats. But, even through those devilish ear fastenings, I heard a woman scream.

Darwent stretched out his hand for the brandy bottle.

The Rev. Horace Cotton would not lift his gaze from the muddy floor.

"A woman, you say," the Ordinary stated without inflection.

"I can swear it!"

"And then?"

"As though the spell had broken, I was suddenly pushed forward and I stumbled across carpet. My wrist cords, with the arms bound behind me, were swiftly cut. By the time I had dragged bandages from my head and eyes, the door was closed and locked behind me. Let me describe it, now:

"It was a fair-sized oblong room with a high ceiling, the

walls papered in dark red patterned with gold. It had a fine Turkey carpet, I remember. Facing me, behind a tortoise-shell wood writing desk in the middle of the room, sat Frank Orford. On the desk in front of him lay a black silk mask.

"Damme, I scarcely recognized the fellow! I had never known him well at Oxf . . . at another time in my life. It was more difficult to recognize him now.

"What kept his head and neck upright, as he sat in a tall thin chair behind the writing desk, was the height and starch of his shirt collar and white cravat . . . as worn by all the dandies, so that a man can't see his own boots. Frank Orford could see nothing, though his eyes looked straight at me.

"He wore a brocade dressing gown, I recall: a fine peacock's-feather color for a skinny figure. He had been run through the heart with a modern French rapier, a cup hilt, pinning him to the back of the chair and protruding in blood more than two feet behind the chair.

"Well, spiritual counselor, what would you have done in my place.

"There was Frank, with his long nose and high shirt collar, and the blood patch just ceasing to spread on his dressing gown. I think he died a moment before I entered; at least, I saw a twitch of the eyelids. High above his head was a glass castle of a chandelier, but with only two or three candles because of Frank's miserliness. On a table stood a bowl of oranges, each looking as though it had been stabbed with a knife.

"Well, I tugged and banged and shouted at the locked door. I also cried, 'Who are you?' and 'What do you want?' and 'Why was I brought here?' But there was no answer.

"Two long windows at the front of the room were closely shuttered. One more window, in the side wall beyond Frank's body, had no shutters. It was moonrise; I could see the lawn round Kinsmere House, and on the lawn a marble statue of the god Pan which, on my oath, I could identify at any time.

"And here was I, locked up in the deep dead quiet of the countryside with . . .

"For, mark me again, this was no duel! Nobody fights a duel sitting behind a desk, with empty hands, and a sneer of boredom even in death. And more! When our fathers ceased to wear swords, towards the end of the last century, the sword went out of fashion in England except in the style of foils for exercise. For duels, it's the pistol now.

"But did I tell you I'm a fencing master? And keep a
26

school near Covent Garden? And had—ay, still have!—a pair of French rapiers in my *salle d'armes*? Fencing is very much the fashion as exercise. If two drunken men bragged and bounced until they fought with real swords . . .

"No matter! As I stood there, with Frank skewered to the chair under the thin candlelight, and a sense of stealthy life somewhere near, all I could think of was escape. That was when a voice spoke out of the air.

"I don't know where the voice came from. There was no one except myself and Frank in the room. The voice spoke in a heavy whisper.

"And it said: *'He must not reach the windows.'*"

Richard Darwent paused.

As his voice broke off, there was a heavy knocking of fist and boot against the iron door of the condemned cell.

"Sir!" called the hoarse voice of a turnkey outside at the iron grill, and keys rattled. "Your Reverence! Dick's got visitors!"

◇ C H A P T E R   I I I ◇

—and with a Room That Disappeared

The Rev. Horace Cotton, almost kicking over the two lanterns on the floor as he marched at the door, uttered an exclamation of annoyance.

The two candles in the lanterns were burning down in broad winding sheets of grease. The Rev. Horace could hear (muffled, though hard by Newgate) the clock at St. Sepulchre's dismally clang the hour of two in the morning.

In both senses, it was later than they thought.

"I believe I gave orders," the Rev. Horace said sternly to the turnkey outside, "I was not to be disturbed. However, open the door!"

The other did so. But this was not the same turnkey whom the parson had left on guard. He was an old hand, a squat hoarse-voiced man nicknamed Blazes. Blazes touched his forelock.

"Sir," he growled, "these visitors is a-waiting in the Chief Turnkey's lodging . . ."

27

"Well?"

"And that means five sovereigns if it means a penny. They're uncommon vexed to be kept waiting. So is the Chief Turnkey."

"Indeed," remarked the unimpressed clergyman.

"True as gospel, sir! Two gen'lemen and a lady . . ."

"It's Dolly!" cried Richard Darwent. A wheel seemed to go round in his brain. "It's Dolly at last!"

The Rev. Horace Cotton bit at his underlip.

"My dear fellow!" he said in* the term of equality rather than condescension, and hesitated. "This—er—Cyprian of yours, this Fair Impure . . ."

"She's not a whore, if that's what you mean."

"Yet she can scarcely be called a lady?"

"You forget she's an actress. She must play a lady before audiences that will howl down Kean himself, if he's less than his best.—Blazes!"

"Eh, Dick?" grunted the turnkey sympathetically.

"Her hair is gold," said Darwent. "She wears it in long ringlets. She is plump, and not very tall. You can feel her look of sympathy as I feel the warmth of that lantern. She has a heart for any blind beggar, and half-dead scavenger round the Theatre Royal. Her eyes are brown. You can't look into them without falling in love with her."

"Begging your pardon, Dick." Blazes was uncomfortable. "But it ain't the same lady."

'"Don't lie to me! I tell you it's Dolly!"

"This lady," Blazes said critically, "is a werry handsome piece. I grant you that."

"Then for God's sake . . . !"

"She ain't too tall, though she looks as if she ought to be. She's a-showing a lot of buzzim in her gown, and fanning herself fit to break the fan. She's got brown hair in short ringlets. But 'er potato-trap. . . I begs *your* pardon, Reverence! . . . 'er mouth's locked up like a moneylender's cashbox.

"Dick," added Blazes simply, "she *ain't*."

Darwent had managed to struggle to his feet. Now he sank down again, and said no more.

"Are you acquainted with this lady" asked the Rev. Horace.

Darwent shook his head.

"Or the gentlemen?" The Ordinary looked at Blazes. "Who are the gentlemen?"

28

"One of 'em is a carrion bird," he meant a lawyer, "named Crockit. But the other! Sir, it's Jack Buckstone!"

"I fear that conveys little to me."

"Buckstone, sir! Sir John Buckstone, to speak him proper. By your leave, Reverence: walk wide o' Jack Buckstone!"

It seemed that Blazes' hoarse pleading was not unmixed with reluctant admiration. His nose bloomed again.

"Ask 'em in Covent Garden," he pleaded. "That gen'leman'll pull off his coat to fight any porter for a pot-of-ale wager. He's been out nine times with the pistol, and never missed 'is man. He always gets wot he wants; and he don't even *notice* 'ooever tries to stop him. I warns you, sir: you'd better see Buckstone. This business . . ."

The Ordinary looked at the turnkey.

"I am about God's business of truth and justice. Who dares interfere with it?"

"Sir, I only meant—!"

"Present my compliments to the lady and the gentlemen," the Rev. Horace added mildly. "Bid them wait until they are permitted to enter."

"*But, sir*—"

"Did you hear me?"

Blazes retreated hastily, slamming and locking the iron door. The Rev. Horace set his back against the door, and drew a deep breath as he studied Darwent.

"Before you say one word more," and his big voice sounded shaken, "I must ask you a question. Who are you?"

"Eh?"

"Who are you? No, don't say, 'It makes no matter,' or some such rubbish! I won't be put off! Is your name truly Darwent?"

The felon almost laughed.

"It's Darwent now," he replied. "I took the name—and there was mockery, if you like—from the title of my uncle's peerage. He's the Marquess of Darwent."

"The Marquess of Darwent!"

"Deuce take it, Padre, don't *you* fall into a swoon at mention of a few strawberry leaves on a coronet. You're a man and a brother. As for the others . . . God rot the lot of them!"

"I will hear no more blasphemy, sir! Especially about—" The Rev. Horace checked himself.

"About great names?" inquired Darwent.

The question darted uncomfortably near the truth. Like Mr. Elias Crockit, the Ordinary felt humility even toward the near-great. A moment ago he had spoken boldly to the turnkey about these visitors; now he wondered. Yet, like Mr. Crockit and most others, his views were quite sincere.

"You told me, sir, you had no person to make interest at your trial."

"That was true, Padre. I should not have appealed to my uncle if I had risked far worse than hanging."

"And why not?"

"A few years ago, as it happens, my uncle and I quarreled. The fault was entirely mine. But I hate the man yet. That's human nature."

"May I ask the nature of this quarrel?"

"I was for some years a fellow at Simon Magus, Oxford. The books, the beloved innumerable books! But I thought Oxford grew stale. I would try my luck in the new states of America. I have always felt a kindness towards them, Padre."

"Indeed."

"You are pleased to be superior, Padre, because you have read so little of temporal government. Well! I have read many manifestoes: thunders, vaporings, prolixities." Darwent's voice grew harsh. "But only their manifesto, through all history, has dared proclaim man's right to the pursuit of happiness."

"Man's duty should be his happiness! That is enough!"

"Your pardon, Padre. It is *not* enough. However," smiled Darwent, "I sailed at a most fitting time, of course, when we were at war with them in '12. I sailed in an ammunition ship bound for Virginia; and hoped to swim ashore without being mistakenly hanged for a spy. But we never reached Virginia. At a place called Crosstree Island, where we were wrecked—" A shudder ran through him. "I hate firearms!" he said.

But the Rev. Horace was paying no attention.

"Sir, sir, attend to me! If you were to inherit the title, if you were to become my Lord Marquess of Darwent . . . !"

And now his companion really laughed.

"Padre," he said whimsically, and scratched his hand manacles at the lice-infested hair, "my uncle is a hale gentleman, scarcely middle-aged, who grows roses in Kent. He has two strong sons to follow him. Even if an earthquake obliterated all three at once, which I consider unlikely, should I be any better off?"

"No. Perhaps not."

"I am condemned, with my death warrant countersigned

by the Regent himself.—Don't ask me why! I don't know! But do you see a loophole now?"

The hours were dwindling, like the candles inside the lanterns.

"And yet," said the Ordinary, "perhaps *I* can be of help."

"You, Padre? And at this time? Come now!"

"Put your trust in *Him*," begged the other, with fierce intensity, "and tell me the rest of your story! I would not hold out false hope. No! But I credit what you say; and I do not think that He is ever mocked."

Here the clergyman held up a big hand.

"You were in a room," he went on, his voice soothing as though to induce sleep, "a room papered with dull red and gold. You faced a dead man, pinned to the back of a chair with a sword. Outside, on the lawn, there was a statue of a foolish pagan deity. Out of the air, or so it seemed to you, you heard a voice speaking. We deal, of course, with no such nonsense as ghosts. But the voice said, 'He must not reach the windows.' "

"Yes!" agreed Darwent, with a short and sharp breath.

Memory, so dreamlike and yet so vivid in each detail, wrapped him round as though by some sleight of the late M. Mesmer at Paris.

"I dislike to recall what happened then," he said, "because from then onwards . . . Well! He took me unawares again."

"Who took you unawares?"

"That coachman! The tall, thin, shabby man, with the scarf round his face up to the eyes: the man who drove me there in the blue coach. At least, I imagine it was the coachman. I never saw him face to face.

"Remember, now, that I had not advanced more than three steps into that room, with the door at my back. When the voice spoke, I looked about me. There was a fireplace in the same wall as the door on my right; against it, upright and unstained, stood a rapier which was a companion sword to the one that killed Frank. I looked back again at the furniture, all buhl and ormolu ornament.

"I had forgotten the door. Someone rushed at me, and struck again.

"When the jarvey attacked me in Hyde Park, it was no love tap. It gave me an aching head. But it was no worse than we get three times a week, if we play at football; and think little of. I could have sworn, that first time, the jarvey murmured an apology, saying this was not customary.

31

"But the second time! It was like to crack my skull, and it almost did. The awakening took a long time, since I had a touch of fever, and what a different awakening!

"First I had a sense that I was in the open air, lying on my back in half-dried mud, with my head against a pile of paving stones. After another long time, or so it seemed to me, I heard the noise of carts on cobbles and familiar street sounds. What I first saw, some distance away to the right and towering up over the houses. were the Greek pillars in front of Covent Garden Theatre.

"It was a smoky pink-and-gray daylight, broadening to sunrise. When I tried to sit up, the sickness came.

"My fencing school, as I told you, is off Covent Garden. On the north side, near the Piazza Tavern, there is a narrow cul-de-sac of an alley named Garter Lane. In our grandfathers' time the place would have been in fashion. But in these days only City bankers and merchants, grave men whom the dandies jeer at, gather at the Piazza Tavern.

"I was lying in Garter Lane, not five yards from my own fencing school: the back of my head caked with dried blood, like—like the bloodstained rapier in my right hand.

"Frank Orford's body, stiff as a board now, lay on its back just in front of me. Damme, I'd heard Frank was so fastidious a dandy he blacked and polished even the soles of his top boots, like Brummell. It was true. I saw the shining soles, and the disarranged embroidered dressing gown with cravat crumpled now, and the unstained rapier in *his* right hand. My shoes were clean too.

"I had only seen that, in daze, when my head split to the noise of a watchman's rattle. There stood the Charlie, in his red waistcoat, and with big gloating eyes, springing his rattle to summon assistance."

Darwent lowered his head.

The Rev. Horace Cotton, still with his back set against the iron cell door, breathed slowly and heavily. Yet he spoke with seeming irrelevance.

"You are too fine-drawn," he said. "Your imagination will not suffer you ever to rest."

"I deny that!" retorted the felon, as though he had been accused of the worst of crimes.

"However!" The Rev. Horace swept this aside. "Undoubtedly you and the dead Lord Francis had been carried to that place?"

Darwent brooded on that charge of being too sensitive.

Though he would not have admitted it, Mr. Cotton was right. He was all sensitiveness and imagination; all loyalties and hatreds: a human being.

"Carried there!" he repeated. "Yes!"

"In the blue coach?"

"I presume so. There were wheel tracks in the lane."

"And therefore," said the clergyman, "it would be assumed that you and Lord Francis, on an evening of drunkenness, had gone out of your fencing school to fight by moonlight in Garter Lane? And that you afterwards fell and struck your head?"

"Yes. Didn't I tell you, Padre? A formal duel with the pistol: yes. With sabers: permissible. But rapiers? Never!"

"This occurred to you, no doubt, when you were roused by the watchman's rattle beside Lord Francis's body?"

"No! I thought of nothing! Nothing at all save my own sickness and a head full of thunder. Do I need to tell you what is hard by Covent Garden? The Charlie, shouting for help as though I were a dozen men, marched me to the Magistrates' Court in Bow Street.

"I only dimly recall walking there. The Charlie would shake my shoulder and repeat, 'You're drunk, ain't you?' I denied it. But I immediately called for brandy, because I had need of it; and the voices of invisible people laughed all about me.

"At the Bow Street Office there was a gentleman (Mr. Birnie, was it?) who spoke fairly and kindly. I attempted to tell my tale, the true tale, but I could not speak with clearness. Mr. Birnie said it would be some time before the arrival of the Chief Magistrate, Sir Nathaniel Conant; and bade me lie down.

"Afterwards, at some time, I was lying on a board floor against the wall of a little room with hats in a row on pegs, and a loud-ticking clock. I think it was a room used by the Bow Street runners. Someone had washed and bound up my head. Squatting beside me was a man whom I later learned was a Mr. Hubert Mulberry. Are you acquainted with Mr. Mulberry, Padre?"

The Ordinary shook his head.

And again Darwent stared at the past.

"He is not prepossessing, it may be. Mr. Mulberry is fat and slovenly, and most of the snuff he takes spills on himself. But he is a shrewd man of the law. And by—no; you don't like oaths; I forbear—by the soul I may or may not have, he has been a good friend to me!

33

" 'Drink this,' says he, and propped me up. He put a bottle of raw spirit to my mouth. Afterwards he gave me a panni-kin of water, and I gulped it down. My wits were enough cleared to tell him everything.

"He said not a word, he asked not even a question, until I had done. He squatted there on his hams, and presently stood up.

" 'I count myself a judge of men,' says he, and went to-wards the door. I asked him where he was going.

" 'Why, damme,' says he, with violence in his bloated face, 'to hire a gig or a curricle! If that country house is where you say it is, then I'll engage to find it.'

"When he had gone, Padre, I had one more visitor. The Theatre Royal in Drury Lane is not far from Bow Street, and news spreads. Dolly Spencer came over a-flying. Mr. Kean was in rehearsal for *Macbeth*. There was Dolly, all strange clothes and glass jewels, with the tears in her eyes, to throw her arms round my neck and put her cheek against mine and—" Darwent stopped.

"Not a lady, of course," he added in a voice of ironic polite-ness. "They removed her, as you may guess. I believe she bit one fellow in the hand. Not a lady. Merely the faithfullest creature alive."

Again, deliberately to hurt himself, Darwent smashed the fetter of his right wrist against the wall behind him. The clergy-man watched with grave, compassionate eyes.

"Mulberry," Darwent went on, "did not return until dusk. He was a trifle in liquor, and stood swaying above me.

" 'Mr. Darwent,' says he, 'you may be an honest man or you may be the prince of liars. But this much I know: we can't tell that story of yours before a judge and a jury. Stick to the drunken duel, my bully; stick to the drunken duel!'—And that, I think, is all."

The Rev. Horace Cotton was jarred with astonishment as though by a blow.

"*All?*" he exclaimed.

"Yes."

"You are mocking me! Unless . . . did this lawyer find the house?"

"Oh, yes. Anyone thereabouts could tell him where to find it. It's a Vanbrugh house: an E-shaped place with domes on pillars atop every corner, and a clock tower in the middle. I have passed it many times myself."

34

"Well!" said the Rev. Horace. "Did he find the pagan statue on the lawn?"

"He did."

"And the room where you found Lord Francis dead?"

"Yes, Padre. Exactly as I described it."

"This is madness!" groaned the Rev. Horace. His expression changed. "Yes, yes, drink your brandy if it comforts you!"

"But," continued Darwent, putting down the bottle after a long draught, "I neglected to tell you what else Mulberry saw. The red-and-gold wall paper was now black with dust. That same dust, undisturbed, covered more thickly the floor and the fine Turkey carpet. Spiders had spun their webs between the writing desk of tortoise-shell wood and the tall chair behind it. Spider webs muffled the dull luster prisms of the chandelier. There was no mark of a sword thrust in the fiber back of the chair.

"Frank's father and mother, the Earl and Countess of Kinsmere, have been abroad for a long time. They ordered the grounds to be kept in order, but the house to be locked up without an occupant. *No man, it seems, has set foot in that room for more than two years.*"

Darwent, half-fuddled now but attempting to look agreeable, watched his companion with close-studying gray eyes.

"Yes, Padre?" he prompted.

"This is a jest in bad taste," the Rev. Horace accused him, not loudly. "You play it, remember, only on yourself!"

"The jest was not of my making. No."

"Some other house, perhaps? Some other room?"

"There was no other house, I fear. And no other room. Yet what I have told you is true. Do you believe me now?"

The Rev. Horace hesitated, and moistened his lips.

"My dear sir," he said gently, "my heart knows that *you* believe it."

"Then you call me mad?"

"No, no! I call you friend. But there are, to speak a truth, varying degrees of . . .of . . ."

"That won't do," Darwent interrupted curtly. "Consider the evidence! We go into the sessions house with this lie of a defense: that Frank and I fought by moonlight in Garter Lane. They accept that. Now it was only natural, you grant, that Frank's relatives should bribe the jury?"

"Not natural!" the other insisted, swiftly and firmly. "But . . . but at least credible."

"Good! Then who made interest at Carlton House?"

35

"I do not understand you."

"Frank's father quarreled with the Regent four years ago. The same year as that famous falling out with the Beau. No Orford, except Frank himself, would dare approach the Regent: even through Ben Bloomfield. Yet here's my death warrant countersigned, and the hanging set forward by at least four days!"

The Rev. Horace's rosy face turned a little away.

"You conceive," he asked, "that someone else is working against you? Someone in addition to the Orfords and this mysterious coachman?"

"I know it!"

"For a little while, sir, I had believed—"

The Ordinary paused. He had seen too many men who thought themselves persecuted; and they went mad, alone, in a little room. Touching the prayer book gently, he moved over and sat down in the niche.

"You have undergone much," he said. "Now forget these worldly affairs in the peace that passeth all understanding!"

"I thank you, no," replied Darwent. "Where's Dolly? Where's Mulberry, even? *He* has been faithful, and come to see me." The chains rattled and jangled. "You tell me I have a soul. I would barter that soul for ten pounds—yes, ten pounds —to leave them a little legacy of my gratitude!"

A new voice, speaking as though out of the air, answered him softly.

"Then suppose," it said, *"you were to be offered fifty?"*

The candle flames had burned down to mere blue hoverings, with a red spark inside each, above masses of grease. Darwent felt his heart contract, and a breath of pure superstitious terror, before he realized the truth.

A jailer's keys rattled. The voice which had spoken, outside the grill, was a thin, dry, elderly voice, very precise.

"My name is Crockit, Elias Crockit," the voice continued. "I am one of those who have been obliged to wait. I offer fifty pounds to the prisoner if he will do a small service which cannot trouble him."

"Fifty pounds!" breathed Darwent.

"Not a penny more," the dry voice warned.

To the amazement of the Ordinary, Darwent did not merely rise up. He sprang to his feet, stung and strengthened by nervous energy and brandy. He stood amid the straw, with an air of lazy lordliness that ill matched his dirt and bloodshot eyes.

36

That spurt of strength would last for only an instant, but it sufficed.

"You may admit Satan," said Darwent.

❖ CHAPTER IV ❖

The Bride of Newgate

Clang smote the distant, muffled bell at St. Sepulchre's Church. It rang out three strokes. In less than an hour, now, there would be daylight.

Mr. Crockit, holding out horizontally a neat leather case which contained writing materials, had just finished a concise, blunt explanation of what he wanted. Fresh candles for the lanterns had been bought from the turnkey Blazes.

"Please come in, Miss Ross," the little shriveled lawyer called. "The condemned man has consented."

"And I should think so!" a woman's voice was heard to mutter.

Caroline Ross entered the cell with (outwardly) an air of careless indifference. Over her white satin gown she had drawn a long gray-silk cape, lined with scarlet, and its peaked hood was now thrown-back to reveal the fair complexion, the short brown ringlets, and the long-lidded blue eyes.

Caroline's white satin slippers had sunk into the mud of the floor. But this, she afterwards confided, was not what turned her stomach and almost made her run away. It was the reek of a condemned cell.

"We must make haste, Mr. Crockit," she said, singling out that unhappy gentleman and pouncing. "Don't *you* find this delay really intolerable?"

"Patience, madam! We must have patience."

Caroline barely glanced at the prisoner; he was not worth noticing. She did not look at him now.

"He . . . does not have to touch my hand, I hope?"

"The bridegroom," answered Mr. Crockit, "must put the ring on your finger. I have the ring here." He tapped the leather case. "It cost only three and fourpence," he added dryly. "You need not wear it long."

"Damme, m'dear," growled a heavy, rather sullen voice

37

from beyond Caroline, "can't you move in and make room for a fellow? I want to see this."

"Ah, and Sir John Buckstone," Mr. Crockit said hastily. "Please enter!"

"Thanks, Little Small-Clothes," observed the voice, with a touch of sarcasm. "Kind of you to let me. Well, what have we got here?"

And Buckstone, Jack Buckstone of legend, ducked his high, buff-colored, heavy-crowned hat under the arch of the door.

As one in the position of being half sporting buck and half dandy, he prided himself that his facial muscles seldom moved. His little black eyes, in the ruddy face of a man who eats too much, would have been bright if he had not kept them under a glaze. There were those who said he had no intelligence, but they were wrong; he had a first-class intelligence. It was merely that he had never been called on to use it, or to use any quality except cunning.

"And that's the bridegroom," said Buckstone. "Gad, let's have a look at him!"

Pushing one of the lanterns to the other end of the cell, he picked up the other and held it high. Buckstone wore the clothes which were almost a uniform of fashion by day: the high collar and white cravat; the blue coat with brass buttons, cut away from the waist and falling into tails behind; the waistcoat colored according to taste—Buckstone's was striped—and the white leather breeches with polished black top boots.

He held the lantern in Darwent's face. He lowered it along the clothes. He moved it sideways, his little black insolent eyes frank with curiosity.

"Sir John!" interposed Mr. Crockit, rather nervously.

"Eh?"

"If you will be good enough to stand back, sir, we may be able to proceed."

"Oh, anything to oblige you," assented Buckstone, moving back. He pronounced it "obleege," and his agreeable contempt for Mr. Crockit was most edifying. "Damme, though,"—he pointed the lantern toward Darwent—"what ails the fellow?"

"Ails him?" repeated Mr. Crockit.

Ever since he had given his assent to Mr. Crockit's bargain, Darwent had not uttered a word. He still stood upright, stricken cold sober. Even under the dirt they could see that he was as white as one of the new candles.

"Jack, be quiet!" interposed Caroline. Despite her imperious tone, she was so badly frightened that she said the first words

38

that came into her head. "Mr. Crockit! Who was speaking to you a moment ago?"

"Speaking to me, madam?"

"In—in this cell. A man's voice. Of rather fine quality, I thought "

Then Caroline's eyes, grown used to the gloom of the cell, suddenly found the Rev. Horace Cotton. The big clergyman, breathing slowly, now stood against the same wall as Richard Darwent.

"Oh, how stupid of me!" murmured Caroline, and gave him one of her archest smiles. "It pleases me you are here already, reverend sir. It was you who spoke, of course."

The Rev. Horace made a violent effort, and remained calm.

"No, madam," he answered. "I did not trust myself to speak."

"You did not . . .?" Caroline's eyebrows went up.

"As I apprehend the matter, Miss Ross, you send this man to his death at least four days too early. You do this, madam, because you are impatient for a hasty marriage, a hasty death, and the fruits of a great fortune."

Mr. Crockit, in his ancient three-cornered hat, intervened smoothly and yet with authority.

"Come now, reverend sir!" he said in his dry voice. "I must remind you that these matters are no concern of yours. They concern only the personage I serve."

"Sir," replied the clergyman, "they also concern the Personage *I* serve."

"Allow me to mention," said Mr. Crockit, "that the act was my own doing. If you blame anyone, blame me."

"Blame you?" exclaimed Caroline, with real surprise. "One moment, Mr. Crockit!"

Her gesture made him subside, with a slight bow. Anger kindled the beauty of her face with soft color, and sparkled in the long shiny-lidded blue eyes.

"For some reason, Mr.—?"

"Cotton, madam. The Rev. Horace Cotton."

"You appear to think, Mr. Cotton, that I am doing some ill service to a wretch who, forgive me, is better dead. Like these other poor degraded people at Newgate."

Caroline gave a shiver of disgust. There was a short, sharp rattle of Darwent's chains, but he did not speak.

"You also appear to think," Caroline went on, with the same faint astonishment, "that I should consider his welfare.

39

Why should I? *I* don't know him. He will get his money." She turned and appealed to Buckstone. "Jack!"

But Buckstone, for the moment, was not listening.

Standing near the door, he still held up the lantern to inspect Darwent against the opposite wall. Buckstone's boots and breeches were dust-stained. He had ridden hard from Oatlands, country home of His Royal Highness the Duke of York, in response to a fast messenger from Caroline. From his right wrist hung a riding crop, with a short thong like a whip.

"But, damme," he insisted, "what does ail the fellow?"

"Jack! If you please!"

"Went to see Bedlam once," Buckstone explained. "Watched all the madmen dance and howl. Damme, that was sport! This ain't. Is the demnition convict a deaf-mute? Why don't he speak? Or can't he?"

This time there was a reply.

"I can speak, sir," Darwent informed him, so that Caroline started involuntarily. "If only to remark that your manners are almost as bad as your grammar."

"My dear fellow!" the Rev. Horace cried out in expostulation.

Buckstone, with a perplexed look, pushed his buff-colored hat to the back of his head.

"Impudent, ain't he?" Buckstone inquired of Caroline.

Buckstone was not angry. He was only puzzled, as though a peaceful-seeming mongrel dog had shown teeth at him. He shifted the lantern to his left hand, and strolled forward. Without rancor, but with a heavily muscled arm, Buckstone lifted the riding crop and slashed it viciously across Darwent's face.

"Jack!" Caroline cried out in protest. She had not meant to speak like this.

They saw the felon's eyes and mouth working with pain. He staggered; the heavy weight on the leg iron nearly tripped him; and his long, greasy hair fell forward. After a moment, with what effort nobody knew except himself, Darwent straightened up.

"May I ask the name of the sportsman," he said, "who strikes a fettered man?"

Buckstone did not trouble to reply. He merely lifted his hand, and again slashed viciously across the face.

Darwent tried hard, tried frantically, but there was no strength left. He fell on his knees, with a bony broken thud, and rolled sideways in the straw.

Buckstone addressed Caroline in a tone of reasonableness.

40

"Gently, m'dear! He's got to learn not to be impudent, ain't he?"

Carefully placing the prayer book in the wall niche, the Rev. Horace Cotton moved out in front of Darwent and addressed Buckstone.

"Sir," the clergyman said quietly. "Observe that I am even less a weakling than yourself." Then his tone changed. "Raise your hand once more; and by God's grace I will flog you through Newgate with your own whip."

Blazes, the turnkey, his fiery nose and popping eyes pressed in the aperture of the partly open door, waited for the explosion. Licking his lips, he felt that this explosion would rock the walls of Newgate.

But, if any man thought he could get the better of Jack Buckstone, that man was always much disappointed.

Pushing his hat back still further, letting the riding crop swing free, Buckstone eyed the Rev. Horace up and down without curiosity.

"Parson feller," he said. "Got to respect the cloth, damme, or where do any of us stand?" Buckstone was not in the least intimidated, for who could defeat him? He merely stated what he thought.

" 'Fraid I can't touch you, old boy," he added coolly. "Now let's have no more nonsense. Fetch out your Bible, or whatever you use, and we'll have done with this business."

"Mr. Crockit, I believe," said Caroline, looking at the parson, "has a document which—which suffices for both Church and State. It *must* be done."

"Not by me, madam. Not by me!"

Mr. Crockit, though rather pale, intervened swiftly.

"You decline to perform this ceremony, Mr. Cotton?"

"No!" interposed a weak, muffled voice from the straw. "Do it, Padre!" Then, after intense struggle: "Assist me. On my feet."

The Ordinary, not without effort, lifted him up. Darwent stood there swaying, with no light in his eyes. Of two weals across the left side of his face, one oozed blood and dirt at the corner.

"You still wish me to do this?" asked the Rev. Horace.

"Yes! Yes! Yes!"

"Then I cannot refuse *you*."

"There, m'dear!" And Buckstone spoke to Caroline, not without complacence. "A taste of the proper medicine, and *he* does as he's told. Never you fear."

41

"Yes. But I rather wish. . ." Caroline paused, and compressed her lips hard.

"What's that, m'dear?"

"Nothing. I am stupid. Must I not think of my own future?'"

Caroline had opportunity to say no more. The clergyman gave curt instructions. Both Buckstone and the turnkey, who had edged into the cell as the second witness, removed their hats with deep solemnity. Mr. Elias Crockit opened his case of writing materials.

" 'Dearly beloved, we are g-gathered here together in . . . in the sight of heaven . . .' "

Up high in the wall over Darwent's head, where no one had observed it until now, was a small, deep, heavily grated window. Mr. Crockit, with an apprehensive glance upward, noticed it only because the sky outside was now faintly gray.

The Rev. Horace's voice, after faltering, went on strongly. Mr. Crockit could have wrung his hands. If Miss Caroline Ross and Sir John Buckstone were seen leaving the prison in daylight, how limitless were the possibilities of scandal! ˗

With a movement of head and eye, Mr. Crockit directed Caroline's attention to the window. He saw her own start of apprehension. Buckstone swore softly, and whacked the brim of his hat against his leg.

"Repeat after me. 'I, Caroline . . .' "

"I, Caroline . . ."

She did not even flinch when Darwent—moving and whispering mechanically, a man who seemed witless—put the ring on her finger. Her eyes would lift toward the window, and back again to the prisoner.

Darwent's brain only partly cleared. He could not explain that, when he fell against wall and floor after the lash, he had reopened the old wound in his head. He heard the scratching of a pen, and presently a pen was put into his hand. Even his blunt senses felt the gasp of thankfulness from the visitors.

"Then that is finished," said Mr. Crockit, too loudly, "in most satisfactory fashion!" Gold sovereigns chinked in a pouch. "I gave you the money, reverend sir. The—the other person seems unable to take it. Pray give me the evidence of marriage."

The Rev. Horace handed it over.

"Turnkey!" he said sharply.

"Sir?"

"Please escort this lady and this gentleman to the wicket; and return here. Meanwhile, leave the cell door unlocked."

"Sir, I daresn't do that!"

"I accept the responsibility. All of it." The Ordinary turned to Caroline and Buckstone, nodding with dignity toward the door. "And now, if you will be good enough?"

St. Sepulchre's clock struck four. The hour of the execution was set at five.

Buckstone, immensely relieved and now in an almost playful mood, strolled up to Darwent.

"A-doo, as the Frenchies say," he remarked without inflection, and playfully cuffed the felon with his open hand. "No hard feelings, I hope? Had to keep you in your place, that's all."

A film seemed to lift slightly from Darwent's eyes.

"You damned swine," Darwent said.

Buckstone's expression did not alter. But his hand swept back. It was Blazes the turnkey, terrified that a too-angry Buckstone would not give him more than a shilling at the gate, who averted danger then.

"Sir John," he bawled, "if you and the lady wants to get out, you'd best get out now! The crowd's a-packing together in the street, and you won't be able to make way through 'em!"

"We must cross the street," Caroline said hastily, "in any event." Suddenly the words seemed to choke her. "After all, have you forgotten our champagne breakfast?"

The iron door shut with a clang behind the three of them. Caroline and Buckstone and the turnkey. Blazes did not lock it. The Rev. Horace Cotton sat down heavily in the wall niche, his prayer book in his hand.

"Padre!"

"Yes?"

"One small matter," the dull voice continued, "which I am now half-ashamed to mention. I can't repent of murder, for I have committed none. But your Deity, Padre: with all my heart I believe in Him."

The Ordinary, in the act of wiping sweat from his forehead with the sleeve of his gown, stopped and stared.

"You believe—" he began with a rush of joy; and then stopped. "Why do you say that?"

"You defended me, Padre. If men like yourself believe in Him, then I were a fool not to believe too."

"Man, man, but this is not faith or belief! This is only foolish gratitude for a trifling . . . a trifling . . ."

The wandering voice paid no attention.

43

"Was the man's name Buckstone? I think someone mentioned it, even before I asked. Was he named Buckstone?"

"Yes, yes! But—!"

"I would give ten years of the life I don't possess," said Darwent, "to meet that coxcomb face to face with sabers. The woman, I think, is worse. I would . . . but it makes no matter. I am beaten. I only dream. Those who are beaten must always dream."

The Rev. Horace stood up.

"I asked for the door to be left unlocked," he said, "because I wish to speak to the Sheriff in his lodgings. Then I shall return."

"Return? Go? But you said—!"

"I wish to speak on your behalf. No! I tell you nothing, because I offer you no hope. But if you would have me credit your so-called belief, show charity even towards the creatures you spoke of."

"Padre!"

The iron door opened and closed softly. Darwent was alone.

The second set of candles had burned out, in gushing smoke which blackened the sides of the lanterns. Through the high window, the gray light was tinged with clear white. After taking a step forward and falling down, Darwent decided it was better to sit down quietly.

"Charity," he thought.

Certain fibers of his brain, or so it seemed to him, were settling back into place after the crack of his head against floor and wall. Only a little blood trickled through scalp into hair: at least, where he could feel it. His eyesight was better, too.

But, when a great shiver ran through his body, it was caused by more than the chill of dawn. A hanged man, they said, could feel his face blackening until the blood spurted from his very eyeballs.

Beside Darwent, upset but still corked, lay the bottle of brandy. He considered it, carefully and deliberately weighing one course against another.

If he swallowed a deep draught now, it would revive him and drive away the horrors. On the other hand, it would almost certainly send him drunk to the gallows. He would stumble and reel, pierced by the ridicule of the mob who came to see him die: an object of repulsion even to himself.

"It is not fitting," he said, and smashed the bottle on the stone floor.

Immediately he regretted it. The brandy splashed out int

44

mud and straw wisps. "You fool!" he said, as though all lost opportunity went with it. But it was done now, and he could go quietly.

The wards of Newgate were already awake, and so noisy that they blotted out other sound. He would not hear the singing that would begin, at any moment now, from the crowd assembled in Old Bailey.

The cold minutes moved on. He could not count them or even estimate them. Over his head the window sent down a slanting shaft of light; as it whitened, it showed the full squalor of the dungeon. His imagination had already compared it to living inside the stomach of a toad.

"Charity!" he said contemptuously. All the lost, impossible wishes rose up again.

To meet Jack Buckstone with sabers, face to face, on firm green turf!

To meet Caroline Ross, and humble her as no woman had ever been humbled!

To find the murderer of Frank Orford, and see *that* person in the condemned cell!

Even, once more, to see Dolly Spencer. . . .

Suddenly, with a wish he had thrown away and despised, he longed for nothing more than ordinary soap and water, to wash himself. To meet his death like this, he saw with clarity, was as bad as to go mouthing and drunken. Last night he could have had soap and water. Now it was too late.

At that moment hurrying footsteps crossed Press Yard outside. Someone, surprised at finding the cell door even a shaving of an inch open, flung it wide and glanced in. The newcomer was Mr. Hubert Mulberry, that somewhat eccentric lawyer who had credited Darwent's account of the murder.

"Mulberry," the prisoner whispered.

The newcomer made no reply. Breathing hard, fat and unwieldy, he moved forward until his face was under the narrow, harsh beam of light from the window. He wore an old brown surtout, and his neckcloth was disarranged. A soiled white hat, emblem of the present-day man of law as opposed to the old school, was cradled in his arm. His somewhat bloated face, with the spikes of grayish-brown hair plastered against the forehead, wore an expression Darwent had never seen there and never expected to see.

Mr. Mulberry cleared his throat.

"I bring great news," he said after a long pause. In a low voice he added: "My Lord Marquess."

45

◇ CHAPTER V ◇

Recounts the End of a Champagne Breakfast

"Make way, there!" shouted Joseph Eldridge, the Chief Turnkey, and leaned out of the window above the Main Gate. "Make way, d'ye hear?"

His words were lost, whirled away in the tumult of the crowd below.

In a large cleared square before debtors' door, they had driven the usual iron posts into the ground between the cobbles, and strung a heavy chain between each of the posts like an oversized prize ring. Into that protected space they would push the scaffold, wheeled and rumbling, after withdrawing the horses.

Six City militiamen, with Brown Bess muskets and fixed bayonets, guarded the chains from inside. A dangerously frightened horse, ridden by a frightened young trainband captain, reared up and clattered down in menace to the guards.

"No bayonets 'less you have to!" The Chief Turnkey whistled into a wind. "No bayonets!"

For a good reason, the crowd this morning were delirious. A dead cat, humorously thrown among them, bounced from hand to hand above women's caps and men's half-crushed hats.

Though the newspapers had not yet appeared, especially the *Times* with its full dispatch dated at Waterloo by Lord Wellington and its casualty list as well, the report of the great victory had already spread.

It was a time for ecstatic rejoicing, a time for taking liberties with the lady who stood next to you in the crowd, a time to sing "Lillibulero," "The British Grenadiers," and "Down to Hell with Boney." More spectators, on the sloping tiled roofs of the houses opposite, waved their arms in tune.

The Chief Turnkey made a last violent effort.

"Make way for the scaffold!"

This time the words had a ripple. And many voices roared back.

"Where's the scaffold?"

46

The Chief Turnkey, exasperated, turned round to a tall, thin, nervous jailer whom he knew only as Jamy.

"Well, where is it?" he demanded.

"Mr. Langley says it's ready, sir. But there's no orders from the Sheriff."

"No orders from the Sheriff?"

"No, sir."

The dead cat danced and traveled. "Boney!" cried somebody. The dead cat, flung high in the air, immediately became Boney. At the window the Chief Turnkey took a double-cased silver watch from his waistcoat pocket.

"Eh, well," he muttered, "they're happy now." His eyes moved up from the watch, and saw Miss Caroline Ross and Sir John Buckstone—much closer than a stone's throw away—at the upper window of the Red Horse Tavern opposite.

Against the harsh dawn, the upper floor of the "Red Horse" showed candlelit windows, with a glimpse of white linen and silver, for a breakfast party of the nobs. Ten or a dozen persons were in the long room. But only Miss Ross and Sir John, who had visited the Chief Turnkey in his lodgings last night, now stood at the window.

Even if there had been no uproar in the street, the Chief Turnkey could not have heard what they were saying. But gestures were eloquent.

The lady had now discarded her gray hooded cape. She was in a white satin gown, and stretched out bare arms toward the street in a kind of ecstasy.

Sir John leaned toward her, said something, and laughed.

"Yes! I almost forgot!" the lady seemed to agree.

With her right hand she touched the third finger of her left hand. She drew off—a ring, of course —and held it invisibly between two fingers. Then, with a delicate gesture, she threw the ring out into the crowd.

Her lips shaped the word, "Gone!"

"Mr. Eldridge, sir!" struck in the hoarse voice of Blazes, at the Chief Turnkey's elbow. "The Sheriff's compliments, and he's got new orders."

"New orders?"

At almost the same instant, in a condemned cell east of where they stood, Mr. Hubert Mulberry looked down at Richard Darwent, and waved his arms in the air as he gave some account of the great victory in Belgium.

"Curse it, Dick!" he exclaimed. "Don't you see they can't hang you now?"

There was a long silence. Darwent opened his mouth, and shut it again.

"No, don't talk." Mr. Mulberry made a peremptory gesture. "*I'll* talk. I always talk."

He turned his fat back to Darwent, as though about to assume a disguise, and then swung round again.

"The battle was fought on Sunday, June 18th. D'ye follow me? No remark! Yes, or no?"

Darwent nodded.

"You may have heard a report, Dick, that two of our lads tried to signal the coast of Kent that same night? And somebody died of heart ailment when the message wasn't plain?"

Darwent shook his head. But Caroline Ross, now lifting a glass above a plate of cold ham at the "Red Horse," could have told him it was true.

"That somebody," said Mulberry, "was your uncle."

Darwent attempted to say, "I am sorry," but the words stuck in his throat.

"And you wondered where *I* was last night, didn't you? Old Bert Mulberry, raised as a charity boy and teaching himself Latin like a beetle crawling up a wet wall! Anyway, I'll tell you. I was at the *Times* office, bribing a friend o' mine to get a list of the killed and wounded."

Mr. Mulberry tossed his white hat into the wall niche, from which it bounced and fell. Taking from the pocket of his surtout a folded piece of paper, he opened it and read.

"'Captain the Viscount Cray, 1st Foot Guards. Killed.'" His voice chopped off the words, like a butcher with meat. "'Ensign Lord George Mercer, 95th Rifles. Killed.'" He crumpled up the paper. "Both your cousins. Both dead."

"They were better men than I am."

"Don't say that. Never say it about anybody Try to use fair play, and a man lands in trouble—like you. You'd care to know, I daresay, how all this affects your trial for murder?"

"Yes!"

"When were you tried and condemned? On what date?"

"The 19th of June. You must know that!"

Mr. Mulberry squatted down in front of him, leering.

"Dick, that trial was illegal."

"Why?"

"Damme, man, on the 19th you were the Marquess of Darwent! And a peer of the realm—eh?—can't be tried for murder except before the House of Lords."

Again there was silence, while Mr. Mulberry chuckled.

"When they do try you," he went on, pointing his finger "they'll acquit you as quickly as it takes to call the roll, from the junior baron upwards. "Not guilty, upon my honor!" They'll more than acquit you; they'll cheer you when they've done with it. D'ye guess why?"

Out of nowhere Darwent remembered a remark the Rev. Horace Cotton had made.

"The House of Lords," he muttered, "fights tooth and nail for the privilege of the duel . . ."

"Eh, and don't they!"

Darwent choked in a senseless kind of mutter. "But there wasn't any duel! Frank Orford was murdered!"

"And who's to know that, Dick, except you and me? We can't change the defense now. And we shouldn't, bully, if we could. I'll acquit you."

Mr. Mulberry, slapping his thigh appreciatively, almost fell over backwards. Then he stood up. His beefy, bloated face, with the bleared yet very shrewd eyes, became somber again. Taking a snuff-box out of his pocket, he thoughtfully tapped his finger on the lid.

"Steady, Dick!"

"Why do you say that?"

"D'ye think I can't see what's in your eyes, every time you look at that door? Lose your fears! They're not coming to hang you. And why?

"Now who would dare," added Mr. Mulberry, "to pull my Lord Ellenborough out of his bed at two o'clock in the morning? *I* would. The writing's in his own fist, and the Sheriff of Newgate's got it now. Today I go before the same noble gentleman, the Lord Chief Justice. I ask for your indictment to be removed, by a writ of certiorari, into the court of the Lord High Steward: that's to say, the House of Lords. Meanwhile, we have someone in to strike off these fetters of yours . . ."

"What's that?"

"Dick! Dick!" Mr. Mulberry took a huge pinch of snuff, only a little of which reached his nose while the rest flew wide on his neckcloth and yellow-striped waistcoat as he sneezed. "Haven't you heard you can live as comfortably at Newgate, on the State side, as in the Clarendon Hotel?"

"No!"

"Ay; well, you can. A private room, with a valet. Your meals from a cookshop. Weston, the Regent's own tailor, to

49

cut your coats. And I daresay"—here Mr. Mulberry's thick lips made a grimace—"you'll want a bath a day?"

"Yes! Yes!"

"A new fashion," the other said moodily, "and I don't like it. Howsoever! You can live like that until your trial. All things are possible, even in Newgate, if you have money."

"And . . . have I money?"

"Money? Boney's teeth! What d'ye say to a hundred thousand a year?—Hold up, Dick! Don't hang your head like that!"

"Forgive me. I was . . ."

"And you have more," said Mr. Mulberry, taking snuff, "that I envy you, Dick, almost to disliking you. Stop; I don't mean that. But I was a charity boy; I can respect an old name, if it *is* an old name."

Mr. Mulberry was a fierce Jacobite, though this issue had been dead for sixty years. His views of the House of Hanover, though from a different side, were those now being freely expressed by many republicans. Even for the old King, George the Third, mad and deaf and nearly blind, he had no sympathy.

"In the Holy Land, near to five hundred years ago, your banner was raised beside Lionheart's own." More snuff flew wide. "What's bloody Hanover against *that?*"

"I . . . I only . . ."

"Stand up, man!" said Mr. Mulberry. "Who cares a fornication if you're weak? Stand up "

Richard Darwent stood up.

"The world's at your feet, lad; and no more gammon about fair play. Is there any person you want to befriend?"

"Dolly! Where's Dolly?"

Mr. Mulberry hesitated and studied him, again tapping the lid of the snuffbox.

"She's not at the theater, as I've told you a hundred times. She's not at her old lodgings. But find her; and befriend her in no niggard way!—Or is there anyone who's used you badly? Anyone you hate with heart and soul?"

Darwent's expression changed. Mr. Mulberry had said these words as the Rev. Horace Cotton, his face radiant with relief after hearing the news that there would be no execution, appeared in the open doorway. The Rev. Horace, hearing the lawyer's grating voice, stopped short.

"Then hit back," snarled Mr. Mulberry, "and have no mercy!"

Clang smote the bell of the clock at St. Sepulchre's, on the first stroke of five. The ensuing strokes quivered over Newgate Prison, over Old Bailey outside its Main Gate, and were heard with aching distinctness in a long room on the upper floor of the Red Horse Tavern.

Caroline Ross and Jack Buckstone, with an almost empty room behind them, stood at one window and looked down into what seemed an eerily empty street.

The crowd had melted away. Half a dozen City militiamen, removing the bayonets from their muskets under the direction of an officer on a quiet horse, alone remained.

The street was strewn with orange peel and empty bottles; a dead cat lay there, and some torn articles of feminine wearing apparel, together with bits of food and a man's shoe. Some one, from the lodge above the arched leaves of the Main Gate, had kept shouting a few words. And the crowd, after a brief hostile demonstration, struggled away by twos and threes.

"Too happy about Boney," growled Jack Buckstone, "to wallop out with a riot. Pity, that. Might have been some good sport."

"But what did the man say?" Caroline kept insisting. "The man who spoke above the gate over there?"

"Can't tell you, m'dear. Couldn't hear. But, gad, now! Why pretend you don't understand? Your husb—"

"Sh-h!"

But, as Caroline glanced round quickly, she saw there was no fear of being overheard. Her guests—the men with groans or curses, the women with sighs or twitters of disappointment—had already stumbled downstairs. The long table, its rush-bottomed chairs pushed back and its tapers flickering in mine host's best pewter candlesticks, showed a ruin of china and glasses.

One last guest, Mr. Jemmy Fletcher, remained face downward across the table, dead drunk and snoring. His fair hair trailed out. His brocaded cocked hat, an article of evening dress so often carried under the arm that it was called a *chapeau de bras*, lay in the butter dish. Young Mr. Fletcher's snores rose loudly against the intense hush of morning.

Both Buckstone and Caroline abruptly spoke in louder voices.

"The fact is, m'dear," Buckstone told her coolly, "your husband's had a what-d'ye-call-it. A reprieve."

Caroline's blue eyes were . . . no, not yet apprehensive. From her wrist now dangled the white fan she had carried at the Chief Turnkey's lodgings. She opened it, and began to fan herself despite the dull cold.

51

"But he will be hanged?" she asked. "Of course?"

"Can't say, m'dear. Pity we couldn't have asked that lawyer fellow to sit down at table. Still! Got to draw the line somewhere."

"No doubt."

"Do you remember what Mildmay said, when some dashed confounded nobody offered Harry the use of his carriage? 'How kind of you!' says Mildmay; 'but pray, sir, where will *you* sit? Up behind with one of the footmen?'"

Since he was alone with Caroline, Buckstone permitted himself to smile. He even threw back his head and laughed loudly, competing with the snores of Jemmy Fletcher. Then he grew serious.

"You've done a bad night's work, m'girl," he observed with critical detachment. "It'd be a rare jape, wouldn't it, if they pardoned your dear husband and set the scum free? Still! It's no affair of mine."

Dismissing the matter, he strolled round to the other side of the table. He picked up a candlestick. For a few moments he found entertainment in tilting it and dropping tallow grease on the drunken man's hair. Caroline watched him, fanning herself harder.

"Jack!"

"Eh? What's that?"

"Do you hold *any* friendly feelings toward me, Jack?"

"M'dear!" protested Buckstone, lifting a wrinkled forehead. "Dash it, didn't I ride all the way from Oatlands to be with you?"

"Then you promise not to sneer if I make a—a somewhat ridiculous confession?"

"Sneer?" repeated Buckstone. "Damme, now!" It would have astonished him if you had told him he was not one of the most agreeable men alive.

"Then you promise not to sneer? Or tell it of me at Almack's?"

"Rot my guts if I do!"

"This condemned man," said Caroline, still plying the fan. "I must own I found him . . . somewhat fascinating."

She had made a mistake. The whole emotional temperature of that room altered, while sodden Jemmy Fletcher emitted a long gurgle of a snore. Buckstone set down the candlestick with a thump.

"Like 'em filthy, don't you?" he asked coolly.

"When I first set eyes on him, I thought him the most re-

52

pulsive creature alive. Presently I heard his voice, and looked at his eyes. Oh, this is stupid! Yet even you, Jack, must have observed that he spoke like . . . like . . ."

Buckstone was almost amused. "Like a gentleman?" he suggested dryly.

"I was about to say: like an Oxford don."

Buckstone ignored this.

"You wouldn't have *me*," he said, fixing his little black eyes on her. "How many times did I propose to you? Thanks; I forget. But you wouldn't have *me*."

"You are a dear fellow, Jack, and it's no wonder your friends love you. But I was obliged to decline the honor."

"Oh, obleeged to *you*, m'dear. You prefer—"

Caroline's face was scarlet.

"Please don't be utterly ridiculous. I said nothing of the sort."

Caroline's wrath, to judge by her expression, was directed mostly at herself. It was evident that she could not even understand herself. She felt bewildered, distressed; in a sense betrayed. And, therefore, she must vent her feelings on someone else.

"I fear you would not understand," she remarked sweetly, and plied the fan until her brown curls trembled. "You came from Oatlands, yes. From your dear friend Frederick of York and his fat wife. How noble a commander in chief of the army, some years ago, was His Grace.

> *'My name is York, I pull a cork*
> *Much better than I fight . . .'*

"And what, Jack, was the scandal which compelled him to resign? Was it not (or do I forget?) that swearing Frederick was too stingy? And his mistress sold commissions in the army, more cheaply than they could be bought at the Horse Guards, with Frederick's full approval? And, with the scandal years blown over, he's back at the Horse Guards again?"

Buckstone stared at her.

"If it comes to that," he lifted his lip, "what about your pet poets?"

"You make yourself ridiculous, Jack."

"Here's George Byron," said Buckstone, "almost new-married but almost ready to separate too, after goin' to bed for years with his half-sister. Poetry! Gad's life, I've written poetry in albums myself!"

53

"You are not quite as good a poet as my Lord Byron," Caroline said gently. "You are not even as good a pistol shot."

But once again, if any person hoped to sting or even ruffle Jack Buckstone, that person suffered bitter disappointment.

"Why, m'dear," he said, with a mouth of sadness, "I can't contradict you."

"Thank you, Jack."

"They're all too afraid to challenge me," said Buckstone, stating a simple truth. "You'd split with laughing," and again, unexpectedly, Buckstone roared with mirth, "to see the poor devil on the field."

"My sense of humor, perhaps, is not well developed."

"No, dash it, I mean that! Poor devil's hand is shaking already. Too anxious, d'ye see, to get in his fire first. Looses off blind, as soon as the word's given, and misses by yards. And there he is sweating, as easy as a wafer at Joe Manton's shooting gallery."

Arm extended and body sideways, Buckstone's finger curled round the trigger of an imaginary pistol. His look of cunning would have delighted his friends. The flat brass buttons glistened against his blue coat, above the head of the snoring toper.

Then Buckstone's arm fell.

"About this husband of yours, m'dear," he began.

"That man is *not* my husband!"

"As you like, pretty. But if you've got into trouble, pretty, I say again it's no affair of mine. You can't expect . . ."

He paused. Both of them had heard clattering footsteps up several pairs of narrow stairs. But both expected it was the tavernkeeper with the reckoning, until the face of Blazes the turnkey appeared in the doorway.

"Ma'am. Sir." Blazes, panting hard, tugged at his forelock. "There's a reg'lar do over there," he pointed, "and a 'ard job I 'ad to get out of the prison and tell you."

As a matter of fact, the Chief Turnkey had sent him. But Sir John Buckstone had given him half a crown on leaving Newgate; and Blazes, though almost in apoplexy from exertion, panted for more.

"Yes?" asked Caroline, with rigid calmness. "What happened?"

"They're not a-going to hang Dick Darwent, ma'am," answered Blazes, so short of breath that his head reeled. "Not now, they says, or ever."

Buckstone whistled. Caroline, without expression, her fan motionless, looked at the opposite wall.

"Indeed?" she murmured. "And why not?"

"It'd seem, ma'am, that Dick's a nobleman. True as gospel! 'E killed another gen'leman in a duel; and now they can't try him except afore the House o' Lords!"

The snores of the stupefied guest across the table rose loudly.

"A nobleman," Caroline murmured. Her blue eyes began to rove round the room, and she breathed quickly. "His title?"

(For the first time now, in anger, Buckstone's fist clenched.)

"Ma'am, I can't tell you 'is title," panted Blazes. "All I know is 'cos I was in the Sheriff's lodgings when they sent me with a message for the Chief Turnkey." He appealed to Buckstone. "What do you say, sir?"

"Don't believe it," Buckstone replied briefly. "Get out."

"But, sir, it's gospel truth!"

"Don't believe it," repeated Buckstone, in the same bored voice. "Now get out."

"Please be quiet, Jack," interposed Caroline. "The news this good man brings is very dreadful, of course. And yet in a way, Jack dear, I find it—well, not ill pleasing. For some extraordinary reason," and she pressed her fingers against her temples, "our Richard Darwent fascinates me."

Buckstone made a short, sharp gesture. Blazes, watching him and raging, saw all hope of half a crown or any tip dwindle away. God's truth, he had nearly killed himself for nothing!

"Begging your pardon, ma'am," said Blazes, "and considering as of wot we all knew happened last night, that ain't wot Darwent thinks o' you."

Caroline was startled. "I beg your pardon?"

"And 'ow do I know that?" asked Blazes, in a passion. " 'Cos I follered the Ordinary, that's the Rev. Mr. Cotton, when he went back to Darwent's cell less'n half an hour ago. Darwent's carrion bird was a-talking to him."

"By carrion bird you mean lawyer? Well?"

" 'Is there anyone who's used you badly?' says the carrion bird to Darwent. 'Is there anyone you hate with heart and soul?' "

Buckstone strolled over to a bench along one wall. From this he picked up his riding crop, turned round, and strolled forward.

"Indeed?" said Caroline in a thin voice. "And what did he say in reply?"

"He didn't say nothing." Then Blazes pounced. "But I've seen all of 'em, ma'am. The savage 'uns, the daft 'uns, the brutes as goes a-fighting to the rope! And I never saw a look on any of 'em like the look in Darwent's eyes."

And the turnkey bolted down the stairs.

Buckstone, thoroughly bored, tossed his riding crop among plates on the table. Mr. Jemmy Fletcher, whose fair hair trailed out into the dishes, gave a prodigious snore like a start of wakefulness, scrabbled with his hands, and rolled out of the chair to the floor like a dead man.

⋄   C H A P T E R   V I   ⋄

Hears the Twittering of Fine Ladies—

That was the morning of June 22nd. On Thursday, July 21st, vengeance began to move swiftly.

It moved, in one place, on a large scale. H.M.S. *Bellerophon*, seventy-four guns, lying off Rochefort in France, weighed anchor for England; and thence to a far place. H.M.S. *Bellerophon* carried a passenger, a little fat man in a green coat and white breeches. In a large flat book, under "Name," Captain Maitland wrote, "Napoleon Bonaparte," and under "Occupation" he wrote: "!!!!!," as you may see in the Public Records Office to this day.

It moved, in another place, on a rather smaller scale. The most Hon. the Marquess of Darwent, two hours after his acquittal before the bar of the House of Lords, sat in his own carriage in Piccadilly, at the top of St. James's Street, just opposite Hoby the bootmaker's.

The carriage was a low, open, fast berline, painted dark red, with no footman up behind but a driver in plain livery on the box. Darwent tried to look sedate, tried not to reveal that he was swallowing the air of freedom and trembling as he did so.

After his thirty-day detention in a clean private room at Newgate, he was used to his new clothes, though the high cravat fretted him. All his wounds had healed. Food and rest filled the wiry figure with its old intense vitality.

Clean-shaven, in new silken shirts, he had taken the air in

the private exercise ground of the State side at Newgate. Purely for exercise, he explained, he resumed practice with the saber. Its straight, pointed, double-edged blade whipped such rapid patterns in the air that they seemed to remain, flashing, when the blade was still.

And then the trial before Peers . . .

Since justice had blundered at the sessions court, the whole matter had been hushed up (or so Darwent and the authorities thought) with expert discretion. No word of it publicly appeared. Even the report of the trial before the Lords was ordered to be suppressed. Darwent marveled that he could emerge, out of darkness and fully habited, as "my Lord Darwent."

But, as usual, he forgot that ear for scandal or unusual behavior which, among the ladies, missed nothing.

Ever since that night of June 21st, a month ago, a buzz of whispering voices had been growing. Nobody knew the story accurately; but everyone knew, or professed to know, some scrap of it. It seemed a story so filled with swoons and romance, so darkling with emotion like *Childe Harold,* that teacups twittered from Hertford House to Northumberland House at dull, dirty Charing Cross.

"My dear," said Lady Jersey (not to be confused with the Regent's former mistress), a dark beauty with an air like a theatrical tragedy queen, "Jemmy Fletcher visited him on the State side in the last week of June. My dear, it does vex me not to know how Jemmy learned he was there. Jemmy says he's positively almost good looking."

"That will be novel," thoughtfully murmured Lady Castlereagh, wife of the War Minister.

"But Caroline?" urged the amiable Lady Sefton. "What of Caroline?"

It was known that Caroline Ross, now the Marchioness of Darwent, had departed for Brighton on the afternoon of June 22nd.

"He is sick for love of her, they say," observed Lady Jersey, posing above the teacups like a tragedy queen. "And I *know* Caroline is sick for love of him. But she won't admit it, and throws brushes at poor Meg."

"He is sick for love of her?" murmured Lady Castlereagh, who had a wandering blue eye and did not like this. "How amusing! But don't you mean 'poor Caroline'? Caroline has always seemed . . . well!"

"Fie, my dear! You must not speak so!"

"Something of a bluestocking, I was about to say."

"It is wonderfully romantic!" sighed Lady Sefton, and added: "Lord Darwent must have a card, of course?"

All the ladies looked at each other.

Lady Sefton referred to a card of invitation for Almack's, that great bemirrored dancing room where they kept the orchestra hung in a kind of wicker basket. These three *grandes dames,* together with Lady Cowper and Mrs. Drummond Burrell and the Princess Esterhazy, were its patronesses and the arbiters of society. They ruled Almack's with such haughtiness that even the Duke of Wellington, arriving one evening in trousers instead of formal black knee breeches and stockings, was turned away from its door.

"God damme!" had said the Duke.

Many persons would have cut their throats for a card to Almack's and walked there afterwards to dance as corpses.

"He must have a card," Lady Jersey agreed firmly. "His name alone . . ."

"Amid other things," murmured Lady Castlereagh.

Amiable Lady Sefton coughed delicately.

"But if the dear man is still in gross confinement," she cried, causing Lady Castlereagh to look at her with a start, "where does one send the card?"

"My dear!" said Lady Jersey. "He has been put up for White's Club by poor Jemmy Fletcher, and seconded by Will Alvanley. Stop! One thinks of a better place. A room has been bespoken for him at Stephen's Hotel. That will do."

The card arrived. But Richard Darwent had not yet seen it.

It was just as well that Darwent, sitting in the motionless red carriage on the afternoon of July 21st, in Piccadilly at the top of St. James's Street, had no notion these whispering voices were making him notorious.

"Hup!" were the cries around him, and, "Mind your eye!"

Past him flowed the rattle of carriages and carts, the clip-clop dance of a showy saddle horse. Against red-brick and dun-colored houses, the shopwindows—with their glass panes set in oblong white window joinings—gleamed amid sunshine and dust. Past the shop fronts moved ladies' bonnets, usually with two or three upright plumes of red or green or blue.

It was as though Darwent had never seen it before. He could hardly sit still in the carriage.

In front of him, unnoticed, a hackney coach pulled up. Fat Mr. Mulberry, tolerably sober, struggled out and paid the fare. A moment later the lawyer muttered an exclamation.

"Dick, Dick!" he protested in a troubled voice. "'Look out for yourself!"

"Mulberry!" said Darwent. "What's the matter?"

"All I did, lad, was touch your arm. You whipped round and showed your teeth like . . . no, no! Don't do it."

"Did I?" asked Darwent, passing his hand across his forehead. "Forgive me. I was preoccupied. After all, they set me free only two hours ago."

Mulberry, standing beside the carriage and watching him in that same troubled way, expressed congratulations.

"I couldn't be there myself, Dick, as you imagine. But I knew they'd do it."

"*I* didn't," said Darwent, and studied his polished top boots. "Each time a voice called, 'Not guilty, upon my honor,' I sweated for the next." His voice rose. "But now, by God, I'm free!"

"Easy, Dick!"

"I beg your pardon. Will you get into the carriage?"

"Are you sure you want to be seen with the likes of me?"

"My dear friend, don't be a fool. Climb into the carriage."

Mr. Mulberry climbed in. Yet his worry deepened. An observer, seeing him with his soiled white hat pressed down on gray-brown hair, would have decided that he knew or guessed far more than he would say.

"I asked you to meet me here," he went on, glancing round at Hoby the bootmaker's, "because I've got two pieces of information that'll set you off a-flying. Wait, now; don't speak!"

For a moment Mr. Mulberry was silent, groping after the snuffbox in the pocket of his long brown coat.

"Dick," he said, "I'm a daft jackanapes when I lose my temper. A month ago, in the condemned cell, I asked whether you had any enemies. 'Hit back at 'em!' says I; 'have no mercy!' "

"Do you see any reason to change those admirable sentiments?"

"No, no! And yet . . ."

"Well?"

"You have an enemy—"

"Only one?"

"Dick," the other persisted doggedly, "you have an enemy you don't know and can't see. If my thinking's right (and it is!), he's the same person who stabbed Lord Francis Orford.

Your life's in danger; and that's a fact. Damme, would it please you to be clubbed to death in a dark lane?"

"It will please me very much," replied Darwent, "if someone tries it."

"Dick, you're a different man!"

"I am what they made me." Presently his expression softened. "Bert, let's speak of this at another time; don't disturb yourself. What's this news of yours?"

"To begin with," Mr. Mulberry said moodily, "your wife has returned to London."

Darwent showed his teeth in what might have been a smile.

"I thank you, Bert. But I've already learned that."

"You've learned it?"

"Yes. It's true," Darwent conceded, "that I have been at liberty only two hours. But I have paid two visits. One was to Stephen's Hotel, to make sure of my accommodation. The other was to number thirty-eight St. James's Square, the home of my dear wife. I wished to make myself acquainted with the servants—if they happened to be there.

"Well, they were there. They explained that 'her ladyship' (my wife, you see) would return today by 'The Age,'" Darwent meant the famous stagecoach, "from Brighton. I propose to call on her this evening."

"Will she know you intend to call?"

"No." Darwent rounded the syllable, lightly touched a side pocket full of money, and said no more. Mr. Mulberry was even more worried.

"Dick, why did she come back from Brighton?"

"Explain to me," suggested Darwin, "the habits of cobras or rattlesnakes."

"No, no, no! That won't do. Damme," said the lawyer, at length producing a snuffbox, "here's a worse tangle than ever! For mark this: when you went to number thirty-eight, did you observe the house next door?"

"The house next door?"

"Ay; number thirty-six! Did you observe it?"

"The shutters were closed; it seemed deserted But not unusual for London in July."

"That," replied Mr. Mulberry, and took snuff, "was the town house of Lord Francis Orford."

Darwent sat upright.

Neither of them heard the clatter of wheels and hoofs about them, nor heeded the fine haze of dust in Piccadilly. Darwent found himself looking at a white signboard above a shop-window; its black lettering ran, SUPERIOR PEN KNIVES RAZORS & PATENT NEEDLES, and next door was an apothecary's.

"This also we can consider afterwards," he said. "What's the rest of your news?"

Mr. Mulberry, taking more snuff and spilling most of it, braced himself.

"It concerns Dolly Spencer, I've found her. And again I say —gently, now!"

"Where is she? Is she ill?"

"Yes, Dick. She's ill."

Darwent smote his fist on his knee. Over his left shoulder was slung a light-gray riding cape, an odd garment for so warm a day; but he drew it up when it threatened to fall.

"I knew it!" he said. "Dolly! Ill for two months . . . where is she?"

"If you'll be quiet, lad, I'll try to be plain. She's not been ill for two months. I had a runner after her: privately paid, in our service, yes. But I learned by accident this morning. Are you acquainted with Mr. Arnold, the stage manager at Drury Lane?"

"Yes, of course!"

"And with Mr. Raleigh, who paints the scenery, and Mrs. Raleigh?"

"I've met them. Dolly . . ." Darwent stopped.

"Ah!" grunted the lawyer, snapping shut the lid of the snuff-box and dropping it into his pocket. "Then you'll understand. Once before, when your—your young lady disappeared for a matter of six weeks, she came back and threw herself on the Raleighs' mercy. At least, so Arnold told me.

"Two days ago, it appears, she fell over their doorstep in a raging fever with some illness the nearest doctor can't understand. He can only let blood and look wise. I'll tell you, Dick: there are pains in her side and she may need a surgeon: The Raleighs have given her their own room. They're not rich people, Dick."

Darwent pressed his hands over his eyes, and then dropped his hands.

"Who is the best surgeon in London?"

"Well! Astley Cooper. Or so they say. *If* he'll see her."

At Hoby the bootmaker's there were two doors, one here in Piccadilly and one round the corner in St. James's street. The former door opened and closed. Darwent heard a now all-too-familiar voice.

"Ah, how do you do, my dear fellow!" called Mr. Jemmy Fletcher.

Darwent, though exasperated, stopped in the act of giving an order to the driver.

Jemmy Fletcher—"only a butterfly, my boy," he would say of himself, though the occasional intelligence of his pale blue eye made this doubtful—strolled up to the carriage, himself agog with news. Jemmy, tallish and thin and with abundant fair hair, lived for the clubs, for the gossip he loved, for the green-baize card table at which he could not afford to play.

He seemed well-meaning, good-natured, and helpful even as a parasite. Meeting Darwent on the State side at Newgate, he had cursed and condoled with the prisoner. Darwent, who thought cards the pastime of a fool when there were books in this world, played piquet with him and deliberately lost large sums—for a purpose.

"Old boy," continued Jemmy, with suppressed triumph, "this is positively providential! On my oath it is!" His slight lisp was the perfection of the dandy, though Jemmy was far from lacking virility. "Old boy," he said in a low impressive voice, "you've been elected to White's. How's that?"

For an instant Darwent wrenched away from his fears about Dolly Spencer.

"I appreciate the honor," he said.

"Frankly, old boy, so you ought to. Nobody knew you. But there was your name. And, of course," Jemmy added, modestly examining his fingernails, "*my* little efforts may have helped."

"Jemmy," Darwent said abruptly, "do you know Sir John Buckstone?"

"Old Jack? Gad, I should think so!"

"I want to meet him," said Darwent. "I want to meet him, so to speak, on his own grounds."

"Now hark to me, Dick!" cut in Mr. Mulberry, with harshness. "If you take one word of advice—!"

Darwent silenced him. Jemmy, who had many times met Hubert Mulberry, nevertheless half-lifted the quizzing glass, which hung on a cord round his neck, as though wondering who this fellow might be.

"Jemmy," said Darwent, "when can I meet Buckstone?"

"But hang it, old boy," Jemmy sounded puzzled, "he's such a dull dog! You must meet Henry Pierrepoint; and Lord Alvanley, who seconded you. And Dan MacKinnon; *he* can crawl all the way round a room on the furniture, and never touch the floor once."

"A magnificent accomplishment. When can I meet Buckstone?"

"Deuce take it, don't press a fellow!" Jemmy, in dandy's uniform except for buff-colored trousers in place of breeches and boots, brought his wits to bear. "Well! Everybody's there between two and four, but it's past four now."

"Can you give me an answer, Jemmy?"

"He'll ride in the park at five. Stop; of course! Jack's always there at six to write letters, deuced if I know why, in the little back parlor."

"Will you meet me at White's, Jemmy? Six o'clock?"

"Well . . . yes. But—"

"One other thing," Darwent interrupted, and consulted his watch. "Jemmy, you're a tremendous fellow. You're acquainted with everybody worth knowing. Don't smirk; it's true. Now if by chance you were acquainted with Mr. Astley Cooper, the surgeon . . . ah, I see you are."

"Only a dashed sawbones, old boy. What's come over you?"

"As a great favor, Jemmy, you must persuade him to come to . . . where do the Raleighs live?"

"Lewknor Lane," grunted Mr. Mulberry, regarding Jemmy with a curiously speculative eye. "Not far from the theater."

"To Lewknor Lane, off Drury Lane, and the home of a Mr. Augustus Horatio Raleigh. Offer the surgeon any fee he likes, and double it if he hesitates. Will you promise to do that, Jemmy?"

"Yes, old boy, if you insist. But—"

"Thank you. Our humblest apologies for leaving you so abruptly." Darwent raised his hat, as the fashion was, and then made a gesture to the watchful driver on the box. "Lewknor Lane!"

And off they clattered, leaving Jemmy Fletcher with his quizzing glass now fully at his eye, his good-natured face slack with astonishment, against clusters of boots in a shop-window.

Though they could make little headway in the throng of vehicles, the red berline presently increased its pace amid the stews and gaming houses of Leicester Square. Somebody of republican tendencies threw a mud ball at the carriage, and it whizzed past Mr. Mulberry's white hat.

He did not even notice. He sat there with his arms folded.

"Well, lad," he said grimly, and broke a long silence, "you've made a fine start."

"I hope so."

"At six o'clock," grunted the lawyer, "you meet Buckstone, I can guess why, at White's. A little later, for what reason I can't guess, you meet your wife in St. James's Square." The bloated face turned sideways. "Rot me, did you engage to meet Frank Orford's murderer too?"

Darwent, his foreboding about Dolly increasing with each hoofbeat of the two black horses that drew the carriage, drummed his fingers on top of the carriage door.

"I should have attended to that too," he said, "if I had known who he was. But we have plenty of time to put him in the condemned cell."

"Let's be open, Dick," Mr. Mulberry spoke with sudden fierce bitterness. "You'll never see him in the condemned cell; and that's a fact."

Though Darwent glanced sideways, this did not seem to surprise him greatly.

"Oh? And why not?"

"Because, lad, you've committed perjury yourself! You've sworn a false oath, in two courts, about fighting a duel with Orford. We had to do it, to save you. But you can't whistle for the magistrate with another story. Has that occurred to you?"

"Yes."

"Eh? It *has* occurred to you?"

Darwent smiled. It altered not only the expression of the thin, fine-drawn face and the steady gray eyes; it seemed to alter the whole air and feelings of the man.

"I have thought much," he answered, "that I can't tell even to you. But what defeats me, everywhere I turn, is this mystery of it!" Again he drummed his fingers on the carriage door. "Why was I taken to Kinsmere House in the blue coach? What cheat was employed overnight to transform a new-furnished room—and the same room, I tell you!—into an old ruin rotted with dust and cobwebs? Who can explain that?"

"*I* can," the lawyer retorted suddenly, and banged his fist against his chest. "Old Bert Mulberry can!" Then out poured the reason for a great deal that weighed on his mind. "The fact is, Dick: I betrayed you."

There was a silence, except for wheels and hoofs. Darwent looked at him, hesitated, and refused to believe.

"You betrayed me? How?"

64

"Oh, the bottle," said Mr. Mulberry.

"Lord, is that all?"

" 'Is that all?' he says!" Mr. Mulberry addressed the driver's back. "I was foxed before I first set eyes on you in that room at Bow Street. When I came back from looking for the country house (d'ye recall?) I was blind-foxed and swaying on my feet."

"I remember, yes. What difference did it make?"

Hubert Mulberry, in a passion of repentance, again hammered at his own chest.

"All through the trial, with Mr. Serjeant Brutable defending you, I sat there with a grin on my face and a head full of grog. How did I instruct the Serjeant? With nothing at all. What do I deserve? Hanging! For it took me near a month (a month, Dick!) to see what I should have seen when you first told me your story."

Darwent's heart seemed to stop beating.

"My st . . . do you know who killed Frank Orford?"

"No. But the rest of it was easy to guess; ay, and I should have proved it at your first trial. They'd have acquitted you, Dick, if I'd had a sober head on my shoulders. That's my confession. That's why I worked to save you. But I couldn't tell you until you were free."

Darwent looked at the floor of the carriage. He drew a deep breath. He touched the gray cape, thrown over his left shoulder, and made sure it was there.

"Well!" he said, and his laugh was real. "Why should you blame yourself? We've done with it. You saved me; and I *am* free."

"Oh, you're free!" roared Mulberry, his face congested. "But I know the truth about that enchanted room! I know why Orford was there! And yet we can never hang the murderer now!"

The carriage, carefully driven through many dismal alleys after they had left Long Acre behind them, swerved to the right into Drury Lane.

—and Love in Lewknor Lane

"No," sighed Mr. Mulberry, losing a little of his haggard look, "you're not thinking on murder now, Dick. But to-night, if you're still alive. . ."

He paused. Down Drury Lane, narrow and not very savory, they could see the big dull-faced theater, wonderfully rebuilt since the fire of '09, with its doors now closed for the summer. Lewknor Lane, of ill repute since the time of Charles the Second, branched left as you faced south. As the red berline swung into Lewknor Lane, half-starved children poured out of doorways and screamed for joy or devilment.

"Pull up!" ordered Mr. Mulberry. "This is the house."

Darwent did not need to be told. He opened the carriage door and jumped down.

"Mr. Raleigh!" he shouted. "Mrs. Raleigh!"

One stone step led up to a door whose frame was somewhat rotted. To the right of it were two windows, giving on ground-floor lodgings of a narrow, scabrous, brick house. At one window—the curtains were painfully clean at both—sat Mrs. and Mrs. Augustus Raleigh, taking a sociable glass of gin-and-water as the heat of the day lessened.

"Emma!" said Mr. Raleigh, in a voice extraordinarily deep for so lean a chest. "God bless my soul! See who's here!"

Every memory out of his old life, everything he had loved when he was a fencing master off Covent Garden, swept back over Darwent as though he had been away for twenty years.

Actors and actresses, they said, were low people. Every respectable merchant knew it. They were still merely Their Majesties' Servants, as they were the servants of every rowdy audience like that one years ago (let wrath try to forget it) which made David Garrick beg its pardon on his knees. It was not much changed now. Old Mr. John Kemble and Mrs. Siddons at Covent Garden Theatre, dimmed in their struggle against the glory of Edmund Kean at Drury Lane, could be honored but regarded as curiosities. No decent woman, of course, could enter the refreshment room at the latter play-house.

Darwent had never noticed this lowness. And Mr. and Mrs. Raleigh were not players. He wrenched open the front door, groped in darkness, and opened the door of the small, clean-scrubbed front room.

"Dick!" began Mrs. Raleigh, but she could say no more.

Alternately he embraced Mrs. Raleigh, who was a little plump woman in a muslin cap edged with lace; and shook hands with Mr. Raleigh, who was a middle-sized elderly man with a bald head and a cadaverous face.

"Those clothes of yours!" gasped Mrs. Raleigh, in a state of fluster. "That carriage!"

"There's not time to explain now," said Darwent, again wringing Mr. Raleigh's hand. He attempted, and failed, to keep his voice steady. "Where is she?"

Augustus Raleigh, who had the stately manner of a player rather than a scene painter, made a ceremonious gesture toward another door. There was only one other room.

Darwent, his hand on the latch, hesitated because he wished to seem calm; but he could not manage it. Lifting the latch, he entered and closed the door behind him in half-darkness.

The back room was so small that most of it was occupied by the wooden bedstead and a tiny chest of drawers. Its window, shut off by a brick house six inches away, showed only a gray soot-drizzled light through which sometimes drifted a gleam of sun. Darwent heard the straw mattress rustle as someone, under a clean and carefully mended sheet, tried to sit up.

"I knew you'd be here," whispered Dolly's voice.

Mrs. Raleigh had combed and curled Dolly's yellow hair, cut shorter than it used to be. Her brown eyes were bright and yet glazed with fever; her face was flushed. Since Mrs. Raleigh's wardrobe did not include a spare nightgown, Dolly wore her shift, or shoulderless undergarment; it was made of silk, but far from new.

It seemed to him a long time he stood there, watching the helpless shining of her eyes. Then he took the warmth of her in his arms, holding her tightly but gently; and her arms went up round his neck, hands pressing the back of his head.

"You musn't kiss me," Dolly whispered, her head tilting back. "I'm not well; I have fever; you might catch it."

Darwent smiled at her.

"Then we'll both have it together," he said, and kissed the lips that were usually moist, but now fever-dry, while her arms pressed him closer and she seemed as always to wish for more intimate contact. When he lifted his head, she was between laughing and crying.

Still he held her with fierce protectivness; those months in Newgate, even the gallows, now seemed a trifle.

"Put your head back on the bolster," he told her. "Don't try to sit up.—What is it, Dolly? What's wrong?"

"I don't know. 'Tisn't much, I expect."

She paid no attention to this, dismissing it while her brown eyes searched his face, and she would not loosen her arms. Her soft voice, carefully and even frantically schooled to elocution as well as grammar by Mr. Raymond, the acting manager, slurred away.

"Chills-and-fever," Dolly said. "That's what Mrs. Raleigh says, and she ought to know. Dick, I . . ."

He smoothed her hair gently, his left arm under her shoulders to support her.

"Dick, I heard they wasn't—weren't going to . . ." Dolly meant "hang you," but she did not say it. He felt her shudder. "I couldn't be near you. Oh, God, I was frightened!"

"Gently, my dear. It doesn't matter now."

"Then I heard someone say they'd shouted out from that place—you know, the prison—and said you were safe. I cried. I couldn't be with you. No, you musn't kiss me!" But she was pleased and smiled, and afterwards laughed, when he did.

"What happened to me," he insisted, "is past and done with. But where were you all this time, Dolly? Where have you been?"

"I can't tell you," whispered Dolly. "I can't tell the Raleighs, I can't even tell you. Not yet!" Then she saw his eyes. "Oh! But 'twasn't what you . . . Dick!"

"Yes?"

"I've known men before I met you. I told you all of that."

He nodded. To men, it is jealousy of the past which stabs; to women, of the present and future.

"But since then there hasn't been anyone else. There never will be." Dolly laughed, not loudly and not for amusement, but at remembrance of things past. She was trembling. "Dick! Do you remember when I saw you the last time?"

"Yes! My God, yes!"

"I was all in costume with glass jewels to play Lady Macduff."

Glass jewels, did she say? It was in his mind to tell her

68

that, if she mentioned Shakespeare, there really was a jeweler named Mr. Hamlet in Cranbourne Alley; and Mr. Hamlet should pour out his boxes for her. But there was a weight in his throat; he could not speak bombast.

"I didn't play it," laughed Dolly, amused at herself as always.

"Why not?"

"They daresn't let me. Mr. Raymond says my voice is 'musical': as though I could ever play a pianoforte or a harpsichord! But I'm no actress, Dick."

"Gently, Dolly!"

Her eyes, with a glazed quality which suddenly alarmed him, wandered up the canopy of the curtainless bed.

"It's awful—awfully funny. When I'm myself I'm natural, like. On the stage I'm wooden." Mirth touched her eyes and mouth again. "Dick! Do you remember the night I played Brutus's wife (me!), and the Roman villa looked so real I leaned on one of the pillars and fell over?" Her memory moved away. "Or the nights we went to Vauxhall Gardens, Dick? And the fireworks? Oh, all the nights!"

"Dolly, I'm going to lower your head. Lie down."

She moved obediently. But as she stretched out her knees, he saw a spasm of pain cross her face. He felt, too late, that before coming here he should have broken the bell wire on the door of every physician he passed.

"Do you feel better, Dolly?"

" 'Tisn't anything," she said, and clearly believed it.

"Before long," he assured her, "the best sur—the best physician in London will be here. And we can't impose ourselves on the Raleighs. Dolly. They're as poor as Lazarus. I want to take you . . ."

As though vaguely remembering something she ought to have noticed before, Dolly half-lifted her head. She ceased to look at his face, and in a groping way she looked at his clothes.

"Dick!" she said. "What's . . . ?"

"The fact is," he said apologetically, and swallowed the lump in his throat, "I've come into some money. I want to take you. . ."

"No, you don't!" Dolly said vehemently, and propped herself on one arm despite his protests. "I don't care if you've come into a hundred pounds! No!"

"It's a little more than that, my dear. You see . . ."

"I told you before!" said Dolly. "I'll go with you, I'll
69

live with you like we did before, becos I love you. But I won't take anything from you except to eat or drink or go a-junketing. I won't take presents. That's wrong.

"Dolly, my dear! Listen to me!"

To demonstrate that she was not angry, Dolly smiled. A film seemed to lift from her eyes, and they brightened.

"Do you recolleck when you won a five-pound note in a wager? And wanted to give the five-pound note to me? And I wouldn't have it? And you were so vexed with me that you tore it up?" Her forehead wrinkled. "What was the wager?"

"I can't remember, Dolly. I can't remember anything except you."

"Oh, I'm stupid" said Dolly. "It was at the fencing school. The son of Gold Ingots Company or suchlike, from Lombard Street, dared you to try him with real sabers . . ." She broke off, with anxiety in her face. "Dick? What is it? You looked at me," she drew back, "as though you hated me."

"Not ever you, Dolly. Not ever you!"

"Then what is it?"

"I was thinking of a certain man named . . . no matter."

"Oh," murmured Dolly, and the fear lest he be angry died out of her eyes.

Propped on one elbow, her yellow hair vivid against the tawny skin, she seemed to press memories against her breast as though in her heart she feared there might be no future.

"Gold Ingots," she said, "kept a-lunging at your chest with the point of the saber. You'd parry, and cut another curl off his head with the edge, and never hurt him, and apologize. I wasn't frightened, Dick. I knew he couldn't touch you."

Pain touched her again as her knees moved. She fell back helplessly. Her companion had become desperate.

"What *is* it, Dolly? Where does it hurt you?"

Uncertainly Dolly put her hand on her right side, moving the hand three inches or so across the abdomen.

"Truly it doesn't hurt," she muttered, "unless I move my legs. It's awful funny. My legs are like boards."

Darwent jumped to his feet. Since he had allowed his lawyer to arrange all things, he was about to call "Mulberry!" when he suddenly realized that Mr. Mulberry was there.

Mr. Mulberry, hat in hand, stood just inside the now-open door to the front room. Mr. and Mrs. Raleigh were in the doorway. At that time Darwent could not understand why Mrs. Raleigh had tears in her eyes, and even her cadaverous-faced husband was not far from this emotion.

"La, now, you've upset her!" said Mrs. Raleigh, and flew across with the lace trembling on her cap. In the half-darkness they could scarcely see each other's faces, and the tiny room was crowded.

"There, now!" Mrs. Raleigh said accusingly.

Dolly, exhausted, had fallen into a doze. As Darwent was about to speak, Mr. Mulberry cut him short.

"No haste, lad," he advised. "D'ye think I'd trust that young what-d'ye-call-it, that Sir Fopling Flutter. . . ."

"Jemmy Fletcher?"

"Ay; Jemmy Fletcher; it's the same thing. D'ye think I'd trust him to fetch anybody we wanted? I sent your carriage to Bart's Hospital as soon as you stepped out of it. It should return at any minute."

Mrs. Raleigh, pink-faced, tossed her head.

"Hark at the man!" she scoffed. "There's nothing wrong with the poor girl but old-fashioned chills and fever. The black medicine will cure her, if it's strong enough and nasty-tasting enough. Wasn't I one of a family of thirteen? Haven't I raised four of my own?"

(Then what had been the other reason for the tears in her eyes, the apprehensive movements?)

"Dick," intervened Augustus Raleigh, in his deep voice like a ghost in a play.

He stepped forward from the doorway. Even his bald head seemed dusty from long work at the theater, but he held himself straight. Though his dark clothes and gaiters were shabby, his neckcloth was clean and his cadaverous face smooth-shaven even from blueness. His dignity was very real.

"Dick," said Mr. Raleigh, "I don't understand. This gentleman," and he nodded in stately fashion toward Mr. Mulberry, "says you have been in prison, but he will say no more. Emma and I did not know of it. We keep ourselves much to ourselves, especially in these days . . ."

"Especially in these days?"

Mr. Raleigh ignored this.

"But, Dick! They speak of 'your carriage'; and I'll swear you wear a hundred guineas on your back." Mr. Raleigh's voice grew less sepulchral and more anxious. "Dick, you haven't taken to thieving or the like?"

"No, of course not!"

"Didn't I tell you?" sniffed Mrs. Raleigh, and began to cry.

"Sir," Darwent continued, with formal respect, "I can't ever repay what you and your wife have done for Dolly."

71

"But that was little enough!"

"Little? Perhaps you think so. But by accident, as I was telling Dolly, I have come into some money. I won't insult you, surely, if I remind you of the old rule of share and share alike?"

Mr. Raleigh gave him a strange look.

"I wish Dolly," said Darwent, "to have more luxury than she has ever dreamed of. I wish to see her, this very afternoon, in a furnished house in St. James's . . ."

"St. James's!"

"And I should esteem it the greatest favor if Mrs. Raleigh could go with her and look after her. With, of course," he added hastily, as he saw a wild glance between husband and wife, "yourself to accompany Mrs. Raleigh. Sir, you will find me not ungrateful."

Then, to his intense discomfort, he saw tears well up in old Raleigh's eyes. But the harsh voice of Mr. Mulberry struck in.

"Pull up, Dick!" the lawyer told him. "D'ye think I can find you a furnished house at an hour or two's notice?"

"Can't you?"

"In a day or two, yes. No doubt! Meanwhile . . ."

"Meanwhile," said Darwent, "it must be managed notwithstanding."

Mr. Mulberry looked thoughtful, pursing up his thick lips. "Oh, it could be managed!" He would not meet Darwent's eye, but stared with a faraway look at the back of Mr. Raleigh's neck. "You already own a house, Dick, which must be tolerably well furnished."

"*I* own a house?"

"Number thirty-eight St. James's Square," Mr. Mulberry said coolly. "Under the law, d'ye see, it became your property when you married."

"So it did," agreed Darwent after a pause, and unholy joy drove the blood to his heart. "I had forgotten. So it did!"

"Married!" almost screamed Mrs. Raleigh. Her husband, who had given a start, backed against the chest of drawers. "Dick! You're not *married?*"

Darwent glanced quickly toward Dolly, who was in a doze and could not hear him. Dolly moaned, turning her head from side to side.

"To speak a truth, Mrs. Raleigh . . ."

A double knock on the street door in the next room, a knock firm yet authoritative, sent Mrs. Raleigh flying to answer it. But old Hubert Mulberry anticipated her. Mr. Mulberry opened the street door to a portly, dignified, fresh-complexioned gentleman whose dark beaver hat and funereal-seeming clothes contrasted with his merry eyes, and who gave his name as Mr. Samuel Hereford, surgeon in chief at St. Bartholomew's Hospital.

Waving Mr. and Mrs. Raleigh away, Mr. Mulberry spoke to the newcomer in a rapid whisper, and the surgeon nodded gravely.

In the tiny bedroom, standing beside the bed and gripping Dolly's hand, Darwent heard the surgeon cough in the doorway.

"Lord Darwent?" he asked in a very low voice, removing his hat with a profound bow. "Your servant, my lord."

"Yours to command, sir." And Darwent poured out Dolly's story as he knew it. "For God's sake," he added, "tell me what is wrong! And if she is in need of surgery."

"We shall do our best, my lord," Mr. Hereford replied cheerfully, but with suitable portentousness. "If your lordship will be good enough to go into the other room, I shall wait upon you as soon as may be."

In the front room, where the Raleighs' most valued possessions were a chiming clock on the wooden mantelpiece and a canary in a wicker cage, both Mr. and Mrs. Raleigh were much agitated. Hubert Mulberry eyed them with a sardonic look.

"I could hate you, Dick," said Mrs. Raleigh, stamping her foot on the floor. "Don't tell me I couldn't! I could!"

"My dear Emma," remonstrated her husband, trying to look very imposing with one hand inside his waistcoat like General Bonaparte, "we had no reason to believe that Dick's intentions towards Dolly . . ."

"Oh, fiddle!" said Mrs. Raleigh. "If two young people choose to enjoy 'emselves, pray what business is it of ours or the parson's? As though we'd never done the same, in our time?"

"My dear!"

"Fie to all hypocrites, I say!" The little, plump, pleasant-faced woman again burst into tears. "But he's *married*, Mr. Raleigh! His wife . . ."

"She is no wife," interrupted Darwent. "She will have a surprise in store for her, I think. Mulberry!"

"Ay, lad?"

"Isn't it true that this marriage can be annulled? Since, to employ a word which has always amused mé, it has never been consummated?"

"It can be annulled; true enough." Mr. Mulberry scowled. "But I've had more than a word or two, Dick, with the old fox Crockit."

"Well?"

"Your dear Caroline's grandfather," said Mr. Mulberry, "made provision against everything except death. Annulment, separation, even a near-impossible divorce that takes an Act of Parliament: she loses her inheritance for any of 'em. She'll fight you, Dick. Don't you see that? She'll fight you."

"In that case," Darwent spoke politely, "we had better begin the fight ourselves. Mrs. Raleigh! Mr. Raleigh!"

Always in his mind, when he thought of Dolly, was the hideous fear of surgery. The surgeon was skilled of course. But, when the patient lay strapped to an operating table, not even laudanum or strong drink could stifle the screams.

"If Dolly's illness be not—serious," he said, "will you come to St. James's Square and take care of her? The playhouse is closed. Surely you can have no duties in midsummer?"

He did not understand the reason for the long silence.

The canary, in its wicker cage hung from the rotted ceiling boards, began to sing thinly. Mr. and Mrs. Raleigh exchanged glances.

"Why, Dick," the deep voice said slowly, "it's plain Dolly never told you."

"Told me what?"

"I have no duties at the playhouse. I was dismissed, we must call it in disgrace, towards the end of April."

There was another silence.

"Forgive the impertinence of the question; but . . . how have you managed to live since then?"

"Well, Dick, there isn't much left." Mr. Raleigh avoided his eye. "Two and eightpence three farthings. Emma and I, like the wasters we have always been, spent fivepence today on a bottle of strong waters.

"You come to us," Mr. Raleigh added suddenly, his dark eyes aglitter under wrinkled and trembling lids, "with this request. You beg it, Dick, as though we were conferring some great favor on *you*. You make a man cease to feel worthless. God bless you."

Mrs. Raleigh had turned away to hide her face, and was looking out of the window.

" 'Cease to feel worthless,' " Darwent repeated bitterly. "Why did they dismiss you?"

Augustus Raleigh did not look bitter: only apologetic. But

74

he could keep up his stately pose no longer. Lifting his hands, those hands so deft to shape and paint a stage-king's throne into living reality, he inspected them and let them fall. The canary trilled a song beyond him.

"I had the misfortune," he replied, "to annoy a gentleman who had gone backstage to the greenroom. I hoped he had not noticed. Indeed, he scarcely seemed to glance at me. I had not meant to spill paint on his boot. But I am told he spoke with four friends, and five complaints were lodged with the directors. What could the directors do?"

"They could do," said Darwent, "what I will not suggest in Mrs. Raleigh's hearing. May I ask the name of this gentleman?"

"I fear he moves in more exalted circles than ours. His name was Buckstone, Sir John Buckstone."

On the sagging wooden mantelpiece, the chiming clock whirred, tinkled twice, and struck the half-hour after five.

Darwent stood motionless, his right hand on the gray cape over his left shoulder. His gaze, which suddenly terrified Emma Raleigh, moved over to the clock, noted the time, and moved back to Mr. Raleigh.

"And has Sir John Buckstone," he asked gently, "as many as four friends?"

"Well, Dick, they admire him. Why speak about this? Let it go! There's not a man in London who isn't afraid of him."

Again Hubert Mulberry's voice cut sharply into emotion.

"Take it easy, Dick!" he begged. "Control yourself. Sit down."

The latch clicked on the door to the bedroom. From the doorway emerged the portly, dignified figure of Mr. Hereford, the surgeon.

"My lord," Mr. Hereford said gravely, causing both Raleighs to twitch their heads round, "you most urgently desired to learn whether the patient had need of surgery. Let me reassure you at once, my lord. The patient has *no* need of surgery."

Darwent's knees weakened with relief, so that unwittingly he followed Mr. Mulberry's advice by groping for a chair and sitting down.

"Do I understand you find it . . . not serious?"

"Not serious, my lord," the surgeon returned dryly, "unless you consider serious a matter of simple indigestion, which (alas!) may attack any of us."

"I thank you." Darwent cleared his throat. "But the fever? The pain?"

Mr. Hereford hesitated, rolling his eyes and pursing up his lips.

"The pain," he said, and pressed his hand to the right side of his lower abdomen, "would seem to be *here.* Yet that must be considered in relation to the other symptoms. Should the patient indeed require surgery, it must be for some operation as yet unknown to medical science."

A subdued twinkle appeared in Mr. Hereford's eyes as he added:

"Now we poor fellows, my lord, consider this to be most unlikely."

The agnostic Darwent offered up a silent prayer of thanks.

"At the same time," said Mr. Hereford, "there are certain matters which (I confess) somewhat perplex me. Alarming? No, no! But curious."

Darwent rose to his feet. From one corner of the room, where he had flung it when he entered, he picked up his hat.

"Would it harm her, do you think, if she were removed to other lodgings?"

"Dear me, no! I even fancy it would benefit her."

"And will you have the kindness, Mr. Hereford, to accompany her there?"

"I shall be honored, my lord."

"Again I thank you." Darwent's tone changed. "Mr. Mulberry!"

"I've been awaiting instructions, my lord," said the lawyer, aping Mr. Hereford's style of speech. "But I'm not happy. It may be I was hasty to suggest . . . Have a care, Dick!"

"Use my carriage," said Darwent, "and take them all to number thirty-eight St. James's Square. I'll go to White's in a hackney coach; my affairs there should not take long; I propose to join you directly."

Mr. Mulberry's voice went up.

"That's all very well! But what if a certain lady (eh?) should refuse to admit us?"

Darwent showed his teeth.

"Should the lady refuse you entrance to my house," he said, "summon the watch and have her put under restraint until I arrive.—She wants the law? She shall have the law!"

Turning round, his hatbrim formally against his chest, Darwent bowed courteously to the others.

"Please forgive my absence for a time," he added. "I have a matter to discuss with Sir John Buckstone."

Displays the Dandy-Lions at Home

"Damme, old boy, but you're ten minutes late," mildly complained Jemmy Fletcher. "Deuced sorry, you know, too. But I'm afraid I forgot to write a note to that surgeon you wanted."

Jemmy, lean and elegant, stood in the doorway of White's Club not far from the foot of St. James's Street. At the foot of the street, back from Pall Mall, was the old red-brick St. James's Palace with its row of mock battlements and its two thin towers at the gate. In the broad street, sloping up to Piccadilly, you might find every club of importance save Watier's.

From Brookes's to the humbler Cocoa-Tree, from the Guards' to the Thatched House Tavern, they closed charmed doors against the vulgar. But White's, where play at the green table ravaged even large fortunes and General Scott had won two hundred thousand pounds at whist, stood above them all.

Jemmy Fletcher seemed to sense this, or imagined he did, as Darwent glanced round.

"I say," whispered Jemmy. "Don't look up. But there it is."

"There what is"

"The bow window, damme! The famous bow window above the door! Only a very select few," Jemmy said with a tinge of envy, "can sit in that window. Or they glare daggers at you until you go away. Here! Dash it! Stop!"

For Darwent, after remarking that he had heard much of the window, was frankly staring upward.

There they sat, behind the glass panes edged with white, only a few of the elect at this hour before sunset. By mutual consent they sat as motionless as a waxworks. They wore their hats indoors, according to club usage. Their fixed unsmiling faces looked out at the street with eyes as glassy as a boy's marbles: seeing everybody, recognizing nobody.

Jemmy Fletcher was almost hopping with discomfort. "Dick! Hang it, man! Don't stare!"

"Why not?" asked Darwent, making sure his voice would carry. "They're staring, aren't they?"

"But, dash it, dear boy, that's their privilege."

"Where's Sir John Buckstone? Is he here?"

"Yes, yes," Jemmy soothed him in a low voice, "since you're so dashed anxious to make friends with him. Here; give me your arm; I'll take you in."

The interior was gloomy, with an atmosphere of starched linen and brushed clothes, threaded through by a whiff of cookery and a fainter whiff of the stable. Darwent, ten seconds after he had entered, received a shock for which he could not account.

Someone, a man of about his own age, crossed Darwent's line of vision and disappeared through a doorway in singularly ghostly fashion.

Now the man was no ghost; the sound of his top boots moved firmly on oak boards. But there was about him something so very familiar that Darwent almost spoke out and addressed him. The same notion must have occurred to the other man, since he glanced round briefly before he vanished.

Distantly, presumably from upstairs, floated the noise of arguing voices.

"What's the good callin' for the betting book?" somebody demanded. "I won't make a wager on that. Ask anybody: what's the filthiest, scurviest trade there is?"

"Moneylender!" Many voices answered him.

"We're all in debt to one of 'em or the other, though there's not a man here who'd admit it. Wager, damme? D'ye think I'm green?"

Darwent disengaged his arm from Jemmy's.

"Wasn't that Buckstone's voice?" he asked.

"No, no, no!" Jemmy assured him truthfully. "Come with me."

He led his companion towards the back of the premises, and opened the door of what was then a small parlor seldom used.

The room was paneled with white-painted wood, and a small bow window looked out on a board fence. A thin carpet patterned the middle of the floor with red and green. Against the right-hand wall, ahead of them, stood a writing desk of grained mahogany inlaid with gilt. Seated at the desk, his back toward them but seen partly in profile, Sir John Buckstone was writing a letter.

Darwent drew a deep breath.

"Ah, how do you do, my dear Jack!" sang out Jemmy's thin, cheerful voice. It was as though he waved his hand to

Buckstone from a great distance. "Hope I'm not disturbing you, am I?"

Buckstone, though exasperated, consented to glance over his shoulder.

"Yes. 'Fraid you are."

But the tall, fair-haired, blue-eyed young man was impervious.

"Sorry to hear that, dear boy," he sang. "I must, positively *must*, make you acquainted with our newest member. Dick loves the pictures on cards, you know. Whist, piquet, écarté, macao: curse me, Jack, he's your man!"

This seemed to alter matters. Buckstone looked at the letter in front of him, and slowly put down the writing quill while he adjusted his ruddy face into an expression of pleasantness. He got up from the chair, and turned round. But carefully, as a matter of principle, he remained by the desk: letting the others approach him rather than taking a step toward them.

"Why he's . . ." Buckstone began; and stopped.

Darwent saw him exactly as Buckstone had been at Newgate: his hat on the back of his head, wearing a striped waistcoat, but with an attempt at joviality now. It was clear, too, that Buckstone did not recognize the former felon.

When last he had seen Darwent, a dirt coating, thick beard stubble and long hair (which seemed black rather than short-cut brown) had formed a gallows mask. Yet Buckstone's eyes narrowed.

"No, you're not Lewis," he corrected himself. "For a second I thought you were. Here, haven't we met before?"

"We have."

"By Jove, I knew it! Where did we meet?"

"Permit me to remind you," Darwent said politely.

His right hand slipped inside the grey cape over his left shoulder. From a deep pocket, where it had lain coiled, Darwent took out a riding crop with a long sharp whip end. He slashed it with pent-up viciousness across the left side of Buckstone's face. Instantly, back-handed, he drove it at the right side of the face with such power that the whip seemed to sing before it struck and drew blood.

"That will remind you," said Darwent.

The stunned silence, a hot heavy quiet of incredulity, seemed to stretch out unendurably. Not one of them moved.

"No!" Jemmy cried out suddenly, with a womanish kind of cry. "He didn't mean it, Jack. I take my oath he didn't

79

mean it. Dick's had rather a rough life, d'ye see? He don't understand gentlemen. He . . ."

Not a muscle moved in Buckstone's face, though a thin trickle of blood ran from his right cheekbone halfway down his face. But his eyes showed he was very much alive, and very much reminded now.

"Who is this . . ." Buckstone began violently; .nd checked himself. "Present him to me, Jemmy."

The newest member of White's spoke in a voice which made Jemmy shy back.

"I am the Marquess of Darwent," he said. "By virtue of my rank, sir, he will present *you* to *me*."

"Sailed in a ship for America," Jemmy was bleating. "Ship with ammunition when we fought 'em in '12. Wrecked, Jack! Rough life. Ship was wrecked; only three survivors. Place called Crosstree Island. Wasn't it, Dick?"

"Present him to me!" replied Darwent.

Faltering, Jemmy did so.

Buckstone and Darwent looked at each other without speaking. Buckstone moistened his lips, his little black eyes straying to the exact center of Darwent's forehead. Buckstone's right hand, hanging at his side, moved as though his finger curled round the trigger of a pistol.

"Jemmy," he said, "ring the bell."

The bell cord hung near the desk, easily within Buckstone's reach. But it was not his habit to do menial service. Jemmy flew at the bell.

"My compliments to Major Sharpe," Buckstone said rather hoarsely, to the impassive waiter who opened the door and did not seem to notice Buckstone's slashed face. "Ask Major Sharpe if he can find it convenient to see me here, as soon as possible."

When the waiter had gone, not a word was spoken until Major Sharpe arrived. All three assumed careless attitudes. Yet in that white-painted room, with the red-and-green carpet, hatred sang like a wasp. It could not have gone on for long, or Buckstone and Darwent would have been at each other's throats.

"No!" Jemmy's mouth framed the word silently. "No!"

But the door banged open.

Major Anthony Sharpe, 7th Hussars, had left the green-baize table and was still scowling at an open fan of cards as he strode into the room. But he closed up the cards, glancing at Buckstone's face as impassively as the waiter.

"Yes?" he asked, rather impatiently.

Major Sharpe, an upright spare-built martinet of fifty, looked frostily from under reddish eyebrows, past a long nose framed by wiry reddish side whiskers. He was very punctilious, very correct. His Hussar tunic, dark blue with horizontal lines of gold braid, ended in tight-fitting blue breeches and gold-edged Hessian boots. From his left shoulder swung the short fur-lined pelisse, though he had discarded his sword and the scarlet busby with the white plume.

"Lord Darwent." He jerked his head as Jemmy made the introduction. "Yes. I see. Well?"

"A little dispute," Buckstone told him, in a bored voice. "You'll act for me, of course?"

Major Sharpe's thumb rippled the cards in his other hand.

"Made you lose your temper, has he?" inquired the Major, forgetting his correct attitude. "Gad, I didn't think it was possible."

Buckstone was rather white in the face. "You'll act for me? You'll call on . . . ?"

Darwent turned to Jemmy. "And you, Mr. Fletcher, will act for me?"

Buckstone seemed on the point of roaring with laughter. But there was more to Jemmy than butterfly wing and sawdust.

"Yes," he said simply. "Got no choice."

"Good!" agreed Major Sharpe. He looked at Jemmy. "Please be in the cardroom, for me to call on you, in half an hour." Something intensely human, even if satiric, peered out from under his reddish eyebrows. "Shouldn't have brought these with me," he added, rippling the cards again. "Nobody'd look at my hand, of course. No, no! Still—! Jack Buckstone sends the challenge, eh? Pray excuse me, gentlemen."

And he strode out of the room.

Darwent looked at Buckstone without appearing to see him, glanced in a satisfied way at the riding crop, and put the riding crop inside his cloak. Then he followed Major Sharpe.

Darwent's step was springy, his heart almost serene. Ever since the lash had whipped across Buckstone, two blows returned for two blows given, he felt a lessening of the tension which had cost him his peace of mind and his sense of humor. Once he met Buckstone in the field, with fair green turf and no favor, he would feel better still.

In this mood, a sort of reversed loving kindness, he suddenly discovered that he had walked all the way to the front door.

81

He stopped in the doorway, with a noise of wheeled vehicles in his ears, and Jemmy Fletcher chasing him.

Though Jemmy's walk was a saunter, his face wore a wild look.

"You did it a-purpose!" he accused Darwent in a low voice. "You involved me, curse you!" Sheer bewilderment seemed to flood out every other feeling. "Dick, what's your game! Are you mad? Why did you do it?"

"Why not?"

"He'll kill you," Jemmy explained comprehensively.

Whereupon, to Jemmy's stupefaction, Darwent beamed at him.

"I'm in two minds about that," Darwent told him, because he had two plans concerning Buckstone. "If you should want me in the next two hours (which you will, since you're to meet Major Sharpe in half an hour), you'll find me at home."

"Stephen's Hotel, you mean?"

"Well—no. I made reference to my own home, and that of my devoted new wife, at number thirty-eight St. James's Square. I am going there to greet her now. Meanwhile, let me give you your instructions."

"Instructions, old boy?"

"In case you've forgotten, Jemmy, you're to be my second in a duel." Darwent considered. "Now let's make sure we have fair play. Buckstone, I daresay, has some knowledge of the sword?"

Jemmy blinked, and half-lifted the quizzing glass on the cord round his neck.

"At exercise, Dick? Lord, yes. Jack's a capital hand with the foil."

"Is he also acquainted with the use of the saber?"

"Why, Dick, he's better with the saber than with the foil. He half-split the skull of some dashed Austrian with a wooden saber; made us all near to burst with laughing."

"Good!" said Darwent, and meant it. "Now as the challenged party, Jemmy, I believe *I* have the choice of weapons?"

"Naturally, old boy. But of course you'll choose—"

Jemmy stopped. Sudden consternation crept into his face.

"The place," Darwent told him, "may be where you like. The time: when you like, but as soon as possible. The weapons: sabers. Good evening to you, my boy."

And he lifted his hat and stepped briskly out into the street.

Behind him Jemmy was bleating some words which he did not hear and chose not to hear. A handsome *vis-à-vis* carriage, its hammer-cloth rich with heraldic designs, its body lacquered black and white with yellow wheels, came spanking down St. James's Street on its way back from the park.

Darwent had to jump to avoid it. But the *vis-à-vis* contained two very pretty, coy and soulful-eyed ladies, in large bonnets with plumes. Though he had no idea who they were, Darwent bowed and smiled. The ladies answered him, one of them turning round, with two languishing smiles (which vanished instantly, as though their faces swam amid the seraphim) before the carriage swung left into Pall Mall.

Taking the same direction, Darwent walked eastward into Pall Mall along the left-hand side. He had now to deal with another handsome lady, Caroline Ross.

It was as well, he thought as he strode along, that he had in some measure recovered his ability to see things in their proper light. He must not appear to treat Caroline too seriously, or he would lose the game.

At this time, a month after he had met Caroline, he did not detest her because she had married a doomed man to get a fortune. After all, what was the world now but a market where harpy mothers clawed and flapped at their daughters to push them into marriage, any marriage, provided the man had money? In most cases the daughter herself, though she might blush and lower her eyes, was in spirit a Roman retiarius with a net to throw and a trident to pin down: *vi*, he thought, *et armis*.

No. He did not blame Caroline for a cruder method.

But he detested her because she seemed as cold as a snake, and because of that happy insolence and arrogance which characterized her tribe.

Caroline's image rose in his mind, her blue eyes looking sideways past brown curls. If he had met her under other circumstances, he admitted to himself, she might have a good deal of fascination. Also . . .

Since he had been put under arrest on the morning of May 6th, he had led a life of enforced celibacy which all but maddened him. If Dolly had been well (though, thank the Padre's God, her illness was not serious), Dolly would have arranged the matter with almost startling haste.

Stop these thoughts? But why should he? Sometimes, when the nerves twitched, it was cold comfort to press vengeance to yourself when you might have pressed living flesh. Nevertheless, Darwent began to think on the situation which—in his own impetuousness—he had brought about.

Caroline Ross and Dolly Spencer were now, or shortly would be, under the same roof.

This would infuriate Caroline as an insult, which was good. But it would also infuriate Dolly who, for all her laughter, was fiercely jealous and had made scenes he preferred to forget.

"What the devil have I done?" he demanded aloud: absent-mindedly, but straight into the face of a bishop who, in full panoply of white wig and shovel hat and black apron, was marching toward him in Pall Mall.

"I ask your pardon, my lord bishop," said Darwent, waking up suddenly as the other stopped short. "But I was thinking deeply on the question."

The bishop, who had a gloomy eye, spoke in a deep port-wine voice.

"Whatever the question, sir, it is a matter for your own conscience."

"My lord bishop, what is your opinion of holy matrimony?"

"Sir," replied the bishop, "it is the only happy estate."

And the bishop marched onward, to be lost among the passers-by. Darwent, roused from abstraction, realized that he had passed the turning into St. James's Square and was walking in the direction of the Haymarket.

Southward across Pall Mall, now sheltered by funereal foliage and backed by deep gardens, rose the round fat pillars of Carlton House, home of the Prince Regent. It was an immense blowsy place, always in need of a coat of limewash or stuck over with ladders for new repairs.

As far as repairs were concerned, he could see enough of them by looking toward his left. For two years' time, up the hill north of the thoroughfare, they had been hacking out a new wide street which they would call Regent Street if they ever finished it.

At this time it was still a covered way, whose houses had been stealthily taken over by gambling rooms and by a more genteel class of prostitutes than you might find in Leicester Square. Its roofs and chimney stacks stood out dark against a smoky golden sky.

Gambling room. Prostitute . . .

Turning round sharply, Darwent walked back in the other direction.

In a few minutes he was standing in St. James's Square, looking up at the stone steps and the three aloof red-brick floors, topped by an attic floor, of number thirty-eight. He smiled again, because his plan was now complete.

The door was opened by Alfred, the first footman, whom Darwent had met here during his brief visit in the afternoon.

"My lord," said the footman, taking Darwent's hat and cape with deep respect in his feelings as well as his voice.

Darwent, though still a trifle surprised when someone addressed him as "my lord," nevertheless was richly and easily at home.

"Has my wife returned from Brighton?'"

"Yes, my lord. Her ladyship returned not an hour ago."

"Ah! As to our arrangement," Darwent meant their financial arrangement, "I trust my wife does not yet know that I intend to call on her?"

Inwardly Alfred felt gleeful. Like almost everyone else, he and the other nine servants knew very little of the facts; he believed The Icicle's sudden marriage to have been a romantic love match.

"No, my lord," he replied, without even a hairline of a smile. "Your lordship will find the secret well kept."

"Good. Where is my wife now?"

"I believe her ladyship is abovestairs, my lord. Shall I . . . ?"

"No, no! Thank you. I wish to go up and surprise her."

"Very good, my lord."

Darwent went to the staircase, and carefully took four steps up before turning round as though he had forgotten something.

"By the by," he said. "Has the other lady arrived?"

"The other lady, my lord?"

"Yes. Miss Dorothy Spencer. I expected her here, together with a Mr. and Mrs. Raleigh and a Mr. Hereford, before I arrived myself."

"I believe there have been no callers, my lord."

Darwent was only faintly disquieted. Though he had been surprised not to see his carriage outside the door, he need not have expected the guests so soon.

"When the lady does arrive," he said, "please arrange for her to occupy whatever may be the best guest room. Mr. and Mrs. Raleigh are to be similarly installed. The other gentleman will not remain."

"Very good, my lord."

"Er—I forgot to inquire whether my wife is served by a personal maid?"

"Oh, yes, my lord! If your lordship will remember, the girl

Meg is one of those to whom you spoke today. Meg did not go with her ladyship to Brighton."

"Then you had better engage a second personal maid. The lady who will arrive soon is my mistress."

There was a perceptible pause, though the footman remained expressionless.

"Very good, my lord."

It was not that Alfred was in the least scandalized. As he afterwards said to the second footman, "Hurrah for the governor!" He was used to such situations, but not to such candor.

"One more question. Where am I likely to find my wife? In the drawing room?"

"I could not say, my lord. But I believe: in her bedroom."

"Where is her bedroom?"

"If your lordship will be good enough to turn left at the top of the stairs, you will see her ladyship's door directly opposite."

"Ah . . . A still better place to surprise her. Thank you."

Darwent sauntered up the stairs, while the footman, after waiting until his head had gone out of sight, bolted belowstairs to tell the others.

It was remarkable, Darwent thought, how the prospect of meeting Buckstone in a duel restored his spirits and his zest for life. It roused more than that: it roused his old, old sense of devilment. Without troubling to knock at the bedroom door, he turned the knob and opened it.

He found himself in a large bedroom, richly furnished but in the severely classical French style. Even the bed was a gilt-scrolled austere white, without posts or tester or curtains.

Caroline was not there. Amid a vast clutter of half-unpacked portmanteaus and boxes, a dark-haired lady's maid, her eyes wide with amazement, stood clutching an armful of billowing gowns.

"My lord," she whispered, though she must have expected him.

Darwent, assuming the role of the dandy, drew himself up in a manner which must have been admired by the acting manager at Drury Lane.

"I take it you're Meg, m'love?" he inquired.

"Yes, my lord," whispered Meg, and curtsied among the gowns. "But . . ."

Here Darwent noticed another door. It was in the right-hand wall. Though the door was closed, a fraction of its edge showed that it was not fastened.

86

"My lord, you mustn't go in there!" whispered Meg in agitation, as though she were speaking of Bluebeard's den. "That's the bathroom. Her ladyship is having her bath."

A look of strong satisfaction crossed Darwent's face.

"You're a good, modest girl, m'love," he declared, as Buckstone himself might have said it. "But after all, you know, the damned woman *is* my wife."

He opened the door of the bathroom, closed it behind him, and bolted the door on the inside.

◇   C H A P T E R   I X   ◇

Tells of a Lady in Her Bath—

The ensuing tableau, as Darwent turned round, might have interested an unprejudiced witness.

Darwent was in a room long but very narrow, since it had been partitioned off from the bedroom. A thin window at the narrow far end admitted light, showing no furniture or fitting except a mantelpiece, two chairs, and the portable but very heavy bath, which had been pushed longways against the same wall as the door.

And thus, as he turned sideways from bolting the door, he found himself at the foot of the bath, looking straight into Caroline's eyes at the other end.

"Good evening, madam," he said pleasantly. He did not believe, after his experience with Buckstone, that she would recognize him.

The bath, made of dark carved wood and lined with copper, was not large but rather high. According to the prevailing mode, it contained six gallons of near-boiling water and two gallons of cold milk. Though all this had to be carried up in buckets from the cellar, Caroline's modesty was considerably aided by the milk and by the height of the water, which was only an inch or two lower than the ordinary evening gown.

But it did not (apparently, that is) aid her feelings of shock and outrage.

Caroline sat bolt upright amid steam from water-and-milk. Her brown hair was severely drawn up on her head, and tied there in a white ribbon with a bowknot. Her eyes, with the long shiny upper lids, were almost wide open. Her face and shoulders were pink-tinted with steam. Her right hand, half-raised and motionless, held a dripping bath sponge.

Thus, while you might have counted twenty, they looked at each other without moving. Caroline's gaze was fixed on his face. She opened her mouth to speak.

" 'How dare you!' " interrupted Darwent, raising his hand. "Forgive me, madam, if I correctly anticipate the remark you were going to make. Do you know who I am?"

"Of c-c . . ." She checked herself. "That is to say, no. How should I?"

If Darwent had been in a mood to observe more closely, he would have seen that Caroline, though frightened, was not very much shocked or outraged. She was angry because he had caught her at a disadvantage, looking like this, with her hair tied up in a white bowknot.

As for Darwent, his first thought had been of how beautiful a woman she was when you saw her like that. The steam mist tinged her to warm color. The white bowknot on the updrawn hair, though tolerably ridiculous, was the very thing which made her seem human and hence damnably desirable.

He crushed out this thought, crushed it as he might have crushed a spider under his boot heel in the floor boards. It was too easy to remember, as so often he had remembered, her lofty voice at Newgate Prison:

"You appear to think, Mr. Cotton, that I am doing some ill service to a wretch who (forgive me) is better dead."

And, thin-echoing through nightmares:

"You also appear to think that I should consider his welfare. Why should I? I don't know him."

Now his smile disappeared, and he looked at her again.

"Don't you glare at me," said Caroline, almost tremulously. She threw the sponge into the bathwater. "Don't you dare!"

"I am your husband, madam."

"How interesting!" observed Caroline, who had known it ever since she heard his voice in the other room.

Darwent, regaining his smile, glanced toward the mantelpiece and empty grate on the wall opposite the long side of the bathtub. A heavy gilt armchair, its padded upholstery a dull purple, stood with its back to the empty grate.

"I observe with pleasure," he said, "that there is no dressing gown or towel in the room. Therefore we can speak together comfortably."

He sat down in the chair, so close to the side of the bath that his boot tops touched it. Caroline looked at him over her shoulder, more flushed and even lovelier.

"Will you be good enough to leave me, sir?"

"No, madam."

"I am helpless," Caroline said tragically. "Have you none of the instincts of a gentleman? I am quite helpless!"

Darwent inclined his head.

"Yes, madam. I was aware of that happy circumstance. Though not perhaps as helpless as I was at Newgate."

"Have you *no* consideration for me?"

"You appear to think that I should consider your welfare. Why should I? I don't know you."

Caroline heard no echo, or seemed to hear none. What she showed was uneasiness growing toward fright.

"You're my husband!" she cried.

"So I am. Your loving care in the past has just reminded me." The snarl in his voice was audible now. "Also, you remind me of one of the matters I wish to discuss. The annulment of our marriage."

Caroline sat very still, her arms extended along the ledges of the bath, looking straight ahead so that he saw her face in profile.

"I don't wish the marriage to be annulled," she stated.

"No doubt you don't. I understand your inheritance depends on the purely superfluous detail of a husband. At the same time . . ."

"Oh. The inheritance." Caroline spoke almost absent-mindedly, and kicked out underwater. She turned her face completely away from him. "Can you think of no other reason," she asked in a muffled voice, "why I might not wish the marriage to be annulled?"

"Yes, madam. I can."

"Oh?" Though her arms and shoulders trembled, she did not look round.

"I ask myself," Darwent continued in a musing tone, "the same question my friend Mulberry asked me today. Why did you return with such haste from Brighton, where (as I now guess) gossip must have told you I should be tried and acquitted today?"

"Then you do begin to understand?"

"Most certainly, madam. It is quite plain."

"Oh, do stop calling me 'madam'! Can't you—say a pleasant word?"

He raised his eyebrows.

"Shall I call you 'my love' or 'my pet'? Thank you, no. And a pleasant word on your lips would be as strange as an honest kiss. As I was saying: to obtain an annulment, I must state why you wished to be married. I have witnesses who can corroborate it. No; you don't want that. It would be simpler to have me killed."

Dead silence. The thin window, on Darwin's right, had its lower half raised and propped up with the window stick. Even the back of Caroline's neck seemed eloquent with shock, as though she had expected him to say something else.

Then there was a splashing and slopping of bath water as she whipped round to face him. Her blue eyes were incredulous; her mouth was open.

"Killed?" she exclaimed.

What an actress, thought Darwent, the lithe rattlesnake was! What craft of pretense she could employ when she liked! A moment ago, from a certain note in her voice, you might have thought she felt some tenderness toward him: even what the Minerva novelists now called a "swooning passion." This amused him.

"Killed?" repeated Caroline, breathing hard against the side of the bath. "Then you do not understand why I returned from Brighton?"

"I know too well. Let me add another circumstance: with your permission, madam?"

"Pray go on."

"When I entered this house a while ago, I forgot to look at the house next door: number thirty-six. Mulberry told me today that it belonged to Frank Orford."

"Whom you killed in a duel?"

"Whom I killed in a duel," lied Darwent, "as all the world seems to know. However! Because you lived next door to Frank, there is no proof you were acquainted with him. But I think you were acquainted with him. You were in some fashion entangled with this mystery of the blue coach and the house near Kinsmere and the dead man in the chair. If a murderer can stab one man with a rapier, he can attempt to kill me too. Surely that would please you?"

"You must be mad," said Caroline, apparently so bewildered that she forgot to be angry. "But you might at least be accurate."

"Accurate?"

"The house next door is the property of the Earl and Countess of Kinsmere, Frank's father and mother."

90

"Well! That is reasonable to suppose. But I believe it has been closed since Frank's death?"

"Do you imagine he ever lived there? Poor, stingy Frank has always had lodgings in Chapel Street. The Kinsmeres' town house next door has been locked up and shuttered for two years."

Darwent lowered his head. Two houses, now! Two houses, one here and one in the country, gathering dust and woven with cobwebs since Frank's parents went to make their home abroad.

"Imprisonment has harmed you," said Caroline, seeing what appeared to be distress. Her voice softened. "It has not brought you to madness; don't think so! I own—yes, I acknowledged— that perhaps I may have behaved badly."

"Thank you," said Darwent, with concealed sarcasm.

Whereupon he lost his head.

"Let me make a confession too," he went on. "Every look and gesture of yours, every nerve of my imagination and every glance of your eyes, brings me closer to the lunacy you speak of. If I remained in your damned room much longer, I should lose my senses; seize hold of you without more nonsense; and (shall we say?) exercise my conjugal rights. But I must not do that, must I?"

"Certainly not!—Why not?"

"Because then the marriage could never be annulled. A simpler means than killing, now I think of it. That's why you behave so very like Aphrodite, I take it?"

Again dead silence.

"You will leave this room, you will leave this house," her voice was thick, "no matter what scandal it costs. I loathe scandal as much as the Kinsmeres have always loathed it, even Frank. But I won't have this." She raised her hand toward a bell rope which hung from the ceiling beside the bath. "I will summon my maid; I will summon all the servants; I will have you put into the street."

"You forget, madam, that I am the master of the house."

"Are you? Let us see!" And she gave a violent tug at the bell rope.

"As you please," Darwent said politely.

Getting up from the chair, he went over to the door, un-bolted it, and opened it. Outside stood Meg, the pretty dark-haired maid, her face now pink-to-crimson. Meg was holding one of Caroline's bonnets, a hat with a fairly high crown like

91

a Hussar's, shaped by wires inside; heavy, blue in color, with two yellow plumes.

"Meg," said Caroline, in a cold and steady voice, "you will first fetch me my dressing gown. You will then inform Alfred and Thomas and Leonard that his lordship has taken leave of his senses, and must be persuaded not to favor us with his company."

Darwent reached out, as though in curiosity, and took Caroline's blue, yellow-plumed hat from the startled maid.

"Meg m'love," he said gently, "stay where you are."

"You heard my order, Meg," Caroline said curtly.

Darwent smiled down at the maid.

"No doubt, my pet, through no fault of your own, you've heard a little of the talk between my wife and myself. I propose to close this door not quite shut, as it was before I arrived. I ask you to sit down there,"—he pointed to the bedroom with Caroline's hat—"and make certain nothing of a compromising sort is heard now. Do you understand?"

"Y-yes, my lord."

"Meg!" Caroline screamed.

"And you'll do this to please me, m'love?"

"Oh, yes, my lord!"

"That's a good girl," said Darwent, and closed the door.

For the first time since she had left Miss Sparerib's Academy as a girl, Caroline had heard an order of hers disobeyed. She was as stunned and incredulous as Buckstone had been when the lash went across his face. Presently tears welled up in her eyes.

"Won't you g-go of your own accord?" she cried. "You said, if you remained much longer—" abruptly Caroline stopped. "Is it your habit to force yourself into ladies' bathrooms like this?"

"Not my habit, no. But I have had some experience. And the practice was never bitterly discouraged by Miss Spencer."

"That's your playhouse wench, is it not?" She opened her eyes through tears.

"Ah, you remember the name."

"Certainly not!" Caroline added, with deplorable lack of dignity: "I'd like to scratch her eyes out!"

"Madam," Darwent said wearily, "stop keeping up this pretense of feeling some kindness towards me."

"You fool!"

"But again you remind me. I neglected to tell you that Dolly,

92

with some friends of hers, will arrive here soon to spend a few nights under our hospitable roof."

Water sloshed in the bath. *"Here?"*

"Only until I can find her a furnished house somewhere off Piccadilly or Grosvenor Square. The girl is ill; she will not trouble you, nor I her. I came to this house merely to give you a taste of your own medicine, and I think you have had it. For the rest, this hat . . ."

Turning the high-crowned blue hat round in his hands, so that the plumes wagged, he moved to the long side of the bath. Caroline shrank back.

"I have never seen a hat worn while bathing," he went on. "But I urge you to put it on. For some reason you seem very distressed about the white bowknot which ties up your hair like a toy steeple. You reach towards it every twenty seconds. Put on the hat, madam, or for God's sake take off the ribbon."

If Caroline had believed the words of fullest insult were past, it was clear that she changed her mind now. It restored her poise, and she remained very quiet. It was as though she searched his mind and heart, seeking where she could best strike and hurt.

"You imagine, then," she asked sweetly, "that someone will kill you?"

"Someone will try."

"Perhaps you are right." She spoke in her old detached way. "I have friends, sir, who will not be happy to hear of your behavior towards me. Would you dare insult Sir John Buckstone as you have insulted me?"

"I spoke very little to him, it's true."

"And that little," smiled Caroline, "was in Newgate Prison?"

Darwent lifted his shoulders.

"Yes, you may well die," said Caroline. "But not from a stab in the back, or a pistol shot from behind, or a bludgeon over the head. Let me quieten your child's fears and your sick fancies. Have courage, sir! Heaven knows you need it. There is enough to trouble you without fretting over assassination. This is London. The possibility of murder is remote. Therefore, dear sir, you are as safe as though . . ."

Once more Caroline stopped abruptly, and started back in the water with a scream and splash.

The report of a heavy cavalry pistol, fired from outside the open window, whacked in their ears even though it was deadened by open air.

The blue hat, with its two yellow plumes, spun out of Darwent's hand as though by a twitch of magic. It struck the wall, and tumbled brim-downwards into the bath. As the milk-white surface of the water heaved, it floated slowly round in front of Caroline. Both Caroline and Darwent could see two holes in the crown that were made by the same bullet.

The bullet, round and heavy, had missed Darwent by six inches and smashed a black gouge in the white wall opposite the window.

◇   CHAPTER X   ◇

—And Out of It

The high-crowned hat, its yellow plumes now grotesque, still rocked on agitated water. Caroline, her face pale, reached out and pushed it away as though its touch would defile her.

"As you were saying," Darwent observed thoughtfully, "the possibility is remote.— I hate pistols."

And he ran towards the window, throwing aside the light chair beneath it. In his mind, as he said that he hated pistols and shuddered in saying it, was a memory of Crosstree Island, where an ammunition ship was wrecked.

Just below the window was the slate roof of the mews, or stable, which stretched behind every house here. The roof sloped, but at no great pitch. Worming his way through the narrow window opening, Darwent jumped out and balanced himself.

He was hemmed in by the backs or sides of high reddish-black brick houses. A narrow alley divided the mews from the corresponding mews of the houses opposite. The windows at the back of the house just opposite were either shuttered or blank with gloom.

An ammoniac odor of horses, and of kitchen slops too, rose up about him. That shot could only have been fired from . . .

The sound of voices in argument floated up from the alley below. Bracing himself against slipping, Darwent walked to the edge of the roof and looked down.

"Did anybody hear that noise?" he asked.

In the alley a groom with uprolled sleeves was currycombing a skittish roan mare. Beside him, watching judicially, stood a very fat man whose coat of many short capes—together with shawls round his neck even in July, and a low-crowned curly-brimmed hat—marked him as a stagecoach driver.

"Did anybody hear that noise?" Darwent repeated.

"Didn't *see* nothing," said the groom, growling. Both he and the stagecoach driver were determined to mind their own business. They knew what the noise had been. "Anyway, what's the odds?"

"Walk-*er!*" jeered Darwent, in the groom's own language. "Nobody was hurt."

"Ah?" inquired the groom, suddenly taking an interest and looking up.

Darwent pointed to the roof of the mews across the alley.

"It was fired," he said, "from that roof or thereabouts. But I didn't hear anyone run across the slates, or jump down. Did you?"

The groom admitted he hadn't.

"Then where was it fired from?"

Up to this time the stagecoach driver, clearly a man of importance, had said nothing. By his bearing he was one of the Mighty Men, idol of small boys, lord of whip and ribbons, who drove a crack mail coach. He spat through filed front teeth, the filed teeth again showing a Mighty Man.

"Winder," he said.

Darwent nodded. By the line taken by the pistol ball, even though it might have been deflected when it struck the hat, it must have been fired from a window on the corresponding floor of the house opposite. Darwent eyed the width of the alley between the mews roofs, finding it not quite so narrow as it looked.

But a good, long jump would do it. Backing up the slates to get purchase for a jump, he ran forward, launching himself into the air, and landed with a crash on the slates of the mews opposite. A pair of closed shutters faced him, and he rapped at them sharply.

The shutters were opened in his face, so quickly that he almost tumbled backward down the roof. In the aperture of an open window stood a middle-aged timorous lady, faded but still pretty, with a bottle of smelling salts in her hand.

"Forgive me, madam," apologized Darwent, on his hands and knees. "But I am not a housebreaker. I only wish to inquire . . ."

"Oh, how you startled me!" the lady said reproachfully,

and inhaled smelling salts. "I can't endure bangs. My family (on my father's side, that is) have always been of the Royal Navy. But I can't endure bangs. Was it a long nine?"

"It was not a ship's gun, madam. It was a pistol."

"My husband," said the trembling lady, "commands the *Swiftstraight* frigate. But I can't endure bangs."

"A distressing experience," said Darwent, finding it difficult to be gallant while on his hands and knees. "But might I inquire whether this house is a private place of residence?"

"It contains most fashionable lodgings, sir, for married couples and single gentlemen. There are no bangs."

"To be sure. Your name alone—er—"

"It is Bang," said the lady reproachfully. "I do not perpetrate a stupid joke, sir. It really is Bang."

"—ensures that no handgun was fired from here, Mrs. Bang. But might I trouble you to ask whether any gentleman, or anyone else, occupies rooms facing opposite?"

"There is only Mr. Lewis, sir. Mr. Tillotson Lewis. A fine young gentleman, though I fear in somewhat indigent circumstances." Tears appeared in her eyes. "You must excuse me. I fear I shall faint."

The shutters were just as quickly and unexpectedly closed.

Darwent backed away from them, though still contemplating them. He knew the sly lurker would have had ample time to get away. But a name reverberated through his mind.

Lewis.

The smoky gold of the evening sky had darkened to pale white and dull blue. There were many shadows. Out of one window a maidservant with cap askew was shaking out a feather bed, preparatory to making it up in the bedstead for the night. Before long the watchmen would go calling the hours; the Bow Street patrols, horse and foot, would prowl on their rounds.

Lewis . . .

He had heard that name, and heard it today. Somebody had spoken it. But Darwent could not pluck it out amid a welter of so many words empty or significant.

Then, as he turned round, took a run, and leaped for the mews roof of number thirty-eight, the memory returned. "Why, he's . . ." Buckstone had begun, in that little white-painted room at the club. And presently Buckstone had added: "No, you're not Lewis. For a second I thought you were." Lewis was no uncommon name; it might mean nothing.

Yet it seemed to Darwent he could feel the repulsive strands

96

of the web brush on his hands and face and body; he could feel the tug of a spider larger than life.

No brooding, now!

Scrambling back up the mews roof, Darwent wormed through the open window into a now-shadowy bathroom. As he had expected, Caroline was gone. Even the bullet-pierced hat was gone. When he opened the door to the bedroom, he saw an empty room still scattered with gowns, frocks, petticoats, shifts, stays, French stockings, not yet put away in cupboards or chests of drawers.

But, as he opened the door giving on the passage outside, he met the first footman at the top of the stairs.

"My lord," said Alfred, with evident relief.

The footman, carrying a long thin waxen spill tipped with tiny flame, was lighting the candles as he passed. He touched the spill along a bracket of five candles, backed by a round mirror, on the wall near the bedroom door. As the flames curled up—how oppressed they seemed, amid a stuffiness of heavy carpets and curtains!—they lighted up Alfred's powdered wig and green livery, no less than his puzzled eyes.

Darwent spoke suddenly.

"Miss Spencer and the other guests. Are they not arrived?"

"Yes, my lord. Long ago. I should have told your lordship, but . . ." Stolid again, his eyes did not exactly indicate the bedroom, though they conveyed an answer.

"Miss Spencer is in the Amber Room," he went on, indicating the floor above. "The—er—Mr. and Mrs. Raleigh are next door. At your convenience, my lord, the surgeon would like to speak with you."

"Good. Where is my wife?" After a pause Darwent added: "Speak up, man! You know you may."

Alfred did know he could. It was another thing he liked about the governor. You could treat him man to man, yet with no familiarity on either side.

"Her ladyship, my lord, is with Miss Spencer.— You spoke, my lord?"

"No, no!"

"Her ladyship gave herself the trouble of hurrying upstairs in informal costume. I have never seen her ladyship so kind and gentle. In five minutes, my lord, she and Miss Spencer have become the best of friends."

"Alfred . . . good God!"

"Yes, my lord."

"Do you understand this?"

97

"No, my lord. A Mr. James Fletcher has called," the footman continued hastily. "Since he said the matter was urgent, I took the liberty of asking him to wait in the drawing room." Alfred nodded toward the front of the passage. "I trust this was—?"

"Oh, yes. Admirable."

Then the details of the duel had been settled. Though Darwent allowed nothing to show in his expression, he could have rubbed his hands together with a savage and lingering pleasure. The footman moved toward the front of the passage, lighting more candles. Darwent was about to follow him when the portly figure of Mr. Samuel Hereford, surgeon in chief at Bart's, appeared past Alfred from the staircase to the floor above.

"Lord Darwent," said Mr. Hereford in a low, grave voice, "this is not a time for prolixity or learned speech. I will be frank with you."

Seeing the look on the surgeon's face, Darwent did not reply.

"If you ask me why we were so long in coming here," continued the surgeon, "I will tell you. At one time I feared the lady might be dying."

"*Dying!*"

"Oh, perhaps not immediately. My feeling was pure imagination, if you like. But born of experence."

"You said it was harmless! What's the matter with Dolly?"

"My lord, I don't know."

The five wax lights, against the round mirror on the wall, shone down on Mr. Hereford's head as he inclined it. Strands of gray-white hair were brushed across his skull to hide near-baldness, and the side hair was brushed out on his cheeks in points.

"However!" he added quickly, as he saw Darwent put one hand against the wall to steady himself, "I think, without giving too much reassurance, I may have found at least some measure of remedy."

"You'll save her?"

"I dare to hope so."

"How?"

"My lord, I count myself a man skilled in my work. But I can only grope in the dark. My colleagues would laugh at me; my reasoning is an old wife's tale. I ventured to send to the Clarendon Hotel for . . . well, it is not usually considered a drug. But already the patient is better!"

In one hand he carried a heavy black-leather bag, in the other his black hat. Mr. Hereford shook them both for emphasis, his plump face full of wonder.

"You are not leaving her now sir?"

"For a brief time only, my lord. I shall return in an hour."

He bowed, marched to the head of the steps leading downstairs, hesitated, and turned round.

"A last word, my lord," he said with an effort. "I mention your personal affairs only because I must. You are married, I understand?"

"Yes."

"Does the patient, Miss Spencer, know you are married?"

"No."

"She must not learn it yet. I have requested her ladyship, your wife, not to mention it. Of course Lady Darwent would not forget herself and drop an incautious word?"

"No, of course she w——!" Darwent stopped. His heart felt as cold as a bitter night on a heath. "I don't know," he said.

The surgeon looked at him quickly.

"Well! Mrs. Raleigh is there; Mrs. Raleigh is vigilant; she will prevent it. Don't fear while Mrs. Raleigh is there. At the same time . . ."

"Yes? What were you thinking?"

"We are men of the world, you and I. Yet I don't understand why you brought the patient here! It was ill-advised, my lord. Very ill-advised. You yourself have an undesirable affect on the patient. I must request you: don't visit her until she is out of danger, or else—we lose her. Good evening, my lord."

There was not a sound as Mr. Hereford went down the carpeted stairs.

Darwent might have cried after him, "You said Dolly wasn't seriously ill! Blame your own lack of knowledge!"

But he said nothing. He stood there for a minute or two, clamping his jaws together and finally pressing his hands over his eyes. Then, with no purpose whatever, he wandered toward the front of the passage. He had touched the knob of the drawing-room door before he remembered that Jemmy Fletcher was waiting there.

Darwent straightened his shoulders, shook his head with an attempt to clear it, and went in.

"I say, old boy," querulously complained Jemmy, who was sitting on a green-and-white-striped sofa and glancing through a richly bound copy of the *Decameron*, "a fellow's time's of value, you know. It's almost dinner hour."

99

"My apologies, Jemmy. I was detained."

It was the *bijou* drawing room, where Caroline and Mr. Crockit had completed their plans on the night arranged for Darwent's hanging. Alfred had lighted the two pairs of candles, each in a delicate glass vase, on either side of the white marble mantelpiece. He had drawn together the heavy green-velvet curtains, bordered in gold, across the two high windows.

There was in Jemmy's manner a certain coolness, an aloof poise, which his companion might have found odd if Darwent had noticed it. But Darwent, trying to clear his mind, snatched at the first thought which entered it.

"Jemmy, are you acquainted with a gentleman named Lewis?"

"Eh? You mean Till Lewis?"

"Tillotson Lewis! That's it! Yes."

"But, damme, Dick, you saw him today! I thought you knew each other."

"I saw him? Where?"

Jemmy threw down the *Decameron* on the green-and-white-striped sofa.

"We'd just gone into White's, old boy, after you'd stared (d'ye mind?) so dashed rudely at those fellows in the bow window; and they don't like it, I can tell you. Anyway, we went into White's. And Till Lewis walked straight across in front of you. Don't you remember?"

"Yes! I remember!"

"Why, Till turned round to look at you. I thought you were both goin' to speak to each other, but you didn't."

Well enough, in imagination, Darwent could see the half-ghostly figure which crossed before him in the gloom, and experienced again the sensation that it was vaguely familiar. Yet he could have sworn he had never met Tillotson Lewis, and never heard the name until it was mentioned by the sad-eyed Mrs. Bang.

"Now, old boy," Jemmy said suddenly. "About that duel."

It was as though, with pleasant shock, someone had thrown a bucket of cold water into Darwent's face. His brain cleared instantly. He was eager, alert, strung to expectancy.

"Good, Jemmy! Have you arranged the time and place?"

"Yes, old boy. Wimbledon Common, not far from the windmill. Five o'clock tomorrow morning, before the magistrates can get wind of it."

Jemmy, his long legs crossed, was in full evening clothes. His black tailcoat, white waistcoat, black silk breeches with

100

diamond buckles and black stockings, were as glossy as though you had just unpacked him. His fair hair, curled *à la mode,* gleamed by the wax lights.

For a moment he studied the carpet. Then he raised his head coolly.

"But there's one thing, old boy, I'm afraid we can't allow. It won't do, you know."

"What won't do?"

"Fighting with sabers. I'm afraid it's got to be the pistol."

A sharp premonition, which should have occurred to him before, spread and blackened through Darwent's mind.

"Who says it's got to be pistols?"

"Jack Buckstone. All the fellows at White's will agree with him, you know."

Darwent walked to the small round table in the middle of the room, while Jemmy examined his fingernails.

"Let me be very clear about this," said Darwent. "As the challenged party, you agree that I have the choice of weapons?"

"Of course, old boy. But naturally you'll choose pistols."

"Why? The dueling code permits sabers."

"Oh, the code!" said Jemmy offhandedly. His blue eyes opened in a vaguely uncomfortable way. "Dash it, old boy, be reasonable! You're not a couple of dem cavalrymen. Got to do what's in fashion, dash it!"

"Tell me," said Darwent, studying him. "I asked you whether Buckstone could use the saber, and you answered that he was a very able swordsman. Did he ask you whether I could use the pistol?"

"No, old boy."

"Let's suppose, for the sake of argument, that I had never touched a pistol in my life?"

Jemmy shrugged his shoulders.

"Well, old boy," he said coolly, "I'm afraid that's your lookout."

Was there, round Jemmy's mouth and eyes, a faint trace of malice? His companion could have sworn Jemmy Fletcher, whatever else he might be, was genuinely good-natured. As Darwent's mind blackened with fury, he hid his thoughts even from himself.

"Major Sharpe," he said, "seemed to me the very best type of army man; and that's saying the best you can say of anybody. You must have dealt with him, not Buckstone. What did Major Sharpe have to say of this?"

"Damme, old boy, that's where Jack's so shrewd! He is, you know. Devilish shrewd. Come, now! Be fair! Admit it even if you don't like it." There was humor in Jemmy's eyes. "Sharpe's a cavalryman. Thinks saber duels ought to be for the cavalry."

"Then it was Major Sharpe who forbade sabers? Is that what you mean?"

"Oh, no. But don't you see, Dick? It don't matter a curse what *he* says. It's what Jack says."

"Is it, by God!"

"Of course, old boy. He'll simpy refuse, and make a laughingstock of you. In fact, he already has."

"After issuing the challenge himself?"

"My dear old fellow, Jack don't need to prove himself. Whereas, if you don't mind my saying so, nobody knows *you*. Jack's a sizzler. He's been out nine times, and never missed."

"Yes, Jemmy. I even remember hearing the same thing from a turnkey at Newgate." Darwent tapped his fingers idly on the table. "How is it," he asked with powerful restraint, "that *he's* never been embroiled with the law? That *his* precious hide never felt the stone of a prison?"

"Shrewd!" remarked Jemmy, shaking his head admiringly. "Shrewd!"

"You have already commeñted on Sir John Buckstone's shrewdness, I think."

"Why, Dick, he's never killed 'em. Except once, when he hated the dem fellow. Then he slipped over to France—that was a year ago; Boney was at Elba—and stayed *mum* (that's the new word) till the row blew over. But if you only wound your pigeon, and the pigeon don't complain, the law won't bother you. D'ye see? Jack lets the pigeon lose his head and fire first. Then Jack fires, and stars the kneecap."

"Stay a moment, Jemmy. What do you mean by, 'stars the kneecap'?"

Jemmy, uncrossing his long black legs so that the diamond buckle glittered, sat up straight.

"Damme, my boy, don't you know *anything* about affairs with the pistol?"

"Nothing whatever. I hate the pistol."

Jemmy looked faintly uncomfortable.

"It means," he said, "to shoot you through the kneecap." Jemmy shuddered. "That can't possibly kill you. But, by jove, the pain! Curse me, it's worse than a bullet anywhere else." He shuddered again. "Knew a fellow; bold as a lion; in the

102

breach at Badajoz; twice mentioned in the Gazette; shot through the kneecap in a duel (accident); heard him screaming all night."

"I see."

"Though I'm bound to warn you, Dick . . ."

"Yes?"

"It won't be a smashed kneecap. Jack means business. He's ordered a post chaise for Dover, and he can be aboard the afternoon packet for Calais."

Darwent nodded, without expression. He walked over to the white marble mantelpiece, his back to Jemmy, and put his elbows on the top as though pondering.

"Of course," murmured Jemmy, glancing at him under lowered eyelids, "you could write a note of public apology. Or you could run away; there's still time. But I can't say it'll suit Jack. And if a thing don't suit him . . . well, the other party's got no choice. Damme, you should have heard him laugh when Sharpe mentioned sabers!"

Darwent remained motionless.

To an unprejudiced observer, in this dim, green drawing room, the figure of Jack Buckstone was as palpable as a third presence. He loomed like a giant, laughing and imperturbable: unbeaten and unbeatable.

Jemmy stirred on the sofa.

" 'Fraid I must take my leave, old boy. What arrangements will you make for going away?"

"Stay a moment, Jemmy!" said Darwent.

And he turned round.

"Present my compliments to Major Sharpe," he went on. "Tell him I withdraw my right to fight with the saber. Tell him I will meet Sir John Buckstone with pistols, and at any distance Buckstone likes."

Jemmy sprang up from the sofa.

A smallish bit of crumpled newspaper, which had somehow become lodged under Jemmy's black double-breasted coat with the pearl buttons, was dislodged now and fluttered down to the carpet. Jemmy did not see it.

"Dem careless of me!" he exclaimed. "Forgot to mention the distance!"

"I said the distance may be what you like."

"No, dash it! Got to get your approval. It's thirty-six feet. Thirty-six feet, not paces; though of course we pace it off. Satisfactory?"

"Entirely."

"Got any pistols, old boy?"

"No."

"Then Jack will bring his. Any objections?"

"None whatever."

"We—ah—in your carriage," said Jemmy, a faint babbling note under his tone, "clear roads; early morning; ought to drive to Wimbledon Common in less than an hour and a half."

"Then meet me at Stephen's Hotel, Bond Street, at half-past three. Is that all?"

"That's all."

"Good night, Jemmy."

Jemmy bowed, took three steps toward the door, and whirled round.

"Don't think I like this!" he babbled. "You got me into it!" His hand went up to his starched collar and cravat. "I'm a second: accessory before the fact. Might mean transportation for life, if you're killed."

Darwent walked past him to a green-and-white-striped chair, which stood under two framed silhouettes on the wall beside the door. On the chair lay Jemmy's brocaded cocked hat. Darwent picked it up.

"Good night, Jemmy."

"Wonderful fellows, the real 'uns," said Jemmy. "Got to do what pleases 'em, ain't I? Or they'd cut me." This horrible possibility made him shiver. "Never be invited to a rout; no card for Almack's."

"Good night, Jemmy."

"Ladies, too: that's worse. Country houses. Never hear the Duke of Argyle say, 'Ah, how do you do, Jemmy?' Or Lady Jersey: 'So pleased.' No, damme! Rather be dead."

"Poor devil," said Darwent, and extended the brocaded hat. "I know you can't help it. Good night."

Jemmy took the hat and went out. Darwent closed the door.

He stared thoughtfully at the floor, the first fiinger of his right hand curling as though round a trigger. His eye caught the scrap of crumpled newspaper, rather soiled, which had dropped from Jemmy's coat; and he picked it up. It was torn from today's *Times,* with datemark and a fragment of newsprint he did not trouble to read. Then a sense of animal nearness, a sense he had known so sharply with only two women, warned him to look round.

In the doorway stood Caroline, in a blue satin gown with white facings; her hair in ringlets, and round her neck a necklace of dark sapphires to match her eyes.

"Then this afternoon you arranged to meet Jack Buckstone," she said.

"Did you hear what was said?"

"Only part of it."

New apprehension seized Darwent. "You'll not lodge a complaint with the magistrate? You'll not have this prevented?"

"I would give a fortune to prevent it," Caroline answered in a low voice, not looking at him. "But if you would have your way, my lord, then you must."

"Thank you, Caroline. I am not permitted to see Dolly Spencer; and now I had best leave."

"You called me by my first name!"

"Did I? Pray forgive me."

From Caroline's right hand hung a blue-and-silver fan. She opened it, not for coquettish purpose but at times to hide expression.

"You have not dined, my lord. Stay and dine with me. I,"— the fan came up—"I half-promised to accompany Will Alvanley to the Italian opera. But I won't, if it's your wish." Then her voice vibrated. "If I ever speak sharp words, as I spoke this afternoon, then kill me!"

"If you speak any word of our marriage to Dolly, you shall have your wish."

"On my word before God, I won't tell her. Stay and dine."

"Pardon me; I have too small an acquaintance with poisons. And I must be awake and ready at three-thirty in the morning. Good night."

One anguished cry followed him out of the dim, green drawing room.

"Dick!"

But he paid no attention, walking stolidly down the stairs.

And so, as the night deepened, all over town there began to stir a furtive night life, as candle or lamp or even gas jet bloomed out, to drunken shouts or the pouring of coffee: in rooms big or little, in rooms painted or mean.

Darwent, partaking of a late dinner in the coffeeroom at Stephen's, wrote and sealed a note to John Townsend, most celebrated of the Bow Street runners, and ordered it delivered by hand instead of by post. He also wrote a particular account of the afternoon's and evening's doings, addressing it to Hubert Mulberry, Esq., 11a Gray's Inn.

At the Italian opera in the Haymarket, Caroline sat in Lord Alvanley's private box, with the round-faced little peer beside

105

her, listening to a new singer named Madame Vestris in *Il Ratto di Proserpina*. Except for a pit, this whole interior was nothing but a tall semicircle of private boxes, like a gaudy beehive. The only light, subdued and mysterious, threw a gauze from hidden lamps behind the scenes. When Lord Alvanley attempted gently to bite Caroline's shoulder, he was amazed to be permitted this and even greater liberties, which argued success at no remote date. Caroline seemed angry, but not with him.

In his lodgings above the mews, young Tillotson Lewis danced for joy. At long last he would receive a generous sum from King, the moneylender, because he had expectations and his father was dying.

Harriette Wilson, a fair charmer who kept a salon-cum-bawdyhouse for the gentry, with suppers in a gilded room, had a number of guests tonight. Jemmy Fletcher absent-mindedly toyed with chicken and champagne as well as with Harriette's sister.

Locked in his chambers at Lincoln's Inn Fields, with a solitary candle burning, Elias Crockit pored late over certain documents.

Sleeping peacefully, her yellow hair spread out on the pillow, Dolly Spencer lay in the Amber Room at Caroline's house. At one side of the bed, which gleamed with Louis XV ornament, Mrs. Augustus Raleigh sat at needlework; on the other side, her cadaverous husband read *Guy Mannering*. Mr. Hereford, his plump chin in his hand, watched from one corner.

In Tom Cribb's public house, the Union Arms in Panton Street, the stout Champion of England smoked his long clay pipe in the snuggery, occasionally glancing toward Hubert Mulberry, who sat in a wooden booth and was more than half-fuddled with hot rum-and-cinnamon.

From the sparring saloon off the snuggery danced a *whick-whack* noise of light boxing gloves. They used the mawleys, of course, only in practice.

In the booth next to Mulberry's, all unnoticed by each other, Jack Buckstone yawned over the advertisements of a three-days-old news-sheet. To him, presently, came sidling up a squat hoarse-voiced man who gave his name as Blazes, and said he had sent a letter to the gen'leman.

The steeple clocks clanged, the watchman cried out, through the wicked hours of the night. In his bedroom at Stephen's, in darkness tempered only by a faint rushlight in a bowl, Darwent sat by the window, fully dressed, and looked down into Bond Street.

"Wimbledon Common, not far from the windmill. Five o'clock tomorrow morning."

A month ago, to the very night, they were going to hang him at five in the morning.

◇ CHAPTER XI ◇

Pistols at Daybreak

Crack went the driver's long whip, as he saw ahead of him a tunnel dimly open in the white world of mist. Bridles jingling, the two black horses of the red berline stretched from a canter into a gallop toward Wimbledon Common.

Darwent, wrapped up in a black ankle-length cloak, stared straight ahead and did not look round.

"Time?" he asked.

Jemmy Fletcher, also in a dark cloak, fumbled inside for his waistcoat pocket. He took out a gold repeater, with a long ornamented fob, and with trembling hands opened its case.

"Ten minutes to five, old boy," he said. Despite himself Jemmy could not keep the quaver out of his voice.

"You were late."

"Couldn't help it, old boy. Positively exhausted. That dem woman . . . dash it! No names."

Crack went the driver's whip.

"You're a man of sense, Jemmy. You take your pleasure whenever it's offered."

The white mist was more than impenetrable, except for its hollows along the white road between hedgerows. The mist was bitter cold; it clammily penetrated through clothing to skin; it fogged the throat; it deadened the noise of gallop and jolting carriage.

"You're a cool one, Dick," Jemmy said rather enviously. "Ain't you afraid?"

"Of course I'm afraid."

"Here!" muttered Jemmy, and squirmed. "Mustn't say that."

"My shirt is sticking to my back with sweat, in spite of this

107

cold. I must take care to speak slowly. Still, if we apply the best outward test . . ."

With an effort Darwent removed his right hand from under the cloak, stretching out the arm and spreading the fingers. The hand was steady, even the fingers as motionless as a statue's.

"That," Darwent said dryly, "is how men gain a reputation for courage when they don't deserve it." *Crack* went the driver's whip.

Jemmy swallowed hard. "Dick, old boy. The fact is . . ."

"Buckstone will kill me? With a bullet through the middle of the forehead?"

"Here, I didn't say that!"

"He probably will." Darwent turned his head toward Jemmy, and forced a smile. "But you're a better man, I think. Will you accept a little wager on the result?"

Jemmy was shocked. "Damme, Dick, I can't do that! You're my principal. Besides . . ."

"How could you pocket the stakes from a dead man?"

"Now, dash it all!"

"Come, Jemmy, don't be so correct! Shall we say a hundred? You can take it out of my pocket afterwards."

"Well!" said Jemmy, after a pause during which he drew a breath of relief. "I must say, old boy, I hoped for something. Bit short, you know; funds locked up in the Controls. A hundred'll take me to France with Jack. Even Paris. I say, d'ye know all the sights in the Palais Royal?"

Darwent looked at him again, and bent forward toward the driver.

"Patrick, can't you drive faster? If they leave the field before we even arrive . . . !"

"It's all right!" Jemmy reassured him. "I can see the dashed windmill now."

The mist had lifted a good deal as they raced up a long gentle rise and moved again on flat ground, the carriage turning left into a smaller road with no hedgerows.

Darwent had no idea of their position, except that they were somewhere in the country on the Surrey side.

"Pull up!" he said.

About twenty yards ahead of them, in the small road, stood a closed black carriage from which three gentlemen had alighted. All three wore cloaks, according to custom. One of them—Sir John Buckstone—moved apart from the others and sat down on a tree stump, yawning as he smoked a cigar.

Though the mist had somewhat lifted, it still clung higher

than ankle deep to the grass, a white restless carpet with a smoky moving top. It hung in shreds among trees, and turned the prospect to gauze.

The red berline jingled to a stop. Before Darwent and Jemmy jumped down, there was dead silence in that unreal world. The sky was gray and heavy, threatening rain. Against it, some distance away, stood up the brownish motionless sails of a windmill.

Of the two cloaked gentlemen who had accompanied Buckstone, one wore a black hat and carried a black case. The other wore a white busby with a scarlet plume; his hands were outside the cloak, holding a flattish rosewood box. They stood side by side, some thirty yards away.

The thud seemed very loud when first Darwent, then Jemmy, jumped down from the carriage.

Patrick, the driver, leaned down from the box. From an apparently inanimate object, Patrick became a thick-set man with a mole on his cheek.

"Good luck, my lord," he said softly. "Shoot the bastard dead."

If Jemmy Fletcher shuddered from head to foot, it was not so much because a servant had spoken out of place. Not now.

"Thank you," Darwent said gratefully to Patrick. "But I don't want to kill him."

All spoke in muttering voices, as though this rich summer expanse of grass and trees had been blighted to deadliness by mist and silence.

"You don't want to kill him?" blurted an astounded Jemmy.

"No. I've never wished to do that. Come on."

They moved toward those who waited, over what felt like rough grass under an impenetrable white blanket of mist halfway to the knees. Darwent's heart began to pound thickly. What he intended to do was so dangerous that it bordered on lunacy.

The face of Major Sharpe, with its frosty brown eyes under reddish eyebrows and its side whiskers brushed out like reddish wires, swam closer and became tight-lipped.

"Good morning, my lord. Good morning, Mr. Fletcher. May I present the surgeon, Mr. Mowbray?"

Major Sharpe spoke quietly but briskly, as though on duty. The surgeon, a kindly-looking man with steel-rimmed spectacles, bowed awkwardly.

Then Major Sharpe glanced over his shoulder toward Buckstone, who still sat on the tree stump yawning over a cigar, and back toward Darwent.

"I suppose there is no question of an apology?"

Neither of the contestants replied.

A slight smile crossed Buckstone's face. That face was gorged with blood, but his eye looked wickedly patient, above the two lash weals dark on his cheeks.

"Very well," said Major Sharpe, weighing the rosewood box in his hands. "It seemed to us that over there," his nod indicated it, "would be a better place. There are no trees close at hand; the mist is lighter; the ground more level. With your permission . . . ?"

He turned round and led the way. All followed him to what seemed a huge open space surrounded by an amphitheater of trees. Opening the rosewood box, he displayed two pistols, beautifully fashioned with mother-of-pearl along the stocks, and embedded in yellow velvet with a small ramrod embedded beneath each. An upper compartment contained powder flask and ball.

"I understand, Lord Darwent, you agree to the use of these pistols?"

"I do."

"Then your second and I will proceed to load them. Or perhaps," said Major Sharpe, with a quick penetrating look at Jemmy, "or perhaps *I* should load them, merely by right as senior second?"

"Yes!" blurted Jemmy.

It was done.

Powder, bullet, wadding torn from newspaper, were deftly rammed into each pistol. The percussion cap was fitted tightly over the firing nipple, hammer resting lightly on it.

Tension was growing, growing nearly to bursting point, during a loading which took perhaps something over a minute and seemed to take twenty. Buckstone and Darwent stood a long distance away from each other, affecting indifference.

But Mr. Mowbray, the surgeon, intercepted a glance between them. And Mr. Mowbray unobtrusively opened his black bag.

"This," he thought, "will not be pleasant."

In addition to knives and bandages, he carried probe, forceps, and a bottle containing a giant's dose of diluted laudanum. A bullet seldom struck through with a clean wound like a sword; it mangled and shattered bone, amid a good deal of mess.

110

"Now, Mr. Fletcher!" said Major Sharpe, handing Jemmy one pistol. "You know your next duty, I trust?"

"Dash it, yes! But I—I had a bad night! I . . ."

Major Sharpe, carrying the second pistol, marched over and handed it to Darwent. The major's eyes were as blank as a blind man's. But a tinge of apology touched his harsh voice.

"My lord, will you be good enough to remove your cloak and hat?—Throw them on the ground; thank you. Now please raise your right arm, and turn your right side towards me."

Darwent did so. "Why are we doing this?" he demanded.

"A mere formality. So that we may be sure there is no padding on the side you turn towards your adversary in—" Major Sharpe, who had been slapping his hands down Darwent's right side between armpit and waist, seemed to remember something. He stood up straight, like a spring released.

"My lord, have you never been out with the pistol?"

"No."

"But I understood . . . no matter now. You will note that Mr. Fletcher goes through the same formality with Sir John.' The scarlet plume on the white busby twitched as Major Sharpe swung his head round. "Satisfactory, Mr. Fletcher?"

"Positively, sir!"

Major Sharpe glanced up at the sky.

"The challenged party has of course the choice of position with his back to the sun. But there is no sun. Have you a choice of position, my lord?"

It was difficult to keep his voice steady, but Darwent managed it.

"None at all," he replied, weighing the pistol in his hand and feeling its fine balance. "Let my second decide."

"Then I think, Mr. Fletcher, we can pace off the distance and place our men?"

That was done, too.

Buckstone's little eye gleamed, and he threw away his cigar.

Darwent found himself standing in the large open space, nearly free of mist except the mist veiling distant trees, and the faint-moving white carpet which sent up smoke round his ankles. The air smelled of rain. Again he tested the fine balance of the pistol. Jemmy Fletcher was whispering and jabbering in his ear.

"No, old boy! No! Don't stand fullface to him!"

"What's the matter?"

"Stand sideways, with the right side of your body towards

111

him! Your right foot a little forward; toe facing him; weight on the left foot. Here, damme, let me place you!—There!"

"Very well, Jemmy. But why?"

"Gives him a narrower target, that's why! Everybody does it. Look at Jack!"

Darwent raised his eyes. At thirty-six feet, and at first glance, Buckstone seemed to be unnaturally close: almost on top of him. Body turned sideways, right knee advanced, Buckstone was listening to a curt word from Major Sharpe.

Mr. Mowbray, the surgeon, was standing a considerable distance back, away from the duelists but at a point midway between.

"Now why," the surgeon was reflecting, *"why* won't they take advice and not stand sideways? A pistol ball through the side is almost certain to strike some vital organ."

Darwent's thumb was on the hammer of the pistol. The hammer drew back with a soft, easy, melodious click. An answering click showed that Buckstone had done the same.

"Got to go now, old boy!" Jemmy was babbling in a thin, high voice. He clapped his principal on the back. "The Major's leaving Jack, d'ye see? Get in first shot and you may wing him. Oh, damme! G'bye."

Jemmy hastened away.

And he was alone with Buckstone, on a fair field at twelve yards, with the white mist drifting about their ankles.

Major Sharpe, swinging the cloak back from his shoulders as he strode toward the surgeon, revealed the dark-blue Hussar uniform with the horizontal lines of gold braid. He took up his position with the surgeon on one side of him and Jemmy on the other. He put his left hand on the hilt of his straight saber under the short dolman over the shoulder.

His voice, though not loud, seemed to rasp and ring in that silent place.

"Are you ready, my lord?"

Darwent drew the rain-scented air deeply into his lungs.

"Ready!"

"Are you ready, Sir John?"

Buckstone, cunning of eye, his beefy figure all in black except for white breeches and cravat, stood sideways with his pistol hand pointed at the ground.

"Any time!" he said.

"Then fire as you please!"

The surgeon's hand, inside the black bag, quickly and in succession touched probe, forceps, and laudanum bottle.

Birds bickered faintly in the trees behind the three witnesses. A light breeze, born nowhere, smoothed across the carpet of mist and sent up billows like smoke. Three seconds passed; then six, then eight. Both duelists were still motionless, weapons pointed at the ground.

Major Sharpe looked from one of them to the other. He had seen many things in an affair of honor, but never this. His wrath boiled over, and all his correctness fell away.

"What the devil's the meaning of this?" he shouted. "Why don't you fire?"

Darwent spoke loudly and very clearly, without taking his eyes from Buckstone.

"Major Sharpe," he said, "I believe Sir John Buckstone is usually good enough to allow his opponent the first shot. This time I await *his* fire."

Buckstone's ruddy face turned livid with rage.

Buckstone, in fact, made a move to dart out his arm rigidly and fire. But he saw Darwent's smile, and wouldn't take first shot.

"Jack's losin' his head!" moaned Jemmy Fletcher, suddenly and incredulously. "Oh, damme, he mustn't lose his head!"

Major Sharpe's head twitched round, the scarlet plume fluttering.

"Are you Sir John's second, Mr. Fletcher?"

"No, no! I . . ."

Major Sharpe, cold and bleak from every wrinkle in his face to every wire of his red side whiskers, again looked from one to the other of the duelists.

"Since you seem to wish for more danger, gentlemen," he said, "then you shall have it. I propose a measure which is not customary. But it is not new, and it is entirely within the code."

Major Sharpe paused, drawing back his lips over well-set false teeth.

"I propose to count slowly to three. This will give you time to aim. At the count of three, you will both fire together. Is it agreed?"

Both contestants nodded. Jemmy moaned. Major Sharpe smiled.

"*One!*" he called curtly, and lifted his right hand.

Buckstone's hand swung up to position, arm rigid and extended, aiming dead for the center of the forehead.

Darwent, thirty-six feet away, saw the steel muzzle of the barrel enclosed in its polished wood and mother-of-pearl. Beyond it Buckstone's little eyes seemed to be glazed with con-

113

centration, the weals on his cheeks stood out, but those eyes flickered when Darwent's weapon remained pointed at the ground.

The light breeze strengthened, drawing veils of mist from trees far away and whispering amid leaves.

"Two!" called Major Sharpe.

Mist rolled before the breeze. Far behind him Darwent heard faintly a new noise: a grinding, then a very slow click-clack. The sails of the windmill had begun to move. A bead of sweat ran down Darwent's cheek.

"This ain't a duel!" cried Jemmy. "This is murder!"

Darwent's hand raised carelessly to about the height of his waist, still taking no aim. Buckstone, eyes bloodshot, tried so violently to keep his aim steady that the pistol muzzle wavered, steadied, and wavered again. Darwent saw it waver. So did Major Sharpe.

"Three!"

As Darwent's hand whipped out to fire, the two shots came so nearly together that only one cloud of birds rose squeaking and twittering from the trees.

Buckstone's aim was a hairline too wide. Darwent heard the hornet hum of the bullet before it screeched past his left ear. At the same moment Buckstone—shot squarely through the right knee cap—seemed to kick out backwards with both legs, his face a mask of wonder, before he fell face down with a thud into the mist-carpet.

His right hand, pistol gone, rose and clawed in the air above the spurting mist. Then he thrashed out with both hands. The surgeon raced toward him, taking out the laudanum bottle.

Overcoming a vast weakness, Darwent walked slowly over to where Major Sharpe and Jemmy Fletcher were looking at him. Darwent's greatest weakness had not yet come.

"It is for your principal to decide, sir," he addressed Major Sharpe, "whether there shall be another exchange of shots."

The other two paid no attention to this. Overhead the sparrows circled, and they heard the slow click-clack of the windmill sails.

"You told me," Jemmy almost whispered, "you'd never touched a pistol in your life!"

"Pardon me. I said I hated pistols. I asked you to suppose, for the sake of argument, that I had never touched one."

Buckstone screamed. He could not help it. Buckstone was fighting the surgeon, rolling, while Mr. Mowbray tried to force the laudanum bottle between his teeth.

Major Sharpe pointed. "Was that shot a lucky accident, my lord?"

"No, sir. I could have killed him when you said, 'fire as you please.' I did not wish to kill him."

"But—!"

"Only to smash his vanity and insolence. To serve him as he served the poor damned pigeons he called out. The score is paid."

Darwent extended the pistol, butt foremost, toward Major Sharpe.

"You told *me*, Lord Darwent, that you had never fought a duel."

"Nor have I." He repressed a shudder. "But on an island called Crosstree, where an ammunition ship was wrecked with no explosion because the powder was wet, there was almost no food. Only scrawny, wild birds as elusive as a speck at twilight. Six hours a day, for eight long months on end, we practiced with the pistol so that we should not starve."

Gravely Major Sharpe took the pistol from Darwent's hand, and bowed.

"You were challenged, Lord Darwent," he said, with what might have been a bright bleak smile. "You withdrew your right to this," he touched the saber at his side, "and agreed to pistols. —Your very obedient servant, my lord!"

"Yours, sir," answered Darwent, returning the bow.

And he turned round and walked slowly, rather unsteadily, in the direction of his carriage. A heavier wind began to sweep away the mist as a broom sweeps, and the world was green again.

◇ CHAPTER XII ◇

Speaks Mainly of Caroline's Eyes

It was a quarter to eight in the morning when the red berline drew up before number thirty-eight St. James's Square.

All through that drive home, trembling from what is nowadays called "the black reaction," Darwent huddled inside his cloak and was silent. Jemmy Fletcher, who sat uneasily beside him, also remained silent until Jemmy alighted in Pall Mall.

"About that wager, old boy. I'm afraid I can't pay you."

"Wager?"

"The wager of who would," Jemmy bit his lips, "fall in the duel."

"You weren't intended to pay it, Jemmy. It was a matter of sarcasm."

"Eh? Oh! Yes. But they won't like it, you know!"

"Who won't like what?"

"Jack's friends," the other burst out. "They won't like it at all. I'm afraid you'll have to look out for trouble!"

"It is a curious fact, Jemmy, that you fail to curdle my blood. Patrick, drive on!"

When the carriage stopped before Caroline's house, under a grayer and heavier sky, Darwent pulled himself together and became his own man. It was necessary. He had scarcely ascended one step before the front door was opened.

But, as a circumstance almost unheard of, no footman touched the door. It was flung open by fat, slovenly old Hubert Mulberry; and behind him stood Caroline.

"Lad, lad, he didn't hit you!" the lawyer croaked hoarsely, and shook his fist in the doorway. "Stop! Are you hiding a wound under that cloak? *Did* he hit you?"

"No. —How's Dolly?"

Slowly Caroline turned away, putting her hand on the newel post of the stairs.

Mr. Mulberry, checked in mid-flight, looked evasive.

"She's dead," said Darwent. "Or dying. *Isn't she?*"

"Now, now, Dick!" urged Mr. Mulberry, as though warning him against such loudness outside a decorous door. "There's no call to think that. The sawbones is locked in the room with her. He won't say much; but sawbones won't, case they're wrong. He says he'll have word this morning. Besides . . ."

"Besides?"

"Well, Dick, don't fret too much before the event! We'll spike his guns. But the fact is: you may be arrested again, and put in Newgate."

"Newgate!" Darwent exclaimed, after a long pause. "Because of this duel with Buckstone?"

"No, no, no!" Mr. Mulberry rubbed at the fringes of hair on his forehead pushing them back so that all his gray-brown hair stood up like a grubby crest. "But—lad!" he added in alarm. "Buckstone didn't hit you. Did you kill *him?*"

"No. I starred his kneecap, as they call it."

"Ah!" said Mr. Mulberry, and a creaky bellows seemed to gurgle in his throat. "Why don't you come in?"

Newgate! Dolly! If the whole half-drunken nightmare began all over again . . .

Darwent went into the foyer. Alfred, after taking his hat and cape, closed the door. Caroline turned round from the newel post, her eyes lowered.

"Have you breakfasted, my lord?" she asked.

"Only black tea at Stephen's. But I don't think I could swallow food now."

"Then at least," said Caroline, her voice rising a little, "sit down with Mr. Mulberry and your other friend." She indicated the front room on the ground floor, at his left. "I ordered breakfast prepared for them in the dining room. They sought you first at Stephen's, and then here."

For the first time Darwent sensed the oddity of the situation. Caroline and Mr. Mulberry, he could have sworn, would be mutually antagonistic from the moment they met: Caroline haughty and indifferent, the lawyer with sulky defiant lip. Yet they stood here like friends.

In fact, everything had changed. From the instant he pulled the trigger and shattered Buckstone's kneecap, it was as though all hatred and even dislike washed out of him. It was as though he really had been suffering, as Caroline had said, from a kind of madness.

"Mr. Mulberry and your other friend," observed Caroline, "think you had better hold a council of war to save you from a new danger." She raised her eyes and cried out, "You have had so much war!"

Darwent looked at the disreputable old lawyer, who was studying both of them.

"Will you go into the dining room, Mr. Mulberry? I shall be brief."

Mr. Mulberry seemed not quite to like this, but the door closed behind him. Darwent looked at Caroline.

"You welcomed my friends," he said in a statement rather than a question.

"Of course. Even—" And her head made a gesture upward, as though to an Amber Room on the floor above her bedroom.

Such a power of sympathy seemed to flow from Caroline that it warmed his heart. Her day dress of sprigged muslin, the sprigs of tiny pink-and-blue flowers against white, glimmered in the dim foyer. She wore her hair in bands across the forehead, drawn to a knot behind: exposing her ears, as he had seen them yesterday evening when a certain white bow-knot . . .

Darwent stretched out his hands, and she took them. He gripped her fingers hard.

"May I speak frankly with you?" he said.

"Need you ask that?"

"In one thing, Caroline, you are right. I have had enough of war. I swear before God that I will never fight another duel as long as I live!"

(He could not guess at the events, rushing toward him now, which would make him break that oath.)

"Yesterday," he went on, "I thought myself a mighty fine fellow, no doubt: stuffed and starched for vengeance, full of hate. I did not even see how ridiculous I was. For what, when you faced them, were these terrors?

"Buckstone, the unbeatable! God's wounds! You had only to take a snap shot at him, when he lost his head as you hoped; and he rolled over like a ninepin and screamed like a snared rabbit. And you, Caroline . . ."

She interrupted him.

"May I speak frankly too? And without namby-pamby words?"

For answer he gripped her hands harder.

"Before I met you—yes, in Newgate Prison! and wondering how you might seem if they cleansed and dressed you—I distrusted all men. Not because I was cold. Not because I had never known desire; yes, and been tortured by it."

Caroline raised her eyes very briefly, but with spots of color under the cheekbones, and lowered them again.

"It was because," she went on, "I thought them oafs and boors, who took a wife as a sailor takes a strumpet. But worse! Since the wife must remain his slave, his servant, the worshipful admirer of his idiocies, until death do them part. You ask me why I changed my mind, or began to change it, when I met you? I don't know why; but I know the truth."

"Caroline, I . . ."

Caroline stopped him, pressing her hands to her temples and shaking her head. And yet, he thought, no man alive could doubt the tenderness of her eyes.

"Acknowledge one thing," she pleaded. "Acknowledge it, even if you speak a lie! You did not truly mean all you said last night?"

"Last night?"

"That I would have you killed. That I would think to poison

118

you. That I would even entice you . . . true; I did; I own it; for a different reason . . . but that I would entice you to keep an inheritance. You don't believe!"

"No! I don't believe it!"

"Then prove what you say."

"How?"

"Escort me," Caroline answered unexpectedly, "to the Italian opera tonight."

"Of course, if you wish it! But," memory troubled him, "wasn't there mention of your going last night?"

"I did. With Will Alvanley. I tried to imagine he was yourself; and oh, miserably, I failed! You'll keep your promise?"

"Yes," said Darwent.

Dropping Caroline's hands, he reached out and gripped her shoulders. At the same moment, the door to the dining room opened. Hubert Mulberry noted the scene, and what it was likely to mean, without remarking on it.

"I'd not trouble you, Dick," he growled. "Or your lady either. But there's a council o' war here, for your benefit."

"Yes. Go!" urged Caroline breathlessly. She turned away, and then turned back again. "But might I," she looked at Darwent, "might I be present?"

"My lady," said Mr. Mulberry, with the corners of his mouth drawn down, "you've been uncommon kind to us. But there's a time for women, and there's a time for reasonable talk. They don't mix."

"If my wife does not accompany me," Darwent replied mildly, "I am in no mood for your talk."

Mr. Mulberry, about to burst out, restrained himself with some mutter about women, and stepped aside. Caroline preceded Darwent into the dining room.

"And now, lad," grunted Mr. Mulberry, "greet a second friend of yours."

The large, lofty dining room, its front windows facing on the square like those of the green drawing room above, was paneled in a strong, light wood colored only by the tan of age. A very long table of polished mahogany gleamed against the Turkey carpet.

Mr. Mulberry, like other relics of the eighteenth century, sneered with violence at the modern breakfast of 1815: "tea and toast, devil take me!" From the sideboard he had removed two large silver platters, one containing a cold ham and the other a cold joint of beef, which he had put on the table beside a delicate glass punch bowl filled with ale.

119

He sat at the head of the table, before a heaped plate. On the far side, at about the middle, sat the Rev. Horace Cotton, Ordinary of Newgate.

"Padre!" exclaimed Darwent.

The Rev. Horace, large and rosy-faced, surged up beaming from the other side of the table. Though he did not now wear gown and bands, and was clad in shabby gray clothes with a black waistcoat, still he was as obviously a clergyman as he was a gentleman.

"My lord," said the Rev. Horace, hastening round the table as Darwent hurried forward with extended hand, "I rejoice to see you freed and happy."

Abruptly the clergyman paused. His large blue eyes clouded.

"That is to say," he amended, "I trust there is no . . . *contretemps.* Our friend Mulberry's message was so urgent that I demanded leave of absence from my duties."

"I have been free," said Darwent, clenching his fists, "for less than twenty-four hours." Visions of past horrors rose up. "They can't drag me back, can they?" He looked at Mulberry. "What do you tell me of arrest and a return to Newgate?"

"Gently, lad! I said we'd spike his guns."

"Whose guns?"

"Your enemy's," retorted Mr. Mulberry. "Your secret enemy's."

While he was speaking, the lawyer stood at the head of the table, cutting slices of ham and beef with a large bone-handled carving knife, and tipping them into an extra plate. He did not touch the large bowl of fruit near the ale bowl.

Caroline, with tact, had ordered that no servant should enter the room. Quietly, unnoticed, she slipped into a chair at the opposite end of the table from Mr. Mulberry. The Rev. Horace Cotton, after a still-dubious glance at Caroline, resumed his seat. Darwent sat down opposite the clergyman.

"Buckstone!" sneered Mr. Mulberry, puffing out his thick lips. "Buckstone's not your secret enemy, and has no connection with the plot against you. Your lady there,"—he pointed at Caroline with the carving knife—"*she's* not your secret enemy, and she's got no connection with the plot either."

Having filled the plate, Mr. Mulberry sent it spinning across the polished mahogany to Darwent. A knife and a two-pronged fork clattered after it. Dipping a deep glass into the punch bowl, and scooping it up full of ale, he sent that spinning wet and splashing into Darwent's hand.

Any conscientious footman would have swooned away. But

the fastidious, delicate Caroline only smiled and did not appear to notice.

Darwent—as the Rev. Horace Cotton observed—gave her a quick speculative glance.

"But what's the charge against me?" demanded Darwent. "What does it concern?"

"The murder of Lord Francis Orford."

Every time that name was mentioned, the image of Frank's long-nosed dead face seemed to leer among them like a satyr.

"But I've been tried and acquitted of that! Can I be tried again?"

Mr. Mulberry ignored this.

"Dick," he said, meditatively tapping the carving knife on the cold beef, "about the *real* story of the murder. Did you ever tell the real story to anybody except this reverend gentleman and me?"

"No. Never."

"Ay; well. Do you recollect, at Newgate, a turnkey named Blazes? A man who'd sell his soul for money? Could he have overheard it while you were telling the parson in the condemned cell?"

"I was not—myself. I don't recollect."

"*I* recollect," interposed the Rev. Horace firmly, and put down his knife and fork. "Come, my lord! When you were in the very middle of your story, the man Blazes came pounding and even kicking (kicking, mark it) at the cell door, as though to say, 'I have just arrived.' Could he not have heard you through the grill in the door?"

"Yes. He could have."

"And think again, my lord! He came there pounding and kicking to announce visitors. But he was an unconscionably long time in fetching the visitors, merely from the Chief Turnkey's lodgings. He could have overheard, my lord."

"In fact," said Mr. Mulberry, "he did. Can ye guess where I was last night?"

"Getting drunk, I have no doubt," observed the clergyman.

Mr. Mulberry was not in the least disturbed.

"Ay; well; true enough. I was at Tom Cribb's public house, as drunk as a Dutchman. But who should turn up there? Blazes. And who, damme, should be sitting in the next booth to mine? Sir John Buckstone."

"Buckstone!" exclaimed Darwent, half getting up.

"Be silent, lad," the slovenly lawyer said magniloquently, "and attend to your betters!"

Darwent sat down.

"Dick, in half a minute I was as sober as an ostler with his head under a pump. Blazes, d'ye see, wrote Buckstone a letter in the hope of a sovereign or a good deal more. From the half-dozen words Blazes does leer out . . . well, he knows the true story.

"And what does Sir High-and-Mighty John Buckstone say?" inquired Mr. Mulberry, scooping his own glass into the ale bowl and tipping off a bumper at a draught. "Why, I'll tell you. 'Not interested,' says he; 'I propose to kill the swine in a duel tomorrow morning.' And he calls for pen and ink. 'However,' says he, 'in case I'm a bit out and only mangle him, here's the name of a gentleman who *will* be interested.' And he writes name and address on a piece of paper."

"Did you see the name and address?"

"And betray meself? No!"

"Then—what?"

"Says Blazes to Sir High-and-Mighty, in a whispery voice, 'Has he got the rhino?' Well! 'It's a fashionable address, ain't it?' says Sir John Buckstone; 'won't he be bound to have money?' And Blazes goes away. Mind, we don't know he went to that address. Still, Dick: that's the enemy."

"But what can the enemy do to me?"

Again Mr. Mulberry ignored the question. His mouth was bitter.

"Yesterday, Dick, I told you I should have seen the evidence you were innocent and saved you at your first trial—if I hadn't been as drunk as a fiddler's bitch? Did you think I was maundering?"

"I didn't know what to think!"

"Ay; well; shall I prove it now?"

"Yes! If you can."

A stronger tension had invaded the light-paneled dining room; behind Mr. Mulberry, the two high windows, curtained in heavy russet velvet, grew darker with coming rain. Dipping again into the ale bowl, Mr. Mulberry drank the next bumper fairly slowly, and wiped his mouth with the end of his neck-cloth.

Then he plumped down in his chair, pointing the carving knife at Darwent.

"Dick, cast your mind back to the morning of May the sixth. When you woke up (eh?) and found yourself flat on your back in Garter Lane near your fencing school. Your head nigh split, and against a pile of stones. And Orford dead as mutton in front of you."

"I can remember," Darwent said grimly.

"Dick, how was that lane paved?"

"It was not paved at all. It was mud only half dry, as I told you and the Padre! The mud stuck to the back of my clothes."

"Ah!" said Mr. Mulberry, pouncing with the carving knife. "And d'ye recollect another circumstance you observed? About Frank Orford's top boots?"

The Rev. Horace Cotton cleared his throat.

"*I* recollect," he said, with a faint dawn of understanding in his eyes. "Lord Francis Orford, like Mr. George Brummell, blacked and polished even the soles of his boots. The soles were clean and shining."

Darwent started to get up from the table, but sat down again.

"Ergo," pounced Mr. Mulberry, "Frank Orford never fought a duel in that muddy lane. He never even walked the five yards from the door of your fencing school. No! He was carried there, no doubt in a coach, and flung down with a sword in his hand.—Stop!"

Here Mr. Mulberry held up the carving knife and leered.

"Will they say, Dick," he asked, "that you killed him nonetheless? That you carried him from your own door? I think not. Your own shoes were clean too, as you said. Ergo, *both* of you were carried there. I've got three witnesses, now, to testify to it. Damme, a jury would have seen the jape in five minutes."

Darwent, throat constricted, swallowed down his glass of ale as though to attain clear speech.

"And all that time," he said bitterly, "it never occurred to me that . . ."

"With a cracked skull and a half-rocked mind, lad? No."

"And that's the defense?"

"The defense?" scoffed Mr. Mulberry. "Why, Dick, that's only the first step in the defense."

"As—how?"

"Didn't I say yesterday," demanded Mr. Mulberry, "I could explain your cursed mystery? Except that I couldn't put a name to the murderer, and I had to guess at one or two details. Ay; I did. But you were too concerned about a wench to heed me. Well! I needn't guess at details now. I've got proof."

"Proof? Who supplied it?"

"You did, Dick."

123

For the first time Darwent became aware of what lay, soiled and drink-splashed, on the table near Mulberry's left hand. He saw the three closely written sheets of the letter he himself had written to the lawyer, describing every event of yesterday's late afternoon and evening, and sent off by hand from Stephen's last night.

"Oh, it's here," said Mr. Mulberry, tapping the letter with his left hand while he pointed the carving knife with his right. "Cast your mind back to this mummer's tale of the blue coach and Frank Orford skewered to a chair in the mysterious house. Now what's the first question you've always asked me about that?"

"I . . ."

"Speak up, lad, and shame the devil! What's the first question?"

"Well, why was I abducted? Why did they take me there? What did they want of me?"

"Why, lad," Mr. Mulberry replied coolly, "they didn't want you. Have you forgotten a gentleman named Tillotson Lewis?"

"Tillotson Lewis?"

"Come, now! You walk into White's Club; you see him; both of you feel you half ought to recognize each other. A minute later, Sir John Bloody Buckstone cries out with, 'No, you're not Lewis; for a second I thought you were.' Dick, Dick! It's because you look like each other."

Mr. Mulberry, his upthrust gray hair a war crest against the gray window, waggled the carving knife.

"I doubt, mind you," he added sharply, "if it's more than a slight resemblance. 'Twouldn't, if you ask Bert Mulberry, stand up against strong daylight or an eye that knew you both. But the driver of the blue coach, in dim light, wanted Tillotson Lewis. He got the wrong man."

Darwent, with a fierce gesture, pushed back his chair from the table.

"You'll serve nobody," roared Mr. Mulberry, "if you rave like a Bedlamite now." Scooping up two more glasses of ale from the bowl, he drank them quickly without troubling to wipe his mouth or the table. "It was plain to Bert Mulberry, as plain as the beak on Old Hookey's face,"—this regrettable allusion to the Duke of Wellington caused the clergyman to quiver—"there's been a mistake between two men. This letter accounts for it. What else d'ye know of Tillotson Lewis, Dick?"

Darwent, standing behind the chair and gripping its back, shook his head.

124

"Only the little I wrote you. Mrs. Bang said he was 'a fine young gentleman,' in somewhat indigent circumstances."

"Indigent, eh?" chuckled Mr. Mulberry. Out darted the gleam of the carving knife. "What's your next question about the mystery, Dick?"

"Well, what was the reason for all the mummery?"

"Gently, Dick! Bit by bit!"

"Why was Frank alone in a big closed-up house? Why was he sitting there, in a dressing gown, behind a tortoise-shell wood writing desk in the middle of the room—yes, and with a black silk mask in front of him!—as though he were waiting for someone?"

"Ah!" said Mr. Mulberry. "You shall answer for yourself, Dick."

"But I can't answer it!"

"Ye lie!" proclaimed Mr. Mulberry, who had taken half a gallon of strong ale for breakfast. "There's the matter that caught my attention, as I daresay it did the Padre's: viz.," said Mr. Mulberry, "who puts a writing desk in the middle of a room?"

"Man, I don't understand you!"

"It's as simple as kiss-your-hand. Answer the question, and you have the key to all. Come! Think of it, now!"

Bending forward, he sighted along the carving knife.

"Who puts a writing desk," he repeated, "in the *middle* of a room?"

◇   CHAPTER XIII   ◇

Reveals a Secret of the Lost House

Darwent looked down across the table into the eyes of The Rev. Horace Cotton. And the clergyman nodded, as though he knew this part of the story only too well; and Darwent recognized that he was deadly in earnest.

Glancing sideways at Caroline, whom the other two men had forgotten, he saw that her head was lowered. Her elbows were on the table, fingers pressed over her ears. A woman should not have been here at all.

But writing desks? All that would shape its image in Dar-

125

went's mind was the picture of Sir John Buckstone, sitting at an inlaid gilt-and-mahogany desk against the wall in the back parlor at White's. And this suddenly opened other thoughts.

"I can't remember," said Darwent, "that I ever saw a writing desk in the middle of a room. It's always been against the wall. Except, of course . . ."

"Except?" prompted Mr. Mulberry, with ghoulish eagerness.

"Except in countinghouses or an office of business. A City merchant's, for instance."

Mr. Mulberry rose to his feet behind the table.

"Well!" he said. "Lord Francis Orford *was* a merchant."

A stifled protest from Caroline, who was apparently scandalized at this suggestion, went unheeded.

"A merchant?" repeated Darwent, not in the least scandalized but much amazed. "Frank? What did he deal in?"

"Come!" sneered Mr. Mulberry, and snapped the fingers of his left hand. "Here's a young man, by your own deposition, so stingy he can't bear to part with a penny. He's rich in his own right; but he loves money as Jove loved wenches or I love Blue Ruin. He has relations in England, ay; but his hoity-toity parents, who fear scandal as they fear the devil—"

"Caro . . . my wife told me that," muttered Darwent.

"His parents, I say, have lived for more than two years abroad and can't keep an eye on him. Damme, what *would* he do? What was he?"

"Well, what was he?"

"He was a moneylender," retorted Mr. Mulberry, and drove the carving knife so deeply into the joint of beef that the knife handle stood upright.

It was as though he had stabbed a living person, to judge by Caroline's look.

"A most despised trade, eh?" grinned Mr. Mulberry. "That is, among the dandy-lions and nobs? Who borrow and borrow, men and women alike, fit for people in a lunatic hospital, but won't ever own they're in debt or to whom? Eh, Dick?"

"So I heard yesterday at White's, yes. But Frank . . . !"

"What a scandal! Eh, Dick?"

"Mr. Mulberry," interposed Caroline, softly but with authority.

Her fingers, spread out on the polished mahogany, looked white and delicate. But the old arrogance touched her features, chilling them, as she lifted her head.

"I fear sir, that what you suggest is so ridiculous you had

126

best not repeat it elsewhere. Even now some corrective action may have to be taken."

For the first time the Rev. Horace turned his eyes on her fully.

"And *I* fear, my lady," said the clergyman, "that what Mr. Mulberry states is all too true."

"*You* say this, Mr. Cotton?"

"I say it, my lady. Because I know it."

Having finished his modest breakfast of beef and ham and ale, the big clergyman stood up.

"It is so difficult," he continued in a repressed voice, which to Darwent was like an echo rolling down the Corridors of Newgate, "it is so difficult to find God's will and one's own duty. Lord Darwent: do you recall what I said to you, when first you told me your story?"

"I had forgotten, Padre, until now. But what you said seemed to have death in it; and doom. 'Other men have seen your ghost coach,' you said. 'Yes, and ridden in it too.' "

A drop of rain stung one of the windows.

"Do you recall anything else I said, my lord?"

"You—let me think! You said you lived amid crime and sin, with even the poor debtor rattling his cup against the door for alms." Darwent broke off. "Debtor!" he muttered.

"True. The debtors, well born or otherwise: Lord Francis Orford had them flung into Newgate or the Fleet. All were fish to his net."

"Now really, Mr. Cotton!" cried Caroline, and rose to her feet. "Do you imagine, if Frank had been what you say, that he would have dared show his face anywhere? That he would not have been shunned and despised, if his friends had known?"

"My lady, they did not know."

"Not know, sir?"

"That was the reason for the mystery, the black silk mask he wore when he faced his clients, the false name and signature he used, even the false teeth removed to change his voice."

Though the Rev. Horace did not wear his black gown and white bands, nevertheless gown and bands were visible to the imagination as his chest swelled out.

"Our Church of England, what the vulgar are pleased to call the High Church, has no seal of confession. But shall I ever betray confidence from a prisoner? No!—except it be life and death. It seemed to me, when Lord Darwent began to speak to me . . ." .

"That it *was* life and death?" asked Caroline.

The Rev. Horace nodded.

"What I learned of Lord Francis Orford," he went on with an effort, "I learned from a debtor whose name I need not speak. But he knew the real name of the moneylender; he knew the moneylender's wheedles and tricks. When I was upon the point of belief in Lord Darwent's story . . ."

Darwent struck the back of the chair.

"I told you a tale, Padre, of a room which had grown thick overnight with dust and cobwebs two years old! And you thought me mad."

The parson inclined his head and spread out his hands.

"For a time, God help me, I did." He faltered. "Afterwards (who shall say why?) I felt in my heart you *must* be guiltless. I hastened to the Sheriff's lodgings, in what I thought was the vain hope of a reprieve. The reprieve had already arrived. I had need to say nothing. But now . . ."

"Now, Mr. Cotton," interposed Caroline, with perplexity and wretchedness tempering her air of coldness, "you merely speak in riddles!"

"Riddles, my lady?"

"Truly. You talk somewhat wildly of a room grown with cobwebs overnight. You attack poor Frank; you attack the Kinsmeres; I won't have it. How could there be such a room, pray?"

"That, my lady, is beyond my knowledge. But I can guess at the reason for it."

"Then do!"

"Why," replied the Rev. Horace, uneasy at so much temporal thinking, "Lord Francis must surely guard against the possibility of being betrayed? Should one of his friends learn the true identity of the moneylender. . . penetrate the disguise . . ."

"That's it, Padre!" said Darwent. His voice was exultant. "That's it!".

Caroline, even as she whirled round toward him, did not forget her formal style of address in public.

"My lord!" she protested.

"I knew Frank," said Darwent, staring at a dead face. "I knew his cursed superciliousness. Suppose someone threatened to denounce him to his friends? 'Oh, indeed?' Frank would say, 'I loaned you such-and-such monies at such a place and such a time? Come; view the premises; then remain silent or be called out.' "

128

"And the dupe," cried the Rev. Horace, "would see a dead room of cobwebs. His tale would sound . . ."

"As mine sounded to you, Padre," supplied Darwent. "It was a trick, Padre! But how was the trick managed?"

"There was no trick," pleaded Caroline. "Lord Francis Orford? Oh, fie? No man of gentle birth would stoop to . . ."

"You observe, Padre," Darwent inquired dryly, "how safe Frank was? My wife cannot doubt your word. But she still won't believe.—Now how was that managed?"

"There was no trick!"

"How was it managed?"

They were interrupted by a low, hoarse, boozy chuckle.

Well over a quart of ale had remained in the immense glass bowl. Mr. Mulberry, leisurely seizing the opportunity, had disposed of it by the simple process of lifting the bowl to his lips and tilting it up.

He stood watching them, licking his lips, with the empty bowl in his hands. Though his eye was somewhat bleary, he retained loftiness because he was much distended with dignity as well as with ale.

"Pah!" he said. "I listen to the prattle of children."

Darwent swung round. "Do you know how the trick was managed?"

"Ay. Didn't I tell you I did?"

"Was I taken to some other room in that place?"

Mr. Mulberry's eye looked cunning. "No," he said.

"Were the dust and cobwebs true dust and cobwebs, gathered a long time?"

"They were."

"Then how. . . ?"

"Damme, I'll not tell you," said Mr. Mulberry, putting back the glass punch bowl with a crash on its glass holder.

"Sir," exclaimed the Rev. Horace Cotton, "you are not yourself!"

"I'll not tell you," pursued Mr. Mulberry, ignoring this remark, "for two reasons. First, Dick, because you ought to see for yourself what's as plain as the evidence of the polished boot soles and the writing desk. Second, because you now know Bert Mulberry's got more up his sleeve than shows on the card table. Good, then! You're not to be afeared if your enemy, your secret enemy . . ."

"If he does what?"

"If he tries to have you indicted for perjury."

In Darwent's mind had mingled so many hags and hun-

129

gry goblins that he heard this with what seemed (at first) a shock of relief.

"Perjury! Is that all?"

" 'Is that all?' he says," mimicked the lawyer, yanking the carving knife out of the beef. "I daresay he thinks, because perjury's a misdemeanor and not a felony, it can't be punished worse than a felony?"

"Bert, I know nothing whatever about it."

"By the present law, laid down 2 Geo. II. c.25, s.2, damme, it can mean seven years aboard the hulks or in an airless hole at Newgate, with no privilege of the State side. How's that?"

Another raindrop stung the window, then a spatter of them. Outside, a carriage rattled past at a quickening canter. The four persons in the dining room stood motionless round the table.

"I won't go back to Newgate," Darwent said quietly. "I'll cut my throat first."

"And you needn't go back, as I tell you! *De minimis*," said Mr. Mulberry, raising the carving knife, "*non curat lex*. If you can show the perjury was forced on you (which I can show, mind!), then you're out of danger. What's more, Dick, I'd lay you a small wager . . ."

"Yes," agreed Darwent, and gave him an odd glance. "This enemy of mine, the 'gentleman in fashionable lodgings,' won't reopen the case."

"Eh, and so you're the lawyer now! Why won't he?"

"Because he daren't. If *I* judge correctly, he was an accomplice of Frank Orford in the moneylending trade. He's afraid of what I know, or may know."

"True as the almanac! But what *will* he do, Dick?"

Darwent did not reply. He was pacing up and down the room, once more trying to conceal his thoughts even from himself.

"Yesterday," persisted Mr. Mulberry, "he fired a barker at you through a window. That's your true danger, Dick. This enemy—whoever he is; and I don't know him!—why, he'll go on trying to kill you until he's got you."

"Or until I've got him. That's fair enough."

"Stop!" protested Caroline.

Darwent stopped short in front of her. Caroline's hand was half raised; her eyes, very seldom wide open under the long upper lids, were open and pleading.

"A while ago," she said, "you promised there would be no more . . ."

130

"How can I help it, my dear? What choice have I?"

That almost absent-minded "my dear" was reflected in Caroline's eyes, and he saw it. Briefly they looked into each other's minds, or thought they did, with an intimacy like a physical touch. Then Darwent addressed Mr. Mulberry.

"In my own bumbling way, I've considered the evidence too. You maintain Tillotson Lewis had an appointment to meet the blue coach; he failed to appear; and I was mistaken for him?"

"That's it, lad, 'Indigent circumstances'!" sneered the other. "Fine fancy words for saying he was hard up."

Darwent pressed his hands against his forehead.

"Much of it," he admitted, "I understand. The secrecy, and the secret appointment. The coachman hidden to the eyes in a muffler, the bandages over my own eyes and ropes on me. But why the ear stoppings? Why the hammock? Above everything, why was I knocked on the head? Surely Frank didn't treat all his clients like that?"

Mr. Mulberry uttered a whistling sigh of satisfaction.

"There's a good answer to every one of those questions, Dick," he replied with great intensity, "if you think deep enough. Hold hard! Except . . . the knock over the head. Ah! There you've got me! It's no way of doing business; and that's a fact."

"May I put a question?" asked the Rev. Horace, his rich voice over-powering them. Darwent nodded. "Doubtless," said the clergyman, "you told the learned gentleman here. But you did not tell me, though I wondered. It was another circumstance which made me . . . made me . . ."

"Doubt my sanity?"

"No, no! Yet you woke up half-dazed in that coach, on the way to Kinsmere House in Bucks. You were not gagged, but you were tied and blindfolded. True?"

"Very true."

"Notwithstanding," said the Rev. Horace, "you swore you knew where you were, and where you were going. How could you have known that?"

"By the simple method, Padre, of working my eye bandage partly loose against the side of the hammock. Didn't I say I knew that countryside well?"

"You did; I allow it."

"Well! When I had one glimpse of a cluster of finger posts, with KINSMERE in reversed letters; when I felt myself carried up the broad steps of the only country house of its kind

131

within fifty miles: what did I know? The coachman adjusted my eye bandages often, but I saw enough. And it brings us to Kinsmere House, and my final query. —Who was the woman?"

"Woman?" repeated Mr. Mulberry, opening bleared eyes.

"What woman?" asked Caroline quickly.

"I stood in front of a door, you remember. The door of the room where Frank was stabbed, before I was pushed inside. And a woman screamed. Who was she?"

Again a dry satisfaction shook Mr. Mulberry.

"Lad," said the lawyer, a bitter misogynist because he had had three wives, "there was no woman."

"So? You credit that? Perhaps I credit it too."

"On the oath of my wits," swore Mr. Mulberry, "no woman was in any way connected with the murder of Orford."

Seeing that there was no ale left, Mr. Mulberry somewhat unsteadily put down the carving knife and took up an apple from the large bowl of fruit near the ale bowl.

"But I'll tell you what it is, Dick," he snapped, when his teeth had crunched into the apple and he swallowed the first bite whole. "Rot my guts! There are two wenches under this roof who'll give you more trouble than your enemy."

Caroline looked at him in disgust. The Rev. Horace was outraged.

"Mr. Mulberry," he said, "you forget yourself. You are drunk, sir. Yet I confess . . ." Angry, perplexed, he fumbled for the sleeves of an invisible black gown.

"Let us hear you, sir," said Caroline, who was furious. "You confess?"

The Rev. Horace turned ponderously.

"My lady," he said, "I should put the matter in less vulgar terms than our friend here. But I am of much the same opinion."

"How dare you," Caroline said flatly, her head back and eyelids drooping.

"I dare, Lady Darwent, because I am the humble personage who united you in marriage to your husband. When I first entered the house this morning, it seemed to me that in some way you had . . . had altered. Have you altered?"

"To the world, no. To my husband—yes."

"Do you love him?"

Caroline's face was becoming pink, though she gave him a sweet smile.

"Really, sir," she chided him, with all the archness and

132

coquetry and battery glances of her day. "You forget that what you ask is not a question one puts to any lady of sensibility. Or do you forget your manners?"

"Here, now, stop!" protested Mr. Mulberry, obviously alarmed at what he had set rolling. For the Rev. Horace Cotton would do his duty, or what he conceived to be his duty, if he smashed the whole house.

"I forget neither, my lady," said the Rev. Horace. "On the contrary, I recall only that you married him, when we all knew he was deeply in love with another lady. It was pitiful, my lady, to see those fifty pounds gained for her legacy."

Darwent intervened wildly. "Padre, for God's sake!"

"Yes," said the Rev. Horace, "for God's sake!" Again he looked at Caroline, and spoke quietly. "Do you love him?"

Caroline had turned her head away. "Yes," she answered.

"That would be a happy circumstance," continued the inflexible clergyman, "if I did not know, from Mr. Mulberry, that the other lady is now upstairs in this house."

Whereupon he swung round to Darwent, and nodded toward Caroline.

"Do you love your wife, my lord?"

"She was one of my enemies, Padre. And yet you yourself . . ."

"I bade you use charity. Not lust. It is in your eyes."

"Oh, this is intolerable!" cried Caroline—which in very truth it was. But she made no move to leave them.

"Do you love her?" repeated the Rev. Horace.

"Padre," said Darwent, "I . . ."

"Let me remind you that the other lady now lies ill abovestairs!"

He had no further need of reminder. The door to the foyer opened slowly. Mr. Samuel Hereford, the portly surgeon, his jowls unshaven and with the look of one who has kept vigil all night, closed the door slowly and bowed.

"Lord Darwent," he said, "I bring you final news of the patient."

The rain, in a fine shower, pattered against the windows; it depressed the foliage and made forlorn the statue of King William the Third in St. James's Square; it shadowed the brownish-tinted dining room.

Mr. Hereford shook his head to rouse himself.

"Last night," he went on, "I told you I believed I had discovered some remedy, though I worked only on feeling and logic against the unknown."

133

"Yes. But it didn't . . . ?"

"Hear me!" interrupted Mr. Hereford. "Have the kindness not to speak until I tell you. My diagnosis, as you heard, was indigestion; what we call, in a general term for many illnesses, inflammation of the bowel. Miss Spencer, I think, drinks a tolerable amount of wine?"

"Well, so do I! So do most of us."

The surgeon lifted his hand.

"Yesterday, in Lewknor Lane, I was about to do what it is our practice to do. That is, apply very hot cloths round the affected place so as to ease pain. At this point I recalled from my experience one or two cases—one or two, I say!—when the pain was right side of the abdomen in that place. We applied hot cloths; it was no doubt a coincidence, but the patient died.

"I decided, mad as you may think me, to try precisely the opposite. That is, extreme cold. I sent to the Clarendon Hotel, where we most easily find iced punch and sherbets and the like, for large quantities of ice . . ."

"Ice?" repeated Darwent. The rustle of the shower deepened.

Mr. Hereford nodded.

"Mr. Raleigh and I," he said, "contrived to smash it in pieces and fit a kind of cloth belt tightly round the abdomen. The ice melts swiftly; we renewed it, and renewed it, and renewed it; for the symptoms were better . . ."

"But your 'remedy' failed," snapped Mr. Mulberry, "and the girl died."

The surgeon roused himself, blinking.

"Died?" He spoke reproachfully to Darwent. "My lord, I can't say why it happened. But I had hoped to receive your thanks." A wry smile crossed his unshaven face. "My lord, the patient is—fairly well."

The half-eaten apple slipped from Mr. Mulberry's fingers, bumped on the floor, and rolled across the carpet.

"Not only is she convalescent, but you may visit her at any time. I remained so secret and even secretive because I failed to credit the good results; not the bad. Let her rest quietly for one day more; keep the ice tightly pressed; and I think she will be cured. But only a short visit now, I warn you!"

Only the rain broke that long silence afterwards.

Darwent, without speaking, grasped Mr. Hereford's hand and wrung it violently until Mr. Hereford protested.

And the surgeon—who never dreamed he had been dealing

134

with a case of appendicitis, and went to his grave without knowing it; or that his guess against the unknown had found the only way to save Dolly—begged Caroline's leave to sit down. He sat with his head in his hands, puzzling at a problem which would not completely be resolved by surgery until eighty-one years afterward.

For it was now the bright-colored, careless present day of '15, with living people who touched real chairs or tables.

"I thank you," Darwent said at length. Bowing to the rest of them, he went quickly to the door, opened it, and closed it behind him.

Caroline's face was as pale as her white muslin dress with the flower sprigs. Disregarding the others, she moved carelessly toward the door; but she followed Darwent with some haste.

Once more Mr. Mulberry uttered his low, hoarse, boozy chuckle.

"Padre!"

"Y-yes?"

"Dick's in love with one of 'em," said Mr. Mulberry dryly. "But rot him if he knows which."

◇ CHAPTER XIV ◇

Of Dolly, and Fond Memory

When Darwent opened the door of the Amber Room, he knew they were awaiting him, even before the cough which answered his knock.

Hangings of amber-colored silk, after the style of Louis the Well-Beloved in France fifty years ago, were draped in folds from the ceiling and covered the walls except at the two windows opposite the door. The big ornate bedstead, its canopy weighted with more hangings of amber silk, had its head set between the two windows and its foot toward the door.

Darwent, as he entered, could not see Dolly. Mr. and Mrs. Raleigh, like a very small grenadier and a middle-sized grenadier, stood at the foot of the bed.

And something was wrong. Not hostile, but wrong.

Mrs. Raleigh, with the lace-edged cap round her plump

face, was ill at ease despite her determined brightness. Mr. Raleigh, cadaverous-faced and bald-headed, held a book with one finger between the leaves; he was on his dignity, but his kindly eyes looked almost frightened.

"La," cried Mrs. Raleigh, throwing up her hands, "and see who's here!"

Augustus Raleigh smiled a sepulchral smile.

"I have been reading," he said, in the bass voice which seemed to rise up from his gaiters, "the new romance by the author of *Waverley*. It is very good. I am told . . ."

"What's the matter?" Darwent demanded bluntly.

"Matter?" repeated Mrs. Raleigh, with a mouth of surprise.

"I am told," said Mr. Raleigh, holding up the book and inspecting it, "that the author's identity is well known to many persons, though it is still officially a secret. Now, Dick." He stopped. "If I may call you so?"

He held up the book with determined cheerfulness. "The new romance, in three volumes, by the author of *Waverley*: whoever he may be. It is very good."

"Thank you," answered Darwent, as he passed Mr. Raleigh on the left-hand side of the bed, and pressed his arm. "Thank you both."

"Why, Dick, there's very little to . . ."

" 'Lo, my dearest," murmured Dolly, smiling as well as she could.

In this line of houses built flat against each other, only the front room and the back room would have been visited by daylight if they had not constructed a narrow air well for the middle rooms. The heavy orange-yellow curtains, touched by the dim gleam of the crimson lamp, showed—on either side of the bed—gray windows spattered with rain.

"I'm awfully sorry," Dolly said apologetically, and weakly stretched out her hand. "I must ha' been more ill than I thought I was."

Her brown eyes were turned up at him, under the shadow of the canopy where the bed curtains were looped back. Her yellow hair, again carefully done in curls, hung well below the ears. Only her white-silk nightgown, clearly belonging to Caroline and cut like an evening gown, showed her uneven breathing. But she still tried to smile.

"I'm as well as beans now, Dick," she assured him. "Truly I am!"

"Well!" cried Mrs. Raleigh, as usual erupting into tears. "Here's the poor girl half recovered, by a miracle it is because

136

they wouldn't give her the black medicine, and she thinks she's well!"

"Emma, my dear," her husband expostulated gently.

For a moment Darwent could not speak. He lifted Dolly's hand, and pressed it to his lips, and sat down on the side of the bed.

In the curtain-hung room, despite its stuffiness, there was a chill of melted or melting ice. The ice had been packed into champagne coolers, which stood on marble-topped gilt tables and dripped with slow monotonous noise on the tables.

"I won't have you troubled," Dolly said suddenly, her eyes searching his face, "I *won't*."

"My dear," he told her, pressing the hand to his cheek, "I've been cursing myself for bringing you here. There is so much I ought to have told you, and told you yesterday. I can't understand why I couldn't tell you."

"About being the Marquess of Darwent?" smiled Dolly, her forehead wrinkled. "*I* could say why you wouldn't tell me."

"You could . . .?"

" 'Cos I know you," replied Dolly, as though it were the simplest thing in the world. "You were afraid we'd think you were lording it over us; and you can't endure to lord it over anybody. But, oh, Dick, that's what I'm a-terrified of!"

"Terrified of?"

Again Dolly's eyes searched his face, and she pressed her hand more tightly against his cheek.

" 'Cos you can't endure for somebody to lord it over *you*." Dolly laughed weakly. "It near crazes you, Dick. It always has. You'd cock a snook at the whole world, and have everybody against you. I—I love that. But you *mustn't*, now you're Lord Darwent." She lowered her eyes. "Didn't you fight a duel this morning?"

He lowered her hand from his cheek.

"Who told you that, Dolly?"

"Miss Ross did."

"Miss Ross!"

"She's been awful—awfully kind to me," said Dolly. "She came in here this morning, a-crying and near a-raving, and saying you were going to be killed and it was all her fault. Mr. Hereford and Mr. Raleigh had to put her out; and, honest-truly, I pitied her. I didn't cry, Dick. Do you know why?"

"Well?"

" 'Cos I knew you'd win," Dolly replied simply.

(How much did Dolly know about Caroline?)

137

Darwent twitched his head round to look quickly at the Raleighs. Emma Raleigh, again seated in a gilt-and-brocade chair at one side of the bed, stabbed rather blindly at a needlework frame. Augustus Raleigh, seated at the other side, was engrossed in reading *Guy Mannering* upside down.

Yet Darwent's unspoken question so burned in the air, where iced water dripped monotonously on marble table tops, that Mr. Raleigh lifted his head.

"Nothing!" Mr. Raleigh said emphatically. "She has been told nothing about . . .!" Mr. Raleigh's expressive eyes meant Caroline. "The rest, yes!"

"About Miss Ross?" asked Dolly, immediately and gently. Tenderness showed in her face, as well as a look of wonder that Darwent could be so stupid. "Oh, Dick, did you think I'd be vexed? Or jealous?"

"Well! In the past . . ."

"I know. I've been dreadful. But—"

Dolly leaned back against the propped-up pillows, and shuddered.

"I nearly lost you to Old Jack." She meant Jack Ketch. "And I wasn't there, Dick. I wasn't there! After that . . . well, was it so very bad if you wanted to lie with another woman? Maybe I was just too awful ill to care; but I don't care, or I didn't. And as for bringing me here," a ghost of the old mirth trembled in her throat, "I liked that best of all."

"*You liked*—" Darwent paused, his wits whirling. "A swine's trick for which I can never . . ."

"Oh, silly!" breathed Dolly, and she shook her head, apologized for impatience, and regarded him with deep sincerity.

"And for some reason you say you liked it?"

"It was the awful, colossal sauce of you," said Dolly simply. "Walking into *her* house." Dolly's eyes brightened with glee, "and saying you wanted the best room for your mistress, and nearly making Alfred drop dead. Maybe she wouldn't be proud of that. But I am."

"Listen, Dolly. About Miss Ross . . ."

"I'm not jealous of her. Truly I'm not!"

"There isn't time to explain the—the situation between Miss Ross and myself!" he went on. "But understand this much: it can be changed." He picked up both of Dolly's hands, leaning forward so that he could press them against his breast, and spoke with all the earnestness in his nature.

"Dolly," he said, "it's a trumpery thing. I mention it, believe

138

me, only because it is the only way I can say it. But will you honor me by becoming the Marchioness of Darwent?"

The aching emotion in that dim, crimson-lit rôom, where iced water splashed unheeded, could be felt with a keen pang even by Mrs. Raleigh, whose needlework ran awry, and Mr. Raleigh, unseeingly concentrated on the uttering of Meg Merrilees' curse against the Laird of Ellengowan. .

Darwent did not even notice them, nor did Dolly. Dolly looked back at him fixedly. Despite herself, despite shame and anger at herself, two tears welled up in Dolly's eyes.

"No, I won't," she said.

"But why not?"

"Becos I shouldn't like it," she answered with that same simplicity, "and neither would you. You think you would; but you wouldn't."

"That's utter nonsense, and you know it!"

"Let's be pleasant!" called Dolly in a voice of sudden cheerfulness. Fiercely she pushed him; and, even as she did so, he saw the stab of physical pain which went through her body under the padded silk coverlet.

How long since that ice bandage had been renewed?

"Let's be pleasant!" Dolly repeated, smiling at him and then turning toward the Raleighs. "Before you came here, Dick, we were speaking of the wonderful times on the stage. Oh, and how we loved it!"

It was not as though an enchanter had brought both Raleighs to life; it was rather as though the enchanter had dug both of them with a long sharp pin.

"We were telling the child, Dick," crowed Mrs. Raleigh, rearing up behind her embroidery frame, "that the stage is not what it was in *our* day."

"Now there, my love," corrected her husband, instantly putting down *Guy Mannering*, "I must ask you to speak for yourself. The giants of today are mightier than those of old."

"Now really, Mr. R.!"

"I affirm it, Emma. I am not, of course," intoned Mr. Raleigh in a voice like a tragedian, "a polished player like Dolly, or a skilled swordsman like Dick. At the same time . . ."

"Mr. R.," cried his wife, "you underrate yourself. I won't have it!"

"Well, well," conceded Mr. Raleigh, with a ghostly smile, "it may have fallen to my lot, perhaps, to amuse the pit during some undue delays in shifting scenes. For juggling ninepins,

139

for throwing up five oranges and catching them on a point, I was perhaps even famous. And you must own I had few rivals at a comic song."

"Fie!" interposed Dolly, catching the spirit. "The comicalest times, Mr. Raleigh, was in the Old Price riots at Covent Garden." She partly turned her head. *"You* remember, Dick? When the fools of managers put up the prices, and people wouldn't endure it? Oh! No. You don't remember. That was six years ago. You were . . . were at Oxford."

"Dolly! Stop this gabble and listen to me!"

"Dick! Dear! Don't!"

"The O.P. riots at Covent Garden Playhouse," cried Mrs. Raleigh, "were a sin and a scandal."

"I quite agree, my love," said her husband, nodding gravely. "Especially when they brought in prize fighters to subdue the audience, with many injured and one dead. It could never have happened at Drury Lane."

As Mrs. Raleigh's emotions veered, the tears smarted into her eyes again.

"Of course, Mr. R.," she observed acidly, "you *would* defend a management that gave you your walking papers overnight, and we without a penny saved to meet it!"

"One must be philosophical about these matters, my love," answered Mr. Raleigh, with a stately wave of the hand. A faraway smile touched his lips. "You are quite right, of course, in your censure of the O.P. riots. Yet nearly seventy nights of fighting in the pit, with post horns blowing and pigeons released, with Lord Yarmouth and the Hon. Berkeley Craven fighting in the pit too . . . well, it was not without its lighter side."

Dolly Spencer looked almost wistful.

"It was lovely," she breathed. "Oh, how I wish there could be a rowdy do like that at the Italian opera!"

"The opera, my dear?" inquired Mrs. Raleigh, her eyebrows seeming to freeze as they rose.

"The opera?" repeated her husband, in a tone almost as freezing. "Pray reflect, my dear Dolly, that this opera is an inferior art."

"Oh, inferior, yes." Mrs. Raleigh shivered. "But—*fashionable*, Mr. R. Fashionable! La, but our quality must wear full court dress; and even in the pit the humbler ones must dress *en grande tenue*. Whereas we at our theater, of course, are mere buffoons."

"But that's it," Dolly protested eagerly. "It's so dainty and

140

prim and deah-me. Lord, how I'd adore to see someone hit in the face with a squashy orange! But it won't ever happen: not there. The opera's for fine ladies and pretty lordlings who . . ."

Suddenly realizing what she had said, Dolly stopped dead. Her mouth opened, and she turned round a face of consternation.

"Dick!" the stricken voice whispered. "I didn't mean you!"

And he smiled at her.

"I know you didn't, Dolly. And, if it pleases you, *I* am entirely at your service to hit someone with a squashy orange." Then he burst out in wretchedness, "Dolly, can't we return to our own affairs?"

"No. I won't. Don't torture me!"

"Have you the least fondness for me, Dolly?"

"I love you," said Dolly, in a puzzled voice. "That's why I daresn't . . ." She stopped. "I'm no good," she said. "You don't even know where I was all that time you were in prison."

"I don't care where you were."

The brown eyes wavered, hesitated, and weakened. Very slowly Dolly stretched out her hand.

At the same moment there was a low but imperative rap at the door. The door opened, and Caroline came in.

Caroline kept her smile and her poise, though in the very atmosphere was the sense that she had overheard much. Both the Raleighs rose to their feet with deep respect.

"Forgive this interruption, my lord!" she addressed Darwent formally. "But Mr. Hereford has just left, together with Mr. Cotton. Mr. Hereford bade me tell you that you have long overstayed your leave with our patient," she looked kindly at Dolly, "and that you *must* go at once."

Darwent rose up from the side of the bed.

It was Caroine's vitality and fresh color which made him understand how exhausted, how spent and used up, were three of the persons in the Amber Room. Even the Raleighs, to say nothing of Dolly, looked haggard after a night's vigil beside that bed. And there was death, still with one foot inside the door.

"I have been clumsy and a fool," Darwent apologized, again lifting Dolly's hand and kissing it. "I will return as soon as Mr. Hereford permits."

"Of course!" murmured Caroline.

"But I'm 'most well," Dolly cried out. "The sawbones said it. This afternoon I'm a-going to get up," she felt her waist

141

under the padded coverlet, "and take off this dreadful ice that makes me drip like a wet fish. I am!"

Mr. Raleigh turned on her his most sepulchral and terrifying look.·

"You will not get up, my dear," he said, "if I am compelled to hold you down. Those were *my* instructions from the surgeon."

"He speaks a truth, Miss Spencer," said Caroline. "My lord!"

Darwent, on his way to the door, swung round.

Caroline regarded him steadily, her blue eyes opaque and the palms of her hands pressed together.

"There is another reason," she told him, as though he might have doubted her, "why I felt obliged to interrupt you. There is a caller to see you." She bit at her lip. "I am sure," Caroline added, "I made little of your conversation at the breakfast table. Yet this gentleman is agitated, he is . . . yes, I *know* you would wish to see him!"

"A caller? Who is he?"

"His name," answered Caroline, "is Mr. Tillotson Lewis."

⋄   CHAPTER ·XV   ⋄

The Coachman from the Graveyard

"Tillotson Lewis!" echoed Darwent.

So elusive had been young Mr. Lewis, so much a pair of top boots striding ghostlike across the passage at White's, that Darwent was as taken aback as though Caroline had mentioned a visit from Prester John or the wily Ulysses.

"May I ask where he is now?"

"I took the liberty of asking him to wait in the drawing room."

"And—er—where is Mulberry?"

Caroline's eyes clouded with uneasiness. She glanced at the door behind her.

"Until a moment ago, he was with me. Unfortunately," and Caroline made a mouth less of repugnance than regret, "Mr. Mulberry was much disguised in liquor. I—I confess I was unwise to return to the drawing room and offer him brandy after breakfast. After your departure, my lord, he made some astonishing statements. Including the fact that he had now solved the mystery."

"*Solved the mystery?*"

"Yes, my lord."

The dull crimson of the lamp darkened the sickly amber hangings of this room in the style of Louis the Well-Beloved. Dolly Spencer leaned back against the headboard of the bed, her long-lashed eyes closed. Mr. Raleigh, in utter weariness, leaned against one bedpost.

"Caroline!" said Darwent. "What did Mulberry tell you?"

"My lord, may I beg you to go downstairs and . . ."

"What did Mulberry say?"

"You may remember," Caroline's eyes shifted, "that he was standing at the head of the table, with a large bowl of fruit in front of him? That he had been eating an apple, which dropped out of his hand after the surgeon entered?"

"I remember it. And then?"

"My lord, I can recount it but imperfectly. After your departure, when Mr. Mulberry drank brandy, he became more and more fond of Latin quotations. I do not know,"—and Caroline smiled uneasily—"whether this was done to impress me. In any case. . . ."

"Go on!"

"He used a quotation which dealt with the sanctity of a Roman villa; and it brought him up as though he had seen a poisonous viper. Twice he repeated 'Roman villa,' and looked at the bowl of fruit as though it enlightened him.

"Whereupon," continued Caroline, throwing out her arms, "to the astonishment of Mr. Cotton and myself, he must produce a number of keys from his pockets—half a dozen keys, at least—and flourish them. He cried out, 'I have solved *all* this mystery,' and insisted that he be taken up to see you."

"Then where is he now?"

Caroline lifted her shoulders.

"As I indicated, he was—was not himself. Thomas," she meant the second footman, "must escort him outside and put him into a hackney coach. My lord, have you forgotten that your life is in danger? Will you not go downstairs and see Mr. Lewis?"

"I will go," answered Darwent; and closed the door behind him.

All over the dim house, as he descended to the first floor

above the ground floor, the rustle of the rain deepened. A grandfather clock on the landing struck twelve noon.

Since the heaviest drive of rain was against the front windows, the curtains had been drawn and the mantelpiece candles lighted in the green drawing room. On the striped sofa sat a frank-looking, clear-eyed young man, reading a copy of Leigh Hunt's newspaper, *The Examiner*.

The young man rose hastily to his feet. "Lord Darwent?"

"Your servant, Mr. Lewis."

Tillotson Lewis, richly but very soberly dressed except for his white red-sprigged waistcoat, was about of Darwent's height and figure. Like Darwent, he had gray eyes and brown hair. Otherwise, Darwent thought, there was no close resemblance between them except in a poor light or when someone was expecting to see it.

And he liked young Lewis instantly; liked his evident straightforwardness and intelligence; liked the fact that he had no lisp, no sour temper, no deliberate eccentricity as cultivated by the dandy to be in fashion.

But Lewis was nervous, twisting and untwisting the newspaper. Darwent waved him back to his seat on the sofa, and himself sat down beside the center table.

"F-forgive my intrusion," said Lewis, conquering his stutter with a ghost of a smile in the plainly friendly atmosphere. "I came here, Lord Darwent, mainly to thank you."

"To thank me? For what reason?"

"I understand from my neighbor, Mrs. Captain Bang, that yesterday someone fired a bullet at you from a window of my lodgings.—One moment!" he added, though Darwent did not offer to interrupt.

"On my oath," declared Lewis, bending forward with the copy of *The Examiner* crushed against his knees, "I am not addicted to casual assassination. And at that time (if Mrs. Bang states it correctly) I was having my dinner, boiled fowl with oyster sauce, at White's."

Darwent laughed.

"You may be easy, Mr. Lewis. I am certain you did not fire the shot."

"Thank God for that! But why are you certain?"

"Let's say I have personal reasons."

"Most men," said Lewis, "would have gone straight to a magistrate, or at least have summoned the watch . . ."

"Now what good are the Charlies," Darwent inquired dryly, "except to show a clean pair of heels when there's trouble?

144

For the most part they are old men who can be beaten sense-less by fine sporting Corinthians such as, for instance, Jemmy Fletcher and Sir John Buckstone."

Lewis glanced at him quickly.

"Don't underestimate poor Jemmy," he advised. "He has a willow-like look, I grant; but he's as strong as a horse. As for Buckstone . . ."

All of a sudden Lewis became conscious of Mr. Hunt's newspaper, *The Examiner,* clutched against his knee. He folded up the newspaper, and put it into the tail pocket of his coat.

"Does it surprise you," he asked half-defiantly, "that a Tory and a member of White's should be reading a paper of such . . . very advanced views?"

"In the case of an intelligent man, no."

"You approve?" exclaimed Lewis. "When the editor was released, only last February, from a prison sentence for writing a so-called libel against the Prince Regent?"

"I applaud Mr. Hunt's good sense, if not his moderation. He called the Regent, I think, a 'corpulent Adonis of fifty'?"

"Something of the kind, yes."

"Better sense, or worse folly, would have written, 'a fat hog who has outlived the great talents he once possessed.'"

Tillotson Lewis opened his mouth to speak, and closed it again. His gray eyes contemplated Darwent with a pinched uneasiness: as though he would have huzzaed, but dared not even commend. Clearly, the candlelight illumined his thin face, with the twitching muscle beside the mouth. Behind closed curtains the rain sluiced down.

"Lord Darwent," he burst out, "you can't do it!"

"I can't do what?"

"Or let me say," amended Lewis, "you must not do it." His voice grew intense. "You mustn't show contempt for society as it is; you mustn't knock over idols; above all, you mustn't touch Jack Buckstone."

All Darwent's laughter, all his momentary happiness, seemed to dry up inside him and turn to a black mud which he could almost taste.

"Buckstone again," he said. "In the devil's name, who *is* Buckstone? Is he too sacred to be touched?"

"Yes."

"And I'm not to be free of him, even when the boasting swine collapses like a bag of wind?"

145

Lewis spoke sympathetically and hesitantly, but with clear truth.

"You will never be free of him, Lord Darwent, so long as he is a symbol of what a fine fellow ought to be. Face that."

There was a silence, broken by Lewis.

"This morning, as everyone now knows, you scored a so-called victory over Buckstone . . ."

"A 'so-called' victory?"

"Yes. It is claimed you fought foul. Today you will be challenged to fight again."

"Challenged by whom?"

When the wax lights faintly flickered, Lewis glanced round the shadowy room as though to make certain they were not overheard.

"The truth is, between ourselves: you're too dangerous a man with the pistol. It won't be pistols. You will have to meet their best swordsman."

"I repeat, sir: who will challenge me?"

"Major Anthony Sharpe. 7th Hussars."

"Major Sharpe?"

"You don't appear to credit me."

"But Sharpe is an honest and honorable man!"

"True," agreed Lewis, lifting his shoulders for emphasis, "as everyone knows! But both Jemmy Fletcher and Jack Buckstone testify you fought foul: they say you swore you had never touched a pistol in your life, and did not even know how to fire one."

"When they say that," Darwent told him agreeably, "they are both liars and damned liars."

Lewis rose in some agitation from the sofa, and paced round behind it.

"My lord," he said, "I make bold to believe you. First because I think you are honest. Second because of . . ." He touched the copy of *The Examiner* in the tail pocket of his gray waist-fitting coat with the black velvet collar.

"But Fletcher and Buckstone," Lewis added, turning abruptly, "have both given their words as gentlemen. Major Sharpe honestly believes them. As for Sir John Buckstone . . ."

"Can't we omit mention of Buckstone?"

But, even as Darwent said this, the hateful words rang in his head like refrain he would now hear without end:

You will never be free of him, Lord Darwent. You will never be free of him. You will never be free of him. . . .

146

"Besides," added Lewis, piercing his thoughts, "there is the question of military preferment."

"I fail to understand you."

"A near friend of Buckstone's," said Lewis, "is His Royal Highness the Duke of York. His Royal Highness of York is no longer head of the army, of course. But his influence is still of great power at the Horse Guards. Major Sharpe is a fine soldier; of good family, related to the Kinsmeres of Bucks; but poor, in debt, with no preferment."

"You intimate, sir, that again 'influence' will . . . ?"

"A colonelcy at the very least," blurted Lewis, "will be his reward-of-merit for cutting you down. —My lord, his second may call here at any moment."

Darwent rose to his feet and went over to the mantelpiece. Just here, last night, he had given Jemmy Fletcher a reply for Buckstone. He turned round to face Lewis, stretching out his arms along the mantel ledge.

And on Darwent's face there was a cold smile which (for some reason) brought out drops of sweat on Lewis's forehead.

"I won't fight him," Darwent said.

"For your kind and mine," the other retorted bitterly, "there is no choice. We accept a challenge, or we are horsewhipped in public. Do you know Ned Firebrace, Major Sharpe's nephew?"

"No."

"Ned Firebrace," returned Lewis, "was—was formerly a cornet of the 10th Hussars, Prinny's own regiment. He's nearly as good a swordsman as his uncle; and he's more malicious than Buckstone ever was. If you refuse his uncle's challenge, he'll take the horsewhip to you; and he'll be justified!"

"Let him try."

"But your *reason* for not meeting his uncle?"

"Oh, I intend to state my reason in public."

"Good! That may be of help. What is it?"

"That I mean to see one honest man, meaning Major Sharpe, uncorrupted by a set of swine who need a taste of the French Revolution."

Another gust of rain drove against the windows. Tillotson Lewis's face went as white as his red-sprigged waistcoat.

"For God's sake, hush!" he implored in a low voice. "You're a worse republican than Tom Paine ever was!"

"I, Mr. Lewis? A republican? Come, now!"

"Then what are you pleased to call it?"

147

"My dear sir," Darwent observed agreeably, and settled himself against the mantelpiece, "let us stop and reflect. All men are not created equal, if only by reason of their intellects. Shall we set up pig-faced York, or Silly-Billy Clarence, or perverted Cumberland, or dough-witted Kent, against the genius of dead Mr. Fox or dying Mr. Sheridan?"

"My lord, this is treason!"

"Treason?" repeated Darwent. "When these dolts are of Hanoverian stock, with not one drop of English blood for four generations? Speak to me of treason, sir, when we serve a British king."

"Man, you are nothing more than—!"

"A Jacobite, like my good friend Mr. Mulberry? I am not sure. But this I do say: that all men are, or should be, equal in their rights before the law."

"Ah, now you speak good sense! I am for truth and justice."

"If you are for truth and justice," Darwent said quietly, "then you can aid me."

"Aid you? How?"

Darwent felt a spell creep over his wits even as he uttered the words.

"On the evening of May fifth, last, were you not engaged to meet the blue coach in Hyde Park? And go out to the moneylender's house?"

Again, as he finished speaking, Darwent half-twitched his head round toward the mantelpiece and the wall behind him. It might have been his imagination, in this shadow-draped room under the rain. But this was a front room, like the dining room below. Its west wall, this wall—with perhaps a three-foot thickness of solid brick between—was built against the wall of the house next door.

Had there been a faint movement behind that wall?

"Forgive me again, Mr. Lewis. Why didn't you go in the coach?"

"Frankly, because I distrusted this moneylender who called himself Mr. Caliban and offered too low a rate of interest. In fact, I wrote to him that I distrusted him; that I should keep the appointment, but investigate him first. I didn't keep the appointment. But I saw the coachman."

"You saw the coachman?" Darwent demanded. "When?"

"Why, on the night you speak of. In Hyde Park."

"Come, sir! Then you must have seen me knocked over

the head and abducted, near the rails of the park on the Piccadilly side?"

"Upon my soul, no! I was at the other end of the park. Behind bushes, with my horse tethered to a tree. I had decided not to go, yet it seemed unfair to send *no* word to the moneylender. I had elected to speak to the coachman; yet . . ."

"Continue!"

"I saw the coach, blue with yellow wheels, coming towards me. It was dusk, but I saw the coachman clearly. He wore a dirty brown muffler round his face, and a low-crowned hat. What turned my stomach was his cloak."

"His cloak?"

"A dark cloak," said Lewis, "stretching to his ankles, making him seem thinner and bigger; yet it was moldy. No, I am not fanciful! The cloak was spotted in places with green mold, as though from a graveyard."

"Ghost coach!" Darwent muttered grimly.

"I beg your pardon?"

"I said, 'ghost coach,' Mr. Lewis, and never understood why I said it! It was that cloak, never noticed except at the back of the mind. Yes! And it explains why the coachman attacked me: intending to attack you. You were suspicious; you might be dangerous; they must treat you as a prisoner, until they found out what you knew. But the graveyard mold . . ."

"It came from no graveyard," cried Lewis. "You have seen such cloaks. They hang for years in a damp cupboard, gathering mildew, until some sporting buck takes them out for a jape or a masquerade.

"The driver of that coach," he went on in a high voice, "was a gentleman masquerading as a jarvey. And what of his partner, Mr. Caliban? I knew no more; I ran from there. King of Jermyn Street, an honest moneylender, has since supplied me with a loan. Besides," and Lewis shuddered again, "it seemed to me I half-recognized the coachman . . ."

"*You recognized him?* Who was he?"

"Stop! I mean only a suggestion, trick of gesture, perhaps an illusion . . ."

A rap at the door, heralding the appearance of Alfred with a letter on a salver, drew a curse from Darwent. But one glance at the letter made him pause.

"It came by hand, my lord," said the footman, "and it is marked 'urgent.' "

The letter, Tillotson Lewis noticed, was rather grubby; its

149

address was squeezed uphill in a half-illiterate handwriting. As Darwent snatched it from the salver, Lewis (into whose thoughts we need not enter) saw that its red wax bore the Crown-and-Broad-Arrow, the seal of the Bow Street runners.

"Forgive me," Darwent muttered.

Breaking the seal and opening out the letter, he glanced down it. His features hardened, perhaps with satisfaction or perhaps with surprise, and then the same cold smile drew back his lips.

"Alfred," he said quietly.

"Yes, my lord?"

"Are you any judge of a sword?"

Alfred smiled a little. He did not mention that his wide shoulders and fine calves had been an asset in the Dragoons as well as here.

"Yes, my lord."

"Good!" said Darwent, fishing a long key out of his waist-coat pocket. "In Garter Lane, off Covent Garden, you will find a fencing school, now shut, with the name 'D'Arvent,' over the door. Everyone knows that all good fencing masters must be French. This key opens the door."

"Yes, my lord?"

Darwent's look changed to one of unholy pleasure.

"Pay no heed to foils or dummy weapons. Choose me a pair of sabers—if the blades be not sharp enough, have them set at a razor maker's—and—yes! a pair of smallswords and a pair of rapiers as well. On your way back; take the carriage; you had better stop at Locke's in Oxford Street and buy me a case of pistols."

Alfred's eye lighted up. "Very good, my lord."

"And . . . Alfred. It will not be necessary to mention this matter to my wife. The weapons had better be hidden where she is unlikely to find them, preferably downstairs."

"Very good, my lord. Are there any other instructions?"

"For the moment, no."

The door closed behind him. Tillotson Lewis felt his rigid shirt collar grow damp and soft with heat.

"Do I understand," demanded Lewis, "that you have changed your mind? That you will meet Major Sharpe after all?"

"Oh, no. I won't meet Sharpe." Darwent's gray eyes had become so intense, so hot with wrath, that the swelling pupils seemed to make them look black. "But there will be a meeting, my friend. There will be a meeting."

"Then what will you say to Alvanley? I told you a while ago that Sharpe's second must be here at any minute! What will you say to Alvanley?"

Darwent, turning toward the mantelpiece, whipped round again.

"Alvanley?" he repeated. "Haven't I heard that name before?"

Lewis stared at him.

"Gad, I should think so! Lord Alvanley seconded you for nomination to White's. What's more, he's one of the few dandy-lions with real ability and wit. And you must trust him a good deal."

"Trust him?"

"Confound it!" muttered Lewis. "You permitted Will Alvanley to escort Lady Darwent to the opera last night, didn't you?"

This was the point at which the door opened, its latch being only partly caught, and Caroline came in. She was at her most stately, with a high color.

"Good afternoon, Mr. Lewis. —Were you discussing, my lord, the state of morals in the private boxes at the opera?"

"To be quite frank, madam," replied Darwent, with a low bow, "we were not. And shall the innocent flee where no man pursueth?"

"Tonight, I think, you go with *me* to the opera?"

"I go with you," said Darwent, having a kind of rapture in his face, "because of your charm, and wit, and the beauty that turns my head; and also, I must confess it," he looked at the letter, "in the hope of a very bloody meeting."

"Meeting!" exclaimed Caroline.

In the open doorway behind Darwent towered the figure of Thomas, the second footman.

"Forgive me, my lord," said Thomas. "But Lord Alvanley is downstairs. He begs the favor of a word with you."

The master of the house drew himself up.

"Ask Lord Alvanley," he said politely, "whether he will be good enough to come upstairs."

151

CHAPTER XVI

Riot at the Opera

As the orchestra soared into the overture of *Il Ratto di Proserpina*, with its clangor of brass softened and without too much tyranny of violins, the Marquess and Marchioness of Darwent groped into the gloom of box number forty-five on the third tier.

Outside the Italian opera in the Haymarket, more properly called the King's Theatre, faint mist had long succeeded rain. Carriages, bright with armorial bearings, crushed together in thick mud to pile up before the doors.

Link boys, who were usually middle-aged men, wove a pattern of torches as carriage steps were let down. In the Haymarket, as far up as the little shop where you might buy the Regent's own snuff mixture, the crowd swayed and grew more restive.

"But where is she?" shouted a voice, affectionate with the loving kindness of liquor. "Where's the princess?"

"Back!" yelled a member of the Bow Street horse patrol, clattering his horse's hind quarters into the crowd. "Back, d'ye hear?"

"The poor little princess: ain't she a-coming?"

"Yes! Soon enough! Back!"

The other voice wept. There could have been no greater compliment to the pious sedateness of the opera than that nineteen-year-old Princess Charlotte—only child of a hate-marriage between the Prince Regent and good-natured, dirty Caroline of Brunswick—should be permitted to attend it. Princess Charlotte had expressed eagerness to hear this new singer who had been praised so lyrically by the *Times,* the *Morning Post,* and the *Theatrical Examiner.*

"But who's the damn singer?" growled another voice, as a stocky gentleman with flaming red hair jumped down from a carriage. The crowd recognized him and greeted him with a derisive shout of "Red Herrings!" which he acknowledged with wolfish tolerance.

Full court dress, of course, was *de rigueur* here. In addition to complete black clothes, with gold or diamond knee buckles, Red Herrings wore small wrist ruffles and a trumpery court sword. He was Lord Yarmouth, whose mother had been another mistress of the Regent; and, many years later, he was to appear as the villain in a novel named *Vanity Fair*.

"Herrings dear," said his wife, nearly falling flat on her face as he handed her clumsily out of the carriage, "the singer is called Madame Vestris. She is Italian, but English-born. They say she has the wonderfullest contralto since Catalini retired to Paris."

"So-and-so to her contralto," said Lord Yarmouth. "Is she goodlookin'?"

"My poor Herrings, the girl is only eighteen. She is married to that divine Frenchman, M. Armand Vestris, who teaches us how to waltz."

"Eighteen, eh?" repeated Lord Yarmouth, and licked his lips. Then he stared. "I say! There's Ned Firebrace, six feet three and lookin' like thunder, with a horsewhip under his clock. What's up tonight?"

Others wondered this as well. Yet there seemed no reason for it. Inside, the benches of the pit—divided only by a center aisle called Fops' Alley—were occupied by as quiet a group as you might find inside a church. At the opera you did not hear, as you heard at Covent Garden or Drury Lane, the vulgar voices of orange girls with their: *"Chase an orange, chase a nonpareil!"* Or, from the other side, *"Buy a bill of the play, buy a bill of the play!"*

Perhaps it was only a reflection of the Italian temperament backstage. Lamplighters and sceneshifters screamed at each other, gesticulating under stage moonlight, which looked like real moonlight. Even the new star, slim and beautiful Madame Vestris, with her dark and shining eyes whose soulfulness seemed to express all the mystery of woman, let the tears roll unchecked down her cheeks.

Her husband danced about her in agony.

"Que tu es belle, chérie," moaned M. Vestris, who would not have to work any longer if his wife scored a success. "M'm, m'm, m'm, m'm, m'm!" repeated M. Vestris, kissing her hand each time he said, " 'm'm.' " "Mais tu es triste, ma petite. Pourquoi? Qu'est-ce que tu dis?"

Elizabetta Vestris raised liquid eyes, and lowered the thrilling voice.

"Je dis goddam," she whispered.

"Mais . . . ma pauvre petite! Pourquoi goddam?"

"C'est ma gorge," sadly replied Elizabetta, touching her breast and indicating what size she thought it ought to be. "Je n'ai pas de gorge. I am not enough develop yet. Oh misérable!"

And then, even as she moaned in self-pity, her mood changed in a flash.

"The princess!" she cried. In her dark trailing robes as Proserpina, Queen of the Underworld, she flew toward the peephole in the curtain. The orchestra had struck up "God Save the King."

Outside, beyond the peephole in the curtain, stretched the stage's immense apron, ringed by a half oval of coal-oil lamps in glass containers. The royal box, of course, reared up inside the apron. Princess Charlotte, bowing and smiling, looked almost handsome against the six frights who had been appointed her maids of honor.

And the occupants of the boxes rose up as one to bow or curtsy.

Of these boxes, set in a horseshoe shape of four high tiers nearly to the roof, sixty-eight out of a hundred were privately owned. They were decorated in white and gilt, with a green laurel pattern in bas-relief on each panel. A small ivory disk, stamped with your name, number, and the season, admitted you to a roomy, draped box, which held six plush chairs as well as a stand bearing oranges (usually rotten) and a small couch.

"Ah," breathed M. Armand Vestris, "quelle vue magnifique!"

In the boxes of the first tier might be seen the daughters of the Duchess of Argyle, said to be the most beautiful girls in London. In the next box sat the equally lovely Marchioness of Stafford, with her daughter, Lady Elizabeth Gore. That belle enfant whom everyone loved, Lady Cowper, was regrettably afflicted with a fit of hiccups.

There was "Monk" Lewis, the moneyed author who had written a novel which pure taste condemned as "lewd and lascivious," and whose crablike eyes now stared at Lady Caroline Lamb. In the box of the Princess Esterházy sat another man named Lewis, Tillotson Lewis, looking steadily up at the box in which the Marchioness of Darwent would presently appear.

So did the Hon. Edward Firebrace, his wide-set teeth fixed at a grin, in the box otherwise occupied only by his new flame, Harriette Wilson, and his old friend, Jemmy Fletcher.

154

There was Scrope Davies, who had once spread the story (untrue, by the way) that Lord Byron wore his hair in curl-papers at night. There (positively) was the great Beau Brummell, thin as a thief, brown hair brushed up to a peak: edging toward ruin, forced to skip over into France the following year. George Brummell had played the fool so long that he had become one now.

And so they rose up, in a sort of feathered silken thunder, as the orchestra played "God Save the King." Faces were mere white blurs, set amid gilt and white and green box frames, against a darkness tempered only by the semicircle of footlights. Gentlemen's white-gloved hands with quizzing glasses lifted, ladies' hands waggling plume-feathered fans, diffused gently over the theater an air like the breath out of a wine vault.

The "God Save the King" faded away. The orchestra swept into the overture from *Proserpina*. Amid much rustling on carpetless boards, the audience sat down.

Caroline and Darwent, who had been waiting in the dim-lit little passage at the back of the third tier, hastened into box number forty-five. In the box adjoining it, separated only by a very thick curtain, sat the three leading patronesses of Almack's: Lady Jersey, Lady Castlereagh, and Lady Sefton.

"My dear Sarah! My dear Emily!" appealed little Lady Sefton. "Acknowledge, now, that your first attitude towards Lord Darwent, when we sent him a card for Almack's, was the correct one!"

Lady Jersey, cost what it might, would never lower her air of a theatrical tragedy queen.

"You are very young, my dear," she smiled.

"Own, now," pleaded Lady Sefton, "that your subsequent suspicions have been baseless, and unworthy."

"Baseless, now!" exclaimed Lady Jersey. "When the wretched man keeps *two* of them under one roof? Oh, filthy!"

"Oh, disgustful!" murmured Lady Castlereagh, who was wearing all the diamonds which had caused such envy. "Nevertheless, Sarah, it shows an initiative which is much to be desired."

"My dear Emily," declared Lady Jersey, peeling an orange and throwing the peel over the edge into the darkened pit, "I do not hold Lord Darwent guilty or even partially guilty. In fact, the blame was entirely Caroline's."

"Caroline's?" Lady Sefton repeated incredulously.

Then came the interruption.

Out of the darkened pit a man's voice, almost lunatic in fury, exploded with an effect as shattering as the explosion of a guardsman's grenade.

" '*Oo the 'ell*," it shouted, "*throwed orange peel on the top of me fornicatin' 'ead?*"

Dead silence, except for noises as though some person or persons had tried to throttle the speaker. It might have been funny, but it was not. No rowdy catcall was hurled back. To box holders, the members of the pit—that buttress of middle-class sedulous apes—seemed momentarily to have lost their senses.

The orchestra, thrown off beat in dim light, slipped again into the smooth iridescent stream of Mozart-and-water. Behind the scenes, old and experienced sceneshifters remembered how few precautions had even been taken here against riot or fire.

"Really," drawled Lady Jersey in a louder voice, and threw more orange peel over the plush box ledge, "they should be more careful to whom they issue tickets. What was I saying?"

"Caroline!" whispered Lady Castlereagh.

"After all, my dear! When she attempts to cuckold her husband on the very first night they are to be together . . ."

"When?" asked Lady Castlereagh, amid a rattle of shoulder diamonds. "Where? By whom?"

"Here," replied Lady Jersey calmly. "And—" she pointed down to a pit box on the ground floor at the left-hand tier, "—and there. Caroline was *almost* indiscreet. The man was Lord Alvanley."

"Lord Alvanley!" almost screamed Lady Castlereagh. All three heads had twitched round toward the door at the back of the darkened box. A narrow vertical line of light opened there, and Alvanley's round good-humored face appeared.

"Your servant," he said. "Your sole wag-dog keeps guard."

For none of the three ladies, tonight, was squired by her own husband.

"I have a small difficulty," smiled Lord Alvanley, intimating it was a very small difficulty. "I shall return at once."

And the box door closed.

It was less warm and stuffy in this passage behind the boxes. Alvanley could hear above his head the stamp and shuffle of late-comers pressing into their boxes on the fourth tier; above that, there was a small gallery for servants and those Italians who had come to live in the Haymarket to be near their beloved opera.

156

Alvanley's smile faded, leaving his face in its usual comic expression, because of a button nose into which he could get hardly any snuff.

"Can't be done," Alvanley muttered. And then: "Got to be done."

Stripping off his white gloves, he slapped them into the palm of his left hand and then stuck them between waistcoat and shirt frill. Almost idly he drew the court sword from its gold scabbard. It was fashioned after the smallsword of the last century: hardly more than an inch wide: no edges but sharp tipped for play with the point: showy, brittle, useless in any hand but that of a master swordsman.

There was a little *snick* of disgust as Alvanley dropped it back into the sheath. At the same time a booming voice carried along the passage.

"Will?"

Since the curve of the back boxes was a half oval, and the front wall of the King's Theatre was a straight line, you could hear a person before you could see him. The windows, beside each of which they had fastened a "safety" lamp, threw a dim white light on the dirty floor.

"Will?" the voice called again.

"Ned?" inquired Alvanley, assuming a dapper air and taking out his snuffbox.

The Hon. Edward Firebrace, nephew of Major Sharpe and formerly a cornet in the 10th Hussars, approached with a leisurely step. He wore a purple cloak, ankle-length, with a high black collar fastened at the neck. Though his two brushes of side whiskers were of a lighter sandy color than his uncle's, his hair at the head-parting was brushed up into a kind of large pomaded spring, coiled along the parting. He was six feet three inches tall, with a reach like the African ape exhibited by M. Saumarez at the Pantheon.

And so he came forward, showing his wide-set teeth in a smile.

"You must have been disguised," he remarked. "Couldn't find you at all, until you looked in at Lady Jersey's box."

"Oh?" inquired Alvanley, tapping his forefinger on the lid of the snuffbox. "Is there any reason why you should wish to see me?"

"Reason?"

"Yes; reason."

Though Firebrace tried to keep his suavity, his wide-set teeth showed through.

157

"This morning, or this afternoon, you carried my uncle's challenge to Lord Darwent. You agreed to act as my uncle's second. . . ."

"Under the code, I had no choice. But I wished it all to the devil."

"Well? What happened?"

"Lord Darwent very courteously refused, and stated his reasons: one of them being that he must first settle accounts with his greatest enemy. I thought them good reasons, and carried them back to your uncle, who agreed. The challenge has been withdrawn."

"Withd . . ."

From underneath his purple cloak fell several lengths of horsewhip, together with its lash end. The horsewhip handle Firebrace still clutched in his fist under the cloak. They could hear, through thin partitions, the overture rising to its close.

"My uncle grows old," Firebrace said dryly. "Old men tend to cowardice. So *I* shall go into the box, Will. I mean to give Darwent a touch of this." He rattled the whip coils on the floor. "If he suffers it meekly, before the whole opera—well! If he calls me out—well! You have seen my sáber-play."

Suddenly, as the shadows towered behind him, you became aware of Firebrace's height and his immense length of arm. His saber-play was all slash and viciousness, to beat down an opponent as Firebrace might have beaten him down with a quarterstaff.

"In any case, Will," he added, "my family honor has its due."

"Your family honor," repeated Alvanley, with a curious inflection.

"At cards, Ned," Alvanley went on, trying to put snuff into his microscopic nose and spilling most of it in spots over his face, "we expect to find only one ace of trumps in the pack . . ."

The whip coils rattled slightly.

"But when the Colonel of your regiment found two aces of trumps, one on the table and one in your sleeve, he was very easy with you in allowing you to resign your commission. Now if you were to kill Darwent, or even humiliate him badly, High Authority would get you back your commission. Eh?"

Firebrace's hand made a short, sharp movement.

The little peer, coolly dusting snuff from his cherubic face with a lace handkerchif, did not even appear to notice.

"Be advised by me, Ned," he suggested. "Don't touch Darwent. If you won't agree for a good reason, you may agree for a bad." Then Alvanley's tone changed. "Did you look in at the pit tonight?"

Firebrace took a step forward, and stopped.

"The pit? No. Why?"

"It's full of prize fighters," said Alvanley, dusting his cravat. "Damme, *you* talk of disguise. I've counted two dozen cropped skulls under more disguises than would fill a shop. Have you forgotten the O.P. riots at Covent Garden?"

"But men like Cribb or Belcher, or even Randall . . ."

"No; they wouldn't touch it. Any more than they'd take the managers' bribes at Covent Garden. But d'ye think I don't know Broad Henchman, when I backed him for two thou in a mill with the Game Chicken: and he fought a cross at that? Or Dan Sparkler? Or the Nottingham Peach?"

Alvanley's voice went up a little.

"They're the scum of the prize ring," he said. "In about five minutes, if not less, this theater will explode as though they'd dug mines under a fort."

The warm passage was silent, for an instant, except for the rustling of gowns and the rush of music.

"But what's the game?" demanded Firebrace. "Nobody's against the Italians. Stop, though! At the O.P. riots somebody did set up a yell against foreign singers. But that was a pretext."

"So is this a pretext," said Alvanley. "To kill Darwent."

Firebrace's eyes widened. "To kill . . ."

"In my opinion, which is only an opinion," said Alvanley, coolly replacing handkerchief and snuffbox, "he'll be found dead of a broken neck or spine at the end of the mill. There was a dead man at Covent Garden, you remember. Who saw what happened? Who could set the blame, in all that confusion? *This* trick would be worthy of Old Q., if Old Q. weren't dead and damned. It was arranged——"

"By the person you call his greatest enemy?"

"Yes. A man dressed like a coachman out of the graveyard." For a moment Alvanley was silent. "Ned, he's in a trap and he can't get out. For God's sake, don't make it worse!"

Firebrace threw back his purple cloak, so that the wings were behind his shoulders. Slowly he coiled up the horsewhip.

"And does my lord,"—there was a grit of hatred behind Firebrace's wide-set teeth—"does my lord know he's in a trap?"

"Yes. I warned him on the staircase tonight. But he merely said . . ."

"Said what?"

"It was his only opportunity to meet the coachman face to face."

Firebrace strolled over to a position beside Alvanley, so that they were both facing in the same direction.

"Oh, he may meet the coachman," smiled Firebrace. "He may meet me as well. Let's see what happens."

His arm snapped back and lashed forward, sending the whip full-length down the passage to crack like a small arm as it curled round an iron joist.

"I wonder," he said, "what Darwent and his dear wife are chattering about now?"

Clang went the last cymbal clash as the overture ended. There was a spattering of applause, which ran through the old wooden shell like rain on a roof.

In box forty-five, Caroline and Darwent were speaking much as they had been speaking five minutes before, when they entered the box. Even at that time their feelings had become dangerously intense.

"Will you look at me?" asked Caroline.

Darwent turned his head.

Caroline wore—deliberately?—the same white satin gown, cut very high at the waist and very low horizontally across the bodice, with the flaming ruby at her breast and the red sash round her waist, which she had worn on the night of the Newgate wedding.

And, now that Darwent turned to look at her, they could not meet each other's eyes.

"You don't love her," said Caroline quietly. "You never have loved her. While you were brooding in that prison, you—you invented an Arcadian cloud cuckooland where there were never any cares; and you put her into it. It was never true."

"Caroline, I . . ."

"What I say is true! You know it! And has ever a woman been forced to shame herself as I have?"

Desperately her companion tried to speak in a light tone.

"If you mean my uninvited visit to your bathroom . . ."

"Oh, no," said Caroline with an unsteady smile. "I give you leave to do that at any time it pleases you. And more! But . . ."

Color reddened her cheeks, hardly visible in the darkened

160

box; but, as though she felt the rush of blood to her face, she put up her hands against her cheeks.

"But *I*!" she said, with self-loathing. "*I* was so hoity-toity, so sure my feelings were above other women's. Men were odious, and I could not endure the touch of one. *My* will power was supreme! My will power would conquer all! Then I must meet you, and my will power was nothing."

Caroline's voice faltered. They sat side by side in two plush chairs well back from the box ledge. Though Darwent tried to stifle her outburst, she rushed on.

"In the ears of everyone—in public!—I acknowledged I loved you. I could have vowed, Dick, the pincers of hell would not make me say that. But I did; I'm glad I did; I'm proud of it. Because . . . haven't you understood from the beginning . . you and I are two of a kind?"

"Two of a kind?"

"You're a rebel. So am I. But I daren't say so."

Then Caroline sat up straight, throwing back her curls.

"What do you believe, Dick?" she asked with soft, fierce intensity.

"In what particular respect?"

"Oh, it's not an absurd question! What does this world mean to you? What do you believe?"

Their box faced directly across toward the drop curtain, at about the middle of the tier. Darwent was vaguely conscious of the orchestra playing the overture, that there had been a brief clamor over someone's throwing orange peel into the pit; little more.

" 'We hold these truths to be self-evident,' " he said, " 'That all men are created equal. That they are endowed by their Creator with certain inalienable rights; and that among these rights are life, liberty, and the pursuit of happiness.' "

Darwent paused.

The slow majesty of the words seemed to hang there like banners, visual images, before they faded away.

" 'Created equal,' " repeated Caroline. "I hate that!"

"Yes; I feared you would."

"But what matter does it make," she cried, "if you and I believe in . . . in . . ."

"The pursuit of happiness?"

"In happiness!" said Caroline. "You would free men. I would free women from being bond slaves: yes, and give them rights equal to men! But this is only illusion." She spoke

161

in a detached, hopeless voice. "Dick, Dick, when will you learn that you can't fight society?"

"I have begun to learn it already."

"Then what will you do?"

"When this affair is over . . ."

"Unless you are dead, of course."

"Yes; unless I am dead. I now own an estate in Kent, with shallow streams and soft brownish-green woods. I spent my boyhood there; I loved it." Darwent paused. His longing for Caroline had gone almost beyond control. "If I could take you there, beyond sight of the world . . ."

"I could live there with you forever," said Caroline. Very quietly she added: "Could Dolly Spencer?"

He did not reply.

"Please believe," insisted Caroline, "I have nothing against her. I—I like her. This evening, when she asked if she could try on some of my gowns, I said she could have half a dozen for her own if she promised not to get out of bed until tomorrow. But could she spend a fortnight in the country, away from London and the playhouses, without screaming from boredom? Have you two anything in common, except—what I . . ."

Again Darwent turned round.

This time he did not realize that Caroline was so close to him. His cheek brushed hers. Then they were in each other's arms, and the ensuing moments closely resembled madness or fury.

"Damn you," Darwent presently said in a choked voice. "I understand you now. I should have understood you long ago."

"Un—understand me?"

"Cold and arrogant? Your trouble is that you're too stimulating. You're a wine that has three stages of headiness. You're Madam Circe and Mother Eve. You're never placid; you're fierce-kiss-and-run-away; you're angel and incubus, enough to—"

"If this is your method of damning me," whispered Caroline, "go on and on and on and on!"

"No! Let's be fair." He seized her arms, and made her sit upright. "This morning," he added, "I told Dolly I was in love with her."

"But you didn't mean it?" A pause. "Did you?"

"I meant it when I said it, yes!" Darwent smote his fist against his knee. "What am, I, what is any man, but a weather

162

vane sported at by his own folly? Yet all the time, Caroline, you were—there. If I told you the same thing now . . ."

"But that's all that matters, isn't it?"

"No. It is not."

"Why not?"

Darwent braced himself.

"I also said to her: if I win free from my present marriage," —he felt Caroline shiver through their clasped hands—"will you honor me by becoming Marchioness of Darwent? Caroline dear, I don't break promises."

Clang smote the cymbal beat as the orchestra soared to the end of the overture. A spattering of applause, a vision of multitudinous hands clapping at innumerable box openings amid the fire-wink of jewels, animated the theater.

"Quixotry again," said Caroline.

"I beg your pardon?"

She did not snatch her hands away, as he had believed she would. Caroline sat motionless, her blue eyes fixed on him; and he could never penetrate to the depths of them.

"How amusing!" she said, and choked back a sob. "One of the first things I l'liked about you was that absurd quixotry. Do you remember Newgate, Dick?"

"Yes."

"You were chained to the wall and as weak as a cat; you had no chance whatever. Yet you insulted Jack Buckstone, in calm and measured language, though you knew he'd strike you senseless in an instant."

Caroline's cheeks were flushed and her eyes sparkled with tears.

"My liking for quixotry has returned to me, I fear," she said. " 'I don't break promises,' you say. As though that were all in the world. Do you love her, Dick? That's the only question? Do you?"

"No. When you spoke of my brooding about an Arcadia . . . that was true."

"Then I won't let you have her," said Caroline. "Whatever I have to do, however low I have to sink, I won't let you have her. I swear this before God."

"Caroline, you must . . ."

Both of them, eerily caught by some subtle sense of wrongness, instinctively glanced toward the stage. Ahead of them, some distance away, was the huge apron with its oval ring of footlights. Well behind it, the green curtain trembled on its rise.

163

The music crept out again, quivering with strings that breathed the melancholy of the Underworld and its dark life. The pit, a motionless blur, scarcely moved. Down the center of the pit benches, as far as the orchestra, lay Fops' Alley.

Yet an intimately sensitive place is the theater. Even thoughts seem to move and have ripples. And these thoughts were ugly and dangerous.

As the curtain creaked up—revealing a moonlit glade which to Darwent in some way seemed familiar—the music quivered up with it.

Two singers, a tenor and a soprano, glided out on the apron. Stage moonlight strengthened, glimmering on leaves. The soprano, in dark clothes like her companion, lifted her voice to sing . . .

A storm of hisses full-voiced and vicious, burst out of the pit and seethed up on the stage like tide on a beach. The woman, her hand at her throat, stopped in mid-flight.

On the left-hand side of the pit, a bulky-bodied man with a thick neck jumped to his feet. On the right-hand side, another man jumped up; and a third followed.

And the third man, with a voice like a bull, made himself heard above the determined rush of the orchestra.

"Let's have native nightingales, not foreign screech owls! Down with Vestris! Kill her!"

◇   CHAPTER XVII   ◇

How Five of the Fancy Fought Two Men's Steel

Darwent had sprung to his feet, his hand on the box ledge. His eyes moved, left and right, across the pit.

He stood with his left side toward Caroline. Something in his pose, something of the way in which his right hand moved toward the trumpery court sword at his left hip, filled her with new terrors.

"Dick!"

"Eh?" He was not even listening; he was studying the pit.

"Dick, what's happening? Madame Vestris is not even *on* in that scene. What is it?"

"Nothing that need trouble you, my dear."

The roar of the pit, to Darwent's ears at least, was almost equaled by the exclamations of outrage from the boxes. In the adjoining box, Lady Castlereagh screamed. The very old Marquess of Anglesea was heard to quaver out, *"You down there, fellow—!"* and an orange came sailing out of half-gloom to burst on the box wall behind him.

"Send the foreign doxy back to Naples!"

"Kill her!"

But the snarlers of the pit were not ready, not yet in action. The general effect was that they were undressing. Greatcoats, fustian coats, wigs, and top hats flew wide. Darwent watched for each emergence of a cropped head.

Every member of the Fancy had worn a cropped head since the day when "Gentleman" Jackson beat Dan Mendoza by gripping him by the hair while smashing his face. They ruled it no foul, though some of us still hold it was the dirtiest of fouls. In any case, the heads stood out white in dimness.

"Her Royal Highness!" bawled a voice. "Make way for Her Royal Highness!"

Four officers of the Life Guards, their red sleeves and steel breastplates agleam under gold braid, quickly whisked away Princess Charlotte and her escort. In the momentary pause after that crying of her name—the mob liked Princess Charlotte, poor girl—nobody noticed a figure which glided from the wings and out on the apron to the very footlights.

The newcomer was not much more than eighteen. She wore heavy black, with black head veils. Tearing off the head veils, jerking open the costume at the throat, she displayed a pallid beauty of face against the stage moonlight and foliage far beyond her.

"I am Elizabetta Vestris," she cried.

What arrested them was partly that dazzle of fascination which springs across a stage and fuses at once with an audience. It was partly the strength and yet softness of her voice: effortless, yet rising gently to every nook of the theater.

"You think I am not English, then?" she asked. "Let me show you!"

She spoke some inaudible words to the orchestra. Straightening up, throwing back her head and hair, she stretched her arms wide. In dead silence the violins wove their snare, the horns crept in beneath; as words soared aloft above the melody, it is a sober fact that not a soul moved. For you may impress men and women with opera. But you can touch their hearts only with a simple song.

165

Oh, believe me, if all those endearing young charms,
Which I gaze on so fondly today,
Were to fade by tomorrow and flee from my arms
Like a fairy gift fading away.......

Six years later, when Elizabetta Vestris was the most famous singer-cum-courtesan in England, there were those who swore that never had she sung so well as she sang one brief verse on that night in '15.

Thou shouldst still be adored, as this moment thou art,
Let thy loveliness fade as it will . . .

Then silence splintered to bits.

Across the song cut the raucous, strident note of a post horn. The man with the bull's voice (he was Dan Sparkler, one of the heavies) roared again.

"That's the foreign screech owl! Why should she have *our* money?"

The post horn blared again. Somebody threw another peeled orange.

But this time it was a rotten orange. It struck Elizabetta Vestris between neck and breast, spattering wide, so that she faltered and stepped back. The spitefulness of it turned that act into an act of obscenity. From then on, it was war.

In the pit a sober-sided young stationer's assistant suddenly whirled round and landed a clinker of a right fist in Dan Sparkler's face, drawing Dan's claret and flinging him asprawl. The Sparkler smashed him down and jumped on him, of course; but another voice, from a second-tier box where Lord Yarmouth of the fiery hair stood with his fists on his hips, added to the din.

"Did you ever," shouted his lordship, "see such a set of damned rascals in your life?"

"Like to get a wipe over the eye, ginger?" a crophead shouted back.

"Ho! Would I?" demanded the Earl of Yarmouth, instantly tearing off his coat and turning to slide down the box pillars into the fight. On the other side of the theater Colonel Dan Mackinnon, being in a pit box, had only to tear off his own coat and hurl himself over the box ledge.

Still Darwent, high above it in the third tier, did not move. Caroline ran round to the other side of him, seizing at his sleeve.

166

"Dick! Listen to me!"

"Well?" He did not look round.

"What did Will Alvanley tell you on the stairs here tonight?" Caroline demanded. Her intuition flew even ahead of her wits. "What was in that letter you had this afternoon, with the Bow-Street-runner seal? Don't deny you had it; Meg told me!"

"Did she, by George!"

"At first you wanted me to come here. Then, just before we entered, you said . . ." Caroline paused.

"You'll be quite safe, my dear, if you follow my orders. What is more, you can help me. Will you?"

"Yes! Yes! Yes!"

"I want you to watch the right-hand side of the pit, as divided by the central aisle. That's where they're struggling," —a woman's scream pierced up, shaking Caroline's nerves— "to get into Fops' Alley and up to the way out under these boxes. But you can see the division?"

"Yes, of course!"

"Watch the cropheads. If they begin to gather near the south door, the one leading up the stairs to the boxes—*thére* —then tell me. I'll watch the door on the north."

"No!" cried Caroline, her eyes inadvertently straying to the stage. "Not fire!"

Under a weird whiteness of stage moonlight, with every lamp turned high, the pit was a fighting turmoil. One crophead, breaking through the orchestra, had hauled himself up on the apron.

Elizabetta Vestris, who had retreated five steps, would not retreat a step further. The crophead's foot crushed a lamp, splintering glass underneath and sending a zigzag streak of fire across tinder-dry boards. Three burly sceneshifters, each carrying the regulation red fire bucket, had already run out from the wings. The first of them, flinging the contents of the bucket in the crophead's face, kicked him below the belt with a hobnailed shoe. The two others sluiced water across the blaze, dousing it in a spitefulness of oily black smoke. The crophead, though barely able to move, launched a roundarm at his adversary and deliberately kicked over another footlight.

"Dick!" said Caroline in the third-tier box. "There's Mr. Mulberry!"

"Where?"

Caroline was pointing downward.

"The aisle end of the second bench from the back. He's

167

got some kind of wet cloth round his head to—to sober himself. He's pointing . . ."

Darwent saw where Hubert Mulberry was pointing. He followed the direction of that stabbing finger.

And then, at long last, he saw the coachman.

The coachman, directly underneath in the pit at the very edge of the way out from Fops' Alley, was staring upward. Tall, lean-shouldered, he stood rocklike in that confusion. Against mad moonlight every detail of the nightmare was kindled or silhouetted: the long cape spotted with green mold, the low-crowned hat, the triumphant eyes above the brown shielding muffler.

Bending over the box ledge, Darwent made a trumpet of his hands so that the coachman would be certain to hear him above the inferno of noise.

"I am here," he shouted, looking straight into the coachman's eyes, "and here I stay. Come and get me!"

In Darwent's voice, for the first time since his meeting with Buckstone, there was again a murderous loving kindness.

The coachman nodded. Already tall, he now seemed gigantic against the distortion of lights. Up went his right hand, high above the crowd, making cryptic signals.

"Dick," Caroline interposed quietly, "they're beginning to move towards the south door to the stairs up to the boxes."

"Yes. I thought they would. And this is your time to go, my dear—don't worry! Alvanley has arranged it all."

Caroline's face was almost as white as her gown.

"Dick, those . . . those prize fighters haven't anything at all against Madame Vestris, have they? It's all a demonstration, arranged by the coachman, to throw dust in people's eyes?" Her voice rose. "Dick, what do they really want?"

And again Caroline, being a woman and therefore sensible, felt maddened by the look of pleasure on her companion's face.

"To be quite frank with you, my dear: I'm afraid they want *me.*"

"That coachman will be up here?"

"Yes."

"And with—with his bruisers with him?"

"Yes."

"You haven't a chance! Any of those men . . . have you seen their arms? . . . could kill you with one hand!"

"Quite probably, my dear."

"And what," screamed Caroline, "have you got to defend

168

yourself?" She saw his right hand dart across to his left side. "Only a little small-sword . . . it hasn't even got edges, has it?"

"No."

"They'll break it like a toy! Dick, I won't let you do it! I won't leave!"

"You have no choice, Caroline. Don't you hear what's happening?"

For a few seconds they had been conscious of a vast irregular shuffling—mingled with women's lamentations or cries of protest—moving in procession, south to north, along the passage behind the boxes.

There was a light knock at the door, which opened immediately.

Lord Alvanley stepped in. The round-faced little peer was smiling, his open snuffbox in his left hand.

"My dear Darwent," he said, as one who utters congratulations, "you were quite right. They're trying an attack on the upper boxes from the south stairs, because the stairs are wider there. Most of the linkmen attached to the theater are guarding the north door. We can get the ladies down quite comfortably."

"Good!" said Darwent. "What about the other tiers of boxes?"

"Warned, my boy. Warned. But all the attacks, except *here*, will be dummy attacks."

From the stage opened a yellow eye of fire, illuminating Alvanley as he lifted a pinch of snuff and really reached his nostrils. There was a heavy crash, amid screaming, as a wooden flat fell. But the red buckets swung in a chain: killing that blaze, strangling it as acrid smoke drifted across the pit.

"And now, my lady?" Alvanley said politely to Caroline.

"I won't go! I won't!"

Through the open box door, at the back, Darwent could see shuffling or hurrying a parade of ladies. Most of them, as they passed the box, glanced in. He saw them dimly, in a haunted light, as though pages flickered in a dim-colored album.

Lady Jersey, head high, marched like Queen Boadicea. Lady Castlereagh, her blue eyes not now fearful but very curious, glanced at Caroline and then at Darwent and then at the couch, before someone shoved forward her diamond-glistening shoulders.

Raising laments about her husband and her dog, little Lady Sefton was hurried forward too. Pretty Miss O'Neil, the female

169

star of Drury Lane, was openly weeping; not because of the fight, but because she had been interrupted in her first visit to the box of a real nobleman.

"I won't go, I tell you!" Caroline was insisting. "They'll kill him!"

"They may not find it," smiled Alvanley, "quite so easy as they think." He looked at Darwent. "But he will need help, I believe."

"I am much beholden to you," said Darwent. "But I think not."

A man's voice, muffled and far away at the south end of the passage, rose above the din.

"Make haste!" it shouted. "For God's sake, make haste!"

Alvanley instantly shut up his snuffbox, thrust it into his pocket, and put his head out past the door.

"What's up?" he called back.

"Five of the Fancy . . . somebody like a coachman . . . halfway up these stairs now. . . ."

Then, sickeningly, a kind of squelch, as of a fist, hit his face.

Sheer panic quivered through that press of rustling skirts and broken fans, and through some of their escorts as well. They did not shuffle; they began to run.

"Gently!" soothed Alvanley. "Gently, now!" Without further ceremony he picked up Caroline by the waist, whirled her out into the passage, and let the rush carry her along. To Darwent it seemed that the whole theater, the tier above as well as the tiers below, shook to a faint thunder as that gay-colored company rushed for the north stairs.

"Gently!" Alvanley cried again.

Plunging in at the end of the procession to shepherd it, he was lost to sight. Darwent followed him at the end, picking up a tearful lady who had lost a necklace, and setting her in the right direction. Over everything a great, calm voice, which was only that of a theater-attendant but sounded like a deity's, spoke in remote bass tones.

"My lords, ladies, and gentlemen. Let there be no haste, I pray. There is not the least occasion for haste."

But there was. Darwent, almost at the north end of the passage, realized he should not have left that box, where he had promised to wait.

He swung round, and hurried back again.

At one step he hesitated, wondering if his courage would hold. Again he touched the small sword at his left hip. It differed from the ordinary court sword only in that it was true

170

steel, and not brittle alloy. Alfred the footman had brought it from the fencing school; and, when Darwent returned to his hotel to dress for the opera, he had contrived to fit it into the gold scabbard.

Darwent resumed his walk along the passage.

Through thin partitions, by yells and the smashing of scenery, he knew that fighting in the pit had redoubled. Yet, as a man walks a tightrope between life and death, he had a strong illusion.

It seemed to him that this passage, this whole tier of boxes, now lay as silent as it was deserted.

On his left curved the wall of box doors, most of them closed. On his right ran the straight façade of immense, arched, dust-furred windows, each with a tiny lamp beside it, which looked out over the Haymarket.

To Darwent it seemed that no one moved, no one even breathed. He could hear his own footfalls on the gritty boards. He could . . .

Look out!

Because of the curve in the wall, he was within a dozen feet of his enemies before he even saw them.

Just in the middle of the passage, some distance back from the door of box forty-five, the driver of the blue coach stood facing him.

Behind the coachman stood three men, features indistinguishable in this light. But at one side of him, next the Haymarket, stood a figure made broader by short fustian jacket and corduroys: Broad Henchman, the lightweight, a harder hitter than many above his weight class. On the coachman's right, next the box doors, stood that powerful so-called middleweight who could never scale below twelve stone; they called him the Nottingham Peach.

There was just room for the three of them—Nottingham, the coachman, and Broad Henchman— to stand abreast across the width of the passage. The coachman's features were masked, except for glistening eyes. All the others wore broad, fixed grins. None of them moved; none of them spoke.

Darwent moved out into the passage, facing them from a dozen feet away.

(*If they make a rush now* he was thinking, *I am finished. I must not even draw the sword yet, lest it bring down a rush. The gamble I take, sixty to forty in my favor, is that the coachman will not wish to act too soon.*)

Still Darwent did not draw

171

Stripping the white gloves off his hands, he thrust them into the open front of his waistcoat. He walked slowly towards the enemy.

And, silently, it was as though his thought were answered.

The coachman's left hand, covered by a rotted leather glove, went up to warning. "Hold hard!" it said, as though he controlled too-eager dogs or held sledge hammers balanced on a cobweb.

(*No*, thought Darwent, *you want no quick face-pulping or snap of a broken spine. You would have the leisureliness which pulls the wings from flies. You would set one of them on me, first. . . .*)

Deliberately, within three long paces of them, Darwent stopped.

Darwent heard their breathing. Very clearly, now, he saw Broad Henchman's cauliflower ear and bony features, upper lip lifting as his fists lifted. He saw the immense bulk of the Nottingham Peach, who often trained on gin and was half-fuddled now: thick neck, thick cropped head a little inclined, as though listening for some very good joke.

But never did Darwent take his eyes from the coachman's. And the coachman's eyes began to turn, which was as good as a signal. . . .

Then Darwent drew.

The rasp of true steel out of a scabbard was like the rasp and flinch of a file drawn across teeth. At the same moment the coachman's right elbow jabbed into the left elbow of the Nottingham Peach.

"Get him!" was the unspoken message.

Nottingham straightened up, his small eyes narrowing. Above the belt round his heavy stomach he wore only a very dirty sleeveless shirt of gray wool. His immense arms, like a man's legs, shaded in color from faint pink above the biceps down to a redness like dried beef at the heavy fists.

"Ho?" he demanded, with a bellow of mirth.

Up went his fists, each a little way out from his face and spread a foot on either side: elbows crooked, a-dance with mirth and gin. The fingers of his left hand were a little open to seize that toy sword blade, his red right fist was a-quiver to send in the gravedigger.

Nottingham took one step forward, he took two steps . . .

Somebody cried out a warning, much too late.

Darwent's lunge and return-to-guard was so adder-swift that

172

the light seemed to flick only once on the blade. All they heard was the slight stamp of the lunge.

But the needle-sharp blade, stabbing under the biceps tendon of Nottingham's right arm just above the elbow, also cut into the brachial artery which feeds blood to the hand. Nobody, including Darwent himself, could have told you those terms. But well Darwent knew the effect of the thrust.

From Nottingham's right arm spurted a long jet of bright-red arterial blood. Another followed, and another, splashing out across the coachman as well. Staring at the arm, Nottingham clapped his left hand over the wound. The blood only flew wide and, as Nottingham moved his hand, spurted up into his own face.

Darwent, facing him sideways at guard position, nevertheless held the smallsword low and unmoving. A little way behind him and to his right was a great arched window. The tiny white lamp by this window threw a single spark of light on the blade.

Nottingham, partly recovering his wits, uttered a roar of rage. He lifted his fists again, and whirled on Darwent.

Again the blade flashed out and back, tearing the artery wider. Blood jetted more heavily: against the recoiling coachman, reddening the cauliflower ear of Broad Henchman. The Nottingham Peach, again arrested, held up his right fist and stared at it with a crumbling look. He saw the red fist turn corpse-white before his eyes.

Darwent spoke clearly.

"Put a turncot on that at once," he said, "or you're a dead man in ten minutes."

Nottingham was almost insensible to pain. It would have taken an ax to fell him. But this was different. This he did not understand. This crazed him.

"Godamighty!" he screamed.

Whirling round, the greasy blood still jetting, he flung past his companions and raced toward the south stairs from which he had come. One of the fighters in the back row—Darwent could see only a white head and a dirty orange neck-cloth—ran after him and tried to stop him.

Nottingham's savage wipe, with the left arm alone, flung him against a closed box door whose panels splintered like matchwood as Orange-Neckcloth went through backwards. Orange-Neckcloth, half-cracking his skull against an overturned table as he fell, rolled over into silence as Nottingham disappeared.

"Well, gentlemen?" inquired Darwent. *"Who comes next?"*

Just behind him he heard the snick of a blade whipped from its sheath. Darwent's heart rose up in fear until he saw it was only Alvanley, breathing hard, at his right side with court sword drawn.

"I told you . . . !" Darwent protested.

"My dear Darwent," said Alvanley, as blandly as he could while panting. "I know you're not in need of assistance. At the same time. . ."

At the same time, the coachman's left elbow dug into the right side of Broad Henchman. And Henchman, either wary of the too-dangerous Darwent or so blind with rage he could make no choice, flew at Alvanley instead.

It was a bad attack, throwing him off balance.

Simultaneously Henchman's left hand shot out to grab the sword blade, while his right fist aimed a round arm at the side of the head. His left grab missed the blade by a foot and a half, as people do. Again the light point winked on a blade. Alvanley, unconsciously dodging the right fist as he lunged, without compunction stabbed him through the heart.

(And now, faintly, the coachman's eyes began to change.)

The two bruisers behind him saw the sword point, almost clean, jump up under Henchman's shoulder blade. They heard the faint bone crack as Alvanley instantly wrenched it out again. The only puzzle was that the brittle steel alloy did not snap off short.

"Think-yer-got-me-eh?" snarled Henchman.

Death was on him like a cold sweat. But a man in a rage is not always stopped by a death wound. Henchman plunged forward between Alvanley and Darwent, both fists flailing. Dimly he seemed to realize he had missed them both: he half wheeled round, seeing before him the great window, dust-covered and with many panes and joinings, where his own image faintly rippled.

"Gotcher!" said Henchman. His sledge-hammer left fist struck that window an instant before his body struck it; and the window, from top to bottom, cracked and splintered.

Link boys, in the wet black street where carriages crushed up against the edge of the pavement, heard the crash from above. Their links, flaring yellow, moved backward in a wide circle, like ripples on dark water. A street organ, so familiar here as well as in Oxford Street, instantly stopped grinding out *Lillibulero*. Henchman fell in the midst of the link circle, and never moved again.

"Alvanley!" Darwent said sharply.

"At your service, my boy." Two swords were at guard-position.

"When I count three," said Darwent, "we charge them together. Agreed?"

"Agreed!"

"Either kill, or put them out of business so they'll never fight in a roped ring again. Agreed?"

"Agreed!"

(*It is impossible to put them out of business without killing, unless your sword has edge as well as point. But will they understand that?*)

"One!" counted Darwent.

The coachman's shoulders, as though twitched by panic, sent a twitch down through the moldy green cloak. Without taking his eyes from Darwent, he stretched his left hand behind him and groped—groped for help, groped for protection, from a flat-nosed, eye-scarred middleweight whose red flannel underwear was stuffed into pepper-and-salt trousers and top boots.

"I ain't afraid of anybody that fights English," suddenly bawled the man in the red underwear. "I'll meet any man wiv 'is fists." His mouth fell open; incredulity baffled him. "But damn French monkey tricks . . ."

"Two," said Darwent—and the scalepans dipped.

Again shouting he feared nobody who fought with fists (which was true) the man in the red underwear turned and bolted. His companion, whose face Darwent never saw or remembered, hesitated, wavered, and bolted after him.

Only the coachman remained. The coachman's right hand, in the rotted leather glove, crept toward the right-hand pocket of his cloak.

Darwent advanced toward him. What weapon the coachman held he did not know, and (in his present light-headed rage) did not care.

"Do you kill him now?" inquired Alvanley, in terms of purely academic interest, "or exactly what?"

Darwent stopped. The coachman's eyes were murderous.

"I should prefer," said Darwent, "only to unwrap him. To hold him out and dangle him, as the image of a so-called gentleman, before I kill him in a fair fight. Only a little injury, now, a *slight* wound . . ."

And then all his plans went wrong.

As Darwent said, "*slight* wound," he made a lightning low

175

lunge to pierce the leg just above the kneecap, where there would be no boot whatever costume the enemy wore under the cloak.

But the Nottingham Peach, old Nottingham's blood, struck back in revenge. Darwent's right foot slipped on the blood-greasy floor. The sword point missed by inches. He fell heavily on his side, bounced to his feet like an india-rubber cat—and was just in time to dodge what the coachman threw full in his eyes.

What flew at him was a thick handful of black pepper, ordinary black pepper. It can drive like a black hornet cloud; the use of it was then a French criminal's trick. Only a few grains pierced the corner of Darwent's left eye, yet they stabbed and maddened like needles into the eyeball.

"Boxes!" Alvanley shouted suddenly.

" 'Boxes,' " mimicked an unrecognizable voice, sneering under the coachman's muffler.

They did not have him trapped, as they thought. He was within door-handle reach of the empty box forty-four. Whipping open the door, the coachman darted inside before you could have snapped your fingers.

Darwent—losing seconds while he vainly rubbed at his left eye—rushed in after him. In the coachman's pocket had been a round tin of pepper, half full and lid off. He had dragged the tin out of his pocket, evidently to throw again. But he dropped it on the floor when he saw Darwent, and leaped for the top of the box ledge.

There, cloak flying like a bat's membrane, he jumped over. From below, even above the fighting turmoil, Darwent heard some one's scream of agony as the coachman's feet struck head or flesh. Craning over the ledge, he saw a circle widen and hack itself out, even among packed heads, for a cleared space in which lay an old man with a curiously twisted neck.

Darwent put down his sword on the box ledge. He picked up the tin of pepper, swearing aloud that somebody should get dose for dose. Then, before the open space should close below him, he vaulted over the ledge.

He landed three tiers below, jarred but without injury, at the back of Fops' Alley. Alvanley, sword sheathed, landed beside him just before the mob closed in. For the first time Alvanley had lost his temper.

"What d'ye play?" he snapped. "Damme, don't you know we can't catch him now?"

"Why not?"

"Because they've hemmed us in. Look there!"

At the back of Fops' Alley there was no ground-floor box. Where there should have been a box, an arched passage led to the outer doors or the way upstairs again. That passage swayed with disheveled pitites, their clothes in rags, who had either joined the fight or struggled to get out.

Over it the heavy gilt-crowned baton of a Bow Street runner rose and fell; rose and fell.

"I made a mistake. But I propose to find the swine," said Darwent, "nonetheless."

"How can you find him?"

Darwent pointed upward.

"Give me a back up," he pleaded. "I can jump and catch the lower ledge of the second box tier. And I can climb up from there to box forty-five."

"For God's sake, why?"

"The coachman wants my neck. I want his. That's where he's headed now: box forty-five! Don't you understand?"

"Yes, and with more of his prize fighters. He's paid 'em."

"Well?"

"You did it once," Alvanley told him quietly. "You can't do it again. They'll pin you in a corner and crush you."

"Will you give me a back up?"

"I rather think he won't," struck in a new voice.

Long and sinewy fingers fastened round Darwent's left arm. Up over the crowd loomed the wide-toothed smile of the Hon. Edward Firebrace, formerly of the 10th Hussars. Though his jaw was discolored and his evening wear torn, Firebrace's coil of reddish hair gleamed untouched. In his own way he was as irresistible as Jack Buckstone.

"This is Lord Darwent, I think," said Firebrace. "And he won't get away from me until we have a small discussion."

Darwent, who had no notion who he was, looked him up and down with detached coolness.

"Your manners are damned familiar, sir," Darwent observed politely—and flung the contents of the pepper tin straight into Firebrace's eyes.

At the same time some middle-aged man who might have been a carpenter (God knows on which side he thought he was fighting) went for Firebrace's throat with both hands. Both Firebrace and his attacker were drawn backwards out of sight in the crowd; irresistibly, as though by suction.

"Will you give me a back up?"

177

"Very well," sighed Alvanley, who had seen his fill of lunatics. "Steady, now!"

The most difficult part was climbing to Alvanley's shoulders, while neither lost his balance. The crowd surged, forward this time, with the heave of a giant's buckler.

But Darwent leaped, caught his fingers round the ledge, and began to climb.

•   C H A P T E R   X V I I I   •

Describes Caroline in the Paneled Room—

"Easy!" shouted Patrick, the driver of the red berline, as it came spanking down the Haymarket for the turn into Pall Mall. "Mind your swingle bar! (No danger, m'lady.) *Mind!*"

Caroline, sitting alone in the carriage with her head back and her eyes closed, did not even hear him.

To Caroline it had seemed several hours, and was actually more than thirty-five minutes, before she could get away from the crush outside the Italian opera. As one difficulty, the carriages were supposed to be summoned in exact order of social precedence, which they were not; it confused even the godlike voice of the carriage caller.

"Her grace the Countess of Bessborough."

"Prinny's mistress," hissed an irate female voice. "Lor, another grandmother. That foul old woman's not called 'Her Grace,' and anyway she has no precedence over . . ."

There was a hair-pulling match between the wife of the Prussian ambassador and the wife of the Russian ambassador, whose names had been mixed up; but, since these ladies were considered little better than savages, it made small matter.

Caroline, numb with fear for Darwent, had been swept along in the press spreading against shop fronts up toward Cranbourne Street. Horsehoofs skittered in mud; link lights dazzled; a street organ kept up incessant tinkling.

"Where is he?" she kept on asking strange faces; and nobody answered.

The fire had been quenched. The Hon. Berkeley Craven, slogging toe to toe on a smoke-blotted stage with Dan Sparkler, had won three rounds over the Sparkler—a round was a knock-down or a fall, whether it took two seconds or ten minutes—before somebody laid out Mr. Craven with a length of gas pipe.

Crash went the glass of a window on the third box tier. A dark figure pitched through, with link flames pressing back against silhouetted hats and bonnets; and Caroline's heart seemed to stop beating.

"Only a prize fighter with a sword thrust through him," somebody called.

Caroline fought her way out to the edge of the pavement and into the gutter, edging down toward the foyer doors. Rolling carriage wheels towered up menacingly in spatters of mud. But she was half-hysterical; she kept on; there *must* be news.

The crowd parted, setting up a cheer, as a platoon of Grenadier Guards poured into the theater with muskets clubbed. Half a dozen Bow Street men, red waistcoats conspicuous under baggy wide-pocketed coats, followed them with batons.

But still the minutes ticked on; the carriages rumbled to cries of the caller; and Caroline heard nothing until, in the literal sense, she caught hold of a chimney sweep.

The boy, chosen for his very small size though he must have been over seventeen, had a startlingly clean face except for black lines round the eyes and a dark neck shading into Stygian clothes.

Caroline took money from her reticule, pressed it on him, and poured out the question.

"Up there?" demanded the chimney sweep, his grown-up voice issuing from a three-foot stature. He pointed to the shattered window. "Up *there?*"

"Yes!"

"Quoz!" the boy laughed scornfully. "That's all over, miss."

"All over?"

"It was Darwent as done it." The boy spoke like one who takes pride in his own achievements. "Him, and good old Will Alvanley. Stick me in a narrow flue, but they made the Fancy run like scalded cats!"

"Then Lord Darwent—isn't hurt?"

"Quoz!" jeered the boy, which meant in general, "Come off it!" And, at the same time, a godlike voice rose aloft:

"The Most Honorable Marquess and Marchioness of Darwent!"

As Caroline was assisted into the carriage—it didn't matter that Dick was not there; he would see her later—she sank back

179

against the cushions in a half-stupor. Patrick's whip cracked; soothingly the carriage rolled.

It was all over. Dick was safe.

Fortunately for Caroline, she failed to learn that it was not all over; that, only a few minutes before, there had been disaster.

Whatever spiteful powers govern the world, this is their trick of management; this is their sleight of hand. It is hope before despair, a tinted-gauze vision hung over the entrance to the cell. Only in storybooks is the hangman too late.

Caroline's head and heart were full of memories which now seemed almost comic, yet which to her were inexpressibly dear. As Will Alvanley had swung her out into the throng shuffling past the box door, she remembered calling out to Darwent, "I love you, I love you, I love you," in the presence of several astounded acquaintances who would have been surprised to hear her speak more than coolly of anything.

Caroline smiled as she closed her eyes. She would not have changed that for the world.

Only one cracked edge marred the sum of her happiness. That was Dolly Spencer.

It would be true to say that, up to this night, she had not even disliked the girl. But it had changed now. Dick was impetuous, but he was wonderfully gentle. He had wisdom, yet he was incredibly foolish. He must not let this stupid, odious, *idiotic* quixotry (thus Caroline arranged adjectives and noun in her mind) make him think he owed anything to Dolly Spencer.

The girl's morals? Damn her morals! It was not that; it was simply that Dolly was not his counterpart. She, Caroline, would prevent it as she had sworn to do. For the first time in her life Caroline realized, with a start, that fiercely she hated some person rather than some abstract idea.

"I loathe her," she whispered.

That was why Caroline, as the red berline rattled down the Haymarket, did not even observe the black-and-silver coach.

The black-and-silver coach smashed at full gallop eastward along Pall Mall—on the wrong side of the road, a four-in-hand team stung by the whip—just as Patrick swung the berline for a wide, westward turn.

"Easy!" shouted Patrick. "Mind your swingle bar!" (No danger, m'lady.) *Mind!*"

The driver of the black-and-silver giant, with the reins laced through the fingers of his left hand while he plied his whip with the right, threw away the whip and seized with both hands a fraction too late. The two vehicles sideswiped with a crash, upsetting the berline on its right side. One horse was down, the other struggling.

"On His Majesty's service!" bawled a voice.

"And are ye, now?" bitterly roared Patrick's voice, as though from a distance away. "Then where's your so-and-so royal arms?"

Caroline suffered no injury, not even a bruise. Afterward she could not even remember what happened. At one moment she was sitting in the carriage. Ahead of her the feeble gas lamps seemed to crumple and blue.

Then, without any apparent change, she found herself sitting in the thick mud of the road, one hand out on either side of her, and a faintly dazed sense that something must have happened.

Reaching up one hand, with a touch of mud against the bright brown curls, she discovered that her hat had gone. Or perhaps she had left it behind at the theater, as she had been compelled to leave her cloak.

Beside her spoke the voice of a middle-aged man, gruff and yet very courteous.

"May I venture to offer you my assistance, madam?"

"If . . . if you will have the goodness, sir."

As he helped her to her feet, she noticed that he wore a military busby and cloak. A withered face and sandy side whiskers showed under the busby. He escorted her to the pavement on the opposite side, while many round, flaring, yellow eyes of carriage lamps looked at them. "Huddup!" growled a voice; and the stream of vehicles flowed on.

Over and over, in a quiet steady voice, Caroline assured her companion she was not hurt.

"No!" he said with some curtness, as she abruptly turned to go back. "Your driver will inquire what happened, and see to the carriage. I believe I have the honor of addressing Lady Darwent?"

"Y-yes?" Caroline spoke on a rising inflection.

"I am Major Sharpe, of the 7th Hussars."

"Major . . . !"

Under the feeble street lamp gleamed a wintry smile.

"Doubtless you heard this afternoon, Lady Darwent, that any fancied differences of opinion I might have had with your husband no longer exist. Lord Alvanley told me much of what your husband told him. I admire him greatly. May I summon a hackney coach for you?"

"No! That is: you are very kind. But for some odd reason I . . . I am afraid to ride in one. It is not too great a sensibility; it's nothing! The distance is short; I prefer to walk."

"May I accompany you?"

"Of c-course."

Not a word was spoken until they reached the Square. Even then Caroline stopped some distance from her front door.

"I must leave you here, Major Sharpe. I am afraid,"—with repulsion she indicated her muddied costume—"I won't allow the servants to see me in this state. I can go in by the back door through the mews. Good night, sir."

"Good night, Lady Darwent." He bowed. "One more word," Major Sharpe added with subdued ferocity, into the collar of his cloak.

"Your husband," he said, "fights a corrupt and evil force. When a man of quality turns moneylender; when another man of quality joins the partnership, even as coachman; then we have . . ."

Major Sharpe's Hessian boot, with the gold trimming, stamped hard into the mud which covered every street after a rainfall. The mud spattered wide.

"Can Lord Darwent clear away *that?* I doubt it! But this particular partnership he may smash."

"He will!" Caroline cried. She was crying, again like one of those women she thought she despised. She told herself that she must hurry, hurry, hurry!

A few minutes later she was entering the unlocked mews. Even with the inheritance of her grandfather's money, she had not yet bought carriage or horses because she had only just returned from Brighton; Dick should choose them now. The back door of the house (always unlocked at this comparatively early hour) opened softly.

Tiptoeing across the housekeeper's now-deserted sitting room, where a rushlight burned, Caroline just as softly opened the door giving on the back of the main hall.

There lay the hall, rather narrow and deserted, stretching to the street door, with a few candles left burning against her return from the opera. It should be easy to slip away unheard up the stairs; only Meg, her maid, would be waiting.

She had taken one soft step forward, when even in her mood of shaken nerves she noticed a circumstance more than odd.

The door of the dining room, which was the front room and

in her present position some distance ahead to her right, appeared to be wide open. From the doorway issued a flood of gentle yellow light.

Whereupon, as startling as a ghost, the voice of an old man —she had never heard it before—rose up clearly from inside the dining room.

"Gummy! You mean there's a-going to be a duel here tonight?"

Caroline stopped short.

Clearly, too, and using informal idiom, rose the voice of Alfred, the first footman.

"Well!" said Alfred. "You know what *you* told us, Mr. Townsend."

"Ah!" rose the richly cryptic inflection of the old man called Mr. Townsend.

"The governor," pursued Alfred, as though with a pounce, "knows 'oo this coachman really is. Leastways, Mr. Townsend, you proved it for him."

"All in the game, lad!" chuckled the benevolent old man's voice.

"The governor," insisted Alfred, "wants to catch old graveyard at the opera and unwrap him, like. But he knows old graveyard won't fight in the open, with saber or barker. If he don't catch graveyard at the opera, he'll lure him back here and finish the business here behind a locked door.

"That's why," Alfred added, and there was a rattle as though steel rattled in a box, "the governor told me to get all this stuff for choice of weapons. Don't you think, Mr. Townsend," he asked very respectfully, "the lower part of this sideboard was the best place to hide it?"

"Here, stop a bit!" interposed the nervous voice of Thomas, the second footman.

"Easy, Tommy!"

"Ah; you may say so! But hadn't we better douse the glim and close the door and make off before they come back from the opera?"

"Quoz!" observed Alfred, horribly as though the chimney sweep spoke again. "It's on the quarter to midnight. Nobody'll be here for another hour at least."

"Ah," persisted Thomas. "But what'll *her ladyship* say?"

There was a silence.

"Tommy, I dunno," Alfred admitted frankly.

Caroline's knees were trembling so much that she was obliged to lean one hand against the wall. Her earlier nerve storm, not quietened by that fall from the carriage, plucked at her body as though with a physical touch.

She was not angry. After all, Caroline was of her generation. If Dick must do this, then he must. But for how long? Each time they turned kindly toward each other, each time they might have been in each other's arms night and day, day and night, then death and danger came to tear them apart as visibly as with a saber cut or the impact of a pistol bullet.

No longer was she conscious of her white-satin gown mud-stained at the back from hem to shoulder blade, of her elbow-length white-lace gloves crumpled and muddy, of her thin shoes and stockings as black as the skirt and petticoat.

She walked swiftly down the hall and faced in at the dining-room door: regally, her eyes seeming pale blue instead of dark.

"What is happening here?" she asked.

Three men faced round from the sideboard, two with their mouths open.

Curtains were drawn on the two tall windows facing St. James's Square. Twenty candles burned in the glass chandelier, brightly lighting a dining room whose floor was bare and scrubbed as though for a dance. All the furniture had been piled against the wall facing the front windows, and the carpet rolled up with it.

Beside the sideboard stood Alfred, formerly of the Heavy Dragoons, with a straight light-cavalry saber in his hands. Near him was Thomas, holding an open rosewood box of pistols. Their companion was a little stout old man, whose paunch seemed endless in a long red waistcoat, and whose baggy coat stretched well down his high-held white trousers.

"What is happening here?" Caroline repeated. She was breathing so hard it was difficult to speak coolly. But her brief glance traveled without sight over the little fat man. "And who, if you please, is that person?"

"My lady . . ." Alfred began.

But out stepped the little old man with the long red-clad paunch. His heavy white hair was fashionably curled, above hard eyes which yet seemed to exude benevolence. "Me? Would *I* hurt a fly?" they seemed to ask.

"Begging pardon, m'lady," he said, thrusting forward his paunch and seeming to speak over the listener's head in so easy a way that it robbed the words of insolence, "but if your lady-ship don't know who I am—why, the Prince Regent does. I carry his purse, m'lady, when he goes out junketing o' nights."

"Indeed."

The benevolent old man proceeded to quote dialogue.

" 'Well, but, Townsend,' says he, taking out a purse stuffed with fifty or sixty pounds, 'you must leave me something to spend, you know.' 'I'll have your Royal Highness's purse and watch,' says I firmlike, 'afore some flash Knuckle gets 'em ten steps inside St. Giles's.' "

Having concluded this anecdote, the red paunch drew itself up with real dignity.

"John Townsend, m'lady," he introduced himself. "Forty year in the runners. Served under blind old Sir John Fielding, almost afore there *was* runners. Confi-dent o' Royalty. And the best thieftaker, not even bar Sayre . . ."

"Thieftaker! Runners!"

"That's it, m'lady."

"Then it must have been you who sent that note to Lord Darwent today?"

"Ah!" replied Townsend, with benevolent slyness. "Can't say it wasn't."

"Why did you send it?"

"We-el, m'lady! It may ha' been becos his lordship wrote to me, late last night, and asked me to search somebody's lodgings for evidence."

"Evidence?"

"Yes, m'lady." Townsend chuckled loudly. "Which *he* did. Which *I* did. Gummy, how easy! Hadn't even to crack a stile or use a dab. But I got the evidence against a certain 'coachman.' "

Some of these words, gibberish to Caroline, went unheeded. She ignored them. Her gaze was fixed so steadily on his that even Townsend, an eccentric character and therefore privileged, shifted and lowered his eyes.

"Then, Mr. Townsend, since you are an associate of criminals . . ."

"Criminals!" said the confident of Royalty, revolted. "I never associate with them low people! Never!"

He touched his fashionably dressed white hair. Though still he exuded benevolence, his eyes were harder.

"But Lord Darwent, m'lady," Townsend went on, "he done me proud in the matter o' money. There's ears at Bow Street, a lot of ears. D'ye think we hadn't heard of this coachman long ago?"

"What do you mean?"

"Why! A gentleman dressed in that rig, who's been a-playing the dirty—thief tricks, but most for spitefulness to enjoy

185

hisself—through Covent Garden and St. Giles's for the past twelvemonth! Not a flash cull, mind; a nob! Knows everybody there, or seems to!"

Suddenly Townsend took out of his baggy side pocket a pistol stamped with the crown and broad arrow. Then, becoming sensible of the impropriety, he thrust it back again.

"Well!" he said. "When this nob hires the Fancy to put the black on Lord Darwent, there's gin inside half of 'em and ale inside the other half. And ears a-listening. What could I do but put a postscriptus on my letter to his lordship? And warn him?"

"Then you . . . you know who the 'coachman' is?"

"I do *now*," chuckled Townsend. "Gummy, how it'll surprise 'em!"

"Who is he?"

"I can't tell you, m'lady," answered Townsend respectfully. "You ain't my client."

This was the point at which Thomas dropped the case of pistols with a crash on the bare floor. He had been holding it too long, like a box of stolen goods, under Caroline's eyes; conscience loosened his fingers.

Again they all became aware that this was a room tidied and swept for death. In the intense hush which followed, while Caroline's hand went to the great ruby hung as a necklace at her breast, they all clearly heard—tinkling and riffling, without attempt at melody—the keys of a spinet.

A spinet.

Caroline looked up at the ceiling. Just behind the green drawing room above her head, there was a music room seldom used except for routs or smaller parties. But it contained a spinet, among other musical instruments.

"Thomas," asked Caroline, "who is playing that spinet?"

It was not being "played": there were only merry and unskilled tinklings of notes picked out with one finger. Thomas, who was as Norman-dark as Alfred was Saxon-fair, exchanged a glance; and in both their eyes was apprehension.

"Who is playing that spinet?"

Alfred took a step forward, still holding the saber.

"May I beg leave to explain, my lady?"

"Pray do. That is what I desire."

"You may recall, my lady, that Mrs. Raleigh was to take precedence over Mrs. Demisham," he meant the housekeeper, "in domestic matters?"

"Yes; well?"

"Both Mr. and Mrs. Raleigh," said Alfred, "fell fast asleep

about ten o'clock." He cleared his throat. "If you'll forgive me, my lady, it's hard to blame them. They'd been for near two days and nights without sleep. Then—er—that is, Miss Spencer got up."

"Got up?"

"Yes, my lady!" Alfred's voice was growing louder. "After all, you did tell Mrs. Demisham the young lady *could* get up and try on some of your gowns . . ."

"I told Mrs. Demisham nothing of the sort," retorted Caroline truthfully. "I said to Miss Spencer that she might *have* half a dozen gowns if she remained abed until tomorrow. She is still in great danger."

Alfred's ruddy face lost some of its color. "But Miss Spencer said . . . !"

"Thomas!" Caroline interposed sharply.

"Yes, my lady?"

"Go upstairs at once. Awaken Mr. and Mrs. Raleigh. The girl must be returned to bed, with the ice bandage about her, if it has to be done by force.—Did you hear me?"

"Yes, my lady!" And Thomas was off at more than dignified speed.

Mr. John Townsend, believing that serious business had now ended and that he could air some of the social graces acquired from the Regent and old King George, uttered a bleat of approval.

"How lovesome a heart is her ladyship's!" cried the old runner, beaming. "Believe me, m'dear, the English language flows more beautiful from me pen than from me tongue. I could write a poem to it. Damme, I did write my memoors, which they asked for; only I thought the Duke of Clarence said amours; and a devil of a scrape it landed me in at home. But this! The young lady who's ill: how fond you must be of her!"

Then he started back involuntarily.

"Fond of her!" said Caroline; and then controlled herself.

"I care not a windlestraw," she added, "what happens to the girl, now or in the future." Caroline was biting at her lips to control her eyelids. "But my husband, if he were here, would wish it so. Very well; that is enough. Now, Mr. Townsend, let us speak of 'clients.' "

Townsend's own expression changed instantly.

"Eh, m'lady?"

"As I have always understood it, you are an officer of the law attached to the magistrate's court?"

187

"Forty years," assented Townsend, cheerfully but warily.

"You are paid your wages for this?"

"Hum! Well! If you could call 'em that."

"But your duty is to arrest criminals? At least to denounce them? Not, in heaven's name, to say you can't speak because you have a 'client'?"

"M'lady, you don't understand!"

"Then make me understand!"

"Come, now," Townsend soothed her, with confidential air. " 'Ow many Bow Street men (the sharp 'uns, that is) can make a living? 'Course,"—and here he meditated—"it's forty pound for a runner as takes a man in highway robbery or housebreaking; and you can always get up evidence against somebody if you need the money bad enough.

"But that's not downright honest, m'lady," declared Townsend, who really believed himself to be a man of honor. "And besides you only touch the real rhino when you 'hire out' to a private person. Which is legal, m'lady; which is legal!"

"My husband hired you. Is that it?"

"That's it, m'lady. Some likes the evidence disclosed; and I discloses it. Some likes the evidence supper-essed; and I supper-ess it. There's a price both ways; but what's fairer?"

"Then you would hide the name of the filthiest murderer who ever lived, if you were paid to do so?"

"Some gets rich," Townsend pointed out, "and some don't."

"Suppose *I* were to hire you too?"

"Ah!" murmured Townsend, and rubbed his hands. "That's different!"

Again Caroline's hand, in the crumpled and mud-stained white lace glove, went to the great ruby at her breast. Her thoughts moved up to the jewel case in her bedroom, and out toward Hookson's Bank by Temple Bar.

"My husband," she swallowed, "is sometimes . . . very foolish."

·"Ah!"

"He *won't* confide in anybody. He *won't* accept help. But he must! We can't live under the shadow of this coachman forever!"

"That's a true word, m'lady."

"Of course," and Caroline drew a deep breath, "he is not in danger now. I thank God for that. He escaped even injury in the riot at the Italian opera tonight."

Outside the street door, clearly heard through the front hall and the open door of the dining room, the door knocker five times rapped heavily and harshly.

Both Alfred and Thomas, the latter of whom had returned unnoticed from his errand upstairs, started for the door. But they had taken only a step when it opened. A man in the conventional black evening cloak, his gold-embroidered cocked hat half squashed over one ear, entered so hurriedly that he left the street door partway open.

Seeing the glitter of the chandelier in the dining room, Jemmy Fletcher turned left and hurried there. But he stopped well short of the threshold.

Jemmy must always be first with the latest tidbit of gossip, of course. Jemmy must be this, Jemmy must be that; his hyacinthine locks must float beside Fashion's. Caroline felt a stab of dread only when he stepped inside the doorway, and she saw his face.

The face, long and blue-eyed, was not that of the court fool. To Caroline it was a face of real incredulity and collapse.

"What is it?" she said. She was not aware that she had almost screamed.

Jemmy moistened his lips. "It's . . . about Dick."

"Yes? *What* about him?"

Jemmy had sworn to himself that he would break this gently: that, afterwards, all men and women should admire his tact and grace. But now he could see only Caroline's expression.

"What about him, Jemmy? What's happened to Dick? What is it?"

"He's dead," blurted Jemmy.

◇ CHAPTER XIX ◇

—and Dolly on the Staircase

An outsider, watching that group who stood silent for perhaps thirty seconds after Jemmy's announcement, might have found it vaguely ridiculous.

There was Alfred, head down, holding the saber as though it burned him. There was Thomas, his gaze on the floor. There was little old pompous Townsend, his hands in the pockets of

the baggy coat, his white trousers three inches above his
ankles, face doleful because he had lost a good client. There
was Jemmy, stricken, his cocked hat half crushed over one
ear.

Finally, there was Caroline.

She showed nothing at all, only blank face and eyes. Perhaps, then, she felt nothing. Caroline stood just under the
chandelier. A drop of hot wax fell on her bare shoulder, but
she did not even notice.

It was Jemmy who broke the silence, babbling as though
words might drive back their feelings like loud-voiced dogs.

"Fool," whispered Jemmy, seizing at the front of his own
cloak to indicate himself. "Wouldn't have said that. Like that.
Not for anything. Positively. No sense. Never had."

He looked slowly round, avoiding Caroline's face. It was as
though muted fierce questions had been flung at him—though
still in silence—and he answered them.

"Dick *was* right as a trivet, you know. Positively. Stake
m'dem life on it! He and Will chased the dem Fancy a-whack-
ing out of the third-floor tier. Everybody says so, anyway.
Then this coachman, the one everybody's talking about . . ."

A kind of shiver went through Alfred. His fingers crept
round the saber hilt. But nobody spoke.

"The coachman," blurted Jemmy, speaking faster, "jumped
over the box ledge into the pit. Dick followed him. So they
say. Anyway," and Jemmy's voice rose with a kind of tearful
but grisly triumph, "I saw the next part from Ned Firebrace's
box. Second tier. Side box. Ned wasn't there. But Harriette
Wils . . ." His delicacy would not let him name a harlot in
public.

The unspoken questions pushed at him, harried him.

"Dick had got back up again to the box. Fact! Don't know
how! Left his sword on the ledge. Picked it up again. Looked
down at the pit. Then this coachman—it was all queer dark
light, lamps swinging backstage—the coachman crept up behind Dick, so quiet and soft you'd hardly see him, and
stabbed Dick in the back with a knife.

"He stabbed three times, I think it was. Oh, damme! Dick
tried to sit down in a chair, but missed it and fell on the
floor. Coachman; dunno. Must have made a flit by the north
stairs."

Now the weight of silence became too heavy.

"Oh, it's true," Jemmy cried almost angrily. "They've taken
his body to Stephen's Hotel."

("They've taken his body to Stephen's Hotel.")

To Caroline, standing there without expression, these were the first words which seemed true. They had finality. They were like limbs straightened, a sheet drawn up over an empty face, the sense of a loved one gone forever.

Believing herself quite calm, she opened her mouth to ask a question. Whereupon, suddenly, it was as though she had lost all control over her muscles. Her lips trembled like a paralytic's; she could utter only unintelligible sounds.

Thomas, after a quick look at her, lifted his hand to draw down a chair from the piled furniture. Alfred, far more tactful, gave him a savage glance which stopped him.

Caroline turned round. As though casually, she moved over to one of the front windows. Her whole body felt drained of blood; she must, *must* reach that little shelter before they noticed. Opening one of the heavy velvet curtains, she slipped inside and drew the curtains.

Caroline pressed her forehead against cold glass. She saw nothing; not even the black night outside. Her mind was too numb. But despite herself a voice (how short a while ago, in time!) would whisper in her ear and in her brain.

"That among these rights are life, liberty, and the pursuit of happiness." Or again, more poignant:

"An estate in Kent, with shallow streams of soft greenish-brown woods. If I could take you there, beyond sight of the world . . ."

Caroline bit at her lips and clenched her hands.

"I could live with you there forever," she had said.

Stop this! Stop it!

Through her dulled mind came one resolution: that she would accept no sympathy, even from a close friend. As soon as she achieved complete calmness, in a minute or two, she would go out of these muffling curtains. She would walk quietly upstairs, and lock herself in her room for days or weeks or months. Let the flapping crows, ill-meaning carrion like Townsend or well-meaning carrion like Jemmy, say what they liked.

Yes, and let the world say what it liked! That was Dick's view; it should become hers.

Whereupon a very small thing, as small things will, almost upset her dry-eyed resolution.

Outside the curtains, in the dining room, silence had become an intolerable weight. Caroline heard the small, soft rattle as Alfred gently put down the saber on the sideboard.

191

She felt she could almost hear Alfred's blunted mind move. Thoughtfully, with intense reserve, Alfred spoke.

"He was a werry brave man, the governor."

Silence.

"Ah," agreed Thomas in the same tone. "Daresn't meet him face to face, did they?"

And the tears *would* sting into Caroline's eyes, and she *would* rage in her heart. Furtively she brushed away tears with one edge of the curtain. But this, she felt, was good; this had brought her to her senses, and away from ignobility.

Before locking herself in her room, two matters she must arrange. She must find a carriage to go to Stephen's Hotel and bring back . . . She closed up her brain. Also, there was another and just as imperative duty.

Throwing back the curtains, she marched out into the room. All four of the men moved back a step. Thomas's foot involuntarily knocked against the fallen case of pistols; and one of the pistols, loose from its bedding in blue velvet, rolled out on the floor.

"Thomas," said Caroline, "you will go out into the street and get me . . ."

She paused. Her eyes lifted toward the ceiling at the back of the dining room, as did the others. The spinet was being "played" again upstairs in the music room. One finger tried to pluck out a tune, merrily, while the other merely ruffled at the keyboard; and the tune, grotesquely, was something like, *A Frog.He Would A-Wooing Go.*

"Thomas," Caroline repeated in a different voice.

"Yes, my lady?"

"Did you deliver my previous message upstairs?"

"Yes, my lady. Mr. and Mrs. Raleigh are awake. But the young lady . . ."

"Well, Thomas? The—young lady?"

"My lady, she says she's well! She says she's not needing that bandage thing! She's put on a very fine gown. She won't . . ."

Caroline raised her hand. "Ignore what I told you a moment ago," she corrected. "Present my compliments to Miss Spencer, and ask her if she will come downstairs at once."

Alfred took a step forward. "My lady! If I may . . ."

Caroline's head twitched round. "Was your opinion called for, Alfred?" she asked gently.

"No, my lady."

"Then have the goodness to keep it to yourself.—Thomas!"

And now, almost as unheard of as unheard, the soles of

Thomas's shoes could be heard clacking on the floor as he ran.

Caroline's soft body seemed now as rigid as marble. Two spots of color burned in cheeks as white as those of one afflicted with the wasting sickness. Will you say that, in sickness of heart, she was striking at the person nearest at hand? Striking at a girl she hated? Well; but that is human nature, too. And another matter burned in her mind.

"Mr. Townsend!"

"Here, dash it, Caroline, now!" interrupted Jemmy Fletcher, taking off his squashed cocked hat and hurling it into a corner. How could there be a fine, touching story for him to tell at the clubs, if the dem woman didn't scream and go off into a fit of the megrims? "Damme, this ain't natural!"

"Please be silent, Mr. Fletcher."

"Dash it, can't you even call me Jemmy?"

All this time, after making a mouth of sympathy at news of Dick's death, the old Bow Street runner had been looking thoughtfully at a corner of the ceiling.

"No doubt, Mr. Townsend," said Caroline, "you are thinking to whom your information about the coachman could best be sold?"

"Now!" protested Townsend, as though shocked. "Come, now! M'lady! 'Ere!"

A film came over Caroline's eyes.

"Di—Lord Darwent," she went on, "had many beliefs which I thought I did not share. Well! For good or ill, I share them now." And Caroline pressed her hand under her breast.

"It's strange," she added in a puzzled way. "Even this morning (or was it years ago?) I thought I did not share his belief in vengeance against those who had wronged him. I pleaded against it. I did not understand." Her eyes moved first toward the pistol on the floor, then to the saber across the sideboard. "But I understand now."

Caroline lifted her hands.

"I can't speak of this now!" she burst out. "I can't! But wait upon me in a few days, Mr. Townsend; a few days, when I am a *little* more sane. Arrest this coachman, let me see him hanged high outside Newgate, and you will find me the most generous patron you have ever known."

Then Caroline whirled round.

"Where is that woman?" she asked.

"M'lady, stop! If you wants . . ." Townsend paused because Caroline did not hear him.

She swept out into the hall, satin rustling. She glanced out

193

of the street door, which Jemmy had left partway open, into an intensely black night scented with rain. Then Caroline turned left, looking up the stairs at the tableau there.

The staircase on the right-hand wall, so high that it looked narrow, was softly lighted by the candles left burning against Caroline's return. There were glimmers on the wooden balustrade and the broad stair rail, on the thick carpet which padded the steps, on the gold frames of the large portraits which hung step-fashion down the right-hand wall.

Mr. and Mrs. Raleigh, standing at the top of the stairs, were out of the light and therefore mere shadows. But the shame which flowed from them, the abjectness of apology, might have tinged the hall with its mood.

Four steps down, within the light, her right hand on the balustrade, stood Dolly Spencer.

Dolly wore the finery she had chosen; Dolly's head was high; Dolly didn't care. Her gown of yellow velvet, with much interlineation of blue color and gold trimming about the waist, was cut according to the usual mode: high at the waist and horizontally low across the breast. This gown had little shoulder puffs, on which Dolly's yellow ringlets rested.

For a moment she seemed to pose, preening herself. And yet, though the brown eyes smiled, her expression was that of one trying hard to hide pain. Then she saw Caroline's face.

"I didn't mean any harm!" Dolly protested.

Caroline looked at her, and made no reply.

"Mr. Raymond," laughed Dolly, a figure of mirth high on the stairs, "said I had a musical voice or was musical or the like of that. I never saw a real spinet, outside the playhouse. I thought . . ."

Dolly paused, her eyes widening and a strange expression round her mouth. Suddenly her hand went to her right side.

"What's wrong?" she cried.

Caroline, almost blind with tears, glanced once more toward the partly open street door behind. She saw only what might have been a vague shape blacker than the night; her mind saw nothing as she looked back up at Dolly.

"My husband is dead," answered Caroline, so coldly and clearly that each syllable was like a snapped icicle. "Yes! I mean the man you call Dick Darwent."

Dolly's hand pressed closer against her right side.

"You will never see him alive again, nor shall I," continued that cold emotionless voice. "I beg of you to leave my house as soon as is convenient."

194

Dolly's mouth trembled, as in a spasm of pain. In the long yellow-velvet skirt she tried to take a step forward. Then she pitched headforemost down the stairs.

Even Alfred and Thomas, plunging out of the dining-room doorway, were far too late.

The staircase was not wide enough for Dolly to roll, or even try to save herself. Even so, it was as though she were inanimate flesh. She fell helplessly, side to side, in a whirl of yellow velvet and yellow-silk petticoat edged with lace. One of her small blue-and-yellow dancing shoes was torn off as she struck the last tread with a thud, rolled sideways, and fell face-down on the floor.

Old Townsend, hardened in the brine of violence since boyhood, merely grunted. He waddled forward, and bent over Dolly, hauling her round on her back as though she were a dummy.

Townsend felt for a pulse at the wrist. Afterward, without ceremony or apology, he ripped open the heavy corsage with a pocketknife, and felt inside for the heart. Dolly's eyelids fluttered; she gave a moan of agony.

The little fat white-haired old man stood up, closing the knife with a click.

"Well!" he said wheezily. "She ain't dead. But I dunno. If you ask me, she's a-dying."

From the doorway to the dining room Jemmy Fletcher uttered a bleat like a scream. The street door had swung wide open.

Darwent himself—disheveled, evening clothes torn, but very much alive and not even injured—stepped inside and closed the door with a slam.

"What is happening here?" he asked harshly.

◇　CHAPTER XX　◇

The Last Bitterness

Nobody answered him.

All of them stood, upright or crouched over, in a little circle round the foot of the stairs where Dolly lay motionless in her spilled yellow finery, her eyes closed and a smudge of dust against her cheek.

Darwent asked no question about why she was there, nor even referred to it. His eyes had acquired a cold, hard look as implacable as the set of his mouth. He looked slowly round.

"I see!" he observed. "Then the report of my death has already spread here?" His eyes flickered toward Jemmy. "*You* brought it, I daresay?"

"But it's true; old boy! I mean: that is . . ."

"I can't blame you," said Darwent, "if you did. I have been denying it ever since."

"Yes; who . . . ?"

"Who *was* killed?" demanded the other. "Can't you think who *was* mistaken for me, in that dim light?"

Whether or not heightened emotions sting wits to greater height, the answer flashed back at him.

"Lewis!" said Jemmy. "Tillotson Lewis!"

"Yes. Tillotson Lewis."

Darwent looked down at his empty gold sword scabbard. His cheek muscles were working, and his eyes blinked.

"Ho, the Reverend Mr. Cotton!" he called, in a way which turned Alfred cold. And though the Rev. Mr. Cotton was miles from here, Darwent seemed to find him in the hall and address him. "Why must the decent people always die, Mr. Cotton? And the rogues stuff their food at Watier's? Tell me that!"

Jemmy Fletcher pressed long fingers together, as though squeezing a gossip orange to the last drop.

"Dick, Dick, what happened?"

"No matter!"

And yet what occupied half his mind so nauseated him that he must speak despite himself.

"I was in the pit. I climbed up the outside of the boxes, to number forty-five: my wife's box."

"Well?"

"It wasn't as easy as I had thought. Some of the projections were rotten wood and crumbled away. It is difficult to get a grip over the padded ledge of a box. I had—had reached my own box with one arm over the ledge, and my right foot trying to brace itself against a pillar, when Lewis came in from the back. He was my friend. 'Darwent!' he said. And, 'Darwent, can I help you?'

"I could not answer. My mouth was pressed against some wooden laurel leaves, and my right foot still groping to get the

196

other arm up. I don't think Lewis saw me, though I saw him. My sword, with the blood on it, was still lying on the ledge. He picked it up, and looked from side to side.

"Seen from behind, turning his head from side to side, even one who knew us both would have vowed it was myself. The coachman slipped in, stabbed him three times in the back, and melted away."

Darwent paused.

"It was a trifle pitiable (or d'ye know pity, any one of you?) to see how Lewis tried to make light of it, though he knew he had death in him. By that time I had got my second arm over the rail, and he saw me.

" 'Fraid I can't give you a hand,' Lewis said. And, ' 'fraid we won't have many more of those political talks.' All this time he was groping and groping for the back of a chair, so that he could sit down and pretend nothing had happened.

"But he missed his last attempt, tried to say something else, and fell down helpless. So died a good man."

Again Darwent glanced down at the empty sword scabbard. Again he seemed to seek the Rev. Horace Cotton in the hall.

All this time Caroline had not spoken. She had backed away almost to the right-hand wall. In tumult she could not decide what was real and what was imaginary. She stretched out her hand.

"Dick!" she said.

He turned his head. To her horror (or was this imagination too?) his face wore the same look of hard, polite contempt he had worn in the cell at Newgate; his voice had the same mockery.

"Yes, madam?" he inquired.

"Dick! What is it? What's wrong?"

"Nothing we cannot discuss later, madam, if indeed we need discuss it at all."

"Dick! No! What's wrong?"

Again he turned his head. Bewilderment, pain, perhaps even a desire to kill her, touched lights of hardness into his look.

"Why did you do it?" he asked. "Why?"

"Do what?"

Savagely Darwent pointed to the closed street door behind them.

"You saw me come up those steps," he said slowly and heavily. "You knew I was alive. But you cried out to Dolly and said I was dead. Why did you make her fall? She never harmed anyone."

197

"But I . . . I didn't see you! Stop! There was some vague kind of black shape; yes, there was. But I never noticed!"

Darwent only made a fierce gesture.

To Caroline this was the ultimate horror, far worse than the news of Darwent's death. She felt like a half-drugged woman stumbling in a dark room, her own room, yet touching no curtain or table top to remind her into what corner she has strayed.

For she and Darwent again looked into each other's minds, with that uncanny insight. What both of them heard (she knew it as clearly as she saw it in his face) were her own remembered words, cried out in the opera when Darwent had reached his worst pitch of idiotic quixotry.

"*I won't let you have her,*" Caroline had cried. "*Whatever I have to do, however low I have to sink, I won't let you have her. I swear this before God.*"

Caroline had not done it. She was guiltless. But at the depths of her heart she suddenly realized another truth. In the shock of cruelty following Darwent's death, she *might,* just might, have done some such trick as this. That was the worst of it.

"Dick, how could I make her fall? You don't think I deliberately . . . ?"

Ignoring her, he turned to Alfred.

"Where's the surgeon?" he demanded. "Isn't Mr. Hereford here? Where is he?"

Alfred stepped forward.

"My lord, Mr. Hereford dispatched a note to say he would be detained at the hospital. He inquired whether it would be too late if he called at past midnight. Knowing what . . . er . . . the circumstances, I ventured to answer that it would not be too late. My lord, it must be nearly twelve-fifteen at this time. Mr. Hereford should be here at any moment."

"Thank you."

Augustus Raleigh, seeming even gaunter from his gaiters to his bald head, and with a pair of steel-rimmed spectacles stuck up on his nose, came hurrying down the stairs. Fiercely Darwent waved him back. He bent over Dolly, who was semiconscious in the pain of that malady nobody understood.

"Poor little . . ." Darwent began, and could not continue.

Gently he bent over and picked her up in his arms. How light she seemed! As he turned to carry her upstairs, he caught sight of the old Bow Street runner.

"You're Townsend, I imagine?"

"At your service, m'lord!" sang out Townsend, with such

grisly cheerfulness that he instantly grew meek and shrank together. "Your lordship writes me a note; I writes back; you writes back again. What's fairer?"

"Have the goodness to remain," requested Darwent. "I may have need of you."

And he carried Dolly upstairs, Mr. Raleigh walking backwards in front of him in case Dolly might fall up instead of down. He carried her, stepping sideways, slowly, so that her feet should not strike against the portraits.

He did not think, or try to think. But, with mind catching at trifles and dully considering the tasteless yellow-and-blue finery which hung from Dolly, it seemed to him that women must gown themselves for their own vanity, or for other women's envy. For a loved one will seem radiant in any old sack cut from coarse serge, but all Sheba's emeralds will not adorn another.

On the second floor above the ground floor, where the grandfather clock fluidly rang the quarter-hour after midnight, he carried Dolly back to the Amber Room. He put her down in the great bed, drawing over her shoulders only a light silk coverlet. Then he stood back, because there was nothing else he could do.

But both Mr. and Mrs. Raleigh were at his side.

"Dick," began Augustus Raleigh in an even deeper voice, "if you could guess what was on *my* conscience . . ."

"Oh, do be silent!" interrupted Mrs. Raleigh. "We—we both went to sleep, Dick. That's the fact of it. But Dolly . . . the girl's willful, you know. She would get up. And, Dick," Mrs. Raleigh hesitated, her muslin cap trembling like her neck, "that lady downstairs. You mustn't blame Lady Darwent. She . . ."

Darwent whirled on her savagely.

"Will you oblige me," he asked in a soft voice, "by not mentioning my so-called wife's name?"

"Dick!"

"Do I make myself understood, Mrs. Raleigh?"

Mrs. Raleigh's hands fell helplessly. Again her neck trembled, sending a quiver through her features and round her lace cap. The dull lamp still burned here. Mrs. Raleigh's tear-smudged gaze moved toward the bed, where Dolly lay and moaned.

"She's dying, Dick. I've seen it too often."

"Yes."

"Then you ought to know," Mrs. Raleigh pounced at him,

199

"what she should have told you. About the time she was two months away from you, and never visited you in prison; and you thought she was keeping merry house with some man?"

"Have I ever asked to learn?"

"We're in God's sight," said Mrs. Raleigh, "or we soon shall be. Listen to me, Dick! It was foolish and it was stupid; but the girl for some shame's sake would have it so."

Mrs. Raleigh looked up, clutching at his sleeve.

"She was drunk, Dick. That's all. Her parents are two sots who live in a foul alley off Bread Street. D'ye recall, Dick? She had just learned she would never be 'of the company,' even to play Lady Macduff? On top of it, they dragged you to prison.

"God forgive me: the girl hadn't strength of will to face it. She went home. She was blind-fuddled on gin, with times when she'd try to get up, until she stumbled back to us. Don't you recall, Dick, how strange about her Mr. Mulberry was? And how the surgeon hinted to you (or Mr. Mulberry says he did) she must have been drinking a great deal of wine? We love her, Dick! But . . ."

Mrs. Raleigh broke off.

Darwent's lips drew back from his teeth in what was not a smile.

"And that," he inquired bitterly, "is her hideous crime?"

"Dick, the poor girl can't face our poor-devil human life. . . ."

"On my word of honor," he snarled, "I have been fuddled for months on end, and three Oxford dons with me, mumbling through our duties and misliking the world without a smirch against our respectability."

"But that's different!"

"How is it different?"

"May *I* be permitted to explain?" interposed Augustus Raleigh.

He walked forward, and his dignity was only a small fraction stage dignity when he put his arm round his sobbing wife. His dark eyes burned with some inner hurt of his own.

"My lord," he said very formally, "you must be told another thing as well. I have no proof of what I say. But when poor Dolly did this, putting on gowns and playing at the spinet, it is my belief she did so deliberately."

"Deliberately? Why?"

"To hasten the end of her own life."

"Are you mad?"

"Have you forgotten," asked Mr. Raleigh, "how changed and even strange she was, when you talked to her in this very room today?"

"Changed; well; in a sense; yes! But she was ill! She . . ."

"No, my friend. You were no longer Dick of Covent Garden, who laughed with her and sported with her and were much loved by her. You were my Lord Marquess of Darwent, with broad lands and gold, as high above her as the sun above a pebble. She was frightened of you. She felt too much beneath you, not good enough for you."

Darwent's face became as white as tallow candle. Augustus Raleigh, dropping his drawn-up formal dignity, spoke first.

"No, Dick, *you* hadn't changed. But a hundred thousand others would change. The world would change; and you can't fight the world. Dolly had already changed. She thought herself only a Bread Street slut, hardly fit enough to . . ."

"You lie," said Darwent. "If you were not my friend, I would take your scraggy neck and . . . I tell you, I knew Dolly too well!"

He struggled a moment, to get his breath.

"God damn you," Darwent said, "if you don't retract those words I'll kill you if I hang for it!"

Augustus Raleigh merely inclined his bald head. He was now no longer a rock of strength; he was only an aging, rather eccentric and gentle man who, as he had said to so many, could save nothing from his wages before he left Drury Lane.

"If you insist, Dick, I retract. As for the blame about what happened here tonight . . ."

Darwent had recovered himself.

"Nobody is to blame; and I apologize." Awkwardly he patted at Mr. Raleigh's arm. "But what I said is true. Nobody is to blame, except myself and—a certain woman downstairs." His voice broke. "And now, for friendship's sake, will you go away and let me be alone with her?"

"Yes, Dick."

The door closed.

This chill room, with its frowsty dark yellow hangings, had become chillier still. Melting ice overflowed the silver buckets; it fell on the table tops, on the floor, with monotonous dull splashes.

Dolly's mouth was moving, as though she tried to speak to him. He hurried to her side, seizing one hand. But he heard no word.

Nor was he left long alone with her. Mr. Hereford, the

surgeon, swept his portly form through the doorway a minute later. Afterward Darwent could not remember that they exchanged four sentences during all the time that ached as it passed.

Mr. Hereford uttered no word of reproach, nor did he waste time. Putting down his hat and case beside the bed, he began his examination of the patient.

During that examination Darwent paced up and down, up and down. Dipping his hands in a silver bucket, he sluiced icy water down his face. His head felt dizzy when he straightened up. He was very tired. Briefly he wondered if he would have strength enough for the final, kill-or-be-killed fight tonight. But all such considerations were swept away when he hurried back to the bed.

The surgeon, having removed Dolly's gown by using a knife as Townsend had, put her under the silk coverlet and now drew it up to her chin with one bare arm outside. With one hand he touched the pulse; with the other he held open a large double-cased gold watch.

Darwent's eyes asked a question: "Is there *any* hope?"

And the surgeon's eyes replied: "None whatever."

Presently Mr. Hereford shut up his watch with a click. It was not all over. Both merely watched, the surgeon sitting on the edge of the bed and Darwent standing behind him.

There she lay, scarce seeming to feel any pain now, as Darwent's hand bent down to take hers. There, with appendix burst in the mysterious malady, she rested under the silken coverlet. There, twenty minutes later, she died.

Darwent knew when she died, though he afterwards wished he had not. The surgeon stood up. Gently Mr. Hereford placed her arm under the coverlet, before drawing the coverlet up over her face.

Picking up his case from the floor, putting his hat under his arm, he glanced at his companion with an unspoken question: "Shall I send someone upstairs?" He received a shake of the head in reply.

"My carriage," Mr. Hereford said aloud, with sudden strong noise, "arrived here at the same time as your lordship arrived. I remained downstairs to question certain persons." He paused. "I regret . . ."

"You need not."

Mr. Hereford bowed. Darwent extended his hand, and the surgeon clasped it; after which he went out and closed the door.

For a little time Darwent stood staring at the floor. Then he moved over to the side of the ornate bed between the two windows. He was wondering whether to remove the coverlet from Dolly's face, for a last look, when he heard a new noise.

He heard it faintly from the square, drifting down the air well. Someone, who had been unable to sleep after that riot tonight, was abroad. It was only a common street organ, tinkling thinly, but he heard it.

> *Oh, believe me, if all those endearing young charms,*
> *Which I gaze on so fondly today . . .*

Darwent swung round, and drove his clenched fist at one of the ornate bedposts. Fortunately, he missed. He needed a sound right hand for the last duel.

> *Were to change by tomorrow, and flee from my arms,*
> *Like a fairy gift fading away . . .*

Since there was nobody there to see him, Darwent pressed his hands over his eyes. He took only one glance at the cold clay which was now Dolly.

> *Thou shouldst still be adored, as this moment thou art,*
> *Let thy loveliness fade as it will . . .*

He tried to shut the imagined words of the melody out of his ears.

Striding out into the center of the room, he knew that he could not evade them. Would Mr. Tom Moore, who wrote the song, ever know that the melody—sorry stuff though the words might be—could hurt like a deep wound and speak like his conscience? Doubtless, in his sentimental soul, Mr. Moore would have been pleased.

> *And around the dear ruin each wish of my heart*
> *Would entwine itself verdantly still.*

There; for a moment the tune had stopped.

For Darwent's difficulty was not that his wits were muddled. They were too clear, or so he imagined. They saw too clearly, with terrifying outline, what was true and what was not true.

Caroline was quite right. He had never been in love with Dolly. As Caroline's grisly carefulness had pointed out, as he himself had agreed, he had transformed Dolly into a nymph for an Arcadia made of sooty-brown Covent Garden, and the Pantheon in Oxford Street, and the Chinese lanterns among trees at Vauxhall.

That was the worst of it. That was the bitterest of it! For he should have been in love with Dolly.

Instead he had elected to fall in love with blue-eyed Caroline, who looked at you past brown ringlets, who could become all Circe and soft words, all seductiveness and passion and a fleshly allure more than Dolly's; yet who, at heart, was as cold as the spade guineas she worshiped. When the time came, she had dealt as ruthlessly with Dolly (why wouldn't man learn?) as she had dealt with him at Newgate.

Could he stamp out this love; quieten the heart, still the fleshly allure? Perhaps not. But, as she loved money, so she could be dealt with.

Darwent walked back to the bedside. Without lifting the coverlet he put the side of his cheek to Dolly's.

"Good-by, my dear," he said, rising a little and holding both her cheeks in his hands. "I rather hope," he added truthfully, "I join you before morning."

Near the door, there was a discreet cough.

"Begging pardon, your lordship," said the heavy voice of Alfred, his eyes fixed steadily sideways, "I took the liberty . . ."

"You were quite right," answered Darwent. He walked out from the bedside, and hesitated. "I shall probably be leaving London for a long time—er—if not for a *very* long time. I shall probably," this had just occurred to him, though it seemed an excellent notion, "buy a commission in the army. I understand you've been in the army. Would you care to come along as my servant?"

Large Alfred's powdered head was lowered. He studied the floor as though he glared at it.

"I expect you don't know it, my lord. But there's several of us 'ud follow you 't'other side o' hell."

Long silence.

"No, I did not know it. But I am grateful," said Darwent, "notwithstanding."

"My lord," blurted Alfred. "Man to man . . . her ladyship . . . she didn't . . ."

Glancing up, he saw that Darwent's face was as inhuman as some monstrosity out of Dean Swift.

"Go downstairs," requested Darwent, as though he had not heard. "I shall follow directly. I expect a visitor soon. Mean-

204

while, downstairs, I have certain business matters to arrange."

"Very good, my lord."

Darwent waited only long enough again to sluice water down his face and this time his head. The water poured gratefully through hair into head, slopping down his clothes. He had long lost hat and cloak. His collar and cravat being long torn away, he had folded over collar and lapels of the dark coat partly to hide this.

When he went downstairs, the hands of the grandfather clock on the landing pointed to ten minutes past one. On the last flight of steps into the lower hall, where Alfred and Thomas stood guard at the dining room, voices could be heard from that brightly lighted dining room.

Townsend and Jemmy Fletcher, at least, seemed in good spirits.

"Damme, Caroline," neighed Jemmy's high voice, "you don't mean *you* were in the carriage that overturned?"

"Yes. I—I fear I was," she replied. Her voice seemed uncertain, even terrified. Now what need, Darwent asked himself, was there for play-acting here?

"Finest jape you ever heard!" giggled Jemmy. "*I* know the truth."

"Ah, sir?" prompted the fascinated Townsend.

"Fact, my good fellow," Jemmy said with gracious condescension. "It was Prinny, d'ye see?"

"His Royal Highness," said Townsend sternly. " 'Cause, sir, if you knows the Prince as a friend . . ."

"Oh, I flatter myself I do," said Jemmy. "Prinny was giving a supper at Carlton House. Pure oversight they didn't have *me*. Anyway, they were hard at iced punch in the Gold Room, when somebody brings the news that the Princess Charlotte's been in danger from a riot at the King's Theatre."

"Ah, but there was a riot!"

"Quiet, my good man. Prinny really is rather fond of that daughter of his; dashed if he ain't. Up he surges like a ghost with frog jowls. First, as usual, he goes and is sick into the hothouse flowers. Then he bawls: won't some friend, some gentleman, save his daughter? Some new 'un, some green nincompoop, dashes out; when the Life Guards have brought the pore ugly gel back to Carlton House an hour and a half before. Damme, ain't it a quiz? I never . . ."

He stopped short. Darwent had come into the dining room.

Caroline, with a look of deep love which Darwent might have sworn was genuine if he had not known better, hesitated

205

and turned away. Townsend looked respectful. Jemmy, having removed his cloak, stood under the chandelier all spick-and-span from shirt frill to diamond knee buckles.

"Ah, Mr. Townsend!" said Darwent, with a broad smile.

Tension relaxed a trifle.

"M'lord," replied Townsend, with a deep bow.

"I fear," Darwent continued agreeably, "I made a grievous error when I tried to take our graveyard coachman alone, and did not call for the help of brisk lads from Bow Street."

"You did, m'lord," Townsend assured him emphatically: "and I'd say it to King George hisself. God bless 'im!"

"Still, since I already know who the coachman is . . ."

Jemmy Fletcher's eyes were agog. He hurried forward to stand in front of Darwent.

"You know who he is?" Jemmy demanded.

"Yes."

"Then, damme, tell a fellow! Who *is* the coachman?"

Darwent looked at him steadily.

"You are, Jemmy," he replied. His right hand suddenly shot out and twined itself in Jemmy's cravat. "And now, my lad, you'll pay for it."

◇ **C H A P T E R   X X I** ◇

The Wrong Murderer

"Me?" blurted Jemmy. There was a horrible illusion that his blue eyes had turned liquid, and were spreading. "Me? A poor butterfly? The coachman?"

"Yes, Jemmy. Shall I prove it?"

As Darwent spoke those five words, a vision of two faces moved as pictures through his mind.

He saw the face of Frank Orford, cold, haughty, long of nose—Frank, who would bite a coin to make sure it was genuine, and throw any poor devil into Newgate or the Fleet over a matter of five pounds—Frank, sitting behind a tortoise-shell wood desk in a lost room, with a rapier skewering him to the chair.

And Darwent saw the face of Jemmy, sitting elegantly last night on the green-and-white striped sofa upstairs, while he gently, gently prodded Darwent into a pistol duel with Buck-stone. He saw the sheer malice which momentarily curled round Jemmy's mouth: melting inward, a bad sign. Against a misty sky at dawn, too, he saw Jemmy's look when Jemmy realized Buckstone might lose the duel.

But Jemmy was already babbling.

"The feller's mad," he cried out to Caroline. And he began to quote. " 'Oh, ye who so lately were blythesome and gay, At the Butterfly's Banquet carousing away . . .' Damme, you can't suspect *me*?"

Darwent stopped him.

"I never suspected you, Jemmy, until last night. Then I tried a sum in addition. My wife, Mr. Townsend, and these two servants shall be your jury now."

With a powerful heave Jemmy wrenched Darwent's hand away. Blocking the doorway were the large figures of Alfred and Thomas, and their faces were not pleasant. Jemmy backed away toward the fireplace across the room from them.

"First," said Darwent, "I was an obscure fencing master, tried, under the name of Dick Darwent. Nobody, except Frank Orford's relatives, paid much attention to that trial.

"How did you learn so much about me afterwards, Jemmy? Until the last moment before the hanging, very few persons knew my name or the reasons for the reprieve. Afterwards everything was hushed up, and even rumors distorted.

"But you knew the truth, Jemmy. How did you know where I was, and how to visit me on the State side of Newgate? Many fashionable ladies, I understand, were distracted with wondering how you knew it.

"Of course, as my wife has told me in the interval,"—Darwent, glancing at Caroline, was disturbed by the sincerity of her eyes—"you were present, apparently dead drunk, at a champagne breakfast to celebrate my taking off. At the end, perhaps, you may not have been so dead drunk as you pretended.

"You *could* have heard a turnkey, named Blazes, blurt out that I was a nobleman named Darwent. This meant an automatic change to the State side, before trial at the bar of the Lords. Burke's Peerage, with hardly any study, would have given you my title.

"But this is not the real mystery, Jemmy. The real mystery lies further back. It begins on the night of May 5th: when you drove me unconscious in the blue coach, and when you killed your partner, Frank Orford."

Jemmy's voice went shrilling up.

"I never killed Frank!" he screamed. Horribly, the ring of truth seemed in it. "Word of a gentleman, egad! I never did!"

Darwent paid no attention. Townsend seemed wickedly amused, and rubbed his hands together.

"You drove me in the blue coach out to Kinsmere House in Bucks," Darwent continued steadily. "I could never swear, either to Mr. Mulberry or the Padre, that two persons lifted me out of the coach; I thought it was two, but I admitted it might have been one. It was yóu alone, Jemmy. You're as strong as a horse. Tillotson Lewis told me so flatly; and I should have seen it before.

"But here's the crux! Here's the riddle! You believed you were carrying Tillotson Lewis. But I discovered Frank's body, and you smashed me over the head again. One good look at me in a good light, and of course you saw I wasn't Lewis."

Darwent allowed the pause to lengthen.

"Jemmy, how could you possibly have known I was obscure Dick Darwent, of Covent Garden? How could you have conceived that ingenious plan of carrying both bodies back to Garter Lane, and pitching them out of the coach without a footmark, very near my fencing school? How could you even have known of the fencing school?"

Jemmy, with sweat· running down his white face, seized at this as though Darwent had been joking all the time.

"I couldn't have known!" he crowed, in giggling gaiety. "It's a dem absurdity, gad! I couldn't have known!"

"Oh, yes, you could," said Darwent. "Townsend!"

"Eh, m'lord?"

"In your letter to me, I think, you said the graveyard coachman had been carousing merrily for a full twelvemonth through Covent Garden and St. Giles's? Playing thief tricks, but chiefly from meanspiritedness or malice? Specifically, that he 'knew everybody there'?"

"Yes, m'lord. That's true as gospel."

"You see, Jemmy? Assuredly you must have known Dick Darwent, though he wrote D'Arvent above his school. God help him, he was a very well-known character in Covent Garden. You, and only you in all your circle, would have known where to throw those bodies! You agree?"

From Alfred and Thomas, moving like tame tigers at the doorway, came a low growl. Caroline was against the curtains of one window, her eyes closed.

But Darwent, though he felt the pain of weariness in his shoulder blades, still spoke agreeably.

"Oh, Jemmy, that's the least of the evidence against you! While I was on the State side at Newgate, I deliberately lost enormous sums to you at the card table: several thousand, to be exact. I wanted you for my bear leader in society. Particularly, I wanted to meet Sir John Buckstone."

Darwent's expression darkened.

"I had little control over my words or inflections then," he said. "You're no fool, Jemmy. You guessed I had no wish to shake Buckstone's hand; a child of ten could have seen I wanted to fight him.

"This was your opportunity, Jemmy. For all your frantic questioning of me, I had told you nothing whatever. Yet I had seen the room with the red-and-gold wallpaper, and the bowl of oranges. I had seen the dead man. If I knew much of you, or even connected you with Frank Orford, you were a dead man. Was it not much better that I should fall by Buckstone's pistol?"

"No offense, old boy!" Jemmy blurted—and Townsend suddenly laughed.

"No offense taken, I assure you," Darwent answered blandly.

For Darwent clearly saw, in Jemmy's down-pulled mouth and hurt eyes, that Jemmy thought himself no hypocrite. *He* was a good fellow. *He* didn't want to do it. If he must conceive the most murderous schemes, and shrink as he carried them out, it was only because poor old Jemmy, the butterfly, must have what he wanted.

"When you presented Buckstone to me at White's . . ."

"I didn't want to do it, Dick! Did I?"

"I wish," said Darwent, "we had a written record. Each bleat you uttered, apparently to make peace, was to goad and sting us further. Afterwards I walked to the front door of White's, and you followed me. Remember?"

"Well, I . . . damme, yes! Why not?"

"We were all alone at that door. Granted?"

"Granted; but a man can walk to the door of his own club!"

"There I told you," continued Darwent, "that for the next two hours I should be at my house, or my wife's house, at number thirty-eight St. James's Square."

"You look a scarecrow! Why don't you have your clothes cleaned!—Well?"

Darwent's smile broadened.

"About three quarters of an hour later," he said, "a pistol ball was fired at me from Till Lewis's window through a window here. Jemmy. In all London you were the only person who knew where I was."

Dead silence.

Little fat Townsend, deeply interested, began to pick his teeth with a small blade of his knife. It contrasted with his fashionably curled white hair.

"How you'll chance your luck!" Darwent exclaimed, studying Jemmy with real curiosity. "Against nonsensical odds, as you will at macao! There wasn't a hundred-to-one chance you would see me at a rear window. But on you came, dressed in shiny smooth evening clothes (forgive the state of mine), with a loaded pistol under your cloak. Your ugly luck-god smiled and then spat at you. You missed."

Jemmy, now very cool, lifted his head high and let his fingers flutter out in a gesture of derision.

"Come, old boy!" he protested. "If I knew Jack was going to finish you next morning, would I have tried to pistol you that night?"

"Ah!" said Darwent. "But you didn't know that, Jemmy!"

"Eh?"

"When I left you at the door of White's, you were nearly in a fit. You couldn't control your speech. You had expected me to choose pistols; but I chose sabers. If I stuck to my rights, as a sword master naturally would, it seemed probable that I should kill Buckstone. You, poor fellow, would be left with nothing but a charge as accessory before and after the fact. So you lost your head and pulled that trigger."

"Dashed clever of you, old boy. But you can't prove that."

"Oh, yes, I can," said Darwent. "Townsend!"

The old runner, carefully putting his knife on the floor, reached into an almost elbow-deep pocket and produced a crumpled, dirty, good-sized scrap of paper.

"When you came to see me afterwards, Jemmy," continued Darwent, "that scrap of paper worked out from under your fine black waistcoat with the pearl buttons, and fell on the floor."

"Come, my dear fellow!"

"Oh, you didn't notice. Now you're aware, Jemmy, that the wadding for pistols is usually torn from newspaper. This fragment, you see, looked as though it had been dirtied by gunpowder and ripped away when a pistol was too hastily wadded. I therefore sent it in a letter to Mr. Townsend, together with a certain honorarium . . ."

" 'Andsome. me lord! Devilish 'andsome!"

"And asked him to search your rooms in Chesterfield Street. Well, Townsend?"

The runner gravely threw out his paunch and spoke as though throwing the words over Darwent's head in a witness box.

"Which on date named," he declared, "me and Tom Gilliflower searched. In one old boot cupboard of accused's bedroom, found old heavy pistol inscribed with accused's name." Out came the pistol, from that capacious pocket, and back again. "A-probing of fouled barrel, done with very small file, picked out unburned scraps of wad. Some scraps of wad, pasted over copy of *Times* that date, just fitted. You'd wish me go on, m'lord?"

"By all means."

"We-el! First scrap of paper, with date on it, exac-a-ly fitted copy of *Times* wrapped round pistol to hide it. Other bits, as spoken, fit as well. Signed statement of finding: J. Townsend, Esq., also T. Gilliflower."

"And when you came to me afterwards, Jemmy," purred Darwent, "what a comedy you played! You must lure me into a pistol duel, eh?"

"Damme. you're twistin' everything to look . . ."

"You were bored; you tantalized; you prodded; you suggested cowardice. How Buckstone was amused at a saber duel! How the *haut monde* would stir its white-faced corpse to smile! Perhaps they did and could. But I had rights, Jemmy, which you tried to persuade me were as airy as your own talk.

"Any fool would have insisted on his rights, Jemmy, unless he were a dead shot with the pistol. But you persuaded me, didn't you? You were almost maudlin when you left me, poor fellow, because of what must be done."

Darwent pushed his hands back through wet hair. His voice began to change.

"But, only a short time before, you had been willing to shoot me in the back."

"Only a butterfly, old boy! No harm!"

Then Darwent's voice rang out.

"How say you, members of the jury? Is the prisoner guilty, or not guilty?"

"Guilty!" replied Alfred and Thomas, who were slowly moving forward from the doorway.

"He's . . ." Caroline could not continue. Her lips formed the word *filthy*.

"Oh, gallows meat," agreed Townsend, who was again picking his teeth with the knife.

"You've got no right to keep me here!" Jemmy almost whispered.

"Not even the right to try you, at the moment," Darwent agreed. "But you will have a fair chance. Look into the lower part of the sideboard, there, and choose your own weapons."

"Weapons?"

"Yes."

Jemmy's tall body stiffened. Slowly he moved forward, to a point under the great chandelier. Among glass prisms many candles were bending or drooping amid their own heat and runs of wax; no host or guest ever minded this; it was too common.

"Hark'ee, old boy," Jemmy gulped. "I'm no coward, mind." He spread out his hands. "It'd surprise you, perhaps, what I can do with a saber. But *dying!*" His voice went up in a half-feminine scream.

"Dying!" he said. "Ged, it's awful. It's unthinkable. Dick, the man's a fool who risks it; he's a fool, Dick. Under the ground; no poetry albums to write in; no fine clothes." Again his voice shrilled up. "I won't fight you! You can't make me!"

The heavy crash, which they somehow associated with Jemmy, made them all jump until they realized it was the flinging open of the street door.

Into the drawing room—majestic, fat, slovenly, his raw-beef face suave and his white hat over one ear—marched Mr. Hubert Mulberry.

"Stand back!" roared Mr. Mulberry.

He was not drunk. He had taken only three or four glasses of brandy to uplift him and strengthen his wits. Most of all, he knew the whole truth. He removed his hat with such a lordly gesture that Thomas instantly sprang forward and took it with deep respect.

But Townsend, who knew him well and knew his intelligence too, made a snarl.

"And now 'oo the devil are you?" he asked.

"Stand back, you Bow Street scum," roared Mr. Mulberry, "and let a gentleman of law expound the evidence!"

Now it was quite true, as Townsend had said, that he was

the best thieftaker of his time. When he died, sixteen years later, he left twenty thousand pounds in fees and royal gratuities. But he gave ground to Hubert Mulberry, because—it spread in the air as palpably as Mr. Mulberry's breath—the slovenly lawyer *knew*.

The lawyer looked at Darwent, and his gaze softened.

"Lad, lad!" he said. "I wasted a lot of time, and that's a fact, going to Stephen's Hotel to discover if they'd killed ye. And now, I take it, you've been expounding the cause to these good people?"

"You heard . . . ?"

"Ay; who denies it? I was listening outside the street door.. You reasoned closely, Dick; you reasoned well." Here Mr. Mulberry prepared for a pounce. *"But—"*

"But what?"

Mr. Mulberry pointed his finger at Jemmy Fletcher.

"Lad," he said clearly, *"you've got the wrong man."*

There was one of those silences which can intensify even the pulse of a heartbeat. Darwent, with the windows at his right hand, had backed away until he was nearly against the wall built against that of the house next door. Then he found his voice.

"That's impossible!"

"Listen, now," said Mr. Mulberry, pointing a none-too-clean finger in his face. "What was your oath, Dick, when you left Newgate? It was to find and hang the person who killed Lord Francis Orford. Wasn't it?"

"Yes!"

Again Mr. Mulberry pointed to Jemmy: on whom, unregarded, the drops of wax were spattering.

"Well!" said Mr. Mulberry. "Your lily friend didn't kill Lord Francis Orford, and in fact he knows nothing at all about it."

"But Jemmy's the coachman! He's as good as admitted it!"

"Burst my bladder," snapped Mr. Mulberry, "but of course he's the coachman! Any soft 'un could see that. At the same time, Dick, he's not the murderer; not even of young Lewis, who's not dead. Stop; no questions; attend to ME!"

And Mr. Mulberry drew himself up, tapping his bulging waistcoat.

"What you said was true, lad, as far as it went. But you didn't tell 'em, which you could have done if you'd only mentioned points you mentioned to me—ay, and the Padre—because you didn't tell 'em the full tale. Shall *I* do it?"

213

"Yes!"

"Imprimis!" said Mr. Mulberry, raising his forefinger impressively. "He drove you out in the blue coach, let's say, to Kinsmere House in Bucks. *Item*: he carried you up the steps. *Item*: he set you down in front of a certain door. *Item*: he cut your leg cords and the door opened."

"Confound it, man, I know all that!"

"Do you?" inquired Mr. Mulberry. "Then, rot my bowels, you saw precious little. When old Bert Mulberry was sober (not until then; I give you that!)—why, lad, it was as plain as poison in a swelled old hag. I thought I could remember even the words you said, and I've compared 'em with what the Padre heard.

"Hark'ee, now!

" 'It seemed that, in an instant,' you said, 'all things stopped as a clock stops. As though these persons with me, if there were more than one,'—which there wasn't!—'stood paralyzed. The hand on my back, impelling me, rested motionless.'

"Just afterwards, you said, you heard a woman scream. But, as I've told you before this, it wasn't a woman. It was . . ."

"Jemmy, of course! I heard him give just that kind of cry at White's Club, when he was apparently trying to soothe down the trouble with Buckstone!"

Mr. Mulberry grunted.

"But why, in that disused house, did the coachman scream?" he demanded. "Why was he struck all of a heap like that? Hey?

"I'll tell you, Dick. He'd just opened a door and seen Frank Orford, his partner, skewered to the back of a chair. He was paralyzed to see a corpse he hadn't expected to see. All he could think to do, in gaining time, was to cut your hand cords, push you inside, and lock the door."

Mr. Mulberry nodded. He made a mesmeric gesture with the snuffbox he had fished out of his pocket.

"Now you'll do me the honor," he said, tapping his finger on the box lid, "to follow closely. This coachman walloped you across the napper in Hyde Park. He drove you to the house. You even saw him, on occasion, when he moved your eye bandages. Damme, he was never *at* the house. By your own testimony, Orford died as you entered that room. *The coachman was the one person who couldn't possibly have killed Frank Orford!*"

Darwent, who had been holding his breath so long that his lungs seemed to burst, now released it.

214

"Agreed," he said in a low voice.

There are some matters so obvious, he was reflecting, that their color or closeness blinds the eyes.

"Then the true murderer . . . ?" he asked.

"Ah!" said Mr. Mulberry, opening the snuffbox and taking a huge pinch, which exploded in a sneeze. But his rheumy little eyes looked apprehensive and evasive.

"You'll have to know, Dick," he went on. "Because why? Because it may stagger you so much that . . ."

"That what?"

Mr. Mulberry slapped at his coat, like a man slapping at imaginary insects in the drink horrors. Abruptly he turned his unwieldy bulk and pointed at Jemmy.

"You have him, anyway! Two charges of attempted murder, one of inciting riot. All of 'em hanging matters. Or, if you want to hush it up and polish off matters in a duel . . ."

"I won't fight him," said Jemmy. Candle grease bedaubed his fair hair and his black-clad shoulders, yet he had regained his light poise. "What's more," and Jemmy laughed loudly, "the implacable Dick won't fight either. Look at him! His strength's so drained he can hardly stand up!"

Though Darwent instantly straightened up, holding his shoulders well back, he was terrified in his heart that this might be true.

"Look at him!" Jemmy jeered again. "He could scarcely even handle a foil, let alone a saber. *I* could cut him down in two passes. But I won't fight him, and that's flat!"

A new voice, from the doorway, struck in with startling effect.

"Then perhaps," observed the voice, with grim pleasantry, "*I* might be allowed as substitute for Mr. Fletcher?"

Hubert Mulberry, who had been facing Darwent, swung fully round, moved aside, and faced the other way.

In the doorway stood the Hon. Edward Firebrace, six feet three and in full pride of strength. His dark cloak hung round him in folds. His large, long curl of reddish hair rose along the parting on his head, with the strong side whiskers framing his cheeks. On his face, as he bowed agreeably, was a smile of wide-set teeth.

Only one evil brush marred that picture. Firebrace's upper eyelids were swollen to a puffy red, more so than the lower lids, where pepper had been thrown at him. Though a chemist in Panton Street had toiled for an hour with water and boracic powder, the reddish eyes were not quite normal in sight. They roved with hatred.

Mr. Mulberry was the first to speak.

"Who are you?" he bawled. "What the devil d'ye want?"

Firebrace, ignoring him completely, spoke across the width of the room to Darwent.

"My name is Firebrace," he said. "You may have heard of me. I am the nephew of Major Sharpe, to whom you deliberately told lies. In addition to this, for no reason you . . ." Firebrace touched his inflamed eyelids. "I require satisfaction for these things, my lord."

"You shall have it."

"You're damned well right I shall," Firebrace told him coolly.

Flinging back over his shoulders both wings of his cloak, he displayed the coiled horsewhip in his right hand.

"As you once introduced yourself to my good friend Jack Buckstone," he said, "let *me* introduce myself."

His arm flung forward with the hiss of the long whip. Darwent felt pain burn his face as the lash snapped just once, more than halfway round.

Caroline cried out. Firebrace, giving a savage yank to wrest back the whip, made Darwent stagger, reel around, and fall to his knees. Darwent put out both hands to steady himself against the floor. Jemmy Fletcher giggled.

(Well, if I'm finished now . . .)

Then it happened.

Often in the life of a healthy man, whether at work or sport, there comes a time when he has driven too hard; when he is beaten, and can go no further. Then mysteriously, no one knows how, there pours into him that quality known as second wind. The breath ceases to choke in his throat. His heart moves to slow, even rhythm. New strength flows into his veins, as though he were re-created, and his brain clarifies to intensity. That was what happened to Darwent, a force gathering at once, as he bounced to his feet.

"Alfred!" he said in a new voice. "Thomas!"

"Yes, my lord?"

"Take his whip away from him."

If Firebrace retreated a step, quickly coiling his whip to strike again, it was not at all in fear. It was in utter incredulity.

"You'd not have a servant lay a hand on me?" he demanded.

Darwent ignored this.

"If he attempts to resist," Darwent said coldly, "knock him flat."

Alfred was moving in at Firebrace's right side, Thomas at his left.

Firebrace hesitated. At each side of him stood a powdered-headed bruiser as large as himself. He could not understand. He had never even noticed servants, let alone thought of them as human beings. It was as though heavy furniture had come to life against him.

"I'm sure you'll give up the whip, sir," Alfred said very respectfully, but with his clenched right against his waist.

"It'd be much better, sir, wouldn't it?" respectfully suggested Thomas, whose eye measured the distance to the side of Firebrace's already discolored jaw.

Firebrace gave up the whip.

"And now, sir," said Darwent, "when we speak of this matter, let us refrain from debating which person is the challenger and which the challenged. I find your notion of the rules somewhat confusing. Still, if you were to choose weapons, which would you choose?"

"Sabers, of course!"

"An excellent choice. And yet,"—Darwent's voice poured with earnestness and even sympathy—"may I not entreat you to postpone this matter until a later day. Believe me, I have two good reasons for this. May I not entreat you?"

Firebrace showed a smile of wide-set teeth.

"And have you," he inquired, "skip over to Calais by the morning packet? No, thanks!—What are your reasons?"

"First, sir, your eyesight is in no condition for a saber duel. Your judgment will be bad."

"Thank you so much. I'll risk that. Any other reason?"

Darwent spoke in a voice of vast, agreeable insult.

"Yes. It is an illusion, sir, that most cavalrymen are good swordsmen. A cavalryman fights and even exercises mainly to fight on horseback, which is a different thing. He does not practice daily on foot, especially if he should belong to a mere fashionable regiment. I give you the warning, sir."

Firebrace's countenance, between the side whiskers, had turned a muddy color. He said, without lowering his voice, some words which are not ordinarily heard in good society.

"Alfred!" Darwent said sharply.

"Yes, my lord?"

"Give him his choice of the sabers," said Darwent. "Then lock the door!"

CHAPTER XXII

Sabers at Late Night

Alfred moved swiftly across to the sideboard, across firm and well-laid boards on which mud-caked shoes would not slip.

"Good!" observed Firebrace, twitching off his cloak and throwing it at Thomas. "We must proceed without seconds, since we have no gentlemen here,"—his eye passed unseeingly over Townsend and sardonic-faced Hubert Mulberry—"for the purpose. Hold! My apologies! There's Jemmy Fletcher!"

"*I* won't do it, old boy!" cried Jemmy. But he ran over toward Firebrace, long black legs a-gangle, as though for protection. "You'll cut him up, won't you?" Jemmy prayed. "You're the man to do it, ain't you?"

Only the pain of Firebrace's eyes marred his joy.

"Oh, I flatter myself on a small victory," he agreed. "Don't fear, my dear fellow. *I'll* shave his pate."

Caroline had run to Darwent, seizing his arms and looking up into his face.

"You won't believe what I say," she told him, attempting with every fiber of her being to make him believe. "But I love you. Don't do it, Dick! Please! You're in no condition to fight."

Despite what he knew about her, he could not help loving her. He wanted to put his arms round her. But he took her hands instead.

"Look at my eyes," he answered, "and tell me whether I'm in a condition to fight."

There was a pause. "Yes," said Caroline. She looked away, and then back at him. Her cheeks were flushed. "May I stay here," she begged, "and watch you win?"

"If that is your desire, you may."

"Now, God's teeth!" roared Mr. Mulberry. Being fond of Caroline, he had been flapping about her like a very large old hen. Now he bawled at the room.

"The lady can't stay," he said. "If you must be fools, if you won't stop to think on more important legal . . . why, damme, you wouldn't let a tavern wench see a sight like this! Even old Bert Mulberry knows it!"

Firebrace lifted his upper lip.

"This man is quite right," he agreed.

Alfred, at his elbow, cradled the hilts of two sabers over his left arm, and offered them. Firebrace chose one at random, and propped it upright against the wall beside the door, while he tore off his own disreputable coat, waistcoat, cravat, collar and slung scabbard.

"Unless," Firebrace's red-stung eyes made him add with a smile, "the rumor about Lady Darwent is really true."

Caroline whirled round. "May I ask what rumor, sir?"

"Since you compel me to mention it, that you would prefer Lord Darwent's absence to his continued existence. In that case, of course, you will remain because . . ."

"No, sir," repied Caroline. She spoke clearly and very sweetly. "I remain because he will make you appear to be an absolute novice."

"Will he?" whispered Firebrace. Then, aloud: "Stand back!"

They stood back, all of them.

While the cambric shirt showed off Firebrace's strength and his immense length of reach, he studied the position. If Darwent insisted in remaining in that place with his back to the wall of the next house, they would fight across the width of the room rather than down its length. And at the end of the room, about six feet out and parallel with the window curtains.

That made no matter! Many an uninitiate would have been surprised at the thoughts in Firebrace's brain.

For duelists with the saber, as with the rapier, seldom move much either backwards or forwards. Saber-play, like rapier-play, is not continuous; it comes in short, sharp bursts. Sabers do not "ring"; their noise is a clunk-clunk mingled with the clang or slither of the parry.

"The saber, my lord," Alfred said at Darwent's elbow.

Darwent, who had been looking at Caroline after stripping off his own coat and waistcoat and empty slung scabbard, drew his eyes back.

"Thank you, Alfred. A very fine balance."

And so it was. The upper edge of the saber was dull, flat, lifeless. The lower edge, razor-sharp, tapered to a sharp point. Darwent, feeling the straight hilt, tightly grasped the leather-bound haft. It was solid, but not too heavy.

From across the room came a burst of laughter.

"Gad, that's good!" exclaimed Firebrace, though his infernal eyes *would* water.

"What is, old boy?" asked Jemmy eagerly.

"Nothing at all!" Firebrace assured him with a very grave face.

For he had just seen his adversary without coat or waist-coat. This fellow, Firebrace admitted to himself, was well made. But he seemed on the slight side, and he was not overly tall; he was just the sort for a battering attack, since Firebrace could not be called fast on his feet.

The beginning of a saber duel, at that time, was almost as standardized as an opening at chess. You led, as a rule, with a forehand cut to the head or shoulder. But Firebrace, the crafty, had devised different tactics.

His custom was to demand: "No salutes or ceremonies?" To which the adversary would almost always agree. Instantly Firebrace, though not quick, would leap forward and send a backhand—not forehand—cut to the head. His battering was under way before the adversary recovered poise.

And Firebrace thought of it tenderly now.

"Ready?" he called across the room, and snatched up the saber from the wall behind him.

Jemmy Fletcher scurried over to join the other spectators just beyond the chandelier.

"Any time at all!" Darwent called back.

The two combatants began to move forward—slowly, in a straight line, guards down.

Both wore sweat-soaked white cambric shirts, with three pearl buttons at the wrist. Both were in black small clothes, Darwent's gold knee buckles gleaming against Firebrace's diamond buckles. The light made a dull shine on the saber blades.

Firebrace towered, his large long curls of reddish hair a-gleam. Darwent risked a side glance toward Caroline, which he should not have done; all noticed the fierce intensity of his gray eyes.

The combatants, moving more slowly, stopped about six feet from each other.

Mr. Mulberry, who contemplated expressing emotion by driving his fist through the crown of his hat, bawled out at them.

"There's work to be done this night! Why must you take so long with your japery?"

"We shall be quick," said Firebrace, with slight moisture in his eyes.

"Agreed!" said Darwent.

"No salutes or formalities?" Firebrace demanded quickly. "Agreed!"

And Firebrace sprang forward, driving a backhand cut to the head.

It was met with a parry which almost numbed Firebrace's arm from wrist to shoulder, with a streak of pain at the elbow. That time, once only, Darwent failed to "carry" a cut, saving strength. But he meant it to warn against battering. Firebrace, off balance, just managed to parry the forehand cut which flew back at him.

Both men hesitated, their heads moving a little from side to side. Then Firebrace lunged with the point. He heard as well as felt through his arm the *sh-r-ung* as the blade went wide. Darwent's saber edge—unorthodox, backhand—seemed to sweep horizontally above Firebrace's eyes as though to cut off the top of his head.

"Oh, Gummy!" blurted old Townsend, who was still picking his teeth with a knife blade. He cut his mouth, and the knife clattered on the floor.

Darwent had leaped back, panting, his saber at guard. Firebrace felt no crush of pain, not even a seeping of blood.

But something, which tickled with a bitterness of humiliation, tumbled and brushed and speckled down over his face. His large reddish coil of hair, shorn off cleanly like other bits of hair, began to unshred before it feathered along the floor.

"I think," Darwent said politely, "you mentioned something about shaving my pate?"

Firebrace did not reply. He merely plunged in to batter.

There was a short, murderous burst of play, two cuts and two lunges on both sides. The *clung-clunk* moved up and then down, each stroke picked out by a dull gleam on the blades. Feet shuffled on boards, and suddenly rose to a maniac stamp-dance which stopped dead.

Abruptly play stopped too. Both adversaries studied each other.

Firebrace's eyes were streaming, either with tears of pepper or tears of rage. He could see, but just barely see.

"Guard yourself!" said Darwent, breathing hard. " 'Ware tricks!"

Instantly, with his own brand of swiftness, he feinted a backhand cut to Firebrace's right shoulder, and lured the other blade wide. His saber swept up vertically, and sliced down the side of Firebrace's left cheek.

Now the best swordsman, in fact, cannot shear off a heavy

side whisker. Hair is too resilient; the blade, for all our talk, not sharp enough; and the steadiest eye may remove the cheek as well as the whisker.

But Darwent's slash was very fair. Large tufts and pieces of hair, as well as the whole end of the whisker, flew wide amid very tiny blood pricklings against a roughened skin.

"You damned . . . !" shouted Firebrace; and stopped for breath.

Four times more the blades hacked or slithered. The terrified Caroline, who could not look but could not keep her eyes from it either, for some reason put her hands over her ears.

Then Darwent feinted again. Firebrace, always rearing up like a great mastiff above a bull terrier, did a half wheel to the right as his saber lashed nearly to the ground. He was wide open. Darwent's crosscut sheared down his right cheek as well, with much the same bits-and-pieces effect as before.

"I say, to all good people present," shouted Mr. Mulberry, as though he were beginning to read the riot act, "this must stop, as in Latin, *instanter*. I further say . . ."

Darwent, who had backed away again, spoke from behind saber guard.

"Listen to that, Firebrace." He spoke quietly, gently, compellingly. "You're blind; you can't see now; I don't want to hurt you. You needn't give up; but give over! There's no dishonor in stopping play now!"

As Firebrace towered over them—his puffy red eyelids streaming, beaten to a standstill, ridiculous with his shorn hair and patchy whiskers—he still had about him some quality of the pig-headed heroic.

"Give over, eh?" he whispered.

Alfred hurried forward toward Firebrace.

"Yes, sir. If you will allow . . ."

Firebrace merely flung out a side swing of that weighted razor edge.

Alfred saved his life only by dropping flat on the floor, and then rolling quickly out of reach. A quivering ran through the prisms of the chandelier, like a chatter of glass teeth. One candle fell, amid grease and fire. Firebrace's dim eyes peered round and round for Darwent.

"Where are you?" he shouted, launching cuts at the air. "Come out and fight!"

Deliberately Darwent threw his saber on the floor. Unarmed, he moved back into that space he had occupied at the beginning, his back several feet out from the wall.

222

"Dick!" screamed Caroline. "What are you doing?"

Curse it, couldn't they understand? If the near-blind Firebrace threw a heavy cut at Darwent, or rather at the wall behind—old unpainted wood backed by a three-foot brick wall of the house next door—the saber would be wrecked or torn from Firebrace's grip. It was the only way to avoid playing Blind Man's Buff against a madman with a saber.

"I'm here!"-Darwent called back, waving his arms in the air. "Can't you see me now?"

"Got you!" gritted Firebrace, craftily finding that dim shadow. And he ran forward, swinging up his arm as he ran.

Darwent, on edge to dodge, picked out every detail of Firebrace's face—red puffed eyes, open mouth, thick-corded neck —as he saw that giant charge straight at him.

If his foot were to slip, or he failed to move at the proper moment . . .

"Got you!" Firebrace repeated.

His saber whirled up, for an overarm cut to split down the middle of Darwent's skull. Darwent, seeing that nightmare face and blade towering at a three-foot distance, slipped out and under just as the strokes fell. Even Firebrace's sight caught the wall looming up ahead. He tried to check himself, but it was too late.

What happened then stunned Firebrace as much as it stunned the watchers.

For there was no brick wall beyond the paneling.

Firebrace's sword sheared through that old paneling, browntinged only by age, as through soft pinewood. It went so far that a part of the hilt got stuck inside; it wouldn't come out no matter how Firebrace tugged.

It was the end of Firebrace. Shoulders sagging, bewildered, he stood there with not even a spark of interest.

And up rose Mr. Hubert Mulberry, pointing with one hand to the saber in the wall and holding up his white hat with the other.

"Ayagh!" he said. "And *now* will you give over, Dick? *Now* will ye stand and hear reason? Don't you see the finger o' the Almighty pointing straight at truth?"

Darwent looked round. Eyes, as bewildered as his own, fixed on that sword cleft and—yes! a very faint glimmer of light shining through.

Caroline's hands, touched with dried mud, were clasped together. John Townsend pressed a reddened rag to the cut at his mouth. Thomas and Alfred stood without expression.

Jemmy Fletcher, it is regrettable to state, lay full length on the floor in a dead faint.

"Listen, lad!" pounced Mr. Mulberry. "Don't you see now what cozened and wheedled you, on the night of all your adventures with the blue coach?"

"No! What was it?"

"It was the power of darkness," the old lawyer said grimly.

"The power of darkness?"

"Ay; just that!" Out thrust Mr. Mulberry's red-roughened face, with the grayish-brown hair stuck to the forehead. "You sought a 'lost room'! A room bewitched and hocussed overnight! Well! D'ye know where it is?"

Here Mr. Mulberry pointed with his hat to the cleft in the wall.

"It's in the front room of the house next door," he said. "And split my britches! you've been sitting beside it the whole time!"

"No!" said Caroline. She hesitated; then there was silence.

But Darwent's mind, as he opened his mouth to deny it too, caught at curious hints and memories which had been swirling there for some time.

"Alfred," he said, "yes; and to Thomas. Mr. Firebrace seems tractable. Will you take him to some other room and bathe his eyes and keep him there?"

"Yes, my lord," answered Alfred. "But if I may suggest it, about the eyes: wouldn't Mr. Hereford be the best gentleman for that?"

"Mr. Hereford! Is *he* still here?"

"Yes, my lord. He has been—questioning. Certainly his carriage is still at the door."

Darwent merely nodded, and they escorted out the numbed Firebrace. Darwent, his mind boiling, swung round toward Mr. Mulberry.

"Stop!" roared that gentleman, facing him like a loaded cannon. "*I'll* speak, Dick, and you'll answer. What did that coachman do to you, on the night of May 5th?"

"But I don't . . ."

"Why, I'll tell you. He drove you from Hyde Park out into the country, though not as far as Kinsmere, and he drove you straight back into London to St. James's Square!"

"He didn't. I can swear—!"

"Stop," said Mr. Mulberry, coolly putting on his white hat. "Now answer your own questions, Dick, which you put to us in this very room at breakfast. Mind, now! Even I ad-

224

mit *I* don't know why they should smash you over the head before Fletcher put you in the coach. . . ."

"But I do," retorted Darwent.

"Eh, lad?"

"I learned it," Darwent replied, "when I was talking to Tillotson Lewis. He suspected the firm of Frank Orford and Company; he was investigating, and he wrote to tell them so. They were compelled to abduct him—or me, as it happened —when they saw him. To knock him out in case he struggled! To treat him as a prisoner until they discovered how much he knew of them!"

"Ah!" breathed Mr. Mulberry with satisfaction. "And now, Dick, to business! To the ordinary customers they didn't have to knock out!—You admitted (eh?) you could understand why they'd be tied with soft bonds, and their eyes tightly bandaged.

"But why did they sling you in a hammock, Dick, when you could just as well have sat in the coach? Above all, why did they stop up your ears so tightly you could only faintly hear a scream beside one ear?"

"Well? Why was it?"

"Because the coachman was driving you back to London," said Mr. Mulberry, "after a small excursion into the country. If you were slung in a hammock, you couldn't feel the difference between the jolt over some bad paving and a jolt on a country road. Above everything, you couldn't hear a street noise to tell you that you were back in town. And you didn't, did you?"

Again the obvious smote Darwent between the eyes. But he couldn't believe it; he wouldn't believe it, because . . .

"I swear to you," he cried out, "that I was at Kinsmere House in Bucks!"

"By your own admission, lad, had you ever been inside it before?"

"No. But I saw the countryside. I saw that signpost . . ."

"Ah!" pounced Mr. Mulberry. "As the sages say, here's it. When you were driven out three-quarters of the way to the village of Kinsmere, you were allowed to work your eye bandages loose once or twice. And you saw the signpost by moonlight?"

"Yes!"

"Now this happened on the drive out there, before you found Orford's body?"

"Yes!"

225

"For the sake of argument, Dick, let me quote your own words. *'I had one glimpse of a cluster of finger posts,'* you said, *'with Kinsmere in reversed letters.'* Reversed letters, Dick? On a finger post?"

White-haired, red-waistcoated Townsend, who had staunched the bleeding at his mouth, emitted what for his voice might have been a crow's note of mirth. It was Caroline who spoke.

"But when you drive towards a place," she said, "the lettering reads forward in the ordinary way! You think you see reversed letters only when you leave. And you know it because they're on a finger post. Dick you were being driven. . . ."

"Back to London," the lawyer growled in assent, "with an aching head and a fuddled sense of time. Ay! And if you don't credit old Bert Mulberry," he added fiercely, again stabbing his hat in the direction of the wall, "I beg you to go next door and see the room you saw that night!"

Darwent went cold to the heart; he could not have said why.

"But that house is locked and shuttered! Who'd have a key to it?"

"I would," said Mr. Mulberry. "Damme, Dick, have you forgotten you told me yesterday to find a furnished house for . . . for . . ."

Hubert Mulberry could not possibly have known Dolly was dead. What instinct, or flow of thought moved in his brain, behind the bloated old face, Darwent could not tell.

But Darwent flung it aside too.

"You didn't mean," he said stupidly, "to get lodgings next door to . . . to . . ."

"No, lad. But when I hear that same day of *another* house that belongs to the Kinsmeres, *another* house shut up for two years: why, I scent the lost room. And I've a devilish good excuse for getting a key."

"Wait!" said Darwent. "When I was in the drawing room today, with Till Lewis, I could have sworn I heard a noise from that house. Was it you?"

"Ay, Dick. I was still as drunk as Davy's whole farmyard; and most uncommon nonsilent. Rot me, why are we wasting time?" Whereupon he lifted up his voice.

"Ho!" bellowed Mr. Mulberry, striking an attitude which he imagined to belong to a Jacobite king and no pig-snouted

Hanover. "Candles for these good people! Lights! A bedroom candlestick, a candle, to see the den of evil and the secret of the lost room!"

And then, for no reason, terror struck into the dining room here.

Perhaps it was Darwent's terror alone. He had lived too long with grisly imaginings. That room had woven through goblin-ridden dreams; it had made him start awake, with sweat on his body; it followed him and tapped his shoulder by day. About it he now felt prophetic. What really frightened him, now, was the feeling that some new catastrophe would spring at them out of the room.

His feeling of prophecy proved to be right. Meanwhile:

"Very well," he said.

The next few minutes, until the time they faced the door of the room, afterwards were confused in his mind. Caroline brought candles whose brass stemholders ended in a kind of brass dish. Grunting some words like, "Allus 'ave me darbies," Townsend bent over the fallen Jemmy and locked the handcuffs over Jemmy's right wrist to his own left wrist. After this he kicked and slapped Jemmy into hissing wakefulness, lifting Jemmy to his feet with an iron-shod toe cap.

Five of them, each carrying a lighted candle in a brass dish holder, went down the front steps of the house into cool air.

It was deathly quiet. Outside stood Mr. Hereford's carriage, driver dozing on the box. In St. James's Square Darwent discerned the movement of a military busby, evidently some officer going home late. The black sky had turned gray, with tinges of dawn.

Dawn. Darwent looked at the sky, and remembered several events.

"This," declared Mr. Mulberry, pointing toward the edge of the pavement outside number thirty-six next door, "is where the blue coach stopped.

"This," he continued, holding the candle flame toward the eight stone steps leading up to the front door, "is the 'staircase' you were carried up. Dick, Dick! You said 'broad' staircase; but how the devil could you have known that? It was stamped on your imagination by that country drive, and also by . . .

"Never mind!" said Mr. Mulberry, unlocking the big front door. "This is the door the coachman opened with his foot, as I do. Now hold up your lights, all of you!"

They obeyed the order. But there was a short, slight struggle

227

between handcuffed Jemmy and handcuffed Townsend, with lights going up and down in two opposite hands, until Jemmy's rib was slightly nicked by the blade in Townsend's left hand. Jemmy began to wail, but fell silent.

"That's order, that is!" Mr. Mulberry said approvingly.

"Thank'ee kindly, sir," bowed Townsend. "Sometimes I slits their wizzends," he explained seriously, "but a flash cull's better took alive."

Darwent's voice was harsh with nervousness. "Can't we get on with this, Mulberry?"

"Observe!" said Mr. Mulberry, sweeping the candle flame inside the hall. "In the two houses, they've built front room against front room, each facing opposite. The first door down, in this house, the door is on the right-hand side as you enter. Now, Dick! Are you ready?"

"Whatever it is, I'm ready! Yes."

"Then walk forward to the first door on the right. . . . That's it; stop! That's where the coachman carried you. Now turn and face the door. That's it! That's where the coachman turned you."

The others had crowded into the hall after Darwent. Caroline's voice rose up.

"Isn't there someone following us?" she asked quietly.

"Gently, now, m'lady!" scoffed Townsend, with a wink meant to be reassuring.

"Dick," said Mr. Mulberry, "open the door and go in. But don't take more than three steps inside. That's all you said you took; remember?"

Darwent gritted his teeth. He felt exactly as he had felt when he prepared himself to go out to the hangman.

"Very well," he agreed.

Shifting the candleholder to his left hand, Darwent opened the door. He took three steps inside, almost nerveless to lift his eyes; then, determined, he looked up. It was the same room.

First he saw the three candles burning in the glass castle of a chandelier, now lightly filmed with dust. But these were even skimpier candles, low-burning and almost ready to go out.

Then, above the Turkey carpet, he saw Frank's tortoise-shell wood desk; with tall chair behind it. Midway down the woven chair back was a dark-brown bloodstain and the thin cut where the rapier had stabbed through. Glancing to his right, Darwent saw (apparently) the same tall, close-shuttered windows.

But worst of all, when he looked straight ahead at the wall, papered in dull red patterned with gold, which faced him from the other side of the room . . .

There was the tall window, in the wall well behind Frank's desk. Through it Darwent saw moonlight falling softly on what seemed to be a lawn outside. He saw the white statue of the god Pan, leering back. He saw the apparently real shrubbery. The power of darkness, to twist and deceive the mind!

"But there's no . . ." he began.

"Yes, lad?" whispered Mr. Mulberry, who was breathing hard.

"There's no open lawn there, as I don't have to tell you! The other side of that wall is the wall of Caroline's dining room."

"Not *quite* the other side," corrected Mr. Mulberry, who seemed half in a fit.

"What do you mean?"

"Why, rot me, Mr. Caliban, the moneylender, wanted to construct a room which should be pretty much like one at Kinsmere House in the country, where there was a real statue outside the window. That wasn't hard, if you have big rooms like the rooms here.

"Don't you see what he did? He had all the bricks removed, and the ceiling propped up with iron and wooden joints. Frank Orford wanted *depth:* eh? He wanted to build a partition wall, a dummy wall of wood, down the length of that side of the room. But he had to have at least four feet depth, or maybe five, behind that wall: eh? So the dummy window could be set in, and a fine illusion behind it would show a country-house lawn? I turned the lamps on, laddie, the way it was when you saw it. Damme, look here!"

Mr. Mulberry strode forward, putting down his candle-holder on the now-dusty desk.

From beside the little table with a bowl of shriveled, moldy oranges, he picked up a chair.

"Don't do it!" cried Caroline, who had slipped in beside Darwent. "I think I understand! We . . ."

There was no reply.

The window was a full-length one, with two sashes horizontal across the middle. Swinging back the chair, Mr. Mulberry drove it at the lower half.

Even as the crash of glass exploded, the moonlight trembled and the statue as well. When the lawyer ducked inside and stood up, the swish of his foot against manufactured glass destroyed reality. He slapped his hand down in the statue; it was plaster. He faced out at them through the upper glass, with that inexplicable wild look on his face and the white hat crammed down on his head.

"*I* saw it," muttered Darwent, "only three feet from the door. *And* (deliberately) in the light of only three candles. Other persons must have seen it closer, I think: but not many feet closer. The power of"—He stopped.

Mr. Mulberry ducked out from under the window.

"Why, Dick, you saw that same effect of moonlight, done with lamps, at the opera! You saw something, maybe, a thought similar in the way o' what they call perspective with greenery." Suddenly he pointed to the window behind. "But was it as good as that, lad? Was it the job of a master craftsman?"

"No, it wasn't nearly as good! But what difference . . ."

Mr. Mulberry regarded him savagely.

"Ask yourself," he said, "how many men could have painted that background, designed each shrub or grass-blade, worked and painted it into a stage scene you could swear was real!"

He pointed to the bowl of oranges on the table.

"Then ask yourself," he snapped, "how many men, potential enemies, would be permitted close to Frank Orford when that man held a sword? Only a man famous for sword-jugglery, Dick! Why were the rapiers there at all? Only a man who could throw up four or five oranges, and catch them on a rapier point when . . ."

"*One moment,*" proclaimed a new voice, just as Townsend dragged the protesting Jemmy into the room.

The newcomer, who also held a candle, straightened up and looked slowly round.

"Oh, I killed Orford," said Mr. Augustus Raleigh, with a look of contempt on his gaunt features. "But why should there be any fuss or sadness at his taking off?"

CHAPTER XXIII

Hopes to Show That We Do Not Always Suspect
Everybody

To Darwent, at least, the shock of that realization came slowly. When Mr. Raleigh spoke, Darwent was looking at the two long, close-shuttered windows in the right-hand wall.

They were only the ordinary windows looking out on St. James's Square. Yet a whisper to the imagination, the power of darkness, even yet conjured up outside the lawns and oak trees of Kinsmere House. Would Frank Orford have risked the noise of carts and carriages out there? Yes; because in summer there were few carts and carriages after nightfall.

But now the new shock, the new spring of catastrophe, was on them again. . . .

"You!" he said to Mr. Raleigh. Since he liked the man, he did not particularly care what Augustus Raleigh had done. But the shock remained. "You killed Orford?"

Mr. Raleigh's dark eyes were steady but very weary in the gaunt face.

"Dick, Dick," he said, "how often I have betrayed myself! How often I have almost told you!"

Darwent turned to Mr. Mulberry. "How long have you known this?"

Mr. Mulberry's expression, Darwent realized, had been one of self-hatred because he must speak.

"Only since this morning, Dick, that time after breakfast you had made haste away from us to see Dolly Spencer." Mr. Mulberry rubbed his nose. "I'd drunk a mort of ale. And your good lady, seeing my needs as she sees all men's needs, outed herself with a decanter of brandy.

"I was foxed, Dick. I admit it. I made some quotation from the Latin (which escapes me now) about the sanctity of a Roman villa. And back it came to me what I'd heard the day before,"—he pointed to Mr. Raleigh—"in *your* house, when Dolly Spencer lay on a bed of sickness, and I was in the room.

"The girl said you'd once built a Roman villa, for *Julius*

Caesar, so real she leaned against one of the pillars and toppled over. I'd already told you I had the rest of the mystery as clear-clean as a line of tulips (though damn the Dutch, says I, for that sour shrunk-faced William the Third). But here! And here, abreast of Roman villas, I was looking at a bowl of fruit on the dining-room table, and remembering the cut oranges in the lost room . . ."

"And remembering," interposed Mr. Raleigh's deep voice, with a touch of bitterness, "how many times you had seen me catch oranges on a rapier point at Drury Lane?"

Mr. Mulberry threw his hat into a corner.

"I did," he roared back, as though confessing a sin. "And at last I knew the assassin of Orford. I tried to send a message to Dick by his good lady . . ."

"And I took the message," Caroline pleaded. "Unfortunately, sir, you were—you were not yourself. I can understand now why you flourished a great number of house keys at the dining-room table. But all you could do was tumble into a hackney cabriolet, and call for cider."

"Well!" said Mr. Mulberry, with a scowl. "The fact is, my lady, I meant the cider cellars in Maiden Lane. I had to sober myself on soda water." Then he glared at Mr. Raleigh.

"But you're an honest man and a gentle kind o' beau," Mr. Mulberry added. "How could I betray you, even if I knew? How did you come to be associated with this firm of Orford and Fletcher?"

Mr. Raleigh quivered.

"Associated?" he said in a voice of such disgust that serpents might have been crawling over him. "In many ways, sir, I own myself to be vile. But those two? No!"

There was a film over Mr. Raleigh's eyes as he turned to Darwent.

"My lord," he said very formally, "when you honored my house in Lewknor Lane by paying a call on Dolly there . . . she is dead now; how curious! . . . you must have been surprised at my unmanned and even unmanly conduct, when you tactfully suggested gratitude (for what service to *us,* my lord?) and a place to live. I was not merely penniless; I was in debt."

Darwent spoke gently.

"And yet not penniless, I imagine," he said, "in the way Jemmy Fletcher there always states he is? Mr. Raleigh, he won several thousand pounds from me at piquet; yet he claimed himself too hard up to pay a wager I made him, on the way to a duel, about my own death. It must have tortured

232

his miserly soul to pay the prize fighters. He's meaner than Frank Orford."

The strength of Mr. Raleigh's voice, in its bitterness and its humility, made even Hubert Mulberry step back.

"No man was ever meaner than Lord Francis Orford!" he cried.

"I ask your pardon," Mr. Raleigh said a moment later, with a faint apologetic smile at the candle flame. "But you will understand if you hear my foolish story. I think I told you, Lord Darwent, I was dismissed from Drury Lane towards the end of April?"

"Yes."

"To be exact, the 21st. Because I had offended a man of title by spilling paint on his boot, I was given no pay in lieu of notice. And I could never save a farthing from my wages, as I have incautiously said to so many."

Mr. Raleigh's gaunt face hardened.

"I wonder that Mr. Mulberry, with all his wit, did not wonder how Emma and I had contrived to exist—to keep even a quartern loaf in the cupboard!—between the end of April and the end of July. Whoever wondered that would have seen all.

"But I spoke to you of other matters!

"Of the five noblemen who lodged a complaint against me at the theater, one was Lord Francis Orford. On the very same night as the day of my dismissal, he sent a carriage for me and requested my presence at thirty-six St. James's Square.

"How I hoped! How I dreamed! How I thought . . . laugh if you like; it was foolish . . . that here had come a golden change of fortune. What things I could do for Emma! Emma —Emma is the Christian name of my wife.

"No carriage (if I may correct Mr. Mulberry, whom I overheard) ever stopped at this house. It stopped a door or two or three away, so that this dark, shuttered place, seldom entered except by the back door, should seem deserted. And in some fashion the horses' hoofs were muffled, so that we made little noise. In this room I met Lord Francis."

Mr. Raleigh paused, swallowing hard. His gaze moved up to the chandelier, where the last low-burning candle had given a leap of smoke and gone out. Then he looked at the desk in the middle of the room, and the tall bloodstained chair behind it.

"Lord Francis sat there," continued Augustus Raleigh,

pointing to the chair. "His dummy partition wall was finished, together with a certain other object. He'd had the materials brought in bit by bit, the workmen cautioned to work quietly, so no one in the neighborhood knew a thing about it. He wished me to construct the window and design the illusion. He wished it done as soon as possible. He was quite open with me. If I wished, I could go to Kinsmere House and copy the statue. For this work, he offered the very large sum of ten pounds.

"Ten pounds! It would support Emma and myself for three months! I promised, and vowed in my soul too, it should be the best work of which I was capable.

"Well! By going without sleep for two days and nights, I finished it. As you see, it is—it is not ill made. On the night I completed it, showing him how to adjust the wick of the lamp, I was desperate. I had spent my own money, as well as borrowed, to buy the materials.

"And I had the temerity to ask for payment. All three of us were in this room; Lord Francis, Mr. Fletcher, and myself."

Darwent glanced sideways at Jemmy.

Jemmy, as though the handcuffs became him, had assumed a jaunty air and waggled the candleholder in his left hand. For some time there had been a curious smile on his face.

"Well, I asked for payment," Mr. Raleigh said heavily. "Lord Francis sat in that chair, reading a newspaper, Doubtless, Lord Darwent, you were familiar with his expression. His eyebrows a little raised; the long nose; the twitch of the nose as though what one just said had offended his nostrils? But it was not that now. It was mere wellbred astonishment.

" 'Pay *you?*' says he. 'Pay a tradesman?'

"He never laughed. But he sometimes smiled, making his false teeth project. Perhaps it was not in his thin-blooded nature to laugh.

" 'My poor man,' he said, 'a tradesman is lucky if he's paid in a year or two.'

"Whereupon, I regret, I lost my head. I said nothing; I only felt. But how shall I explain? *How?*" demanded Mr. Raleigh, in a puzzled tone. "How shall I gain your ear, much less your sympathy, for this feeling?

"You see, I had never thought of myself as a tradesman. Though that is honorable work too." Suddenly his voice throbbed with a drum note of pride. "I had thought of myself as a master craftsman, proud of his hands' work, who would

234

have been honored by the guilds of olden time, and yielded the wall to no man save in the way of friendship!

"But sometimes it is good, perhaps, to have pride chastened.

"All this time, I noticed, Lord Francis Orford had been regarding me in a very odd way. I guess the reason now, of course. In a short time I had learned much of 'Mr. Caliban,' who was now in business. Lord Francis and Mr. Fletcher had talked as carelessly in front of me as in front of Pan's statue. But this never occurred to me then.

"Lord Francis, as pleasantly as he could, made an apology which pleased and surprised me. I was quite right, he assured me. If I would return the next evening, he said, I should be paid.

"You may be sure I was there. The money lay on the desk. Might he trouble me for the formality of a receipt? Of course!" Mr. Raleigh hesitated. "But I am not perhaps," he added superfluously, "a good man of business. What documents I signed, or the nature of them, remains a mystery to me.

"I took my ten pounds, and forgot the matter.

"That was the night of April 24th. Just a week later, the—the horror (forgive such a big-drum word for my small affairs) came on me. I received a letter from Mr. Caliban.

"It reminded me of our agreement, evidently made a week ago. It seemed Mr. Caliban had loaned me twenty pounds on my note-of-hand: this sum was to be paid back, at one hundred per cent interest, in quarterly installments. The letter did not ask for payment, as yet; it merely reminded me."

Mr. Raleigh moistened his lips.

"And again—how shall I explain?" he asked. "My first impulse, as usual, was to slink away and in some fashion make my peace with Lord Francis. This soon passed. Run to a magistrate? Cry for a help which would now be useless? You may call me bookish-minded and crazed. But this is what I thought."

Mr. Raleigh's whole bearing changed.

"I thought to myself: what would Shakespeare have said? Or Kit Marlowe? Or rare Ben Jonson? Or manly Wycherley? Or even those authors, of our own day, who have given us *Marmion* and *Childe Harold*: what would *they* have said? 'Forbear, old hunks!'—would they have said?—'slink gently and timorously away.'"

Then again the deep drum roll thundered in his voice.

" 'No, by God!' they would have said. 'Let the dog be run through with a sword!' And so I determined to kill."

Mr. Raleigh lowered his bald head, all triumph gone. He was only a tired, aging man who for a brief time had opened his locked-up heart.

"The rest," he added, "is short and simply told.

"I had learned so much of their affairs through one circumstance, viz: that you must not suppose Mr. Caliban new to this business. Their firm had been at work upwards of seven months, from a house near Hyde Park. This house here, if they changed, would be more daring with no rent to pay. When they discussed small changes in their plan of action, I knew the plan itself.

"No one ever entered this house save Lord Francis and Mr. Fletcher, and then by the back door. There were no servants. The 'servant' who drove me on the first night had been Mr. Fletcher. The caretaker, paid by Lord Francis's father, had been sent away. On the night they expected a client, the front door would be left unlocked for the coachman to open.

"Lord Francis Orford would sit in this room, wearing a black mask and with false teeth removed to disguise his voice. The coach always arrived at midnight, when no one would see it or no drunken wanderer even pay heed to it.

"I chose at random the night of May 5th. I carried with me two old rapiers in their long heavy-headed leather case. The front door was unlocked. As St. James's Church clock struck the quarter-hour to twelve, I went in.

"Lord Francis had not yet put on his mask or removed his false teeth. He was surprised to see me, but not alarmed.

"For I was humble. I made apology, God forgive me. I said I had tried to be too sharp in asking payment for my work, and had been taught a deserved lesson. This pleased him; he thought it his just due.

"But, I added, I had just procured a new fine employment at the Pantheon, at ten pounds a week; we should soon have done with money troubles. He wished to know my new work; he was curious about the case; I knew it would be so. I said I had newer, more amazing feats of sword-jugglery with oranges. I demurred from showing them until he grew angry, and ordered me. . . .

"Have you wondered why there were *two* swords?

"I had oranges in my pockets. But he bade me bring a handful from the bowl over there. One rapier I placed on the desk at my right hand. With my left hand—explaining how much more difficult this was; a lie—I used the other sword when I tossed up oranges and caught them.

236

"Lord Francis was absorbed. His attention was fastened on my left hand. He paid no heed to my right. But with my right hand I caught up the other rapier. I lunged across that narrow desk. And I stabbed him through his poisoned heart.

"This was when I heard, too soon, the very faint sound of muffled horseshoes as the coach returned.

"Dick," added Mr. Raleigh, dropping all formal address and speaking heavily, "only one more thing you must have noticed. Look there!"

And Mr. Raleigh, lifting his candle, pointed toward the doorway of the red-and-gold-patterned room.

"The fireplace! The chimney piece!" said Darwent.

Well he remembered it, on the right side of the door as he entered. The stone fireplace, with its long tapering hood, from which . . .

"If you had stopped to think," Mr. Raleigh said gently, "you would have known it for a dummy. What lunatic, at least in our age, builds a fireplace with its *back* to the wall of a main hall? Lord Francis's masons built it, because the other fireplace had been cut off by the partitioned wall. One can climb up inside, stand on a ledge, and hear without being seen. Then, with the aid of a folding trap, the hidden person slips down into the main hall behind."

"And you climbed up there? It was you who—" Darwent stopped.

"I climbed up," assented the other. "I took my leather case. But I left the two rapiers, to suggest a duel and no murder. I wanted one last bitter word with the coachman."

He glanced toward Jemmy, whose agreeable smile was edged with hatred.

"I could see nothing," said Mr. Raleigh. "Dick, how could I guess it was you? When the door clapped to, I imagined the coachman to be there with some poor devil. I gave the coachman my final taunt. Down the chimney I said . . ."

"'*He must not reach the windows,*'" repeated Darwent.

"With Orford dead, I wrongly believed, their whole filthy lost room' would explode like a powder magazine. Let a client touch one of the windows, and . . . well, that was my taunt. Afterwards I had only to slip out through the folding trap, and leave by the front door.

"That is all I have to say. You have heard my confession; do as you like. I killed him. And, as God sees me, I would do it again."

237

A long silence, except for heavy breathing, held silent the dingy room.

Except for the dim moonlight glow over the statue of Pan, looking on derisively, six candles—five held in hands, one on the desk with the bloodstained chair behind it—made a dull ring of light as though for a council circle.

The silence was broken by Jemmy Fletcher, who looked down at Townsend.

"And now, my dear Charlie,"—to call a runner a Charlie was the deadliest insult at Bow Street—"hadn't you better unlock these darbies, and put them where they belong?"

" 'Ad I, now?" whispered Townsend, as though holding his breath.

"Come, dear lad, what have *I* done?" crowed Jemmy. "Dick's alive. Till Lewis, somebody says, is still alive. It was larks, Charlie; only my larks! I have friends, influential friends, who will show it." Then Jemmy nodded toward Raleigh. "But him?" His voice went up to a scream. "They'll hang him! They'll hang him! They'll hang him!"

Darwent moved toward him with a soft, dangerous step.

"Oh, no, they won't," said Darwent.

Round that intent group went a faint sibilance of approval, as though of breath released, in a kind of hiss; and Caroline's was the most approving of all.

Darwent turned toward Mr. Raleigh. The candleholders they carried were close together, throwing weights of shadow underneath. Nobody saw the treasury notes Darwent slipped into his companion's waistcoat pocket.

"Go home, forget all this, and sleep," he said gently. "You will not be arrested. You will not even be suspected."

Mr. Raleigh regarded him with a stupid, bewildered look. He could not meet anyone's eye.

"Dick, I . . ."

"No," said Darwent firmly. "You committed no murder. You trod on an insect. Sir, even before the matter of—of Dolly Spencer, I saw you were under some great strain as soon as I mentioned number thirty-eight St. James's Square. Go in peace. When you have rested, we will speak of the matter of finding you employment."

The other's mouth worked. "Dick, to thank you . . ."

"No!"

Hesitantly, Mr. Raleigh turned toward the door. He turned there, and spoke in an apologetic but sincere voice to them all.

"Believe me, I should not mind. . . ." His hand went up

to his throat, as though there were a rope there. "Except for one thing, again no doubt foolish. It would leave Emma alone. Good night."

He moved away, one thin light leaving the group, and they heard him go faltering down the hall. Darwent whirled round to Townsend and Jemmy.

"Take off his handcuffs," he said to Townsend.

" 'Ere! M'lord!"

"Take off his handcuffs."

Jemmy assumed a half-sneer of virtue as the catch clicked.

"Listen to me, Jemmy," said Darwent. Again his hand shot out and gripped Jemmy's cravat. "I desire to know whether you have understood anything, *anything*, of what has been said tonight. Do you believe in hell?"

"How should *I* know? Ask the parson fellows!"

"Let us suppose, for the sake of argument, there is a hell. Do you know why Frank Orford's soul rots deep in it? Let me tell you. It was not because Frank cheated a poor devil like Raleigh. Not in the least. It was because Frank thought he had a *right* to cheat him.—Do you understand that, my soaring songbird?"

"No, I see you don't," Darwent added. "Mr. Mulberry?"

"Aye?"

"Speaking as a lawyer, how much evidence have we to hang this beauty?"

Gathering up his white hat from a corner, Mr. Mulberry sat down in a dead man's chair at the desk, glowering at the candle there.

"Why, Dick," he grunted, "if we had more evidence, you couldn't use it; it'd be too much. For that affair at the opera, there's half the Fancy to swear he hired 'em (inciting to riot: stretched neck). There's five who've already sworn he stabbed Mr. Lewis (attempted murder: stretched neck)."

"Have you anything to add, Mr. Townsend?"

"Well, m'lord," said Townsend, dropping the handcuffs into one pocket and then patting both, "me and you and 'er ladyship together, we could show in ten minutes 'ow he tried to shoot you in the back. At Newgate they don't like people as shoots friends in the back. He'll have things thrown at him afore Langley scrags him outside debtors' door."

And Jemmy's eyes began to turn one way, turn another way. . . .

"Now go free," said Darwent, dropping his hand from the cravat. 'I release you because I must. But one little word

239

from me, Jemmy. If you ever so much as breathe a hint of Raleigh's guilt . . ."

"I won't, old boy! Word of a gentleman!"

"Remember, I shall hear it. And the law works too slowly for me. I mean to call on you one night. When I leave, Jemmy, you will not be alive."

And now Jemmy's knees gave way. These threats of the law, though frightening, seemed remote and scarcely touching his cosseted life. But Darwent was different. Darwent he understood perhaps less than the former understood him. In Jemmy's eyes Darwent was inhuman, like one of those iron figures they exhibited: a monstrosity who never missed with the pistol, never missed with the sword, never failed to keep a promise of death. And something in Jemmy Fletcher cracked across, cracked with terror, and was never the same again.

"Mum's the word!" he babbled, and hurried for the door. But, at the door, he remembered his position as a dandy. Moistening two fingers at his mouth, he manipulated a few strands of his fair hair so they stood up like a flower.

"Ill-breeding!" sneered Jemmy, and ran for the street door as though pursued, taking another light with him.

"Mr. Townsend," Darwent said gravely, "I am told you gentlemen of the runners have a certain admirable code. If evidence be necessary, produce it; if not . . . exactly! It being always understood that the honorarium shall not be so high as to be called by an unpleasant name."

"M'lord," crowed Townsend, pleased by such a word as "honorarium." "You couldn't ha' said it better, Lord Darwent, if you'd been Lord Malmesbury hisself!"

"Thank you. If you will do me the honor to call on me next day . . . ?"

"I'll do *meself* the honor," returned Townsend. At the door, candle illuminating his red waistcoat, he gave his best evidence of sincerity.

"I'd ha' done it for nothing, damme!" he declared, "if times wasn't so hard and my wife so devilish agg-a-ravating ever since she cotched me a-writing my amours. M'lady: m'lord: yours very truly: good night."

Another light moved away, adding to the gathering darkness. For some time Mr. Mulberry had been sitting behind the desk, thick arms folded, blinking rheumy and brandy-filled eyes at the candlewick.

"Ayagh!" he growled. "And I daresay I'm next?"

"Bert! Listen, and stop your posturing. Yes, posturing:

240

stop it!" Darwent paused for a moment. "What I owe you," he said, "I can never repay. There's not another man in London with the brain to solve that mystery."

"Ayagh!" growled Mr. Mulberry, trying to look as though he scoffed at this.

"I won't insult your present mood by offering you payment; though you deserve it and you shall have it whether it suits you or not."

"To buy my silence about tallow-faced Fletcher, who ought to hang higher than Haman?"

"No. To protect an old friendless man, who would be dealt with as the law dealt with me.—You will be silent, Bert, for two reasons. First, because you are my friend; and, second, because you know that this is just."

Now, for a time, Mr. Mulberry blinked at the tip of the candle flame. Presently, grunting as he rose, he took his hat in one hand and the brass candle dish in the other.

"Ay, lad," he said as he passed Darwent, "I'll stand by ye. You know that."

But, at the door, *he* turned round, shifting the battered hat in his fingers.

"My lady," he said, with that maudlin fondness for Caroline, "I have at the moment a great thirst for cold rum punch. This, perhaps regrettably, I propose to satisfy. But, by God," said Mr. Mulberry, rapping his knuckles against the side of his head, "I *have* reason to be proud of this old noggin!"

And, hat on the side of his head, he marched down the hall.

Caroline had been expecting, had been waiting for, what would happen then. For some time she had known only one emotion. It was not pity for Mr. and Mrs. Raleigh; she had felt that, but it was gone. All her feelings had concentrated into a blind, mad hatred of Darwent.

Caroline did not know why she felt this. She never stopped to think. She did not reflect that—with all questions answered, with the great wheels stopped—there must flow back more strongly than ever what had been strongest from the first: what had been only turned aside, momentarily deflected, by the clash of blades or the wildness of emotions.

That night . . . how she had loved him! When she heard the news of his supposed death, she had known an agony as close to real heart-break as mankind can feel. She had not shown it: no! In this modern year 1815, one must only creep into a corner and weep until the eyes are blind.

And then—he was alive. And *that creature* was dying. Dick
241

had believed that *she,* Caroline, would stoop to ensure that creature's death. When he questioned her, his disbelief was like a slap across the face.

Even this she would not have minded, or at least could have endured, if he had not shown he had loved the creature . . . all the time. He loved the creature. There was the burn of hatred, the crux of misery, the last bitterness!

These would have been Caroline's thoughts, if she had even tried to put them together, as Mr. Mulberry marched away down the hall. Only two candles now burned in the dim room.

To hide the expression of her face, Caroline blew out her own light and put it down. She moved across to the desk and stood with her back to it. Some distance behind her was the moonlit window, and the statue of Pan.

When Caroline spoke, she hoped her voice would not tremble. It did not. It was deadly cold and full of acid.

"Then I am honored, sir, by being reserved as last?"

He did not reply, lifting his candleholder as though to study her.

"And in what manner, sir, can you procure *my* silence?"

Still, maddeningly, he gave no reply. Caroline spoke as though wonderingly, from the depths of her being.

"God, how I hate you!" she said.

Darwent inclined his head. His voice, though perfectly level, was colder and more acid-stung than hers.

"Then you make my task easier, madam."

"True, perhaps. You wish always for easy tasks. You have no courage; you never had. Then shall *I* tell you the threat you mean to use in compelling my silence?"

"There is no threat, madam."

"Come, come! How clumsily we lie! You would threaten me with annulment of our marriage, so that I should be shamed and humiliated and mortified by having to tell why I married you. I much fear, my lord, you can never fight fairly. It gives you no satisfaction if you cannot stab in the back."

(Even as she heard herself crying out these words, Caroline was amazed and somewhat appalled. She did not mean them. She had not meant to say them. But she must strike, wound, hurt with *any* weapon.)

"Two days ago," she said, "that threat might have had force. But not now, my lord. Not now! Rather than humble myself before you in any way, I would give up two fortunes and be arrested for a common slut in Charlotte Street! Pray try your threat; it won't work."

Darwent looked at her steadily.

"I had thought of such a threat, I confess. But have no fear. I can't do it."

"Oh, and he can't do it! And why not?"

"Because I love you," Darwent answered quietly. Where-upon his own temper burst, and he yelled at her. "Now have done, you bawling fishwife, until I say the last word I mean to say to you."

There was a small rattle, as though Caroline had bumped against the desk. Beyond her smiled the great god Pan.

"I do not expect you to understand." Darwent went on with polished courtesy. "Doubtless, in the strictly anatomical sense, you possess that organ known as the heart. In the happy event that you were to die and be dissected, they would probably find it. I have seen no other evidence of its existence.

"That is the fact: I love you. Everything I said in that opera box, or you wheedled out of me (God knows why), was strictly true. Even when I stood beside that girl's death-bed, and cursed myself for I-don't-know-what, I knew I had never cared for her.

"No: I must choose *you*. Very well. Accept my curses; but don't ever fear harm or threat from me. That's the trouble. Even knowing what you are, I couldn't bear to see you hurt, humiliated, even touched; and make no wagers on the life of anyone who tries it. Such is my form of folly."

He was so infuriated, a trifle light-headed, that he did not hear the tone of Caroline's voice.

"Dick! Wait! You never said . . ."

"And now," he concluded, "pray take your beloved money and go to the devil. Cram your pockets with it; eat it; may good digestion wait on appetite, and health on both!—Eh?"

Suddenly he discovered that Alfred, who had appeared at his elbow like a genie, was pressing on him a letter sealed in green wax with Caroline's crest.

"From Mr. Hereford, my lord," Alfred told him. "If you listen, you can hear Mr. Hereford's carriage driving away. I believe it's *very* urgent, my lord."

"Urgent?" he repeated dully.

Alfred slipped away. Still holding the light in his right hand, Darwent broke the seal and clumsily spread open the letter. The neat, small handwriting would persist in blurring, until words leaped out at him;

MY LORD:

If I venture to intrude into your lordship's affairs, it is because long experience has taught me that my skill does far less good than those who surround the patient do harm.

Had you troubled to question Mrs. Demisham (housekeeper) and Meg Saunders (maid), you would have discovered the wonder that the late Miss Spencer remained so long on her feet. She was more than due for a collapse at any time. Her hearing and eyesight were already affected.

Had you further troubled to consult any sober-minded witness to the scene on the stairs . . .

Darwent's eyes opened. The black letters were as clear as newsprint.

. . . you would have found that it was several seconds before Miss Spencer could see your wife (as her questions show) clearly enough to ask if something might be wrong. In my opinion, she scarcely heard what your wife said. Her collapse was long overdue, and it occurred.

Again Darwent paused. He glanced over toward the faint moonlight glow, where Caroline stood silhouetted against the statue.

As I think I reminded you, I myself arrived in my carriage just as you walked up the steps. If you will accredit me as a witness, I saw a great deal myself. If you can explain how a tear-blinded lady in a lighted hall can recognize a man dressed entirely in black, with even the shirt front covered, mounting a stairway against a pitch-black sky, I feel sure your theories would interest a student of optics.

As we grow older, my lord, we know that we are all fools. The solace of wisdom lies in learning, for the most part, how to avoid being a damned fool.

I beg to remain, my lord,
Yr. obdt. servt.,
SAMUEL HEREFORD

Darwent lowered the letter slowly. He lowered his head to look at the floor. To his surprise, Caroline—all changed, the blue eyes softened and frightened—came hurrying across the room.

"Dick! What is it?"

Silently he handed her the letter.

"If we take the term 'damned fool,' " he said bitterly, "and build it up high with every strong adjective we know, how high could we make a man's foolishness go? As high as Babel? As high as Mt. Blanc? It still would not reach *me*."

244

He turned away from her as she glanced at the letter.

"Caroline, I . . ."

She looked at him only with fierce tenderness tinged with wonder.

"But what difference does it make," she held up the letter, "if you really do care for me?"

"Difference! Caroline! It . . ."

"Why don't you ask me what *I* think? What *I* want?"

"What do you think, then? What do you want?"

"Your love."

"You have that already."

"Then that's all that's necessary.—Oh! Wait! Except . . ."

"Yes?"

" 'An estate in Kent,' " she said, " 'with shallow streams and soft brownish-green woods. If I could take you there, beyond sight of the world . . .' "

"You meant that too? You'd go?"

Her actions left him in no doubt of it. So long they remained there, locked together, that time did not exist. Presently, in their happiness, all things seemed new and fresh and full of discoveries. Someone noticed a glimmer outside the door, and he hurried her out into the hall.

"But . . . it's dawn!" Caroline exclaimed, though it had been dawn for some time.

The front door stood wide open. Clear, white light, with a tinge of pink, flooded into the dusty hall. Darwent blew out the last candle, and set it on the stair post. A faint, warm breeze moved the trees in St. James's Square.

"Your arm, Lord Darwent?" smiled Caroline, with mock formality.

He gave her his arm formally, and her hand rested lightly on it. He smiled back at her.

"Your whole being, Lady Darwent?"

"That, of course," murmured Caroline, "was always understood."

And with her hand on his arm, their eyes raised and their faces smiling, they went down the front steps into the dawn.

THE END

Let us have all things but pedantry. The author respectfully requests that no critic, or reader, will mention the pages that follow.

Though many readers will already know, it may interest some to learn how much of *The Bride of Newgate* is imagination, and how much true. The author, now relaxed and comfortable, is happy to supply such information.

Most of the main characters are fictitious. All but two incidents are fictitious.

But no house, club, theater, tavern, street, hotel even a shop or a place of amusement, or the windmill near which duels were fought, or the opera and its description, is in any way fictitious.

It will have been noticed that no famous historical character appears in the story at all. Many are talked about. But they are seen at a distance—on a balcony, or in an opera box—so that they never speak and never enter to clog up the action.

But a great many of the minor characters were very much real persons, as we shall discuss in a moment.

As one who has been browsing through the annals of the Regency for the past dozen years, the author need scarcely mention that its best contemporary historical backgrounds may be found in the *Creevey Papers* (notes and diaries of Thomas Creevey, 1768-1838, first edited by Sir Herbert Maxwell in 1838), and the *Croker Papers* (notes and diaries of John Wilson Croker, 1780-1857, first edited by Lewis J. Jennings in 1887). Creevey is Whig, Croker Tory, and Creevey almost modern in his outspokenness.

But for men and manners, for intimate social background by a man who knew these people well, we must seek out *The Reminiscences and Recollections of Captain Gronow, 1810-1860* (2 vols., London: John C. Nimmo; New York: Charles Scribner's Sons, 1900).

It is true that Gronow will sometimes stretch a point to make a good story, and you must often compare his account with another's. For example, to take a very small point: it is Gronow who makes Scrope Davies tell the story about Lord Byron's curl papers. But this is denied by Lord Lovelace, Byron's grandson, in *Astarte* (new edition; London: Christophers, 1921). And anyone who sees the locks of hair in the famous room of Byron relics at the firm of Messrs. John Murray, 50 Albemarle Street, can see that Lord Lovelace was right.

Next, regarding the bucks and dandies whose dress and manners Gronow has so accurately described:

It is curious that so many vivid accounts of them may be found in books centering round Beau Brummell. The author begs leave to consider Brummell a dull dog, to be thrown away in a couple of sentences. But other personalities appear round him, from William Jesse's standard *The Life of Beau Brummell* (2 vols., 1844), to an excellent modern study in Willard Connely's *The Reign of Beau Brummel* (Cassell & Co., London, Toronto, Sydney & Melbourne, 1940).

Lewis Melville's *Beau Brummell* is chiefly notable for its careful tracing and plotting of house numbers and club numbers (London: Hutchinson & Co., 1924). And, though intended only for light popular entertainment, E. Beresford Chancellor's *The Regency Rakes* (London: Philip Allan & Co., 1924) is admirably accurate.

As for Newgate, the "foul, heynouse jail" of the chronicle, there is enough material so that we can walk its corridors blindfolded in 1815.

To W. Eden Hooper, when Newgate Prison was demolished in 1903, fell the task of gathering and sorting the accumulated papers. Mr. Eden Hooper published his subscription volume, *The Central Criminal Court* (London: Eyre & Spottiswoode, 1909, eight guineas). Later he condensed it into *The History of Newgate and the Old Bailey* (London: Underwood Press, 1935).

The pictures and sketch plans make several Newgates unroll as on a dark screen. See also Albert Crew's *The Old Bailey* (London: Ivor Nicholson & Watson, 1933), and that grisly but pleasant volume, Horace Bleackley's, *The Hangmen of England* (Chapman and Hall, 1929).

It has been stated that only two true historical events occur in the story. The account of how the news of Waterloo was brought to Lord Castlereagh (technically still "Foreign Secretary," but referred to usually as the War Minister) comes from contemporary newspapers. The author would raise his hat to another and much fuller modern description in, Miss Carola Oman's *Britain against Napoleon* (London: Faber and Faber, 1942).

For the second event: the O.P. riots at Covent Garden happened just as they are described here. See the monumental work first published in 1863, Dr. Doran's, *Their Majesties Servants, or Annals of the English Stage* (London: John C. Nimmo, 1897).

A third historical event might have been permitted to occur if—regrettably—the author had not spoiled it by introducing a fight at the opera. Fortunately, however, on the previous night Lucia Elizabetta Vestris did score her first triumph in

Il Ratto di Proserpina. You may read about her in Charles E. Peace's *Madame Vestris and Her Times* (London: Stanley Paul, no date on title page or following page).

Excellent descriptions of the opera, too, have been left by both Hazlitt and De Quincey; and a line from the Opium-Eater has shamelessly been borrowed for the first paragraph of Chapter XVI. Should anyone wish a vivid and accurate picture of the purely literary or theatrical side of the age, he is heartily recommended to Miss Amy Cruse's *The English-man and his Books in the Early Nineteenth Century* (New York: Thomas Y. Crowell, no date given).

But this last-named book concerns very genteel society; it does not deal with the boozing and the wenching which were the other side of the Regency. As an antidote, read about the prize-fighters—"Gentleman" Jackson, Tom Cribb, Jem Belcher, Jack Randall were of course all real—in the often inaccurate but always stimulating works of Pierce Egan.

On that note, let us take stock of those persons in the story who really lived and breathed in that gaudy, beginning-to-be-clean Regency.

The Rev. Horace Cotton, Ordinary of Newgate, was very much real. See the account of him, together with picture, in Bleackley's, *The Hangmen of England.* Also he bobs up at intervals in a curious set of volumes, *Celebrated Trials and Remarkable Cases, with Testimony, from the Earliest Records to the Year 1825* (6 vols., printed for Knight and Lacey, Paternoster Row, 1825).

All the dandies, bucks, and fine ladies, whether mentioned in the text or seen at the opera, were real persons—except Jemmy Fletcher, Tillotson Lewis, Major Sharpe, and Ned Firebrace.

Therefore it may not be necessary to add that Ladies Jersey, Castlereagh, and Sefton really were the patronesses of Almack's, and have been described from contemporary observation. They may well have spoken in the way they are made to speak.

Lord Alvanley, too, was bouncingly real. All diarists and memoir writers unite in their praise of his good nature as well as his talents and his ram-you-damn-you spirits. He is one of the few persons who honestly would have assisted Darwent.

John Townsend, the old Bow Street runner, would fight his way out of the grave if you denied his reality, or the speech he uses in the story. For this see Gilbert Armitage's *The History of the Bow Street Runners* (London: Wishart & Co.,

1920) or George Dilnot's *The Story of Scotland Yard*
(London: Geoffrey Bles, no date in book). The latter book
contains Townsend's picture.

All names of contemporary magistrates and justices are
real, up to and including Lord Ellenborough, the Lord Chief
Justice. The device by which Darwent is saved from Newgate,
of course, is legal to this day.

Nor is it at all necessary to point out that Edmund Kean,
Mrs. Siddons, John Kemble—to say nothing of Mr. Arnold,
the stage manager, or Mr. Raymond, the acting manager, at
Drury Lane—bustlingly moved within their own world.

Enfin, we come to the speech of the year 1815.

It has been attempted here to reproduce the authentic
speech of the time. Where do we find it?

For his own sanity's sake, the reader is entreated not to read
their novels. He is especially warned against the Minerva
novels, from the Minerva Press, which poured into the circulat-
ing libraries—yes, they had such libraries then—and which
talked on stilts as high as a house. Intelligent people, of course,
knew these novels were funny. Macaulay, even as a boy, jotted
down on the last page of Mrs. Kitty Cuthbertson's *Santo
Sebasiano* a sentence which particularly delighted him.

*"One of the sweetest smiles that ever animated the face of
mortal now diffused itself over the face of Lord St. Orville,
as he fell at the feet of Julia in a deathlike swoon."*

Poor goop. Is this the language or behavior of the Regency?
No. But—

We find it in letter writers and diarists, though often
polished up to be what really was the language of good society.
We find a larkier sort in the newspapers. Finally, we hear it
very clearly in the testimony at trials.

This does not mean that writer or reader need shut himself
up with *The Newgate Calendar,* the best version of which
brings together the works of Captain Johnson, Captain Smith,
George Borrow, Knapp and Baldwin, and Camden Pelham in
The Complete Newgate Calendar (5 vols., London: privately
printed for the Navarre Society Ltd., 1926). He will find little
word-for-word testimony here.

But, in addition to Knight and Lacey (see above), he can
accumulate dozens of pamphlets containing the testimony of
crimes committed during this period. A man on trial, usually
for his life, puts on no airs. Educated or uneducated, his
language is real. So is that of judge, counsel, witnesses, and
parson afterward, as Darwent found it.

250

Indeed, some of these musty pamphlets should be shaken out and filled with color. There is the murder case of Thomas Patch (1803), with the most curious alibi on record. There was Bedworth (1815), who was driven by a ghost to confess murder. There was Eliza Fenning (also 1815), and any man in his five wits could prove—*pace* Mr. Roughead's fumbling —that this beautiful girl never poisoned the dumplings. But our friend the Rev. Horace Cotton escorted her to the gallows.

Stop! This note grows garrulous. The writer apologizes; it is only enthusiasm from one who, after dark, likes still to re-people the old streets with the old ghosts. Eyes may be wide open to the injustices, the brutality, the essential falseness. Yet those same may linger there, and ever rejoice, though all its arches be dust.

FINE MYSTERY AND SUSPENSE
TITLES FROM CARROLL & GRAF

- [ ] Allingham, Margery/NO LOVE LOST $3.95
- [ ] Allingham, Margery/MR. CAMPION'S QUARRY $3.95
- [ ] Allingham, Margery/MR. CAMPION'S FARTHING $3.95
- [ ] Allingham, Margery/THE WHITE COTTAGE
      MYSTERY $3.50
- [ ] Ambler, Eric/BACKGROUND TO DANGER $3.95
- [ ] Ambler, Eric/CAUSE FOR ALARM $3.95
- [ ] Ambler, Eric/A COFFIN FOR DIMITRIOS $3.95
- [ ] Ambler, Eric/EPITAPH FOR A SPY $3.95
- [ ] Ambler, Eric/STATE OF SIEGE $3.95
- [ ] Ambler, Eric/JOURNEY INTO FEAR $3.95
- [ ] Ball, John/THE KIWI TARGET $3.95
- [ ] Bentley, E.C./TRENT'S OWN CASE $3.95
- [ ] Blake, Nicholas/A TANGLED WEB $3.50
- [ ] Brand, Christianna/DEATH IN HIGH HEELS $3.95
- [ ] Brand, Christianna/FOG OF DOUBT $3.50
- [ ] Brand, Christianna/GREEN FOR DANGER $3.95
- [ ] Brand, Christianna/TOUR DE FORCE $3.95
- [ ] Brown, Fredric/THE LENIENT BEAST $3.50
- [ ] Brown, Fredric/MURDER CAN BE FUN $3.95
- [ ] Brown, Fredric/THE SCREAMING MIMI $3.50
- [ ] Buchan, John/JOHN MACNAB $3.95
- [ ] Buchan, John/WITCH WOOD $3.95
- [ ] Burnett, W.R./LITTLE CAESAR $3.50
- [ ] Butler, Gerald/KISS THE BLOOD OFF MY HANDS $3.95
- [ ] Carr, John Dickson/CAPTAIN CUT-THROAT $3.95
- [ ] Carr, John Dickson/DARK OF THE MOON $3.50
- [ ] Carr, John Dickson/DEMONIACS $3.95
- [ ] Carr, John Dickson/THE GHOSTS' HIGH NOON $3.95
- [ ] Carr, John Dickson/NINE WRONG ANSWERS $3.50
- [ ] Carr, John Dickson/PAPA LA-BAS $3.95
- [ ] Carr, John Dickson/THE WITCH OF THE
      LOW TIDE $3.95
- [ ] Chesterton, G. K./THE MAN WHO KNEW
      TOO MUCH $3.95
- [ ] Chesterton, G. K./THE MAN WHO WAS THURSDAY $3.50
- [ ] Crofts, Freeman Wills/THE CASK $3.95
- [ ] Coles, Manning/NO ENTRY $3.50
- [ ] Collins, Michael/WALK A BLACK WIND $3.95
- [ ] Dickson, Carter/THE CURSE OF THE BRONZE LAMP $3.50
- [ ] Disch, Thomas M & Sladek, John/BLACK ALICE $3.95
- [ ] Eberhart, Mignon/MESSAGE FROM HONG KONG $3.50

☐ Fennelly, Tony/THE CLOSET HANGING	$3.50
☐ Freeling, Nicolas/LOVE IN AMSTERDAM	$3.95
☐ Gilbert, Michael/ANYTHING FOR A QUIET LIFE	$3.95
☐ Gilbert, Michael/THE DOORS OPEN	$3.95
☐ Gilbert, Michael/THE 92nd TIGER	$3.95
☐ Gilbert, Michael/OVERDRIVE	$3.95
☐ Graham, Winston/MARNIE	$3.95
☐ Griffiths, John/THE GOOD SPY	$4.50
☐ Hughes, Dorothy B./THE FALLEN SPARROW	$3.50
☐ Hughes, Dorothy B./IN A LONELY PLACE	$3.50
☐ Hughes, Dorothy B./RIDE THE PINK HORSE	$3.95
☐ Hornung, E. W./THE AMATEUR CRACKSMAN	$3.95
☐ Kitchin, C. H. B./DEATH OF HIS UNCLE	$3.95
☐ Kitchin, C. H. B./DEATH OF MY AUNT	$3.50
☐ MacDonald, John D./TWO	$2.50
☐ Mason, A.E.W./AT THE VILLA ROSE	$3.50
☐ Mason, A.E.W./THE HOUSE OF THE ARROW	$3.50
☐ McShane, Mark/SEANCE ON A WET AFTERNOON	$3.95
☐ Pentecost, Hugh/THE CANNIBAL WHO OVERATE	$3.95
☐ Priestley, J.B./SALT IS LEAVING	$3.95
☐ Queen, Ellery/THE FINISHING STROKE	$3.95
☐ Rogers, Joel T./THE RED RIGHT HAND	$3.50
☐ 'Sapper'/BULLDOG DRUMMOND	$3.50
☐ Stevens, Shane/BY REASON OF INSANITY	$5.95
☐ Symons, Julian/BOGUE'S FORTUNE	$3.95
☐ Symons, Julian/THE BROKEN PENNY	$3.95
☐ Wainwright, John/ALL ON A SUMMER'S DAY	$3.50
☐ Wallace, Edgar/THE FOUR JUST MEN	$2.95
☐ Waugh, Hillary/A DEATH IN A TOWN	$3.95
☐ Waugh, Hillary/LAST SEEN WEARING	$3.95
☐ Waugh, Hillary/SLEEP LONG, MY LOVE	$3.95
☐ Westlake, Donald E./THE MERCENARIES	$3.95
☐ Willeford, Charles/THE WOMAN CHASER	$3.95

Available from fine bookstores everywhere or use this coupon for ordering.

Carroll & Graf Publishers, Inc., 260 Fifth Avenue, N.Y., N.Y. 10001

Please send me the books I have checked above. I am enclosing $_____ (please add $1.25 per title to cover postage and handling.) Send check or money order—no cash or C.O.D.'s please. N.Y. residents please add 8¼% sales tax.

Mr/Mrs/Ms _____

Address _____

City _____ State/Zip _____

Please allow four to six weeks for delivery.